BACKSHOOTER AND TEXAS IRON

A Robert J. Randisi Classic Western Double Draw

ROBERT J. RANDISI

WOLFPACK
PUBLISHING
— EST 2013 —

Backshooter and Texas Iron: A Robert J. Randisi Classic Western Double Draw
Paperback Edition
Copyright © 2022 (As Revised) Robert J. Randisi

Wolfpack Publishing
9850 S. Maryland Parkway, Suite A-5 #323
Las Vegas, Nevada 89183

wolfpackpublishing.com

Paperback ISBN 978-1-63977-770-9
eBook ISBN 978-1-63977-769-3

BACKSHOOTER AND TEXAS IRON

BACKSHOOTER

FINAL SHOWDOWN

Maddux waited until he saw his men in place on the roof.

"Stay here and cover me," the ex-lawman said to Wilkes. "I'm going to get closer and draw them out."

The wounded Pinkerton agent grimaced from his shoulder wound as he grabbed his gun.

Maddux took a deep breath and ran out from behind the trough they were using for cover.

Running diagonally, he fired on the move, taking down one man. He headed for a doorway as the rooftop shooters opened up with a hurricane of hot lead.

As Maddux reloaded, he saw several of the outlaws fall, their guns firing wildly into the air. But through the clouds of gray gunsmoke, he noticed a big man running toward the livery. "The yella bastard's trying to get away!" he shouted to his men. "Keep them pinned down, and I'll get him!"

To Dale Walker, from one Sutphen boy to another.

PROLOGUE

Maddux was in a bad position.

In fact, this was as bad a spot as he'd found himself in in a long time.

He was lying on his back in a gully. He was holding his gun in his left hand, because he was carrying a bullet in his right arm. There were three men out there who wanted nothing better than to kill him after first stringing him up to a tree.

He didn't know why two of them were so mad. He was only after Lucas Freeling. Unfortunately, Free-ling's friends were loyal to Lucas, who was a rapist and a killer. Maddux wondered how a man like that could command loyalty—unless the other two were just as bad as he was.

He'd tracked Lucas Freeling and his friends for over a hundred miles, and they had probably gotten pretty damned tired of him dogging their trail. So they'd lain in wait for him here, and before he knew it there was a bullet in his right arm and he was lying on the ground, his horse having reared at the sound of the fust shot.

Actually, the horse rearing had probably saved his life, because the two subsequent shots had sailed harmlessly over his head as he was falling off his horse.

He had rolled immediately, coming to a stop on his hack in the gully. He'd pulled his gun out right-handed and switched it to his left. His right hand was already starting to go numb, which could have meant that there was some serious damage done to his right arm.

Using his bandana he tied off the wound in his arm as well as he could, enough to staunch the flow of blood for a while at least.

Now he had to concentrate on getting out of this situation alive.

———

LUCAS FREELING NARROWED his eyes as he peered toward the gully that Maddux had scampered into.

"Did you see him roll into that gully?" he asked the others. "He's hit bad."

"Let's go in arid finish him off, Lucas," Harve Morrow said.

Freeling looked at both Morrow and Slim Drake.

"*I* want that lawman alive, boys," Freeling said. "I'm gonna hang him up by his balls as a message to other lawmen."

"Wouldn't the message get across just as well if we killed him?" Drake asked.

"We'll kill him," Freeling said, "when he begs for it."

Both Morrow and Drake had winced when Freeling mentioned hanging Maddux up...that way. No man, they thought, deserved to have that done to him. If they'd ever needed further proof that Lucas Freeling was a cruel, heartless bastard, this was it. More than loyalty *to* Lucas Freeling, they responded to their fear *of* him.

"All right, Lucas," Drake said, "if that's the way you want it."

"That's the way I want it."

"How do we get him out of that gully then?" Morrow asked.

"He'll come out on his own," Freeling said. "He's hit bad, so he's gonna have to try to get away. All we have to do is wait."

———

MADDUX HAD ONE MAJOR ADVANTAGE, and one major disadvantage. He wasn't sure that one successfully offset the other, but they were both there and he had to examine them.

His disadvantage was the fact that he was wounded. He couldn't afford to wait them out, because he was the one who was losing blood. Freeling would surely be content to wait him out, biding his time until Maddux made his move to escape.

His advantage was the fact that Freeling wanted him alive. He'd shouted as much to him just moments after he'd crawled into the gully. Maddux had winced at the thought.

Still, when *you* were willing to kill someone, while *they* were trying to take you alive, *that* was an advantage.

"What do you got against this lawman?" Drake asked Freeling.

Freeling looked at Drake, then at Morrow. Both men were watching him curiously. They'd been waiting an hour now, and maybe they weren't criticizing him, maybe they just wanted to talk.

"Let me tell you about this bastard," Freeling said. "He's killed three of my old partners, three good men who could take almost any man face to face—except Maddux. Now he's been on my trail for better'n a hundred miles, and I'm gettin' damned tired of looking over my shoulder."

"Who were your three partners?"

"Joe Santos, Kenny Muldoon, and Whip Wilcox."

"Didn't they call him Kid Whip?" Drake asked.

"They did," Freeling said, "until Maddux killed him."

"You rode with those three?" Morrow asked.

"*I* did, and he killed them," Freeling said. "He's not gonna kill me. I'm gonna do something those three couldn't do. I'm gonna kill me a lawman named Maddux." He looked at them again and said, "You know what killin' him is gonna do for me?"

"Make you famous," Drake said.

"It sure as hell is," Freeling said, "but taking him alive, torturing him, and *then* killing him is gonna make me in-famous."

"What's m-famous?" Morrow asked, frowning.

"That's when you're more than famous," Freeling said, "and that's just what I'm gonna be."

Privately, Drake and Morrow wondered if being present when he did it would make them in-famous as well.

———

MADDUX WOKE WITH A START.

Jesus, had he really fallen asleep? If he ever needed proof that this game was for younger men, this was it. His wife kept telling him that this was no business for a man nearing fifty. For once he was thinking that maybe she was right.

He turned and peered out to see if the three men were still there. One shot was fired, just to let him know they were still there.

Christ, they could have walked right up on him while he was asleep.

Maddux tried to move his right arm and found that it had stiffened up on him. He passed his left hand over his eyes and forehead and it came away wet. There was heat throbbing behind his eyes and he knew he had a high fever.

He had to get out of there and get some medical treatment. He stood to lose the arm, or his life, if he didn't get help—that is, if he didn't get killed trying to get away.

Get away? Shit!

He was thinking about getting away from these three when he should have been thinking about a way to get them. If word got out that they had gotten away from him—that *he* had gotten away from *them*—he'd lose all the respect he'd built up over the years. In this business that respect—that *fear*—could mean the difference between living and dying.

Maddux finally decided that he had little to lose and a lot to gain. If he died, he died. It had to happen to everyone at one time or another. But this time wasn't what he had in mind.

———

"WHAT THE—" Morrow said.

He'd been watching while Freeling and Drake sat with their backs to him. Now Freeling turned at the sound of his voice.

"What is it?"

"You'd better look at this, Lucas."

Freeling got up onto his knees and peered over the rocks they were using for cover.

"What the—" he said.

What he saw was Maddux standing up in plain sight, holding his gun jammed underneath his chin. He looked for all the world like he was gonna blow his own head off.

"What the hell is he doing?" Drake asked.

"What's it look like," Freeling said. "He's gonna steal my moment from me. If he kills himself I'll never be in-famous."

Freeling started to stand up, and both Morrow and Drake said, "What are you doing?"

"I'm gonna talk to him."

Freeling moved out from behind the rocks, his gun holstered.

"Maddux, what the hell do you think you're doin'?" he demanded.

"What does it look like I'm doing, Freeling?" Maddux asked. "I don't relish begging to die, and I don't think I can get away from you. Not in the condition I'm in. So I guess I'll just blow my own head off."

"Don't do that!" Freeling said.

Behind him both Morrow and Drake moved out from behind the rocks, watching.

"What do you care?" Maddux asked. "I'll be dead and off your trail."

"I want the pleasure of killing you myself," Freeling said. "You ain't gonna steal that from me, Maddux."

"Watch me."

"No, wait!"

"What are you going to do?" Maddux said. "Stop me by killing me?"

"I'll make a deal with you," Freeling said.

"What kind of deal?"

"I'll kill you quick," Freeling said.

"You'll kill me quick?"

"Yeah."

"Shit," Maddux said, "I can do that myself."

As Maddux's finger tightened on the trigger of his gun, Freeling shouted, "No!" and started forward.

As Freeling charged him—obviously intending to try and stop him from blowing his own head off— Maddux lowered the gun and pointed it at the man.

"What—" Freeling said, trying t6 stop his forward motion.

"I changed my mind," Maddux said, and squeezed the trigger.

Morrow and Drake, seeing Freeling shot down, decided that it would be best for them to get out of there.

Maddux watched as the two men ran for their horses,

mounted, and rode off. Then he went over to Freeling's body and nudged it with the toe of his boot.

"Lucky for me," he said, "that you had more guts than brains."

Maddux turned his back on the downed man and moved to take a step, but his legs would no longer hold him. Suddenly, he felt as if he were floating. He heard a shot and felt a sharp pain in his back. He didn't even feel it when his face hit the dirt.

CHAPTER ONE

KANSAS, THREE YEARS LATER

The pain was back.

No, Kyle Maddux thought as he straightened up, that wasn't exactly right. The pain was *always* there; some days it was just worse than others.

Today was just one of those days.

"What are you doing, Kyle?"

He turned and knew that the look on his face was one of guilt as he stared at his wife, Laura. Now in her early forties, Laura was still a handsome woman. When he looked at her he could still see the woman he'd married more than fourteen years ago. He would sail never know what such a woman saw in a man ten years her senior. Back then Laura's hair had been black as the wings of a raven. Now there were streaks of gray in it, but he didn't care. When they walked down the street in town he saw that she still commanded admiring looks from other men, and he was proud of her.

He was also a little afraid of her, but what husband isn't a little afraid of his wife? The man who said he wasn't was a liar.

"We need wood," he said lamely.

"That's what Shadoweyes is here for, Kyle Maddux!" she said, scolding him. "Now put down that ax—your back hurts, doesn't it?"

He could never hide it from her.

"It aches a bit," he admitted, dropping the ax to the ground.

"Come inside," she said. "I've made some coffee."

He smiled and followed her into the house.

The town of Cromwell had given them this piece of land and the house, after he had recovered from the wounds he'd received while chasing down Lucas Freeling. It was lucky for him that his deputy back then had been almost as stubborn as he was. Joe Hannibal had trailed Maddux while Maddux was trailing Freeling. If Hannibal hadn't found him he probably would have died from those wounds. He owed Joe a lot, and one of the things he did was endorse Hannibal for his job when he'd retired, three years ago.

The house was as it was three years ago, built of fine pine lumber, with three rooms. The bank had taken it over when the old owner had died, and would have sold it had they not turned it over to the Madduxes. The banker, Charles Timberlane, had come up with the idea of giving it to Kyle and Laura in gratitude for the twelve years that Kyle had been marshal there, and the rest of the town council had gone along with it

Kyle sat down at the table and Laura put a steaming cup of coffee in front of him.

"You didn't sleep very well last night, did you?" she asked.

"I tossed some," he said, looking into the coffee cup.

"Did you have the dream?"

Yes, he'd had the dream. It was amazing how he was always able to feel the impact of the bullet, and the pain, over and over again in The Dream.

The thing that really bothered him was that he never knew who had shot him. When Joe Hannibal had found him, he and Lucas Freeling were lying on the ground, both looking good and dead. Freeling *had been* dead but, by some miracle, Maddux had still been alive. It was even more of a miracle that he'd survived the trek back to the nearest town, being dragged on a litter behind Hannibal's horse.

"Maybe Freeling lived long enough to plug you one more," Hannibal had said at the time, but Maddux always doubted it. He had shot Freeling, and he'd been certain the man was dead. Those other two who were riding with him—it was possible that one of them had sneaked back and done the deed, but he doubted that too. When they'd lit out they'd looked like they'd never want to come back.

"I had the dream." He hated admitting it to her. He took the dream as a sign of weakness.

He appreciated that Laura did not fuss over him. Instead she simply asked him if he'd like a piece of pie with the coffee, and he said yes.

When she had placed the hunk of apple pie in front of him he said, "I think I'll take a ride into town after this."

"What for?" she asked.

"*I* need some tobacco," he said, which was true, but not the real reason. He just felt he needed to get away for a while, have a beer, maybe see Joe Hannibal.

"Well, take the buckboard," she said. "You know your back can't take you sitting a horse anymore."

Little did she know that he sometimes sneaked away just to ride again.

"I'll take the buckboard," he promised, and hacked off a piece of that pie.

———

THE TOWN COUNCIL had given Ben Tibbs some trouble when he'd first put up the sign bearing the name of his saloon. In the beginning the sign had said HORSE'S ASS SALOON and it had had a big horse's hind section hanging right over the entrance. But the women of the town had started to complain to the council, and the council had taken it up with Tibbs, who'd reluctantly agreed to move the horse's ass inside-"With all the *other* horse's asses"—where it now hung over the bar.

Maddux always figured that he'd put the horse's ass on the outside in the first place just so he'd have something to bargain with when the complaining started.

And it worked like a charm.

Maddux entered the saloon and went directly to the bar. Sam Waters was tending bar as usual, and gave him a surprised look.

"What brings you to town, Marshal?" Most of the people in town still called him Marshal. He had protested at first, but had decided that if Presidents can stand to be addressed by their former title, who was he to complain?"

"Supplies," Maddux said, "and a cold mug of beer."

"I can help you there," Waters said, and drew Maddux a cold one.

Sam was a tall, emaciated-looking man in his mid-fifties. He worked the day shift in the saloon. The night shift belonged to Dog Nichols. Dog was six and a half feet tall and almost as wide, and was able to handle the rougher shift more effectively than Sam.

A door in the back wall opened, and Ben Tibbs stepped out. When he saw Maddux he sauntered over to the bar.

Tibbs was a gambler, and a fancy dresser. A man in his mid-thirties, he had an eye for the ladies, and the eye was usually returned. In the six months since he'd opened the saloon, Maddux had become friends with Tibbs and Sam Waters. He was still working on Dog Nichols, who had the disposition of a three-legged dog. His name was actually Doug, but where he'd grown up everyone had pronounced it "Dog" and it had stuck.

"Afternoon, Marshal," Tibbs said.

"Ben." Maddux looked up at the stuffed horse's ass hanging over the bar and said, "I don't know how you manage to keep the flies away from that thing."

"I just charm them away, Marshal," Tibbs said, smiling.

Looking at Tibbs's best smile, Maddux could believe it. He'd seen many women charmed by that smile, even when they disapproved of Ben's profession.

"How's the ranch coming?" Tibbs asked.

"It's coming along."

"Did you ever hire any help?"

"Got a feller helping me."

"Oh? Anyone I know?"

Maddux hesitated and then said, "John Shadow-eyes."

"The breed?" Sam Waters asked. "He'll rob you blind, Maddux—"

"John's a good man, Sam," Maddux said. "All he needs is a chance."

"And you're giving it to him, huh?" Tibbs asked.

"Someone's got to."

"You know, another time you might have been hunting John Shadoweyes," Tibbs said.

"Well, this isn't another time, is it?" he said.

"No, it damned sure isn't," Tibbs said. "If it was, I'd be

standing in my own place in Portsmouth Square, San Francisco, that's for damned sure."

Ever since Maddux had met Tibbs, the man had talked about owning his own place in Portsmouth Square.

"That beer's on the house, Marshal," Tibbs said. "Sam, he pays for the second one. All right?"

"That's fair," Maddux said.

Tibbs slapped him on the shoulder and said, "I've got a little filly waiting."

"That's no surprise," Maddux said to Waters as Tibbs walked out. "Is this one married?"

Waters shrugged and said, "I don't rightly know which one he's got waiting, but there's a fifty-fifty chance that she is."

"He might get shot by a jealous husband long before he ever gets to Portsmouth Square," Maddux said.

"That's the truth."

Maddux made some more small talk with Sam until he finished his beer, and then declined to take a second one.

"I'll tell Ben you had your free one and took a walk," Sam said.

"Tell him I'll be back later," Maddux said.

When Maddux left the saloon he headed for the marshal's office to visit with Joe Hannibal. Joe had been Maddux's deputy for five years. All during that time they had maintained a relationship of marshal and deputy. Since Maddux's retirement, however, they had become friends.

As Maddux entered the office Hannibal was at his coffee pot, which was where he spent a lot of time.

"That stuff is going to kill you one of these days," Maddux said.

"Coffee?"

"*Your* coffee."

"In that case," Hannibal said, "I'll pour you one so I don't die alone."

Hannibal turned with two cups in his hands and Maddux accepted one. Hannibal sat behind his desk and Maddux took a seat across from him.

"What brings you to town?"

"Tobacco."

Hannibal was in his late thirties, not tall, and very powerfully built. When he'd first laid eyes on him, Maddux had likened him to a bear, and had seen no reason in the ensuing years to change his mind. Hannibal had a short beard and a deep, drawling voice. His brutish appearance belied the sharp mind he possessed, and usually made people underestimate him.

"What else have you got on your mind?" Hannibal asked as Maddux sipped the coffee.

"What makes you think I've got something else on my mind?" Maddux asked.

"Because you really only brave my coffee when you've had the dream and want to talk about it."

Maddux was in the middle of another sip, and made a face. He leaned forward and put the cup down on Hannibal's desk. "You're right, I had the dream," he said, "but I don't want to talk about it."

"Fine," Hannibal said. "We'll talk about something else."

"What are you reading there?" Maddux asked. Hannibal had the newspaper opened on his desk.

"Ah, I'm reading about this Backshooter varmint."

"Did he kill someone else?"

"Yep," Hannibal said.

"Where this time?"

"A little town just this side of the Rio Grande."

"He must be taking his act into Mexico."

"Yeah, well, they can have him," Hannibal said, closing the paper.

"Let me see it," Maddux said.

"What for?" Hannibal said, holding the now-folded newspaper. "It's all the old stuff."

"Let me see it," Maddux asked, again.

Hannibal sighed and handed Maddux the paper. Maddux immediately turned to the Backshooter article and started reading it.

"You're becoming obsessed with this thing, Kyle," Hannibal said.

Maddux didn't answer, but Hannibal knew he was right. Ever since the Backshooter had claimed his third victim, Kyle Maddux had taken an interest in the case. Now that the man's list of kills was up to an even dozen in a two-year period, Hannibal was afraid of what Kyle Maddux might do.

"Kyle—"

"Shh."

Hannibal leaned over and slammed his pawlike hand down on the newspaper.

"What the—"

"Just because we never found who shot you in the back doesn't mean it was this fella."

"It's a possibility," Maddux said.

"This fella didn't claim his first victim until more than a year after you were shot."

"What if I was his first victim, only nobody knows it?" Maddux asked.

"There could be *hundreds* of victims before his acknowledged first," Hannibal said, "but that still doesn't mean you're one of them."

Kyle frowned and looked away from his friend.

"You know this is getting to be an obsession," Hannibal said, "and you know where it's going to lead."

"Where?"

"I know you, Kyle,' Hannibal said. "Retirement hasn't set well with you. You're looking for an excuse to get up on a horse and go looking for this jasper."

"Bull," Maddux said, but even to him his tone sounded unconvincing.

"Sure," Hannibal said, "it's bull." The marshal leaned forward and said, 'I'll bet if I searched your house I'd come up with a map of this fella's movements. Am I right? Huh?"

"Damn you," Maddux said, "you're too damned smart, Joe Hannibal."

"I learned from you, Kyle," Hannibal said. "I learned to know my subjects."

"You been studying on me?"

"I've been watching you, my friend," Hannibal said, "and I'm gonna keep on watching you."

"You do that, *friend*," Maddux said, "and you're going to get pretty bored."

They sat in silence for a few moments, and then Hannibal said, "You still got that breed working for you?"

"John Shadoweyes? Yeah, why?"

"If you knew how many times I've had him in a cell for—"

"He's not drinking anymore," Maddux said.

"He's gone off the bottle before, Maddux, and he's gone right back on again."

Maddux shrugged. "He's good with horses."

"When he's sober."

"I guess we'll just have to wait and see. I'm not losing anything by giving the man a job."

"He gets real violent when he drinks," Hannibal said, warningly.

"So I'll watch him," Maddux said, standing up. "Come on, let's go over to the hotel and get some real coffee."

"You buying?"

"Since when did a lawman buy?" Maddux said. "Of course I'm buying."

As they left his office Hannibal said, "You know what you need?"

"What?"

"A woman."

"In case you forgot, Joe, I have a woman."

"No, I mean a younger woman," Hannibal said. "Somebody to take your mind off of things."

"You got somebody in mind?"

"Sure," Hannibal said. "Susan, over at the hotel."

"Stop playing cupid, Joe," Maddux said. "Susan is a nice girl, and a good waitress."

"That's my point," Hannibal said. "I mean, that she's a nice girl."

Maddux waved his hand at Hannibal in a "shut up," gesture and walked ahead.

CHAPTER TWO

Sue Daniels saw Maddux as soon as he entered the hotel
dining room, and hurried over to his table.

"Hi, Kyle."

Maddux looked up at Sue, struck as usual by her freshfaced
beauty. She was blonde and had a peaches-and-cream complex-
ion. She was twenty-eight, old enough for him to notice her all
the time, but young enough for him to do nothing more.

On the way over to the hotel someone had called out to Joe
Hannibal, who had told Maddux to go on ahead and get a table.

"Hello, Susan."

"Would you like to order now?"

"I'm, uh, waiting for Marshal Hannibal."

"Does he know you're in here?"

"Yes, he knows."

"Coffee while you wait?"

"Yes, thank you."

He watched her walk away, admiring the way her behind
looked in her dress, and then chiding himself for being a lech-
erous old man. She was, after all, about twenty-five years
younger than he was—give or take a year. He loved Laura and
would never do anything to hurt her, but Sue Daniels's atten-
tions whenever he came to town boosted his ego in a way that
he sometimes needed.

He hoped he never had to explain *that* to Laura.

The dining room was doing a brisk business as it was

dinnertime, and almost all of the tables were taken by this time. Maddux knew that, despite the fact that she was very busy, he'd be getting Susan's very best service.

After almost three years it still felt odd not to have his gun on his hip, not having to shift every so often to accommodate it. He was grateful, however, that in his new life he didn't have to carry it anymore.

He was thinking about that when he saw the two men enter. They moved through the doorway from the lobby to the dining room and stopped. It appeared that they were looking for a table, but there was something about them that alerted Maddux. Later, he'd be surprised that the old instinct for survival had not gone stale in retirement, but right then he didn't have time to think about that.

He could see things developing very clearly. Sue was on her way to his table with his coffee, and another waitress was moving toward the two men to see if she could help them. Maddux was seated just about in the center of the dining room, with people behind him, in front of him, and on both sides.

The potential of the situation couldn't have been worse.

He sat watching the two men, peripherally aware of the movement of the two women. He forgot everything else in the room, all the idle chatter and clinking of glasses and silverware. Perspiration broke out on his brow, and he was trying to think of a way out when the two men moved.

Sue had reached him by this time and was saying,

"Here's your coffee—"

"Down, Sue!" he shouted.

"Wha—"

"Get...down!" he shouted, pushing her.

The two men saw him moving and the one on the right—the left-handed one—would have had him if it wasn't for the other waitress. She reached them and put her hand on the man's left arm, saying, "Can I help—"

Angrily, the man pushed her away from him, and it delayed his move to his gun.

The other man just wasn't very fast.

By the time both men had their guns out, Maddux had overturned the table and had it in front of him, at the same time yelling, "Everybody down!"

Everyone in the place looked up as he shouted, and then the shooting started and screams of fear and cries of pain began.

Maddux felt the table jolt as each slug pounded into it, and knew he had to do something before an innocent bystander got killed. He grabbed a table leg in each hand, lifted the whole table, and ran towards the two men, screaming at the top of his lungs.

The table shook in his grasp as they continued to fire, and then suddenly the firing stopped as they ran out of bullets.

He ran into them then, ramming them both with the table and forcing them back into the lobby, where they went sprawling. He tossed the chewed-up table away and charged them.

He pulled one man to his feet and hit him in the face, then turned to find the second man up on one knee. He launched a kick that caught the man in the jaw, snapping his head back, and his jaw closed so hard that he bit through his tongue.

He turned on the first man then, and the man had his gun in his hand. It was obvious from the way he trained it on Maddux that he had managed to reload.

"Shit!" Maddux said.

Joe Hannibal charged into the lobby, assessed the situation quickly, and reacted the only way he could.

He shot the man with the gun.

Maddux watched the man fall and breathed a sigh of relief. Only three years into his retirement he'd almost bought the farm, after cheating death for years.

Jesus, he thought, it makes a man think, don't it?

CHAPTER THREE

Several people were injured, including Sue.

Maddux had rushed back into the dining room to see who was hurt, hoping that no one had been killed, and found Sue sitting on the ground, bleeding from a scratch on her left arm. She had her hand closed over it as he lifted her to her feet.

"Are you all right?" he asked, anxiously.

"I'm fine," she said, her eyes shining as she stared at him. "You were wonderful."

He hugged her to him then, not even thinking of what consequences might result from the move.

———

LATER HE AND Hannibal went over to the doctor's office to check on the second man.

"We'd like to talk to him, Doc," Hannibal said.

The doctor's name was Algis Cleaver, but everyone called him Doc. He was in his sixties and had seen it all. Nothing surprised him anymore, not even a man with a near-bit-off tongue.

"Can't," Doc said.

"Why not?" Hannibal asked.

"He's got a pretty bad neck injury, and he bit through his

tongue so bad he might lose it, *and* his jaw's broke. You *could* talk to him, but he can't answer you."

"Shit!" Maddux said.

"Easy," Hannibal said. "Can he write his answers down?"

"Nope."

"Why not?" Hannibal asked. "Is his hand injured?"

"Nope."

"Then what is it?"

"First thing I asked him was could he write down his answers to my questions," Doc said. "Your man don't know how to write."

"Shit!" Hannibal said.

"Easy," Maddux said, mimicking Hannibal.

"Let's go to my office, Kyle," Hannibal said. "Keep me informed on his condition, huh, Doc?"

"Sure, Marshal, sure." Doc looked at Maddux and said, "What did you do to him?"

"*I* kicked him."

"You near killed him."

"*I* was trying to," Maddux said, and followed Hannibal out

———

"DID YOU KNOW HIM?" Hannibal asked in his office.

They both had a glass of whiskey, and the bottle was on the desk. Maddux's hands were shaking now that the danger was over, and his back was aching from lifting the table off the floor. But he also felt something else.

He felt exhilarated! He had never felt more alive in the past three years than in that dining room a little while before.

"Kyle?"

"What? I'm sorry."

"Did you know them?"

"No," Maddux said, frowning.

"Neither of them?"

"No."

"Then it can't be that they recognized you and felt they owed you, can it?"

"Sure it can," Maddux said. "Just because I don't know them doesn't mean they didn't know me. I've arrested a lot of people over the years, Joe, here and before I came to Cromwell. After thirty years of toting a badge, I can't be expected to remember all of them."

"Jesus, you're a talkative cuss tonight, ain't you?"

Maddux looked at Hannibal and said, "I'm sorry, Joe. I'm just a bit shook up, is all."

"Why? You been shot at with bad intentions before, ain't you?"

"Not in the last three years I ain't," Maddux said. He held up his whiskey glass so Hannibal could see that his hand was shaking, and then drained it. Hannibal emulated him, and then picked up the bottle and filled both glasses again.

"Kyle..." Hannibal said.

"Yeah, I know."

"Those fellas could have been hired to kill you."

"That's a possibility," Maddux said. "They did walk into the place, spot me, and open fire right away."

"Why?"

Maddux shrugged. "Like I said, a lot of people could have a lot of reasons for wanting me dead."

"I was hoping we could find out for sure from the other one."

"It don't look like we're gonna find out anything from him, not for a while anyway," Maddux said.

"I guess not."

"You could of took it easier on him."

"No, I couldn't," Maddux said. "Not in that situation. There were too many people around."

"Well, luckily no one was killed. The worst hurt was Bill Fowler. The rest was just scratched, scared, or got trampled."

"That doesn't make me feel any better."

"Hey, it wasn't your fault."

"Sure."

"It wasn't," Hannibal insisted. "Two hardcases come in and start blasting at you, how could you know that was gonna happen?"

"I could have figured it would happen sometime or another."

"Okay, and then what would you do?"

"Stay on my ranch."

"And do what? Send Joe Shadoweyes in for your supplies? He's a *real* welcome sight around these parts."

"All right, all right," Maddux said. He drained his glass and put it on the desk, waving off another drink. "I'm going to check on Sue."

"That gal's sweet on you, Maddux," Hannibal said. "You know that, don't you?"

"That's just plain sill—"

"And now you're her hero."

"Her hero," Maddux repeated bitterly. "I almost got her killed."

"Maddux—"

"Yeah, I know, not my fault," Maddux said, heading for the door. When he reached it, he turned and said, "Hey, Joe."

"Yeah?"

"Did I thank you for saving my life?"

"Not yet."

"Oh," Maddux said, "well, remind me to do it sometime, okay?"

"Gotcha."

"Good night."

"Night, Kyle."

Maddux went outside, and for a moment he felt some panic. What if there were others in town, men brought in to back up the first two shooters? What if they were drawing a bead on him right now?

Jesus, he told himself, you're seeing ghosts and goblins where there ain't any.

Nevertheless, as he walked down the street his aching back was stiff and erect and felt as if it had a target painted on it.

————

WHEN MADDUX GOT BACK HOME he told John Shadoweyes what had happened.

"That mare is gonna foal soon," Shadoweyes said. "I will keep an eye on her tonight."

"Did you hear what I said?" Maddux asked.

"Yes," Shadoweyes said, "you had some excitement in town."

"Two men tried to kill me, John," Maddux said. "If they were hired, then there'll be more on the way."

"So?"

"So maybe you better hightail it."

Shadoweyes gave Maddux a baleful stare and asked, "To where? This is the only home I have."

Shadoweyes had been working for Maddux for six months, and was worth his weight in gold. It was hard for Maddux to gauge his age. He could have been forty, or sixty. His long black hair had some gray in it, and he stood ramrod straight at about six-two. He was thin, but not as thin as when Maddux had hired him. Shadoweyes had been eating pretty good since he started working for Maddux. Maddux was glad to hear that he thought of the K & L Ranch as his home. Maybe he would stay off whiskey for good, but in this situation...

"John, you may be buying into trouble that's not yours," Maddux said.

"If anyone comes here looking for trouble," Shadoweyes said, "they are looking for me too."

"Is that your final word?" Maddux asked.

"It is."

"Well then," Maddux said, "we'd better get to work."

Shadoweyes nodded, and Maddux turned to go into the house. He had to break the news to Laura, and he decided to do so without repeating any of the conjecture he and Hannibal had gone through.

It was bad enough he had to tell her someone had tried to kill him, let alone that they might have been hired to do so.

CHAPTER FOUR

Over the next few days Maddux was tempted several times to go into town, but the incident was still fresh in his mind. Marshal Hannibal had said that as soon as the injured man could talk he'd question him, and if he found something out he'd come out to the ranch, but Hannibal had not shown up yet either. He also knew that if he decided to go to town it would precipitate an argument with Laura. She had not taken the news of the shooting well.

"Look at you," she'd shouted at him after he'd told her. "You haven't been this fired up in a long time. You liked it, didn't you?"

She had run into the bedroom and slammed the door before he could answer her.

He hadn't *liked* it—not exactly.

"Why don't you go into town?" Shadoweyes asked when he found Maddux standing on the porch, staring at the main road.

"And have somebody else get shot because of me?"

"That kind of talk is useless."

Maddux looked at Shadoweyes and said, "Yeah, I know it is. And we've still got some horses to break, and that mare has to foal—"

"She did," Shadoweyes said. "Last night."

"You didn't tell me."

Shadoweyes shrugged. "You have other things on your mind."

"How are they doing?"

"Mother and son are both fine."

"A colt, huh?" Maddux said. Thinking about the Arabian stallion the mare had been bred to, he said, "He's going to be a beauty."

"He already is," Shadoweyes said.

"Yeah," Maddux said. He tore his eyes away from the main road and said, "Come on, let's have a look at him."

———

LATER THAT NIGHT, after Laura was asleep, Maddux took out what he had come to think of as his Backshooter map. He had traced the path of the Backshooter, from his first victim to his eleventh. Now he took his red marker and wrote in the twelfth victim.

It would be a long ride dogging the Backshooter's trail from victim one to victim twelve, but that would be the only way to find out who he was. Given the two-year period over which his twelve victims had been claimed, the man must have spent a reasonable amount of time in each area, establishing himself under one name or another. Somebody had to remember him. All Maddux would have to do was start matching names and descriptions. Pretty soon he'd know what to start looking for, even if he didn't know who.

That is, if he was going.

All the law knew was that people were being killed, shot in the back. The lawmen of each town were going no further than their own territory.

Maddux wondered why a federal marshal hadn't been sent to trail the Backshooter. Maybe the federal government didn't see this killing spree as a problem. Maybe that was because nobody important—like a banker, or a politician—had been killed yet. First time one of *them* bought the farm, you'd see how quick a federal marshal was on the scene.

Maybe that was why the Backshooter *hadn't* shot anyone important...yet.

Maddux folded the map and poured himself a cup of coffee from the bottom of the pot. He had the itch, all right, that was for sure. The question—if he was on the verge of making a decision—was whether or not he had the physical stamina for the job.

Laura would say no, but that was because she loved him and wouldn't want him to go.

If she loved him enough, though, maybe she *wouldn't* say no.

And maybe he'd go no matter what she thought.

A hell of a lot of maybes.

———

THE NEXT AFTERNOON Shadoweyes came walking in from the barn and said, "Visitors coming."

"It's probably the marshal," Maddux said. "Maybe he got some information out of that fella."

"More than one rider," Shadoweyes said.

"*I* can't see anything yet."

"*I* can."

"The first rider?"

"A big, bulky man."

"Hannibal."

"Yes."

"And the second?"

"Not so big and bulky."

"Have Mrs. Maddux put up a pot of coffee, John."

Shadoweyes went inside, and Maddux watched until finally he too recognized Hannibal. He didn't know who the other man was.

He waited on the porch until both men reached the house and dismounted.

"Kyle," Hannibal said, by way of greeting.

"Afternoon, Joe," Maddux said. "You got any information for me?"

"Sorry, but Doc don't think that fella's ever gonna talk right. The swelling hasn't gone down on his tongue, yet, and he doesn't know how to write."

"Maybe I'll come on into town and ask him some yes-or-no questions. He could shake or nod his head."

"Could be," Hannibal said. "You're welcome to try it."

"Who's your friend?"

"Oh, sorry," Hannibal said. "This here is Mr. Glenn Wilkes, Kyle. Mr. Wilkes, this is Kyle Maddux."

The two men sized one another up.

Wilkes had the look of a dandy. Even his trail clothes were expensive, although they were covered with the same dust that Hannibal's clothes were. He was tall and slender, and Maddux noticed that he had soft hands. He wore a gun, but Maddux doubted that he knew how to use it."

"Mr. Wilkes," Maddux said. He moved to the edge of the porch and shook hands with the man. The handshake was firm enough.

"Mr. Maddux."

"Kyle, Mr. Wilkes came into Cromwell looking for you," Hannibal said.

"Really? We haven't met before, have we, Mr. Wilkes?" The question was a polite one. If Maddux had met this man before, he'd remember it.

"No, we haven't, Mr. Maddux," Wilkes said, "but I've heard all about you."

"Is that a fact?"

Hannibal, sensing that the meeting was not going well, said, "Can we take this inside, Kyle?"

"Sure, Joe. I've got coffee on—real coffee, not that piss you drink."

Maddux checked Wilkes to see if his language shocked the man, but his face never changed.

"Just tie your horses off. Shadoweyes will take care of them."

"Shadoweyes?" Wilkes said, frowning, looking at Hannibal.

"John Shadoweyes," Hannibal said. "He works for Maddux."

"With," Maddux said. "He works *with* me."

"With," Hannibal said. "Sorry."

Maddux moved into the house, followed by Hannibal and Wilkes.

Maddux sat in an old stuffed chair that he had gotten from the hotel when they were going to toss it out.

"Have a seat," he said to the other two men.

Laura came into the room and all three men stood up again. Maddux could see the look of admiration on Wilkes's face.

"Hello, Laura," Hannibal said.

"Marshal."

"Mr. Wilkes," Maddux said, "this is my wife, Laura."

"Mrs. Maddux," Wilkes said, "a pleasure."

Maddux noticed that Laura was dressed to go out.

"Kyle, I'm going to see Mrs. Hodges. She's ailing and could use some help around the house."

"All right," Maddux said.

He saw the look she gave both Hannibal and

Wilkes. She knew something was up, but she didn't want to hear about it now. She'd wait until she heard it from Maddux, later.

"Johh," Maddux said to Shadoweyes, "hitch up the buggy for Mrs. Maddux."

"Right."

That was the first time either Hannibal or Wilkes noticed Shadoweyes was in the room.

"Hello, John," Hannibal said.

"Marshal."

Shadoweyes went out, followed by Laura Maddux.

"You staying dinner, Joe?" Maddux asked.

"Who's cookin?" Hannibal asked, since it was obvious Laura wasn't going to be there.

Maddux laughed and said, "Shadoweyes."

"Then we'll stay."

Wilkes didn't seem to mind not being consulted.

Maddux brought three cups and the coffeepot to the table and sat down with them.

"Why don't you tell me what this is all about, Joe?" he asked.

Hannibal looked at Wilkes, who shrugged, indicating he didn't care who did the talking.

"Mr. Wilkes came to Cromwell looking for help, Maddux."

"Mine, or yours?"

"Yours."

"What seems to be his problem?"

"He's a Pinkerton agent."

"Is that a fact?"

"Maybe I should speak for myself," Wilkes said at this point. He looked at Maddux and said, "I'm after this fella some of the newspapers are calling the Backshooter."

"I've read about it," Maddux said. "What's Pinkerton's interest?"

"We've been hired by the family of one of the victims."

Maddux raised his eyebrows in surprise. "One of the victim's families is rich enough to afford Pinkerton?"

"*I* suppose so," Wilkes said. "I couldn't even tell you which family it was. All I know is that I've been assigned to track him down."

"And why are you here?"

"To ask you for your help."

"Why me?"

"Frankly," Wilkes said, "*I* didn't know who you were until Alan Pinkerton told me."

"Pinkerton and I are acquainted," Maddux said. Actually, he and Pinkerton knew each other very well. They didn't necessarily *like* each other, but they had respected each other over the years, and still did.

"What did he tell you?"

"He told me that since the Backshooter's trail started near here, in Abilene, that you were probably following the progress in the newspapers."

"Did he say why I might be doing that?"

"Yes," Wilkes said. "He said that in retirement you would have little else to do."

Damn him, Maddux thought.

"What do you want from me?" Maddux asked. "Advice?"

"No, sir," Wilkes said, "*I* want you to come with me."

Maddux stared at the man for a few moments, then looked at Hannibal, who just shrugged.

"Why?" Maddux asked.

"Frankly? I'm a city boy, Mr. Maddux. I need someone who can track him."

"Track him?" Maddux said. "How do you expect to follow a two-year-old trail?"

Wilkes cleared his throat. "Mr. Pinkerton said that no one can follow a cold trail like Kyle Maddux."

"Mr. Pinkerton is being very kind," Maddux said, sarcastically.

"Will you come?"

Maddux opened his mouth to say no, and then closed it. "Let's discuss it again after dinner," he said.

CHAPTER FIVE

After dinner Hannibal joined Maddux out on the porch. Inside, Wilkes was having a cup of coffee, being watched closely by John Shadoweyes.

"Give it all to me, Joe," Maddux said.

They hadn't discussed it over dinner because Maddux needed some time to digest the information that had been sprung on him.

"All I know is what the man told me, Maddux," Hannibal said. "He came to my office, introduced himself, and told me he was a Pinkerton agent and he was looking for you."

"Did he tell you why?"

"I wouldn't bring him out here until he did."

"What else did he tell you?"

"He thinks the Backshooter is more than one man."

"What makes him say that?"

Hannibal hesitated, "He thinks some of the Backshooter's killings were done by Walker Bogart."

"Walker—" Maddux started, looking at Hannibal. He paused a moment, then said, "Well, now this makes a little more sense."

Walker Bogart's name had started hitting the papers just about the time Maddux had retired—and about the same time as the Backshooter. During the past year his legend had been growing, to the point where his name was being mentioned in the same breath with the great ones—the James boys, Billy the Kid, and Clay Allison as an outlaw, and Hickok as a gunman.

"This Wilkes is after the reward on Bogart," said Maddux, "and he's disguising his hunt with this Backshooter business."

"Why would he do that?" Hannibal asked. "Why not just go after Bogart?"

"Maybe this was the only way he could get Pinkerton to foot his bills."

"Wait a minute," Hannibal said, suddenly excited. "This might be making more sense than we know."

"How do you mean?"

"What if Bogart heard that you might be coming after him?"

"How would he hear that?"

"Never mind how," Hannibal said. "What if he did? What would he do?"

Maddux knew what Hannibal was getting at. "Maybe he'd send some hired guns to kill me."

"Right."

"Well," Maddux said, "we'll have to ask the one we have in town."

Hannibal agreed.

"What's the price up to now?"

"Bogart?"

Maddux nodded.

"Five thousand. He's murdered seven people, among his other crimes."

Maddux rubbed his hand over his face. "Nineteen between him and this other crazy man."

"What if we took Wilkes's theory a step further?" Hannibal asked.

"How?"

"What if he and the Backshooter are the same person?"

"And what if there's no connection at all?"

"If Wilkes's theory is right, and it's not just a dodge, then there's a possibility that when we find Bogart we'll find the Backshooter. If not, then we'll just find Bogart, and maybe along the way you'll get a clue about who the Backshooter is."

Maddux turned and stared at Hannibal. He had noticed that Hannibal was saying "we" a lot."

"You're the marshal of Cromwell, Joe. You can't go off hunting a deadly killer because of another man's theory."

"I could, if a friend asked me."

"Meaning me?"

"You are gonna go, aren't you?"

"For him?" Maddux asked, jerking his head in the direction of the house.

"For him, for your friend Pinkerton...for yourself."

Rubbing his mouth with his hand, Maddux said, "I thought I had my last hunt, Joe."

"Three years ago."

"Yeah," Maddux said, thinking back. "That was a bad one, you know?"

"I know," Hannibal said, "I'm the one who found you, remember?"

"That one made me realize that after thirty years of hunting men for a living—among my other duties— the odds were definitely not in my favor anymore."

"What odds...for what?"

"Survival."

"You mean that even if you hadn't been shot in the back you might have retired?"

"It's possible."

Maddux looked straight out over his land, and Hannibal gave him a moment with his thoughts. Hannibal doubted that Maddux would have retired if his back hadn't forced him into it. Kyle Maddux had enjoyed the work too much, even after thirty years. It was the back injury—and Laura, of course—that had forced him into it.

Now he was going to have to defy both.

"There's a catch to this," Hannibal said, breaking the silence, "if you do agree to go."

"What catch?"

"Don't forget that Wilkes will be going along."

Maddux snorted derisively. "He'd get his clothes all dirty!"

"I guess that don't matter to him much," Hannibal said. "If he finds Bogart he gets the reward. If he finds the Backshooter, Pinkerton will reward him. Either way he can't lose, can he?"

"Only we can," Maddux said, "if he gets us killed."

Maddux took a moment to think, leaning against a post with his right thumb hooked into his back pocket. "Well, I've got a catch of my own then."

"What's that?"

"Shadoweyes comes."

"Shadoweyes?"

"He's a damned good tracker."

"When he's sober."

"I told you—"

"I know what you told me," Hannibal said.

"You can stay behind, Joe," Maddux said. "No point risking your job—"

"My job'll be there when I get back," Hannibal said. "Besides, who else would want to be the marshal of a town called Cromwell?"

"You've got a point there."

"Well?"

"Well what?"

"Are we going?"

Maddux made a face. "Let's go in and see if we can't talk the damn fool out of coming with us and slowing us down."

"And do his work for him?"

"If we're going to go, Joe," Maddux said, "what do we need him for?"

Hannibal smiled.

"Don't forget who'll be footing the bill," Hannibal said. "I know enough about you and Pinkerton to know that you won't mind taking advantage of *that*."

As it turned out, Glenn Wilkes was adamant about Shadoweyes not going. He had an Easterner's distrust of Indians.

"There's really no good reason for the Ind—uh, for Mr. Shadoweyes to come, is there?"

"There is," Maddux said.

"And what would that be?"

"Because he can track a mountain cat through a stone canyon."

"I'm...not sure I know what that means."

"It means he's an expert tracker, Mr. Wilkes," Hannibal said.

"That's what I said," Maddux said.

"I see," Wilkes said. He looked at Maddux and said, "I thought you were the expert tracker."

"Four eyes are better than two," Maddux said.

"And you, Marshal?" Wilkes asked. "Do you vouch for Shadoweyes?"

All eyes were on Hannibal now, waiting for his answer. To

his credit he gave it with only the slightest hint of hesitation. "He's a good man, Mr. Wilkes."

"Well, all right," Wilkes said, "but I will not pay him. That will be up to you, Mr. Maddux."

'If he'll come at all, Mr. Wilkes," Maddux said, "you'll pay him, or I won't come."

Shadoweyes sat in a corner of the room and didn't say anything. Maddux knew he'd come, and that was all that mattered.

"Well," Wilkes said, grudgingly, "all right, Marshal, can we get back to town now? I have some wires to send."

"Sure, Mr. Wilkes," Hannibal said.

"Joe," Maddux said, "Shadoweyes and I will be along at first light. We'll want to talk to Doc's patient first."

"Patient?" Wilkes said.

"Another matter, Wilkes," Hannibal said.

"Mr. Maddux, I'll expect your full attention to *this* matter," Wilkes said pompously.

"You'll get it, Wilkes," Maddux said. "My undivided attention."

"We have not settled on a fee—" Wilkes started.

"I'm sure you'll pay me fairly, Mr. Wilkes," Maddux said, "with Mr. Pinkerton's money."

Glenn Wilkes looked puzzled at Maddux's attitude when it came to the money. It was probably an attitude he had never encountered before in the East.

"I'll walk you gentlemen out."

———

WHEN MADDUX WENT BACK INSIDE, John Shadow-eyes had the place cleaned up and a fresh pot of coffee on the stove.

"Cup?" Shadoweyes asked.

"Sure."

Maddux sat down at the table and Shadoweyes set a cup of coffee in front of him.

"Are we going?" Shadoweyes asked.

"I'm going," Maddux said, sipping the coffee. Shadoweyes made the best coffee he'd ever tasted, and the Indian refused to tell him what he put in it.

"Whether or not you're going is up to you," Maddux said,

putting his cup back down. "You hired on to break horses and help me run the ranch, not hunt men."

"If you are going, Maddux," Shadoweyes said, "I am going."

Maddux looked at John Shadoweyes and then decided not to ask why.

The answer might embarrass both of them.

"What are you going to tell Mrs. Maddux?" Shadoweyes asked.

Maddux looked at the other man and said, "I've been wondering the same thing myself."

CHAPTER SIX

I n the morning Maddux and Shadoweyes closed up the house. Laura, incensed that Maddux had decided to go, said that she would be staying with Mrs. Hodges until Maddux returned.

She also hinted that she might not be ready to come back when Maddux returned. "But we can talk about that, Kyle. Go and get this out of your system, and we'll talk about it *if* you come back."

On the way to town they stopped off at their nearest neighbor's and asked Tom Seals if he'd come over and pick up the horses that were in the corral. Maddux trusted Seals to complete his transaction with the Army. It was one of the things that made this life so different from his other life— trusting people.

He was preparing to move back into the old life, though, and evidence of that was the gun on his hip and the anticipatory emptiness in the pit of his stomach. He did not feel particularly comfortable with either one of them at the moment.

After leaving Tom Seal's place they rode directly to Cromwell and stopped in front of Marshal Joe Hannibal's office. Inside Hannibal was talking to his two deputies, Ed Gorman and Al Collins.

Gorman was the older of the two and would be the man put in charge until Hannibal returned. He was in his mid-forties, and this particular star was just one of many he'd worn over the years. His scarred face and hands were evidence of the fact that there were times he upheld the law without the use of a gun.

Al Collins was in his thirties, and yet he could have passed for a youth in his early twenties. He was one of those men who always look ten years younger than they were. Of course, when he was seventy, that wouldn't matter much.

"Come on in, Maddux," Hannibal said. Shadow-eyes had remained outside with the horses. Maddux knew that the man had no desire to step inside the marshal's office.

"All right," Hannibal said to the deputies, "you boys know what to do."

Gorman and Collins nodded, greeted Maddux, and wished him luck on their way out.

"Have you talked to the town fathers?" Maddux asked.

"Yesterday evening, after Wilkes and I got back," Hannibal said. "They didn't like it, but then they don't have to."

"Joe, tell me your read on Wilkes."

"Self-important," Hannibal said, ticking points off his fingers, "a real pain in the ass—"

"Come on, Marshal," Maddux said, "don't hold back. Tell me what you really think."

Hannibal scowled at Maddux's humor, but was unable to hold it for very long.

"Where's Shadoweyes?" Hannibal asked after the laughter had subsided.

"Outside with the horses. Have you arranged for supplies?"

Hannibal nodded and said, "There'll be a pack horse waiting at the livery. Uh, Susan would like to see you before you leave."

Maddux stared at Hannibal and said, "How did she find out I was leaving?"

"Well, uh..." Hannibal stammered, looking sheepish.

"You told her, didn't you?"

"It slipped out last night, while she was serving me dinner."

"Shit."

"She's working this morning."

Maddux shifted his feet and said, "Yeah, all right, I'll go and see her."

"That's a right nice gal, Maddux," Hannibal said. "You could do a lot worse—"

"Believe me, I've got enough problems with one woman, Joe," Maddux said, holding both hands up to stop his friend from going any further. He told the lawman Laura Maddux's feelings about the trip.

"Doesn't sound like you got much of a send-off," Hannibal said, commiserating.

"I didn't."

"Well, maybe Susan can—"

"I'll meet you at the livery. Can I trust you with Shadoweyes? I mean, you won't arrest him or anything?"

"What for?"

"I don't know," Maddux said, shrugging. "You're just ornery enough to think of something."

"I ain't ornery—" Hannibal was saying as Maddux went out the door.

"John, I have to go over to the hotel," Maddux said to Shadoweyes outside. "Why don't you take the horses to the livery. There should be a pack horse waiting. Check it out, okay?"

"Yes."

"I'll meet you and the marshal and Wilkes there." The Indian scowled, and walked into the office without another word.

CHAPTER SEVEN

As luck would have it Glenn Wilkes was seated at the table Susan was serving when Maddux entered. She saw Maddux and motioned him over. Reluctantly, Maddux approached the table.

Wilkes had been speaking, placing his order, and had not seen Susan wave Maddux over. When he looked up and saw Maddux, he assumed that Maddux was coming to see him.

"Maddux," he said, his tone scolding, "I don't make a habit of discussing business at breakfast."

"Well that's good, Wilkes," Maddux said, "because I'm not here to see you." He looked at Susan and asked, "Do you have his order?"

"Yes."

"Well, let's go put it in."

He took her arm, careful of her injury, and led her to the kitchen. Before talking to him, she gave Wilkes's order to the cook.

"I understand Hannibal told you we were leaving.

"Yes," she said. "I wanted to see you before you left. I want to...to..."

She was faltering and he decided to let her work it out on her own. "I wanted to tell you to be careful."

"Did he tell you where we were going?"

"No."

"Or why?"

"No."

"Then why do you feel the need to tell me to be careful?"

"Well, he's leaving with you. The marshal wouldn't do that unless whatever you were doing was important—or dangerous."

"Susan..."

She smiled at him and touched his mouth with her hand. He was as startled as if she had kissed him, and looked appropriately guilty.

"I won't embarrass you," she said, "I just wanted to say good-bye, and to ask you to be sure to come back."

"I have every intention of doing that."

"Fine," she said, and went back to work.

Maddux stepped out of the kitchen and saw Wilkes standing outside waiting for him.

"Saying good-bye to your lady friend?" Maddux did not like the look on Wilkes's face, as if the two of them now shared a secret of some sort.

"Saying good-bye to a friend," Maddux said. "What's it to you?"

"I'm just not used to being ignored by my employees, in favor of a waitress," Wilkes said, "although I must admit she's very—"

He stopped short when Maddux's forefinger poked him hard in the chest. "Let's get something straight here, Wilkes," he said, pressing hard with his finger. "I am not your employee. I work for myself."

"I understood that—"

"You understood wrong."

Rubbing his chest where he'd been poked, Wilkes said, "You're taking my money."

"*I* haven't taken a cent yet," Maddux reminded him, "and it remains to be seen if I will—and if *I* do, it will be Alan Pinkerton's money, not yours. Now, we're ready to leave. Are you coming?"

"I've just ordered breakfast."

"Fine," Maddux said, "you stay and have your breakfast."

Maddux headed for the lobby, unaware that Susan was watching his progress.

"Now, hold on," Glenn Wilkes called out, following him.

Maddux turned on Wilkes in the lobby.

"The marshal, Shadoweyes, and I will be at the livery stable for the next fifteen minutes," he said. "If you're coming, you'll be there by then."

He turned and left the hotel without giving the man a chance to reply.

If it hadn't been so early, and the street so empty, Maddux might have died right there and then. As it was, Maddux detected a slight movement from the comer of his eye as he left the hotel and threw himself into the street. If nothing had happened he would have looked pretty silly—but it was better than being dead.

The man he had seen began firing the exact second Maddux dove from the boardwalk. As Maddux landed he pulled his gun, came around on his knees, and fired twice at the man. The first shot caught the man right in the belly, the second in the heart, killing him instantly.

People came running out of the hotel, and Marshal Hannibal came from his office.

"Jesus," Hannibal said, "another one?"

"Somebody wants me dead pretty bad, Joe," Maddux said, reloading his weapon, his eyes sweeping the street for further danger.

"Could be Bogart."

"Could be anyone," Maddux said. "It's not going to be so safe to be riding with me."

"Safe is just another word for boring," Hannibal said, "and I hate being bored."

"All right," Maddux said, snapping the gun shut. "Maybe you'd better get someone to clean up here and then meet me at the doctor's."

"I won't be long," Hannibal said.

Maddux started for the livery, wondering if someone was stepping out of his past with these two attempts on his life, or if it really was Walker Bogart. If it was the latter, then the man feared him for some reason.

Or maybe he was just sending him a calling card.

CHAPTER EIGHT

Maddux had to wake the doctor and apologized for it.
"Don't apologize," the doctor said. "Usually people wake me up because somebody's hurt or dead. I prefer your reasons."

"Can I talk to him?"

"I imagine he's asleep," the doctor said, "but I don't think that will stop you, eh?"

"No, it won't."

"He can't talk very well," the older man said. "He's developed an infection and I'm afraid I'm going to have to take his tongue."

"The man tried to kill me, doc," Maddux said. "The last thing I'd feel for him is pity."

"Go on in, then," the doctor said, scratching at his head of gray hair.

Maddux entered the room where the injured man lay sleeping. He walked over to the bed and slapped the man in the forehead.

"Uh—" the man said, coming awake. His eyes, fuzzy with sleep, cleared when he saw Maddux.

They cleared even more when Maddux put the barrel of the gun up against his jaw.

"I'm going to ask you some questions," Maddux said. "They are yes-or-no questions. You answer with a nod for yes, or a shake of the head for no. Do you understand me?"

The man's eyes, wide with fright, fastened on Maddux's face as he nodded.

"Were you sent to kill me by Walker Bogart?"

The man closed his eyes. He started to lick his lips, and then hissed at the pain the move caused.

"If you're worried about Bogart killing you," Maddux said, pressing the gun tightly against the man's chin, "you better worry some about me. I'll ask you again. Were you sent by Walker Bogart?"

The man opened his eyes, looked into Maddux's eyes, and was moved by what he saw there to nod his head.

"Well, that's good," Maddux said. "That's real good." Now he didn't have to rack his brain trying to figure out who was rising up out of his past.

"Do you know where Bogart is now?"

A shake of the head indicated no.

"Did you get paid in advance?"

A nod, for yes.

"How many of you—did he send two of you?"

The man shook his head no.

"Three?"

A nod.

"And you decided that one of you would lay back, in case the first two failed?"

Another nod.

"All right," Maddux said. He cocked the hammer back on the gun and the man began to whimper. When the man closed his eyes, Maddux took the gun away from his face and brought the hammer back down.

"Think of me when the doctor cuts off your tongue, and don't be here when I get back."

The man remained with his eyes closed, his face drenched with sweat, as Maddux left the room.

———

"AND YOU BELIEVED HIM?" Hannibal said back at the livery.

"Yes," Maddux said. "He wasn't in a position where he could afford to lie."

"*I* won't ask what that means."

"Have you got paper on Bogart?"

"I was waiting for you to ask," Hannibal said. He took a folded poster from his back pocket and handed it over.

Maddux opened it up and looked at it. As usual, the drawing of a man's face could have been anyone. The physical description said Bogart was six-four, with sandy-colored hair and a scar on the right side of his neck.

"Bogart is supposed to be good with a gun," Maddux said.

"Very good."

"That's odd for a big man," Maddux said, thoughtfully. "Can I keep this?"

"Sure."

Maddux refolded it and put it in his back pocket.

"You've got a funny look on your face," Hannibal said.

"I do?"

"Yes, you do," Hannibal said. "You're feeling it again, aren't you?"

"Feeling what?"

"The thrill of the hunt."

"Could be," Maddux said. He realized that this was not a denial, but then he couldn't very well deny it. There had been a surge of something when

Hannibal handed him the poster, and it had nothing to do with the five-thousand-dollar reward.

John Shadoweyes was standing in the shadows, listening to the conversation, saying nothing.

"Where's Wilkes, I wonder?" Hannibal said then.

"If we're lucky he decided to have his breakfast," Maddux said. He looked at Shadoweyes and asked, "How is the pack horse?"

"The marshal picked him out."

That was the way Shadoweyes would say he hadn't checked the animal.

"I know horseflesh, Maddux," Hannibal said.

"If you picked him out, then I'm satisfied, Joe," Maddux said.

Maddux saw Hannibal looking over his shoulder, and turned to see Glenn Wilkes hurrying toward them.

"I'll saddle his horse," Hannibal said.

"Let him saddle his own damned horse!" Maddux said.

Hannibal just gave Maddux a look and went to saddle the horse.

CHAPTER NINE

CEREMONY, NEW MEXICO

Walker Bogart was enjoying his breakfast.

He was eating with the hearty gusto of a man who had no worries in the world.

In fact, as far as he was concerned, he *didn't* have any worries. He was eating in the dining room of the Ceremony House Hotel, and was far from finished when his man Jerry Parnell entered and approached his table.

"You ain't gonna tell me something that's gonna ruin my appetite, Jerry, are you?" he demanded before Parnell could speak.

"Uh, it ain't my fault, Walker," Jerry Parnell said, whining.

"Jesus," Bogart said, dropping his fork in disgust. "I can't eat when you whine like that. What the hell is the problem now?"

Parnell shifted his feet, then blurted out, "Maddux ain't dead."

Bogart stared at Parnell long enough for the man to start to fidget from foot to foot.

"And why ain't Maddux dead?" Bogart finally asked.

"Well—"

"How many men did you send to do the job?"

"Three to do the job, and one to report on it."

"And what happened to them?"

"Two of them are dead."

"And the third one?"

"He was hurt."

"How bad?"

"I—don't rightly know, Walker."

"So Maddux took all three of them?"

"Yep." Pamell shuffled his feet.

"And whose decision was it to send three men to do the job on him?"

"Uh, mine."

"And who was wrong?"

"*I* was."

"Remember that, Jerry," Bogart said.

"Remember what, Walker?"

"That I'm always right and you're always wrong."

"Aw, Walker—"

"Shut up," Bogart said. He was a big man, broad across the shoulders and chest, and even seated he seemed to dwarf Jerry Pamell—but it wasn't the sheer size of Bogart that frightened Parnell. It was the fact that Parnell had personally seen Walker Bogart kill six men—two of them with his bare hands, and one of those just for spilling coffee on him.

"Shut up and get out of here," Bogart said. "Find out about that third man, and whether or not he's gonna talk to the law."

"Right."

"*I* want to know if Maddux's coming after me."

"I'll find out."

Parnell didn't move. Bogart picked up his fork, saw that Parnell was there, and then put it down again. He fixed the man with an impatient stare.

"Now what?" Bogart asked.

"What about the girl?"

"What about her?"

"What do we do with her?"

"You do what I said to do."

"Uh, why don't we just kill her, Walker?"

Bogart assumed an expression not unlike that worn by a schoolteacher addressing a slow-witted child.

"I told you, Jerry, she's just too damned pretty to kill."

"She's dangerous, Walker."

"*She* ain't so dangerous where she is now, is she?" Bogart asked.

"No, but—"

"Jerry, I'm gonna be known not only as the man who brought Maddux out of retirement, but as the man who killed him as well. Do you understand that?"

Parnell didn't. If Bogart wanted to kill Maddux himself, then why did he have Parnell send the men to Cromwell to bushwhack him?

"I still think she's dangerous on her own—" Parnell began.

"Jerry?"

"What?"

"Who's always right?"

Looking sheepish Parnell said, "You are."

"And who's always wrong?"

In a low voice the other man said, "I am."

"Get out!"

"Right, Walker."

"Jerry!"

Parnell, already a few steps away, turned and came back. "Yeah, Walker?"

Bogart beckoned to him and Parnell leaned over the table, very conscious of the fact that he was now within the big man's reach.

"I don't want her hurt or killed—"

"Sure, Walk—"

"—and I don't want her touched either. Do you know what I mean by *touched?*"

"Uh, sure, Walker, I know. You don't want her, uh...touched."

"Right. You'll pass that along to those two idiots you have watching her, won't you?"

"I sure will, Walker."

"Good," Bogart said. "Now you can get out."

The other diners in the room did not hear the conversation, but when they saw the smaller man hurriedly scurrying from the dining room they knew he was propelled by fear.

The big man looked down at his breakfast then and frowned. He called for the waiter loudly and told him that his food had gone cold.

"But sir," the waiter said, "it got cold while you were talking to you friend—"

"I don't care *why* it got cold," the big man said, frowning. "I just know that it is."

"I'll...have it reheated for you, sir."

"I don't want it reheated, man," Walker Bogart said, "I want it replaced." He held the plate aloft and said, "I want a fresh plate. I'm a guest of this hotel. Don't you take care of your guests?"

"Uh, yes, sir, we do."

"Well, then?"

The waiter smiled nervously and picked up the plate from the table. "I'll bring you a fresh plate, sir."

"Thank you very much."

As the waiter headed for the kitchen another diner called out to him.

"Yes, sir?" the waiter said, holding the big man's plate away from him.

"Waiter," the man said, rather timidly because he wasn't sure if this was going to work or not, "my breakfast seems to have gotten cold."

The waiter frowned at the man and barked, "Eat it anyway."

CHAPTER TEN

They rode into New Moon, Texas, sixteen days after leaving Cromwell. They had stopped first in Abilene, where the Backshooter had claimed his first victim. The second victim had been killed in New Moon.

"Small town," Hannibal commented.

"Big enough to have a telegraph office," Maddux said, pointing to it.

"What are we going to do here?" Glenn Wilkes asked impatiently.

The man had asked a lot of questions all along the way. Things like "Why can't I drink more water?" and "How do you expect me to eat that?" and "Are you sure we're going the right way?"

Maddux looked at Wilkes and said with as much patience as he could muster, "Right now we're going to have the horses taken care of, and then get us a couple of hotel rooms."

"A couple of rooms? Don't we need four?"

"Two will be plenty."

Wilkes look appalled.

"Don't worry, Mr. Wilkes," Maddux said. "You can bunk in with the marshal."

That didn't seem to appease the man any. In the end Wilkes offered to pay for three rooms so he could have his own.

"That's up to you," Maddux said. "John and I will share a room anyway, though."

So Marshal Joe Hannibal ended up with a room of his own.

When they got to the livery John Shadoweyes said, "I will see to the horses."

They all gave their mounts over to Shadoweyes and Maddux said, "Meet us at the nearest hotel."

"Right."

As Maddux, Hannibal, and Wilkes walked away from the livery to find the hotel Wilkes said, "Shouldn't we go to the telegraph office?"

"All in good time, Mr. Wilkes," Hannibal said. He replied because he knew that Maddux's patience with the man was just about at an end. "There are some other things we have to do first."

"Like what?"

"Like—" Hannibal began, but Maddux cut him off.

"Look!" he said, whirling on Wilkes. "We're going to get along a lot better with each other if you'd stop asking so damn many questions."

"I'm just concerned—"

"Being concerned is my job," Maddux said. "All *you* have to do is follow me. Understand?"

"Look, Kyle," Hannibal said, "why don't you go to the saloon and wait for us there. We'll take care of getting the rooms."

"I'm going to check in with the local law, Joe."

"Shouldn't I do that?" Hannibal asked. "After all, I'm a lawman—"

"Not on this trip you're not," Maddux said. "I'll check in with him and then meet you at the saloon, like you suggested."

"All right, Maddux," Hannibal said. "It's your show."

"Thank you," Maddux said, and walked away from them.

Maddux found the sheriff's office with no trouble and entered without knocking. He caught the man behind the desk in the act of pulling on one of his boots. It was a difficult act because the man's mountainous belly was getting in his way.

He finally slid the boot on and then slammed his foot onto the floor.

"Damn marriage!" the man said, and then noticed Maddux standing there.

"What has marriage to do with getting a boot on?"

"I'll tell you, stranger, so you can keep it in mind before *you* ever marry," the sheriff said. "Once I was as slender as you, and then I married a woman who could cook. Now I got this gut."

"I see."

The sheriff straightened behind his desk and said, "But you didn't come here to talk about my problems. What can I do for you, mister?"

"My name's Maddux, Sheriff..."

"Oh, sorry," the lawman said. "Name's Kiley, Andy Kiley."

"Sheriff Kiley, my name is Kyle Maddux. I'm here in town with a Pinkerton agent."

"Really? I ain't never met a Pinkerton agent."

"I'll be sure to introduce you."

"That's right nice of you. Just what are you fellas doing in New Moon?"

"Sheriff, you had a murder here a couple of years ago."

"That?" the sheriff said.

"You know which one I'm talking about?"

"We ain't had that many murders in this county, Mr. Maddux. You're talking about old Pop Wingate bein' shot in the back by that fella they're callin' the Backshooter. Right?"

"That's the one," Maddux said.

"Why you here lookin' into that after all this time?"

"It's a long story, Sheriff," Maddux said. "Let's just say I'm dogging a cold trail."

"You sure are."

"I wanted you to know that we'd be talking to people in town about it, and probably the family as well."

"Only family Pop had was his daughter, Patricia, and she left after he was killed."

That didn't surprise Maddux. They had run into the same situation in Abilene. The man who had been killed there had been a young man, and his wife had left town soon after.

"That's all right," Maddux said. "We'll still be talking to the townspeople about it—that is, if you don't mind."

"Suit yourself," the sheriff said with a shrug. "That's all old business to me."

That was the attitude Maddux had expected to run into dealing with local law. He'd have been surprised by anything else.

"Well, thanks very much, Sheriff. I appreciate your time." .

Maddux turned and started for the door.

"Maddux?"

Maddux turned and said, "Yes?"

"Uh, will you and your friends be staying in town long?"

"Just a few days, I think," Maddux said, his hand on the doorknob. "Long enough for my friends and me to talk to most of the people who knew Pop Wingate."

"Well then, good luck," Kiley said. "And if you're interested in knowing, the Hotel of New Moon has a fine dining room."

As the man spoke he rubbed his belly, and Maddux knew he was speaking from experience.

"Thank you, Sheriff," Maddux said. "I'll keep that in mind."

Maddux left the office, and the sheriff sat back in his chair and assumed a worried look.

CHAPTER ELEVEN

Maddux walked into the saloon and found Hannibal and Wilkes at a table, sharing a bottle of whiskey. Actually, Hannibal was drinking the whiskey, and Wilkes was complaining that the saloon didn't have any brandy.

"It's a small town, Mr. Wilkes," Hannibal was saying as Maddux approached the table.

If Wilkes was going to reply, he was interrupted by Maddux's appearance.

"Kyle," Hannibal said, "take a chair."

Maddux sat down and Hannibal filled the glass he'd provided for him.

"Thanks," Maddux said, taking a taste.

"Did you find out anything from the sheriff?" Hannibal asked.

"Oh, he had some words of wisdom about marriage, and eating, and putting your boots on—"

"What?" Wilkes said.

"—but he had nothing to say about the murder, except that the dead man's daughter left town soon after. He didn't know anything about the murder."

"Did you believe him?" Wilkes said.

Maddux didn't answer right away.

"*I* have no reason not to believe him, Wilkes," he finally answered, wearily. He looked at Hannibal and asked, "Did you get the hotel rooms?"

"Yes," Hannibal said.

"Good. I'll see you back there. I figure we'll have dinner in the hotel dining room."

"That's fine," Hannibal said.

Maddux stood up and left the saloon, leaving his drink unfinished.

"Mr. Wilkes," Hannibal said, "you're gonna have to try and get along with Maddux."

"Why?" Wilkes asked. "I am employing him. *He* should be trying to get along with *me*. If he's not careful, I'll fire him."

"If you fire him you'll never find...what you're looking for."

"You mean you couldn't find Walker Bogart?" Wilkes asked with disdain. "Or the Backshooter?"

"Mr. Wilkes, I'm a good lawman, but when it comes to tracking there ain't a better man than Maddux."

"If he's so good, why did he retire?"

"Well, I guess that's something you're gonna have to ask him—but he sure won't answer that question while you and him are sniping at each other."

Hannibal picked up the bottle and poured himself and Wilkes another drink. It occurred to him that he had left Cromwell to play nursemaid to two men who were just as likely to kill each other as not.

CHAPTER TWELVE

When Maddux left the saloon he decided to take a turn around town and try to talk to some of the people about Pop Wingate. It was something he had also done in Abilene, talking to people about Del Kilmer, the man who had been killed there.

In both cases people were fairly willing to talk about the two men, indicating that the victims were, for the most part, well-liked men. But when he started asking about people who might have been hanging around the two men, that's when people didn't have much to say.

Maddux was looking for someone who might have noticed a stranger who had come to town and become involved with the dead man. He was also looking for information on someone who might have left town right after the killing—other than family, that is.

As he had in Abilene, he came up empty in New Moon. The killings had simply happened too long ago for people to remember anything other than the people who were killed.

When Maddux got to the room he was sharing with Shadoweyes, he found the man sitting on the floor, even though there were two beds in the room.

"Bad mattresses?"

Shadoweyes looked at him and said, "They are almost like lying on the ground."

"But not as comfortable, huh?"

"No."

Maddux sat on one of the beds and discovered that Shadoweyes was right. He took a moment to sit there and close his eyes, trying to will away the pain in his back. Stretching would do no good—about as much good as willing the pain away did.

"Is it bad?" Shadoweyes asked.

Maddux looked over his shoulder at the man and said, "It's there."

"The riding—" Shadoweyes started to say, but Maddux cut him off.

"Hasn't made it any worse...yet," Maddux lied. He knew that his back *was* hurting more because of the riding, but then so was his backside. It had been a long time since he had done any serious riding. He was hoping that his back and butt would hurt less after a few more miles in the saddle.

"Bad news?" Shadoweyes asked. Maddux knew they were off the subject of his back and onto the subject of what he had found out.

"No news," Maddux said.

Briefly, he told Shadoweyes about his visit to the sheriff, his conversation with Wilkes, and then his talk with some of the townspeople .about Pop Wingate.

"People will remember more when we get closer to Mexico," Shadoweyes said.

Maddux frowned. By the time they reached the site of the twelfth and-most recent murder, it would be almost three months old—and there might be another one in the meantime.

"Maybe," he said. "I'm having dinner in the hotel dining room with Hannibal and...Wilkes. Do you want to come?"

"I do not think so," Shadoweyes said. "I do not think Mr. Wilkes and I should sit at the same table."

"Look, John," Maddux said, "if he doesn't like it, then he can go and sit somewhere else."

"No, I do not worry that he will not like it," Shadoweyes said. "I know I will not like it."

"All right then."

"*I* will find someplace else to eat, and keep my ears open."

"Okay, you do that," Maddux said. He walked to the window and looked down at New Moon's main street. "We'll meet up here later and see if either of us has come up with anything useful."

John Shadoweyes nodded and stood up.

"I wish you luck," Shadoweyes said. "I do not envy you having dinner with that man."

"I don't know what it is, John," Maddux said. "We've just taken an instant dislike to each other."

"That is easy to understand—on your part."

"Yeah, well, maybe I should just make more of an effort to be civil with him."

"I am glad the effort is yours to make," Shadow-eyes said, "and not mine."

"Yeah," Maddux said as Shadoweyes went out the door.

At dinner Maddux decided that if he couldn't say anything civil to Wilkes, he wouldn't speak to the man at all.

"Where's Shadoweyes?" Hannibal asked.

"He's eating somewhere else."

"That's just as well," Glenn Wilkes said. "I don't relish having my meals with an Indian."

"Shadoweyes is a half-breed," Hannibal said, correcting him.

"That is even worse," Wilkes said. 'There's *nothing* worse than someone whose blood isn't pure."

Maddux held his tongue.

"What's Shadoweyes really doing?" Hannibal asked.

"Keeping his eyes and ears open."

"Excuse me," Wilkes said, "but I'm not paying—"

"Shadoweyes works for me," Maddux said, forestalling any objections Wilkes might have.

"Very well," Wilkes said. His tone was imperious, as if he had just given his permission for something.

Maddux held his tongue.

"What are we going to do?" Hannibal asked.

"I'll talk to Shadoweyes in a few hours," Maddux said. "If he hasn't come up with anything, then I'll make another visit to the sheriff and see if I can't jar his memory a little."

"We'll be leaving tomorrow?" Hannibal asked.

"I think so," Maddux said. "There doesn't seem to be much reason to stay any longer."

"One day doesn't seem like very much effort," Wilkes said.

Maddux gave Wilkes a cold look. "Are you really a Pinkerton?" he asked.

The man looked surprised at the question.

"Of course I am."

"I never did see any of your papers."

Wilkes's chin seemed to stiffen as he fished his wallet out of his pocket and showed Maddux his certification that he was a Pinkerton agent.

"What do you want?" he asked Wilkes, passing the wallet back.

"What?"

"I asked you what you want? Why you're here?"

Wilkes looked at Hannibal, then said, "I want to find the Backshooter."

"Or Walker Bogart."

"Yes."

Maddux shook his head and said, "It doesn't figure."

"What doesn't?" Hannibal asked.

"Him being a Pink," Maddux said. "He hasn't done a lick of work either here or in Abilene."

"I beg your pardon," Wilkes said. "My methods happen to be subtle."

Maddux studied Wilkes, nodding his head to himself, and then said, "It just doesn't figure."

"And why not?" Wilkes asked, stiffly.

"You're not Alan Pinkerton's type," Maddux said. "Who hired you?"

"I was hired by William Pinkerton."

"Out of Chicago?" Maddux asked.

"Yes."

"And sent to the St. Louis office?"

"Yes."

"That explains it then."

"Explains what?" Wilkes asked, frowning.

"You're not Old Alan's type, but you are William's."

"And what type is that?"

Maddux studied Wilkes for a moment and then said, "If I told you that, Mr. Wilkes, it would ruin both our meals."

Maddux put his napkin down on the table and stood up. "I'm going to take another turn around town." He assumed that Wilkes would take care of the check. Expenses were part of the deal.

As he was leaving the dining room he heard Wilkes asking Hannibal, "What did he mean by—"

Maddux smiled.

CHAPTER THIRTEEN

Walker Bogart's dominance over the town of Ceremony was spreading. By virtue of force he was already the most feared man in town. People stepped aside when he walked toward them, storekeepers served him without ever asking for payment, and even the law in Ceremony turned the other cheek when it came to Bogart and his men.

Part of Bogart's dominance was in being able to take over the largest house in town, which had formerly belonged to the mayor of Ceremony. Bogart had simply arrived on the mayor's doorstep one morning and announced that the house was his. The Mayor and his wife had then moved to the hotel. Mayor Perry had assured his wife that this was just a temporary situation.

"Just until we can figure out what to do about Bogart and his men, dear," he'd said.

"You and the others will continue to do what you've been doing," Janet Perry had said.

"What's that?"

"You'll let him walk all over you."

And, indeed, that was what Walker Bogart was doing, walking all over the people of Ceremony.

And to a man they were too frightened to do anything about it.

———

WALKER BOGART WALKED into his house and nodded to the man he had watching the door. Inside, there was a man sitting in the living room, reading a newspaper.

"Where is she?" he asked.

"Upstairs," the man said.

"How is she?"

"Quiet."

"Has she eaten?"

"I brought her something a little while ago, but I don't know if she ate it."

"Has anybody touched her?"

"Geez, Mr. Bogart," the man said, "you told us not to, so we ain't."

"Good."

Bogart went upstairs to his bedroom, but she wasn't in there. He went to the other bedroom in the . house and found Anne Redman there. She looked up as he came in, and there was no expression on her face. He saw the untouched tray of food on the top of the dresser.

"Miss Redman."

She didn't answer.

"You haven't eaten."

No reply.

"You should eat, you know," he went on. "You have to stay healthy."

No reply.

"If you don't eat you'll lose weight, and if you lose weight you won't do those clothes justice."

"You call these clothes?"

Bogart had gone to all of the saloon girls who worked in the town and asked them each for their most revealing piece of clothing. He'd then taken Anne Redman's clothes away from her and provided her with garments he'd appropriated from the saloon girls.

Anne Redman wore those garments only because her only other choice was to go naked. At the moment she was wearing a rather gaudy red corset with black nylon stockings and garters. It was the least revealing thing she could find to wear, but her creamy breasts still threatened to spill out of the top of the corset.

"Those are the clothes I've chosen for you to wear," Bogart said. "Of course, I wish you would alternate the clothing a little more. You've been wearing that same outfit for weeks."

"And I'll keep wearing it until you take it away from me."

"Well, I'll have to do that eventually. Will you eat this food?"

"No."

"I'll leave it here in case you change your mind."

He turned to walk out of the room and Anne sprang off the bed, took hold of the tray, and threw it after him. It missed him and struck the wall on the hall, spewing food all over the floor. Some of it did get on Bogart's shoulder, but his reaction was surprisingly calm.

Bogart looked into the room and said, "I'll send someone up to clean this mess. You'd better close your door, though, because if he sees you like that he might get some ideas."

Bogart was going down the steps when he heard the door slam.

———

ANNE REDMAN WAS FURIOUS.

Some of her fury was directed at Walker Bogart, for forcing her to dress up like a whore, but most of her fury was aimed at herself. She'd been dogging Walker Bogart's trail for weeks, and had finally decided that she might need some help. What she had not known was that Bogart was on *her* trail by that time, and consequently she had been taken—and taken rather easily. They had been waiting for her at the livery stable when she'd tried to leave the town of Kent's Fork, to pick up Bogart's trail again. Bogart hadn't been with them, but they'd made it clear to her whose men they were, and where they were taking her.

She had felt all along that Bogart was headed for New Mexico. Bogart's men had taken her directly to Ceremony without blindfolding her or making any attempt to keep her from knowing where they were taking her.

She had assumed that this meant she was going to be killed.

And there were days when she wished they *had* killed her.

Walker Bogart had been immediately taken with her, and had decided to keep her. He'd set her up in this house, and forced her to dress up in whores' underwear. For any normal woman that would have been demeaning, but to a woman in her line of work it was...downright embarrassing.

The odd thing about Bogart was that he basically left her alone. He protected her from his men—who would have liked nothing better than to take turns raping her—and had never once touched her, or even tried to.

In fact, most of the time—in spite of the way he forced her to dress—he treated her with an almost reverent attitude.

She thought he was mad, and expected him to kill her at any time.

The prospect of dying did not bother her so much.

It was the damned waiting.

CHAPTER FOURTEEN

Maddux's second turn around town yielded him nothing but an opinion that there were certainly not many decent-looking women in New Moon. For a town with such a pretty name, he thought that a shame.

He went back to the hotel after dark and found Shadoweyes waiting in the lobby. This apparently did not sit well with the clerk, who kept throwing the half-breed nervous looks.

"Come on," Maddux said. "Let's get a drink and talk somewhere else."

Shadoweyes stood up and followed Maddux out.

"What did you see or hear?" Maddux asked.

"Nothing much."

They went to the saloon and walked to the bar. As soon as they entered they attracted attention as strangers in town. John Shadoweyes, in particular, drew disapproving looks.

Maddux knew trouble was coming, but he was looking for trouble just about now.

"Two beers," he said to the bartender.

"One beer," the bartender said. "We don't serve Indians."

"Does he dress like an Indian?" Maddux asked.

"Just because he dresses like a white man don't make him one," the bartender said.

"Two beers," Maddux said.

"One beer," the bartender said again. "I told you we don't serve Indians."

"He's not full-blooded Indian," Maddux said, half serious.

"That don't make no—" the bartender started, but Maddux reached out and took hold of the front of the man's shirt. He made no move to resist when Maddux pulled him halfway across the bar.

"I said draw him a beer."

As the man's left hand came out from below the bar Shadoweyes reached out and caught it by the wrist. In the man's hand was a billy club, which he'd intended to use on Maddux. Shadoweyes took it from his hand.

"Now," Maddux said, "draw two beers."

"The sheriff's gonna hear about this."

"I know," Maddux said. "I'm gonna tell him." He released the man and pushed him so that he slammed against the shelves behind him, rattling the bottles.

The man drew two beers and put both of them in front of Maddux. Maddux pushed one of the beers over to Shadoweyes, and they drank.

Maddux looked the place over through the mirror behind the bar. Once he and Shadoweyes were served their beers, the rest of the men in the place seemed to sense that the entertainment was over, and they went back to their conversations, or their games, or their flirting with saloon girls.

There was a table in the back that was empty, and Maddux gestured towards it with his beer. He and Shadoweyes went and sat down.

"Tell me," Maddux said.

"I talked to the children in the town."

"Ah," Maddux said. Shadoweyes had always gotten along with children.

"Children see everything, and will talk to anyone who is willing to listen."

"That's true," Maddux said. "Now what did they see?"

"Pop Wingate owned the General Store," Shadow-eyes said. "The children say he hired a man to work for him before he was killed."

"How long before?"

Shadoweyes shrugged. "What do children know of time?"

"What happened to this man after Pop Wingate was killed?"

"He left town."

"What did the man look like?"

"The children I spoke to were mostly girls," Shadoweyes said.

Maddux thought that would have thrilled any of the townspeople or parents who'd seen Shadoweyes talking to their little girls. He hoped they weren't going to run into trouble over that.

"They said he had dark curly hair, nice eyes, and was very handsome."

Maddux frowned. "Was he young? Old?"

"To children," Shadoweyes said, "we are all old."

"That's great."

"They said he was not so old as Pop Wingate."

"All right, so we've got a man younger than the victim—let's say that makes him under fifty—with dark hair and nice eyes."

"And he is handsome."

"And handsome."

Shadoweyes looked across the table at Maddux and said, "It is not much."

"Hell," Kyle Maddux said, "it's a hell of a lot more than we had when we came here."

CHAPTER FIFTEEN

Maddux and Shadoweyes finished their beers and Maddux was trying to decide whether he should go up to the bar for two more when the sheriff walked in, followed by two deputies. The sheriff looked around the room until he spotted Maddux, and then approached the table. His deputies stayed at the door.

"Sheriff," Maddux said.

The sheriff looked at him, and then at Shadoweyes. "I thought Bert didn't serve Indians."

Maddux smiled. "Bert changed his mind. What can I do for you, Sheriff?"

"I just thought I'd check on you," the sheriff said. "You know, do my job."

"Why don't you sit down and have Bert bring three more beers?"

The sheriff licked his lips, then said, "Why not?" He turned and called to the bartender to bring three more beers, and then sat down.

"I'm glad you came here, Sheriff," Maddux said. "I have some more questions to ask you."

Maddux looked past the man to his deputies, who were still standing at the door. "Why did you bring your deputies?"

The sheriff looked over his shoulder for a second, then turned back. "We were just making our rounds."

"Together?" Maddux said. "Small town like this and it takes three of you to make rounds?"

"I...like to be careful...and your friend here was seen talking to some little girls a while ago."

"Is that so?"

"Their parents were worried."

"The same parents who let their children out on the streets late at night?" Shadoweyes asked.

The sheriff stared at Shadoweyes and said, "We got a safe town here."

Shadoweyes looked away from the man.

"What questions you got?" the lawman asked Maddux.

"We heard something about a man Pop Wingate hired before he was killed."

"Pop was always hiring drifters to work for him. There might have been one here when he was killed."

"You don't remember."

"I told you," the sheriff said, "that's old news to me."

"I see."

"I'm sorry I can't help you, Mr. Maddux," the sheriff said. He drank down his beer and stood up. He was about to leave when he said, "Say, are you the same Kyle Maddux who was marshal up in Cromwell for some years?"

"A lot of years."

"Yeah, well," the sheriff said, "I heard you was dead."

"As you can see," Maddux said slowly, "I'm not dead."

"Retired, then."

"Yes."

"Then why are you looking for this feller who's shooting people in the back?"

"Let's just say I don't like backshooters."

"You huntin' bounty now?"

"There isn't a price on the man's head that I know of."

"Maybe that's because nobody knows what the hell he looks like."

"Maybe that's why," Maddux agreed.

"Well...you know when you'll be leaving town?"

"More than likely in the morning."

"See if you can't keep your breed away from the kids in town until then, huh?"

Maddux was about to say something when the hand of

Shadoweyes fell on his arm and squeezed.

"I'll do my best, Sheriff," Maddux said.

The overweight sheriff nodded and, waving at his two deputies to follow, left the saloon.

"Buffoons like that give the job a bad name," Maddux said.

Maddux and Shadoweyes stayed a little longer at the saloon. Maddux turned away the advances of one saloon girl. He had the feeling that she would rather have offered herself to Shadoweyes, but was afraid to.

On the way back to the hotel Shadoweyes said, "What do we do about the tail?"

"You know," Maddux said, "I've had a feeling— how long has he been with us?"

"Since we left Cromwell."

"Why didn't you say something before now?"

Shadoweyes looked at him and said, "I assumed you knew about it."

"I should have," Maddux said, chiding himself, adding with feeling. "I had a feeling, damn it, but I should have known."

"It has been a while since you were on the trail," Shadoweyes reminded him.

"Let's assume he's an observer," Maddux said, waving the excuse away. "He was probably sent to Cromwell to report on whether or not I had been killed. Since I wasn't, he is now just following us."

"Why doesn't he try to kill you?"

"Three men have failed, and now I'm traveling with three men myself."

"All right," Shadoweyes said. "What do we do now?"

"Well, as of now we do nothing," Maddux said. "We get some sleep and an early start. Tomorrow, one of us will hang back and see what kind of answers we can get out of our friend the observer."

"I will do it."

Maddux studied Shadoweyes for a moment, then decided that it was a good idea. Up to now it had been all Maddux could do to stay in the saddle. Sneaking up on someone was just not something he felt capable of doing—not just yet, anyway. "All right."

Maddux had no illusions that he was as good or as quiet as Shadoweyes, even in his prime.

CHAPTER SIXTEEN

E arly the next morning Maddux banged on the door of Joe Hannibal's room. When the door opened he saw that Hannibal was dressed and ready. He hadn't spoken to Hannibal the previous night before turning in, so he was pleased to see that his friend had anticipated him.

"I figured you'd want to get a very early start," Hannibal said.

"Did you tell the city boy that?"

"I did," Hannibal said, "but we'd better bang on his door anyway."

"I'll do it," Maddux said. "Shadoweyes has already gone to the livery to get the horses ready."

"Did you find out anything else last night?"

"Yeah," Maddux said, "I'll tell you about it later."

Maddux went down the hall and banged on the door of Glenn Wilkes's room. When there was no immediate answer he forced the door open. The flimsy hotel lock did little to keep him out.

Wilkes was sprawled on the bed, fast asleep. Maddux looked around, saw the pitcher of water on the dresser, and couldn't resist.

He walked over, got the pitcher, and then very deliberately poured the water over Wilkes's head.

Wilkes came up sputtering, looking around the room frantically.

"Wha—wha—" he blubbered.

"Let's go, Wilkes!" Maddux called out. "We don't keep bankers' hours out here, you know."

Wilkes sat up and glared at Maddux. "You—you didn't have to do that."

"Well, I knocked," Maddux said, "and I called and I shook. This was my last option before I fired my gun in your ear."

"Damn you."

"Look," Maddux said, "Hannibal told you we wanted to get an early start."

"Yes, but I expected someone to wake me up."

"Well, we don't have a wake-up service, Wilkes. Now, we're all ready to roll, so you only have a couple of minutes to get dressed...and dried."

Maddux turned to leave and Wilkes said plaintively, "What about breakfast?"

"You'll have to wait until lunch," Maddux said over his shoulder, and closed the door behind him.

MADDUX, Hannibal, and Shadoweyes were mounted and ready to leave by the time Wilkes showed up at the livery. He was trying to control his breathing so that they wouldn't know that he had run from the hotel.

"Well, at least you saddled my horse," he said mounting up.

"Shadoweyes did it," Maddux said.

Wilkes didn't reply.

"I told him not to," Maddux said.

Again, Wilkes made no reply.

"You could say thank you," Maddux said.

Wilkes frowned at Maddux, then turned to Shadoweyes. He seemed about to say something when Shadoweyes kicked his horse in the sides and started forward.

"Let's go," Maddux said, and followed Shadow-eyes out.

Now as they rode out of town Shadoweyes, who had taken the lead, rode further ahead of them, as if he were riding point. His plan was to ride far enough ahead to be able to circle back and come up behind the man who was following them.

Then he would ask him a few friendly questions.

Ed Chartman's back hurt. That came from sleeping in a

doorway across the street from the hotel where Maddux and the others were staying.

Charterman had ridden to Cromwell with three of Walker Bogart's men, to observe while they tried to kill Maddux. After Maddux had shot the three of them, killing two, Charterman had sent a telegraph message for instructions—sending his message to a town in Texas, from where it was relayed to Bogart in New Mexico, so it couldn't be traced—and his instructions were to follow Maddux when he left, and keep an eye on him. If and when he started to get close, Charterman was to send word.

Charterman peered ahead now, making sure that he was close enough to follow, but not close enough to be seen. The terrain was mostly flat, with some stands of trees and rock formations, and he had to maintain a respectable distance to avoid being seen. Charterman was not a gunman, and was only kept around by Bogart to do menial tasks. He had felt that this job was a way to move up in Bogart's estimation, and he was determined to do it right.

Walker Bogart didn't like his men to make mistakes. When they did, they generally ended up dead, like the men in Cromwell.

Ed Charterman had no hankering to end up dead.

CHAPTER SEVENTEEN

Hannibal rode up on Maddux and asked, "Where did Shadoweyes go?"

"He's going to ask our friend some questions," Maddux answered.

"Our friend?"

Maddux jerked his thumb behind them and Hannibal understood.

"What's going on?" Wilkes asked, riding up next to them on Hannibal's side. "I don't like being left out."

"Nobody's leaving you out, Mr. Wilkes," Maddux said.

"Where did the half-breed go?"

Maddux ignored him.

Hannibal said, "He has a name, Mr. Wilkes."

"I know he has a name, for Chrissakel"

Now he was ignored by both Maddux *and* Hannibal.

"All right," Wilkes said. "Where did Shadoweyes go?"

"We have a tail," Maddux said. "He's gone to find out what the man knows."

"A tail?" Wilkes asked, turning quickly in his saddle to look back. "I don't see anything."

"He's far enough back so that you wouldn't."

"How long has he been there?"

"Since we left Cromwell."

"And you didn't know it?" Wilkes asked Maddux.

"Of course he knew it," Hannibal said. "He *and* Shadoweyes

knew it."

"And the marshal," Maddux said.

"Well, that's fine," Wilkes said. "Everyone knew it but me."

"We all saw it on our own," Maddux said. "We didn't discuss it until we got to New Moon."

"And none of you did anything about it?"

"He was just watching us, Wilkes," Maddux said. "He was doing no harm so long as we knew he was there."

"And now?"

"Now we want to see if he knows where Walker Bogart is. Maybe he knows something about the Backshooter too."

Exasperated, Wilkes said, "There's no price on *his* head. We don't even know what he looks like."

"We have a partial description," Maddux said, and gave it to the man.

Wilkes stared at Maddux openmouthed, and then said, "And how long have we had *that?*"

"Since last night. Shadoweyes got it from some children in town."

"Children?" Wilkes said. "Oh, for Christ—"

"Mr. Wilkes," Hannibal said. "I'm a God-fearing man and I'd appreciate it if you didn't keep using the Lord's name in vain."

"Oh for—" Wilkes started, and then thought better of it. "Shouldn't we stop, or go back, or something?" he asked.

"No," Maddux said. "Shadoweyes will talk to the man and then catch up with us." "Meanwhile, where are we headed?" "Southwest, to the town where the Backshooter

claimed his next victim," Maddux said. "That *is*

where we want to go, isn't it?"

———

ED CHARTERMAN DIDN'T KNOW what hit him.

One minute he was riding along on his horse, and the next he was sitting on the ground.

He looked up and saw an Indian dressed like a white man drop down from a tree. Obviously, the man had kicked him off his horse from up there.

Charterman had an idea of going for his gun, but the Indian spoke just then.

"Don't try it," Shadoweyes said.

Charterman looked at the gun on the Indian's hip and froze. He didn't know if the Indian knew how to use the gun or not. "What do you want?"

"Just some simple answers to some simple questions."

"I don't know you."

"You should," Shadoweyes said. "You have been dogging my trail—and the trail of my friends-ever since we left Cromwell."

"Cromwell? I don't even know where that is."

"We will not get anyplace if you continue to lie," Shadoweyes said. "If you do that I shall have to force the information from you."

The man swallowed and eyed the Indian with fear.

Shadoweyes could see that this was not a brave man, and knew that he could find out what he wanted—if the man was also not a foolish man.

"I want to know about Walker Bogart," Shadow-eyes said.

The man shook his head, closing his eyes.

Shadoweyes knew the man's quandary immediately. He was afraid of Shadoweyes, hut he was also afraid of Bogart.

"I want to know about Walker Bogart," Shadow-eyes said again.

"Jesus," the man said, "I can't—Bogart will kill me."

"I will not kill you," Shadoweyes said, "but I will make you long for death."

"But..." the man said again, and it was like a sob.

"Where are they?"

"N-New Mexico," the man said, almost blubbering now.

"Where in New Mexico?"

Charterman closed his eyes, and he could see Walker Bogart. If Bogart ever found out that he talked...he couldn't...he had to do something...

When the man opened his eyes Shadoweyes saw something there. "Don't," he said.

The man ignored him. His fear of Walker Bogart gave him the courage to draw his gun.

Shadoweyes was not a gunman, he did not possess fancy shooting skills. He did what he knew how to do. He drew his gun and fired first, the bullet going into the man's chest.

He looked down at the dead man and holstered his gun.

"Foolish."

———

MADDUX HEARD THE SHOT, as did Hannibal and Wilkes.

"What was that?" Wilkes said.

Maddux reined his horse in, and the others stopped behind him. It wasn't easy to tell, but he felt sure the shot had come from behind them.

He looked at Hannibal and the marshal said, "Shadoweyes can take care of himself."

"I know that," Maddux said. "I just hope he learned something before he killed the man."

"Killed him?" Wilkes said. "He was supposed to question him, not kill him."

"If Shadoweyes killed him," Maddux said, "he had a good reason for it."

CHAPTER EIGHTEEN

Maddux, Hannibal, and Wilkes were camped when Shadoweyes caught up to them. They had found a formation in the ground that was almost like a small basin, and had scared up enough brush and chips to build a fire.

"Coffee's ready," Maddux said.

"I can use it," Shadoweyes said. "Let me settle my horse."

"I'll take it," Hannibal said.

Shadoweyes looked at Hannibal for a moment, then handed him the reins. He then accepted a cup of coffee from Maddux and hunkered down by the fire.

Glen Wilkes was sitting off to himself, and he was staring at Shadoweyes.

"What is wrong with him?"

"He thinks we're hiding plans from him."

Shadoweyes sipped the hot coffee without blowing on it first, the way a white man would. "You heard the shot?"

"Yes," Maddux said. "I figured you had your reasons."

"The best reason," Shadoweyes said. "A desperate man tried to kill me."

"Did he say anything first?"

"Yes," Shadoweyes said. "New Mexico."

"He didn't say where?"

"That was when he drew," Shadoweyes said. "He was more afraid of Walker Bogart than he was of me.

Maddux had beans on the fire and they were ready. He spooned some out and handed the plate to Shadoweyes.

"Come and get it!" he shouted to the others.

Glenn Wilkes came over grudgingly and spooned some into a plate for himself, then went back to where he had been sitting.

"He should do that more often," Shadoweyes said.

"What?"

"Stay off to himself."

Hannibal came over at that point. "The horse is taken care of."

Shadoweyes looked at him again, then said, "I thank you."

"Forget it. Let me get some of those beans." Hannibal helped himself, then sat back. "What did we find out?"

"We're going to New Mexico."

"Do we know where in New Mexico?"

"No," Maddux said. "The man pulled a gun and Shadoweyes had to kill him."

"Damn fool," Hannibal said. "But at least Shadoweyes here found out something. In fact, he's been finding out damn near everything."

"That's why I wanted him along."

Shadoweyes said nothing.

Hannibal looked at Maddux. "How are we going to play this?"

"You know what Bogart looks like?"

"Only from the poster."

"Yeah," Maddux said, "me too, and that could be anybody."

"We can't go riding around New Mexico asking if anybody's seen him," Hannibal said. "Word will get back to him faster than you can spit."

"We'll have to play it by ear," Maddux said. "We'll continue to dog the Backshooter's trail, because it will take us to the border of Mexico and West Texas. New Mexico's a hop, skip, and a jump from there."

"Maddux, I'm sorry to bring this up…"

"Go ahead."

"What if Bogart is fishing…and he's got us hooked…and he's reeling us in."

"It's possible," Maddux said.

"Maybe he's after you."

"Me?" Maddux asked. "What the hell for?"

"Come on, Kyle," Hannibal said. "You put a lot of people away. And Bogart has been building himself a hell of a reputation for the past three years. If he draws you out of retirement and kills you—"

"A lot of people will be saying 'so what.'"

"I don't think so," Hannibal said. "I've got another question."

"Go ahead."

"If Walker Bogart *wants* you to come to him, why did he send three men to kill you."

"He didn't."

"What do you mean, he didn't? Then who were those three guys—"

"He sent three guys to *try* and kill me."

"Wait a minute," Hannibal said. "I'm just a poor dumb country lawman."

"Yeah," Maddux said, "you may be poor. Okay, let me explain it to you. I think Bogart sent them after me to see if three years of ranching had made me rusty. If it had, they would have killed me."

"And since they didn't, he knows you're coming for him."

"Well, wouldn't you?" Maddux said.

Hannibal leaned forward and said, "And what about Wilkes over there?"

Maddux shrugged and said, "There's a joker in every game, Hannibal."

"Yeah," Hannibal said, "but in some games the joker's wild."

Maddux laughed and said, "Not in any game I ever played."

CHAPTER NINETEEN

"Why can't we go into town?" Glenn Wilkes complained.

"Because it's not on our list," Maddux answered.

"Look," Wilkes said, "I don't see why we can't go into town and sleep on real beds and eat a decent meal at a table with—"

"Joe," Maddux said, "See if you can explain to Mr. Pinkerton here," and walked away from the two men. Maybe Hannibal could talk some sense into Wilkes. Maddux was tired of trying.

"What is he complaining about now?" Shadow-eyes asked.

"He wants to sleep on a mattress."

"He should have brought his own." Shadoweyes smiled, then looked at the ex-lawman. "Maddux."

"What?"

"I know you don't believe in fate."

"So?"

"So this Glenn Wilkes shows up in Cromwell to ask for help in finding the Backshooter and, oh, by the way, maybe Walker Bogart too. At the same time Walker Bogart sends three men to kill you—or *try* and kill you. Now you figure Bogart *wants* you to find him."

Maddux stared at Shadoweyes.

"What is wrong?"

"That's the most I've heard you say at one time."

Shadoweyes frowned. "Who is Glenn Wilkes, Maddux? How do we know he is telling the truth?"

Maddux shrugged. "We'll let him go on for a while longer. As long as he's in front of us he can't hurt us."

"Whatever you say. I will just keep my eyes on him from now on."

"Well, that'll make me feel better," Maddux said, truthfully. "I wonder if him being such a pain in the ass is part of the act, or if it comes natural."

"It comes natural."

"What makes you say that?"

Shadoweyes gave Maddux a solemn look and said, "He is too good at it."

———

SHADOWEYES COOKED DINNER THAT NIGHT, keeping one eye on the pan and the other on Glenn Wilkes. He was making beans, but he put some bacon in also. When the coffee was ready they all took a cup and drank it while waiting for dinner to be ready.

Wilkes went off and sat by himself while Hannibal pulled up a log by Maddux.

"What's with Shadoweyes?" he asked.

"What about him?"

"He's been watching Wilkes pretty closely."

"He doesn't like him."

"There's more to it than that."

"He doesn't trust him."

"That I can believe."

"He thinks it was too much of a coincidence that Wilkes appeared in Cromwell just when Bogart sent some men to try me."

"Well...Bogart could have heard he was coming to see you to get your help."

"How? Unless Wilkes isn't the Pinkerton he says he is."

"Then what is he?"

"We'll ask him, in due time."

"So what are we gonna do until then?"

"Exactly what Shadoweyes is doing," Maddux said. "We're gonna keep an eye on him."

Later, while Maddux was eating, Wilkes came over and sat by him.

"If you're gonna complain about the accommodations—" Maddux started.

"No, no," Wilkes said, "no complaints. I just have a question."

Maddux sighed and said, "What is it?"

"Shadoweyes."

"What about him?"

"He's been watching me all afternoon."

"Maybe he doesn't like you."

"I'm sure he doesn't," Wilkes said, "and that doesn't bother me at all, but somehow I don't think that's the reason."

"Then what do you think is the reason?"

"I don't know," Wilkes said, "unless he doesn't trust me, for some reason."

Maddux ate some beans and said, "John Shadow-eyes doesn't trust too many people."

"He trusts you."

"Maybe that's because I'm the only white man he knows who doesn't look down on him."

Wilkes grinned and said, "Well, you certainly have him fooled, eh?"

Maddux turned his head slowly to look at Wilkes and said, "Wilkes, you'd better go back where you were sitting."

"Please," Wilkes said, "if he's your friend then I'm sorry I said anything. I certainly didn't come over here to offend you."

"He *is* my friend."

"Okay," Wilkes said. "He's your friend."

Wilkes took a forkful of beans, made a face, and swallowed. "Say," he said, "just out of curiosity, what kind of Indian is he anyway?"

"His mother was a Kiowa."

"Kiowa," he repeated. "Are they, uh, vicious...I mean, are they a warlike tribe?"

"Very," Maddux said. "They don't like white men at all."

"I see."

Wilkes looked over at Shadoweyes then and saw that the half-breed was staring at him.

"Well, if he hates white men, then how come he's not staring at Hannibal like he is at me?"

Maddux waited a beat, then said, "Some white men he likes less than others."

CHAPTER TWENTY

alker Bogart had taken over the Ceremony Saloon
—literally taken it over. He had walked in with two
of his men, entered the office of owner Jim Barnes,
and told him that he was buying the saloon—and then given
Barnes a dollar!

Bogart was sitting in "his" saloon, at a back table, enjoying
the fact that the money all the people were spending was going
into his pocket. He'd gotten rid of the bartender and put his
own man behind the bar. He'd kept the four girls who worked
there, though, and since they needed the job they'd stayed.

They'd also stayed because they were afraid not to.

Ginger, the oldest of the girls, a thirtyish redhead, went
past, and Bogart put his big arm out to ensnare her and draw
her into his lap. She put up some token resistance, but no real
fight, as he buried his face between her big breasts.

At the bar Jerry Parnell said to the new bartender, Billy
Cowen, "He's got that Redman woman back at the house and
she makes any of these four look like cows. How come he paws
these girls, but he doesn't touch her?"

"She's a lady," Cowen said.

Parnell snorted. "A lady? When did Walker Bogart ever treat
a woman like a lady?"

"I guess this is the first time," Cowen said. He looked over
at Bogart with Ginger in his lap and said, "I tell you, I wouldn't
mind rubbing *my* face in that a little."

"Yeah," Parnell said, "neither would I—although this one's not bad either."

He grabbed one of the girls who was going by, a blonde named Maxie, and pulled her to him. She was about twenty, short and almost plump. He shook her a little and watched how her breasts jiggled.

"Look at that, will you?" he said to Cowen.

Maxie lifted her foot and brought her heel down on Parnell's instep. He howled, released her, and began hopping around. The man standing nearby began to laugh, and some began to clap in time with his hopping around.

"I ain't no stuffed toy," Maxie spat at Parnell. She turned to Cowen and said, "Give me two beers, Billy."

"Sure, Maxie."

Cowen drew two beers and put them on a tray for Maxie to deliver.

"Bitch!" Parnell said, ceasing his hopping and moving back to the bar. "I'll show her a thing or two."

"Yeah, well, before you do maybe you better give Bogart that news you was talking about."

"Yeah," Parnell said, "after I have another drink. Pour one, will you?"

Parnell picked up his drink, walked over, and stood in front of Bogart's table.

"You're blocking my view," Bogart said. "Sit down, for Chrissake!"

Parnell sat.

"What do you want, Parnell?"

"I have some news for you."

Bogart moved his eyes from the crowd to Pamell, who looked nervous. "You're nervous, Jerry," he said. "That means that I'm not going to like what you have to tell me."

"It's not my fault, Walker."

"Did someone touch her?"

"No, nothing like that," Parnell said. "We haven't heard from Charterman."

"Is that all?"

"We should have heard from him by now."

"So?"

"So he's probably dead, seeing as how he was dogging Maddux's trail."

"I repeat, so?"

"Well, we've got no one watching Maddux now, if Charterman's dead."

"So what?" Bogart said. "We know he's coming, don't we?"

"But how does he know where to come?"

"He'll figure it out," Bogart said. "If Maddux is so damned good, he'll figure it out."

CHAPTER TWENTY-ONE

It was less than two months later when they rode into Kent's Fork, Texas, just a few miles from the Mexican border and the New Mexico border.

They put their animals up at the livery, got their hotel rooms, and then repaired to the saloon to wash away some trail dust and consider their next move.

This was the town in which the twelfth victim had been claimed. Traveling through Texas, from northeast to southwest, they had continued to ask questions in each of the towns where a victim had lived. In five of those places people recalled a dark-haired stranger coming to town, staying for a period of time, and then leaving after the murder. In one town he had gone by the name Bart Silver, in the other Billy Salt.

"We have a dark-haired man, thirty to forty, who has worked at a passel of jobs," Maddux said. "He has always been described as pleasant and well mannered. Whether or not we find out anything here, we're going to have to decide what our next move is, Mexico or New Mexico."

"New Mexico," Wilkes said.

"Why?" Maddux asked, even though he knew the answer.

"Because that's where you said Bogart was—at least, he was a couple of months ago. He could be anywhere by now."

"That's true," Maddux said. Privately, he did not think so. He thought that Walker Bogart had probably dug in somewhere, waiting for him to come and get him.

He had decided that Hannibal was right. If Bogart could kill Maddux it *would* make his reputation. History would forget that Kyle Maddux was fifty-three and was suffering from a bad back. All history would show was that Walker Bogart killed Kyle Maddux.

If it happened that way.

Maddux was going to do his best to see that it didn't—but he wasn't going to go running headlong into Walker Bogart's arms. Let the man wait and wonder, and if he got tired of waiting, let him make the first move.

"Let's all move around town and see what we can find out," he said, standing up.

"I haven't finished my beer," Wilkes complained.

No one paid any attention to him. They had long since decided that this was the best way to handle him.

———

"HOW LONG WE GONNA WAIT, WALKER?" Jerry Parnell asked.

"As long as I say, Parnell," Bogart said, staring across the table at Parnell.

"He ain't comin'," Parnell said.

"He'll be here."

"If he was comin' he would have been here by now," Parnell insisted. "We got to get moving."

"That's the reaction he wants," Bogart said.

"What?"

"He wants me to react the way you're reacting now," Bogart said. "He's a smart old man, that Maddux."

"Why do you have to kill him?" Parnell asked. "Why do we have to wait here for him, especially since he *is* an old man?"

"Because old or not, he's got a reputation," Bogart sid, "and I want it."

"You already *got* a reputation!"

"Sure, mine," Bogart said, "but I want to add *his* to it."

Parnell sagged in his chair, surrendering. He wasn't going to talk Bogart into leaving Ceremony. In fact, Bogart had so completely taken the town over that Parnell was starting to think he'd never leave. "What about the girl?"

"What about her?" Bogart asked.

"Well, the men are startin' to talk—"

"About what?"

"About what you're gonna do with her after all this time," Parnell said. "I mean, if *you* don't want her, we—I mean, they do."

Bogart, who had been sitting very relaxed in his chair at the saloon—sitting at *his* private table—now sat up and glared at Parnell.

"The woman is mine, Parnell," Bogart said. "Any man who touches her will have to face me. Do you understand?"

"Sure, Walker, sure, I understand," Parnell said hurriedly.

"And you'll make sure the others understand?"

"Sure, Walker, you know I will. You know you can count on me."

"Sure, Parnell," Walker Bogart said, sitting back,

"I know I can."

Parnell turned to leave and Bogart called out his name.

"Yeah?"

"You know that town where we picked up the girl?"

"Sure, Kent's Fork."

"Put a couple of men on the border near there."

"The Mexican border?"

"No, stupid," Bogart said, "the border between New Mexico and Texas."

"What are they looking for?"

"Jesus," Bogart said to himself, and then he barked at Parnell, "Figure it out!"

The sheriff at Kent's Fork remembered the stranger.

"Now that you mention it there *was* a stranger in town who fit that description," Sheriff Wade Miller said to Maddux.

"Did he know the victim?"

"Everybody in town knew Sam Rosen," Miller said, "but it sure didn't make any sense for anyone to kill him."

"Why not? Did he have a position in town?"

"Oh, he had a position, all right," Miller said. "He was the town drunk!"

"The town drunk?"

Miller nodded. "Why would anyone want to kill him?"

Maddux didn't have an answer. "Would you have any idea where the man went?"

"He was just gone the morning after the murder," Miller said.

"Excuse me for asking you this, Sheriff," Maddux said, phrasing carefully, "but didn't it occur to you that this stranger might have been the killer?"

Miller stared at Maddux for a few moments, then said, "No," thoughtfully.

Maddux watched with interest as the man mulled over the suggestion.

"I mean," said Miller, "I couldn't understand why *anyone* would want to kill poor Sam, let alone a stranger who had only been in town a few days, but I never really figured anyone in particular for it."

Maddux frowned. This was a departure from what had happened in the other towns. Here the dark-haired Backshooter had not bothered to become acquainted with victim, and he had not spent as much time in Kent's Fork as he had in the other towns.

"All right, Sheriff," Maddux said, standing up. "Thanks for your time."

"Sorry I can't help you, Maddux," Miller said. "I don't even know the feller's name."

"That's all right," Maddux said. "We've got a ton of names for him, and it hasn't helped so far."

"Good luck," Miller said as Maddux left his office.

CHAPTER TWENTY-TWO

"All right," Glenn Wilkes said, "we're in New Mexico. Now what?"

They were camped one day into New Mexico and Shadoweyes was making some rabbit and beans for dinner.

"We just have to keep moving, Wilkes," Maddux said.

"Moving where?"

"I don't know."

"Tell me something, Maddux," Wilkes asked with some doubt. "Before you were retired were you *really* good at this?"

Wilkes was holding his plate out for Shadoweyes to fill. Shadoweyes spooned out some hot food and deposited it on Wilkes's exposed wrist.

"Ow, damn!" Wilkes said, pulling his scalded hand back. "You did that on purpose, you heathen!"

"I think it was an accident, Wilkes," Hannibal said.

"No," Shadoweyes said, "it was not."

"You see? What the hell is wrong with you, man?" Wilkes demanded of Shadoweyes.

"I am getting tired of you constantly digging at Maddux, Mr. Wilkes," Shadoweyes said. "I thought someone should teach you some manners."

"By burning me?"

"It is something you will remember."

Maddux was watching carefully, thinking that the incident

would go a long way toward showing them what kind of man Wilkes really was.

Shadoweyes stood up, inviting Wilkes to make a move on him.

Wilkes mistook the move and thought that Shadoweyes was going to take some action against him. "I have no gun."

"I do not need a gun," Shadoweyes said.

The two men regarded each other over the fire, and then Wilkes backed off. He leaned over and picked up his plate and made a show of trying to clean it.

Hannibal stuck his plate out and Shadoweyes filled it. Maddux was next, and then Shadoweyes looked at Wilkes expectantly.

"I'll get it myself," Wilkes said.

Shadoweyes shrugged, filled his own plate, and then left the spoon in the pan. Wilkes took his fill and then walked off to eat on his own.

"Nice move," Hannibal said to Shadoweyes.

"Thank you."

"I just had a horrible thought," Maddux said.

"What," Hannibal asked.

"If Wilkes is not who he says he is," Maddux said, "I don't think I'm going to get paid one red cent for this trip."

"Whoever he is," Hannibal said, "make him pay anyway."

"I guess I could do that."

"Besides," Hannibal said, "you're not doing this for the money anyway."

"Yeah," Maddux said, "good point."

After dinner Maddux said, "I think we should start setting watches."

"Three?" Shadoweyes asked.

"We should make him take a turn," Hannibal said.

"Sure," Maddux said, "and then we'll take turns watching him."

In the end they set four watches, although Wilkes complained—as usual. Something about how his paying the way should earn him a good night's rest.

"We all pull our weight, Wilkes," Maddux said, "no matter who's footing the bill."

"Very well," Wilkes said, agreeing reluctantly.

Although Wilkes apparently had no handgun, he did have a

rifle. Maddux told him to make sure he had it at hand while he was sitting watch.

They gave Wilkes the first watch, and then Maddux, Hannibal, and Shadoweyes put their bedrolls down in a row. They were each going to take an hour to watch Wilkes, waking each other up with a nudge for relief. This was to be done without Wilkes's knowledge. They didn't want him to know that they were watching him.

Not yet anyway.

Maddux was about to lie down when he saw that Wilkes was settling himself down in front of the fire.

"Don't sit in front of the fire."

"Why not?"

"If you sit and stare into the fire you'll have no night vision," Maddux explained. "Find a spot away from the fire."

"Jesus—" Wilkes said, but he got up and went to find himself a comfortable spot.

"And don't get too comfortable," Maddux said, before lying down.

———

WILKES WOKE Maddux for the second watch. Maddux had been asleep for two hours, having taken the first hour watch on Wilkes.

"Anything?" Maddux asked.

"What was I supposed to hear?"

"There should be some noise out there," Maddux said. "There are varmints out there, you know."

"Oh, I heard them," Wilkes said, with disdain. "I thought you were talking about two-legged varmints."

"Sometimes two-legged varmints can sound like four-legged varmints."

"Well, how the hell am I to know the difference?" Wilkes demanded.

Maddux shook his head, wondering if they should leave him off the watch.

"Go to sleep, Wilkes," Maddux said. "We're getting an early start in the morning."

"Are we going anywhere in particular?" he asked, sarcastically.

"There's a small town ahead of us a few miles," Maddux explained patiently. "We're going to stop there for supplies."

"Well, thank God," Wilkes said. "A real bed and real food."

"We may have a meal there, but we're not staying overnight."

"Why not?" Wilkes asked. When Maddux stared at him the man backed off and said, "All right, all right. Forget I asked."

Wilkes took his bedroll and set in on the other side of the fire, away from Hannibal and Shadoweyes.

Maddux walked away from the fire and found himself a rock to sit on. He hoped no one heard him groan as he sat down. His back was killing him after more than two months, in the saddle, but he was happy to see that the other aches and pains—the ones that were a result of years of soft living—had subsided. His joints didn't ache so much anymore, and his ass didn't hurt as much.

Now if only the back pains would let up.

Sitting alone, he thought about Laura. He wondered if this trip, this search for a killer who shot his victims in the back, would be worth throwing away his marriage.

So far, it wasn't.

Parnell entered the saloon. Bogart was sitting with a drink on the table and a cigar in his hand. It was a position he seemed increasingly satisfied with. Parnell could remember a time when it was impossible for Walker Bogart to even stand still.

"What is it, Parnell?"

"The two men we had on the border?" Parnell said. "They just rode in."

"And?"

"Four men crossed into New Mexico not far from Kent's Fork."

"Is one of them Maddux?" Bogart's eyes glittered with eagerness.

"One of them is in his early fifties, the others are all younger," Parnell continued. "One is an Indian, the other two are white men. One's wearing a badge."

"Is the older man wearing a badge?" Bogart asked, frowning. Was Maddux coming after him with a posse—a posse of bounty hunters?

"No."

That satisfied Bogart for the moment that Maddux wasn't

heading a posse, but he still had a lawman riding along with him.

"Tell me about the older one."

"He's tall, no gut, and like I said, in his fifties."

Bogart smiled around his big cigar and said with great satisfaction, "That's got to be him."

Parnell waited a few moments, then said, "He's got three men with him, Walker."

"I heard you."

"What do we do about them?"

"You and the others can kill them," Bogart said. "But make sure everyone knows—and I mean *everyone,* Parnell—that the old man is mine!"

"Don't worry, Walker," Parnell said, "they'll all know."

"It's gonna happen, Parnell," Bogart said, staring at something only he could see. "I can feel it in my bones."

CHAPTER TWENTY-THREE

The first town they came to in New Mexico was called Silver's Fork. Unlike Kent's Fork, this town took its name from an actual fork in the road. The fork was away from the town, but both parts of the fork led to the town. One just took longer than the other.

As they rode into Silver's Fork Glenn Wilkes looked around and said, "This is a town?"

"Well, it used to be," Maddux said. "Now it's just sort of a supply station for people entering New Mexico at this particular point."

"Does anyone live here?"

"Last time I was here it had a population of about fourteen. That includes the man who runs the general store and the fella who runs the saloon."

"You've been here before?" Wilkes asked.

"Many times."

"Then they know you."

"Yes."

"Well, maybe you could ask then about Bogart."

"Yeah, maybe I could."

Maddux reined his horse in and they all stopped.

"What's wrong?" Wilkes asked.

"I want to get something straight before we go into town."

"What?"

"*I* do the talking."

"Are you afraid I don't know how to talk?"

"I *know* you don't know how to talk to these people. Now, either you agree to keep quiet, or I'll have Shadoweyes cut out your tongue."

"You—you wouldn't dare," Wilkes said, looking at Shadoweyes.

"No, I probably wouldn't," Maddux said, "although I'm sure Shadoweyes would like it, but you get my point."

"Yes," Wilkes said, "I get your point."

"Good," Maddux said. "Just remember it."

They rode into Silver's Fork single file. Maddux, Hannibal, and Shadoweyes were on the alert for trouble, although they didn't really expect any. Bogart wasn't going to send men to every possible entry point. That would spread his forces too thin.

The buildings were all run-down wood structures, some boarded up and obviously empty, some not so obviously empty, and a few of them still open for business.

Maddux led them to the general store, where he dismounted.

"I'm going to go in here alone," Maddux said. "Why don't the rest of you go over to the saloon and I'll meet you there."

"Won't you need help with supplies?"

"I'm not going to buy that much. In fact, I think we should leave the pack animal here so we can travel more freely."

"What about our food?" Wilkes asked.

"We'll just have to eat less from here on in," Maddux said.

"I'll take the pack horse to the livery," Shadoweyes said.

"All right," Maddux said, "you do that. Divide the essential supplies among our four horses and put the animal up at the livery."

"Should I sell it?"

"If you can get a price, yes."

Shadoweyes nodded.

"Hannibal, take Mr. Wilkes over to the saloon and get him a drink."

"Right."

"I'd rather have something to eat," Wilkes was complaining as Hannibal led him away.

"Maybe they'll have some hardboiled eggs," Hannibal said.

Maddux entered the general store. Even though it had been

a couple of years since he had last been through, he'd swear the same supplies were lining the shelves.

He walked to the counter and slapped his palm down on it, raising a small cloud of dust. After a moment the curtained doorway behind the counter belched forth a tall, gangly man with big ears and hands and a long jaw.

"Hello, Rufus," Maddux said.

Rufus Walter stared at Maddux for a moment, then said, "I'll be...Kyle Maddux."

"How are ya?" Maddux asked, putting out his hand.

Rufus took Kyle's hand in one of his huge ones. The man had the largest hands Maddux had ever seen. "How long has it been? A year?"

"More like three."

"Three? I heard you retired, someplace in Texas."

"Kansas."

"What brings you through here, then?"

"I'm looking for somebody."

"Anybody I know?"

"Walker Bogart?"

Rufus whistled soundlessly and said; "The worst. He's come a long way since you retired, Maddux."

"So I heard. I need some supplies, Rufus."

"Just tell me what you need."

"Some canned peaches, a pound of coffee, some beef jerky, beans, and some licorice."

"Licorice?"

"Doesn't take up much room and you can chew it for a long time."

"Licorice it is."

While Rufus was moving from shelf to shelf Maddux said, "What do you know about Bogart, Rufus?"

The man's back was to him but he saw his shoulders hunch for just a moment.

"Nothing much," Rufus said over his shoulder.

"Oh, come on, Rufus," Maddux said. "You know everything —especially everything that goes on in these parts."

Rufus put some supplies down on the counter and looked at Maddux. "I also know how to keep my mouth shut, Maddux," he said "You know that."

"I do know that, Rufus, and I wouldn't ask if it wasn't important to me."

Rufus slumped and stared at Maddux.

"Rufus, I think Bogart wants me to find him."

Rufus thought about it, then said, "I can see that. He's done everything he can do to make a name for himself. Drawing you out of retirement, and then killing you...well, that would just about make him a legend."

"I don't know about a legend," Maddux said. "You have to kill a legend to become a legend."

"Don't underestimate your reputation," Rufus said.

"Well, are you gonna help me?"

"You want to know where Bogart is?"

"Yes."

Rufus thought a moment, then said, "I don't know exactly where he is, but I guess I can give you a general idea."

"Thanks, Rufus."

"Let me get you the rest of your supplies."

Maddux waited while Rufus collected all of his supplies, and then paid the bill. He had Rufus write out a receipt so he could give it to Wilkes.

"Rufus, you been reading the newspapers?"

"Sure," Rufus said, "but by the time I see them they're usually a couple of months old."

"That wouldn't matter," Maddux said. "You been reading about this fellow likes to shoot people in the back?"

"Oh, yeah, I read about that."

"You know anything about it?"

"Like what?"

"Like who he is maybe? Like if he's been through here? Like whether or not he works for Bogart?"

"I don't know any of that, Maddux," Rufus said. "I'll tell you all I know, though, you can count on that."

"Okay, Rufus," Maddux said, folding his arms, "I'm listening."

CHAPTER TWENTY-FOUR

When Maddux entered the saloon, Hannibal and Wilkes were seated at a table with a beer in front of each of them. Maddux went to the bar and said, "Beer."

There were a few more tables scattered around the room, and in one corner some two- and three-legged tables and chairs were stacked like so much firewood.

"Hello, Maddux," the bartender said, putting the beer on the bar.

"Toke, how are you?"

"Could be better."

Toke Marlowe was sixty if he was a day, but he could have passed for eighty easy—or maybe it was the other way around. As many years as Maddux had been passing through here, Toke was always behind the bar, and they always had the same exchange.

Maddux took his beer over to the table and sat. "Shadoweyes must be dickering," he said.

"You find out anything interesting?" Hannibal asked.

Maddux took a moment to sip his beer. It was as cold as he remembered. Possibly the best beer he'd ever drunk was right here in Silver's Fork.

"Yeah, I found out something interesting," Maddux said. "It seems Walker Bogart has taken himself a town."

"What do you mean, taken?" Wilkes asked.

"Just what I said," Maddux replied. "He's taken the town."

"You mean...a whole town?"

"Sure," Hannibal said, "he's got enough men to do it."

"Well, what do we do now?" Wilkes asked. "What's the name of the town?"

"That we don't know," Maddux said, "but we do know that it's west of here."

"So we just ride west?" Wilkes said.

"He's learning," Hannibal said to Maddux.

"There's something else."

"What?" Hannibal asked.

"Some of Bogart't men were through here some months ago, maybe three."

"So?"

"They had a woman with them," Maddux said, "and she wasn't along willingly."

"Oh, that's fine," Hannibal said. "What do you think Bogart and his wild bunch will have done to that woman by now?"

"I don't even want to think about it."

"What are we worried about some woman for?" Wilkes asked.

"If Bogart has a woman and is holding her against her will," Hannibal said, "it will be up to us to get her away from him."

"Why?" Wilkes asked.

"Because," Maddux said, and when he didn't elaborate, Wilkes just frowned even more.

"Well, all right," Wilkes said, finally. "I mean, if we take Bogart, that'll set her free anyway."

Maddux didn't reply. For the first time since he knew him, Wilkes had said something that made sense.

Maddux was about to get up and go looking for Shadoweyes when the half-breed walked in. "What happened?"

"The liveryman wanted to buy, but he didn't want to pay a fair price."

"That would be old Jeff Kanaly," Maddux said. "What happened?"

"We dickered," Shadoweyes said, "and we finally agreed on a price."

"If you beat him I'll be impressed."

Shadoweyes stared at Maddux and then said, "You did want to get rid of the animal."

"Well," Maddux said, "as long as you got a *decent* price. Get yourself a beer."

Shadoweyes went to the bar and came back with a beer. Maddux told him what he had just told the others.

"Then we have a definite direction," Shadoweyes said.

"Yes," Maddux said.

"Then we leave?"

"We leave," Maddux said, "but there's something we've got to clear up first."

When neither Maddux nor Shadoweyes asked, Glenn Wilkes said, "What's that?"

"We may be in a little trouble where this Backshooter is concerned."

"How's that?" Hannibal asked.

"It's been two months since his last victim in Kent's Fork, and we just left that town."

"So?" Wilkes asked.

"So, we may have a direction on Bogart, but we've got nothing on this other boy."

"So then we go after Bogart," Wilkes said, "and forget about the other one."

Maddux shifted in his chair, trying to ease the pain in his back. "I'm not about to forget someone who shoots people in the back," he said.

"What do you want to do, Kyle?" Hannibal asked.

"I don't know," Maddux said. "I guess what I *don't* want to have to do is wait for him to take his next victim."

"Kyle," Hannibal said.

"I know, I know," Maddux said, "that's about what it's gonna take for us to get a bead on him again."

Maddux sat sipping his beer, with the others all watching him.

"So?" Wilkes said, the first to become impatient. "What do we do now?"

Maddux turned his head and looked at Wilkes. "Let's clear something else up."

"Like what?" Wilkes asked.

"Like just who the hell you are, and what you're doing here."

Glenn Wilkes stared at each of them in turn, and for a

moment Maddux thought he was going to try to go on with the pretense.

But he didn't.

"All right," Wilkes said, "my name *is* Glenn Wilkes."

"And?" Maddux said.

"And I am a Pinkerton agent," Wilkes said. "You saw my identification."

"Get to the parts you lied about," Maddux said.

Wilkes looked at the three of them again and then sighed and said, "I'm not after the Backshooter."

"Pinkerton wasn't hired by one of the families?" Hannibal asked.

"No."

"I figured that," Maddux said.

"How?" Hannibal asked.

"I've talked to the families of six of the victims, and none of them hired Pinker ton."

"What about the other six?"

"Three of them had no family, and the families of the other three had left town, and they didn't figure to have that kind of money."

"So what are you after?" Hannibal asked Wilkes.

"The reward on Bogart."

"The five thousand dollars?" Hannibal asked.

"No," Wilkes said, "the paper you have is outdated. The bounty on Bogart is fifteen thousand." He took a folded-up poster from his back pocket and put it on the table.

"Fifteen thousand?" Hannibal repeated in awe, picking up the poster. He unfolded it, then showed it to Maddux, who nodded. He passed it to Shadow-eyes, who couldn't read, so he just handed it back to Glenn Wilkes.

"If you're hunting Bogart," Maddux said, "why the pretense? Why get me involved?"

"I've heard Alan Pinkerton talk about you, Maddux," Wilkes said. "I knew that the Back-shooter's trail started in Kansas, and I knew you'd been shot in the back."

"How'd you know that?"

"Like I said," Wilkes said, "Pinkerton. He was always saying he wouldn't be surprised if you took off after this fella sooner or later."

"So you decided to play on that to get me to go with you?"

"Sure," Wilkes said. "Hey, this is your contry, Maddux. I'd be lost out here without you. I mean, listen, I was going to split the reward with you."

"Five thousand dollars," Maddux said.

"What?"

"You were gonna split five thousand dollars with me, right?"

"Well...no, I was going to split the entire reward with you."

"And what did you figure as a fair split?"

Wilkes fidgeted. "Well, I figured we'd splilt down the middle."

"Two ways?"

"Sure, you, me."

"And what about Hannibal and Shadoweyes?"

"Well," Wilkes said, fidgeting some more, "I didn't expect them to come along. I guessed you'd pay them from your share."

Maddux remained silent for a moment, then finished his beer before speaking.

"Here's the way I figure it," Maddux said. "We could leave you here and go on without you, and when we find Bogart we could split the reward three ways."

"You'd leave me out?" Wilkes demanded, outraged.

"Well, that's just one way of doing it," Maddux said.

"And what's another?" Wilkes asked suspiciously.

"We all leave here together," Maddux said, "and when we find Bogart we split four ways."

"*Four* ways?"

"Even split," Maddux said.

"Sounds fair to me," Hannibal said.

"I'm not done yet," Maddux said. "After we split the reward four ways, you're going to pay me for my time out of your share."

"What?"

"That way," Maddux said, "you'll still come out with something."

"That's not fair!" Wilkes said. "I brought you into this."

"By lying to me," Maddux said. "Usually, when people lie to me, it gets real expensive. You're getting away cheap."

"Cheap, hell—"

"Or we could go back to the first option," Maddux said. "That way you'd get nothing."

"All right," Wilkes said, waving his hands. "Let's go back to the second option. I mean, four ways that still comes to three thousand seven hundred and fifty dollars—"

"He did that in his head," Hannibal said sarcastically.

"—and then how much is your fee?"

"I'll set my fee when the job is done," Maddux said. "I mean, if we all get killed, there's no use in my setting it now, is there?"

"Killed?"

"Killed," Maddux said. "That's the third option, and that way we all lose."

Wilkes looked away nervously.

"Tell me something else, Wilkes," Maddux said.

"What?"

"Just how good a detective are you?"

"Well...I'm pretty good, I guess."

"Well, I hope you're a better detective than you are a bounty hunter."

CHAPTER TWENTY-FIVE

They left the saloon together and walked back over to the general store, where they'd left their horses. There were white sacks hanging from each saddle, with each man's share of the supplies to carry.

"Do you know how to use that rifle?" Maddux asked Glenn Wilkes.

"Sure I do."

"And do you have a handgun?"

Wilkes nodded. "In my saddlebag."

"Well, put the damned thing on. We're going to need every gun we've got."

They all mounted up, and Maddux turned towards Wilkes again. "I've got one more thing to say to you, Wilkes."

"What?"

"You lied to me, and you got caught at it." Maddux waggled his finger in Wilkes's face to keep him from cutting in. "That means that every time you open your mouth to me from now on, you might be lying to me again."

"I wouldn't—"

"Shut up!" Maddux snapped. "That means that from now on you speak only when you're spoken to, understand?"

"I don't—"

"Understand?"

Wilkes lapsed into silence, his eyes wandered around a bit, his face flushed, and then he said, "Yes, I understand."

"That's good," Maddux said. "Now let's ride."

———

BY THE TIME they'd put ten miles between themselves and Silver's Fork, Maddux had made up his mind about Glenn Wilkes. He was a leech, a parasite. Maddux had known his type before, bounty hunters who would think nothing of stealing from another bounty hunter, given half a chance. He saw a chance to make some money, and he wasn't above using another man to do it.

Maddux would have to watch Glenn Wilkes even more carefully now that he knew what he was, and he knew that Hannibal and Shadoweyes were thinking the same thing.

When they stopped that night to camp, Wilkes sat at the fire with Maddux and Hannibal. It was Shadoweyes who went off on his own to eat this time.

"So that's why Shadoweyes was watching me so intently," Wilkes said.

"Why?" Maddux asked.

"Because he didn't trust me."

"None of us did," Maddux said. "In fact, none of us do."

"Hey—"

"I'd be very careful about what I say and do for a while, Wilkes," Maddux said. "Real careful."

"I told you fellas the truth."

"Sure, after we demanded it," Maddux said. "Would we have heard it otherwise?"

"Well, you would have had to hear it once we found Walker Bogart."

"Sure."

Wilkes fell silent.

"How would you collect the reward without us knowing about it? You haven't figured that part out yet. Had you, Wilkes?"

Wilkes hesitated, then said, "No. I didn't know what I was going to do when we found Bogart. I...don't know how to collect a bounty."

"That shows what an amateur you are," Hannibal said. "You've got know what you're going to do every step of the way in any plan you make."

"I'm an amateur, huh?" Wilkes said. "And what are you, some small-town lawman? What do you know?"

Hannibal fixed Wilkes with a hard stare and said, "I wasn't always a small-town lawman."

"Oh yeah, well—"

"That's enough, you two," Maddux said. "When we find Bogart and his men we're going to have to depend on each other. Let's not say some things we're gonna be sorry for later."

Hannibal and Wilkes fell silent, eating and occasionally looking across the fire at each other.

After they'd eaten, Maddux set up the same watches. Wilkes was first.

CHAPTER TWENTY-SIX

Walker Bogart now owned the mayor's house, the biggest saloon in town, the local cathouse—with free access .to the girls, of course—the livery, and now he had his eye on the bank.

"I won't have it," Douglas Bent, the president of the bank, said. "We have to call in some help."

"What kind of help?" Mayor Perry asked. "Gunmen? Do you know how many gunmen we'd need?"

Jack Barnes said, "Well, something has to be done. I want my saloon back."

"Well then, go and tell him," Perry said.

"Sure, and you go and tell him you want your house back," Barnes said.

"I'm not the one who's complaining, Jack."

"Oh? You like living in the hotel?"

"There are worse things," Perry said. "He could have killed us all."

"Sometimes I wonder if that *would* really have been worse," Sam Amory said. He had been the owner of the livery before Bogart "bought" it for a dollar.

"Come on," Perry said. "Dying is always worse."

"This whole town is dying," Jack Barnes said.

"We were growing by leaps and bounds, and now with Bogart here we're stagnant."

"Maybe," Perry said, "he'll just go away, eventually."

"All by himself," Barnes said. "Do you really believe that?"

Perry hesitated, then said, "Damn it, no."

———

"WHERE ARE THEY?" Bogart asked Parnell.

"In the town hall," Parnell said. "That's where they hold their town council meetings."

Bogart ignored Parnell's sarcasm. "All right," the big man said, "let's go to a town council meeting."

———

THE FOUR MEMBERS of the town council were startled when the door to their meeting hall slammed open and Walker Bogart walked in, followed by his man Parnell.

"Well, well," Bogart said, "what have we here?"

'This is a town council meeting, Bogart," Mayor Perry said.

"So?"

"You're not on the council."

"You mean I wasn't on the council...until now," Bogart said.

He walked over to where Perry was sitting, at the head of the table, and loomed over him.

"Now I am a member," he said. "In fact, I think I'll be the chairman of the council. Would that be the chairman's seat you're in, Mayor?"

Perry had to try twice before he said, "Y-yes, it is."

"Then I'd like it, please."

Perry hesitated, and then stood up and moved to one of the other chairs at the table. Bogart sat down in the vacated chair and regarded the other members of what was now a five-man council.

"Now what were we discussing?"

No one answered.

"It wouldn't by chance have been how we could rid the town of some of its more...negative influences, could it?"

Again, no reply.

"Well, if we have nothing further to discuss, then," Bogart said, "I declare this meeting to be ended."

He made a show of looking around the table for something,

and then said, "A gavel. I don't have a gavel so I can call meetings to a close. Parnell?"

"Yeah, Walker?"

"Make a note. I have to get a gavel for future town council meetings."

"I'll make a note, Walker."

"Gentlemen," Bogart said, drawing his gun, "in the absence of a gavel this will have to do. I now declare this meeting...adjourned."

He punctuated the remark by firing the gun.

————

ANNE REDMAN HEARD THE SHOT, and since she was already sitting in front of the window she saw the men running from the town hall.

Apparently, Walker Bogart had declared himself mayor, or leader of the town council, or something.

She watched as Parnell came out of the hall, followed by Bogart himself, who seemed to be laughing.

She was amazed that Bogart still had not touched her. She wondered how much longer that could go on. The man's eyes were like fingers on her whenever he was in the room. Surely he wouldn't be able to contain himself for much longer—especially if he kept taking clothes away from her. She was now reduced to wearing a very flimsy red nightie through which she—and Bogart, and all of his men—could see her dark nipples and the firm curves of her breasts. She saw the way Bogart's men looked at her. How long would it be, she wondered, before someone decided to go ahead and try to rape her?

How long before her almost naked charms made one of Bogart's men forget that he was afraid of his boss?

How long would it be before Bogart himself decided to have her by force, instead of waiting for her to offer herself willingly?

She knew that she would never do that, and as soon as Bogart realized it, her time would be up.

Still, she sat in front of that window, waiting for somebody to come riding to her rescue.

She looked inside herself at that moment as something occurred to her. Maybe she should be working on a plan to get herself out, despite the fact that the town was full of Bogart's men.

There had to be a way.

All she had to do to find it was stop thinking like a victim and start thinking like what she was.

An experienced bounty hunter!

CHAPTER TWENTY-SEVEN

Every town they came to, they decided that one of them should first ride in and take a look around. If it looked all clear, then he would signal to the others and they could ride in. This way the same person wouldn't always be seen asking questions.

Even Glenn Wilkes, although reluctantly, had done it once.

Once they were in town they would split up and go to the saloons, barber shops, and restaurants and just listen to the conversations that were going on. You could learn more from just listening than you could from asking questions, sometimes.

"Somebody's got to know something," Maddux said. "A man cannot take over a whole town with a gang of men and not have word get out."

They were in the saloon in a town called Wadsworth.

"Maybe we're just not close enough to where it's happening," Hannibal said. "We'll just continue to ride south and see what happens."

Was he getting impatient? Maddux wondered about himself. After three years out of the business, had he lost that most valuable commodity of patience? The very thing that had made him as good as he was?

"You're right," Maddux said. "We just keep riding, and we keep listening."

"I don't know if I have the patience for this," Glenn Wilkes said, and just hearing the man say that seemed to strengthen Maddux's own resolve.

"If you don't have the patience, Wilkes, you can always walk away."

"You'd like that, wouldn't you?" Wilkes said. "You'd like me to ride away and leave a full share behind, wouldn't you?"

"Wilkes," Maddux said, "I'd just like you to ride away, period. Hell, I'd even send you your share."

"Sure," Wilkes said, "sure you would. Well, I'm sticking around to look after my interests, and that's that."

"Then do it quietly," Maddux said.

Wilkes opened his mouth to answer, but thought better of it.

"What's the next town?" Hannibal asked.

"They said in the last town that the next one is called Dennison."

"Sometimes I wonder where people get the names for these towns," Hannibal said.

"Look who's talking," Maddux said. "Cromwell?"

"Hey, Cromwell is a *fine* name for a town," Hannibal said in defense of the people who had named the town where he was marshal—even though he wasn't there when they did it.

"Do I have to listen to you two argue about the names of towns?" Wilkes said.

"Wilkes," Maddux said, "if you were sitting somewhere else, you wouldn't have to listen to anything we say."

"All right, all right," Wilkes said, standing up, "I'll go and sit over there." He started to walk away, and then realized that Shadoweyes was sitting over *there*. "I'll sit over there," he said, and walked the other way.

"What are we gonna do with him?" Hannibal asked.

"I've been thinking about that a lot and I don't rightly know what we should do," Maddux said. "What do you suggest?"

"Well, you're not really going to give him a share of the reward, are you?"

"Why not?" Maddux said. "How else is he going to pay me what he owes me?"

"Well, what about me?" Hannibal said.

"What about you?"

"I can't take any of that reward. I'm an officer of the law."

"*Officially* you can't take any of the reward," Maddux said. "I'll give you some, don't worry."

"I don't know if I want it."

Maddux studied Hannibal's face and saw that he was serious.

"Well, if you don't, I'll hold it for you," Maddux said. "Someday you might need it."

"What about Shadoweyes?"

"What about him?"

"Does he need the money?"

"Probably not," Maddux said. "He's got everything he wants, but I'll hold his share too, in case he ever needs it."

"You'd do that, wouldn't you?"

"Do what?"

"Hold over seven thousand dollars in cash and never spend it, just in case we ever want it."

"No."

"No?"

"No, I wouldn't do that," Maddux said. "I'd put it in the bank and let it collect interest."

———

WILKES TOOK THE FIRST WATCH, and Maddux the first watch on Wilkes.

When Wilkes woke Maddux for the second watch he stayed up and had a cup of coffee with him.

"You know, you fellas don't have to keep watching me," he said.

"Why not?"

"Because we're partners in this," Wilkes said. "Partners have to trust each other."

"If we were partners, then you wouldn't owe me any money, and you do."

"You mean you're gonna hold me to the deal we made?"

"I made that deal in good faith," Maddux said, "even if you didn't, and yes, I'm going to hold you to it."

"You know, I really figured when you saw the size of the reward you'd be a little more understanding."

"When I retired from this business—the man-hunting part

of it," Maddux said, "I meant to stay retired. You made me break my word to myself."

"For money."

Briefly, Maddux gave the man a humorless, almost pitying smile. "No, not for the money."

"So then what brought you out of retirement?" Wilkes demanded.

"Certainly not your offer."

"Why'd you take my offer, then?"

"Because I figured if I was going to go looking for the Backshooter," Maddux explained, "I might as well let you foot the bill."

"You know, I've heard a lot about you—"

"Then you know I mean what I say," Maddux said, fixing Wilkes with a hard stare.

"Yeah," Wilkes said, after a moment. He dumped the rest of his coffee into the fire and said, "Yeah, I know you mean what you say. Don't worry, Maddux, I'll hold up my end."

"That's good, Wilkes," Maddux said, "that's real good."

CHAPTER TWENTY-EIGHT

Dennison was like a lot of New Mexico towns, small and just marking time.

Hannibal had gone in first and had found the town clean, so he'd ridden back to the town boundary and signaled the others to come ahead. Now they all rode down the main street to the livery stable.

"I never saw so many nothing towns in a row in my life," Wilkes said.

"New Mexico has its share of large towns," Maddux said. "We just haven't been traveling that route."

They left their horses at the livery and went in search of the saloon. It was midday and there were only a few patrons there drinking. They each got a beer from the bartender and took them to a table.

"We're not going to find out much here," Hannibal said, looking around.

"We might have to stay overnight," Maddux said, "maybe get into a poker game later."

"A poker game?" Wilkes said.

"Lots of gossip in a poker game, Wilkes," Maddux said. "You play much?"

"No, I don't."

"Why not?"

"I was never very good at it."

"Well then, I guess I'll do the playing," Maddux said. "Unless..." he added, looking at Hannibal.

"My poker-playing days are long gone," Hannibal said.

Maddux didn't bother asking Shadoweyes. The only poker the half-breed ever played was pass-the-time two-handed poker with Maddux.

"I guess we ought to get some hotel rooms," Hannibal said.

Hannibal looked at Wilkes and asked, "You still want your own room?"

Wilkes looked at Shadoweyes doubtfully and Maddux said, "Don't worry, you can share a room with me."

"Okay," Wilkes said. "I mean, I don't want to be difficult."

"Since when?" Hannibal said.

Hannibal seemed to be especially peeved at Wilkes, because Wilkes's deception had begun with fooling the marshal of Cromwell.

"Now look—" Hannibal said.

"Let's hold it down, shall we?" Maddux said.

"I'll go and see about the rooms," Hannibal said, standing up.

"I will take a walk around town," Shadoweyes said, also rising.

As they left Wilkes said, "I'm getting a little tired of being treated like I got the plague or something."

"You brought it on yourself," Maddux said. "Don't expect to come out of this thing with a lot of friends."

"As long as I come out with some money."

"You should be worried about coming out of this with a whole skin."

"Hey," Wilkes said, "I got the best manhunter in the business as a partner. Why should I worry?"

"Just remember," Maddux said, "I've been out of action for three years."

"*I* saw you in action in Cromwell, Maddux," Wilkes said. "You ain't lost a step."

"How would you know?" Maddux said. "You didn't see me three years ago—or ten years ago."

Maddux watched Wilkes's face as he digested the words, and was satisfied to see a small worry frown crease his brow.

———

MADDUX HUNG around the saloon until early evening. By that time there were enough townspeople and cowboys in the saloon for someone to suggest a poker game, and he worked his way into it.

Wilkes took up a position at the bar and watched.

"Five-card draw is the game," one man said, explaining the rules. "No wild cards. Jacks or better to open, three-raise limit Stakes are whatever you've got on you."

"Check and raise?" Maddux asked.

The man looked at him and then smiled and said, "Yeah, we check and raise."

It seemed that at least two or three of the men played regularly. In fact, Maddux was probably the only stranger to the game, which was at the moment five-handed.

The man who had explained the rules was Taggett The other three men in the game were Cable, Crawford, and Mandon. Taggett and Crawford came from the same ranch, while Gable and Mandon were town merchants.

Maddux had been hoping to find a drifter or two in the game, men who were perhaps working their way north and who might have some news. As it turned out, this game was the only game in town.

He played for an hour, staying even. The big winner seemed to be Taggett, who kept up a steady chatter in between hands and while he dealt, but fell silent after all the cards were dealt out.

During the second hour of the game Hannibal walked in and positioned himself at the bar, away from Wilkes. Shadoweyes had still not reappeared.

During the third hour Maddux finally decided to say something about the game.

Maddux had been dealt a pair of aces, but he hadn't had a chance to open because Taggett had, while Crawford was dealing. Maddux called for three cards, and drew a third ace. Taggett announced he was breaking openers and made a one-card draw.

"Opener bets twenty," Taggett said.

Mandon and Gable dropped, and Maddux raised. Crawford, the dealer, dropped out.

"See your twenty, and raise forty," Taggett said.

"Your forty," Maddux said, " and raise forty more."

"Last raise is mine, I guess," Taggett said. "Your forty, and two hundred."

Maddux counted the money he had on the table and it didn't add up to two hundred.

"Well?" Taggett said.

"I'm going to call," Maddux said, "but first I want to ask you a question."

"What?"

"You fellas always cheat?"

The action at the table stopped and everyone stared at him.

"Who are you talking to?" Mandon asked.

"These two," Maddux said, indicating Taggett and Crawford.

"They're cheatin'?" Gable asked.

"You better be sure about what you're saying, fella," Tagget said.

"Oh, I'm sure," Maddux said. "See, you just split openers, and I don't think you had openers."

"What?"

"I think if we look at your hand, and at what you discarded, we'll see that you didn't have openers, so you opened illegally—and then he dealt you the card you needed for your straight, or your flush, whichever you have."

Man don looked at Taggett and said, 'Is that true?"

Taggett ignored Mandon.

"You're startin' trouble because you can't call the raise," Taggett said. "You better be ready to back it up, friend."

"I am," Maddux said. "You call it."

Mandon and Gable stood up and moved away from the table. Crawford started to get up and Maddux said, "Don't move."

"I ain't got a gun, mister," Crawford said.

"Just stay there."

"He made me do it," Crawford said, whining now.

"Sit."

By now they had the attention of everyone in the saloon, and Maddux hoped that someone had been smart enough to send for the sheriff, and that the law would arrive before he had to kill someone.

"Look," Maddux said, "a card game is a poor reason to die."

"Ha! You're backin' down."

"No, I'm not," Maddux said. "I want you to."

"You called me a cheater, friend."

"And I can prove it."

"If you live that long."

"He will," Joe Hannibal said, and put his gun to Taggett's head.

Taggett's eyes went wide, his back stiffened, and he said, "This ain't fair."

"I'm saving your life, mister," Hannibal said. He reached over Taggett's shoulder to turn over his cards. He had a heart flush.

Maddux reached across the table and turned over his discard, which was a five. It matched the five in Taggett's hand, which meant that he had opened on a pair of fives in a game where you needed at least a pair of jacks to open.

"Like I said," Maddux said, looking at Crawford, "do you fellas always cheat?"

"How do you like that?" Mandon said. "They *was* cheating."

"The pot's yours, mister," Gable said.

Maddux put down his three aces and raked in his pot. At that point the batwing doors opened and the sheriff came walking in.

"What's going on?" he demanded.

"Why don't we take these two fellas over to your jail, Sheriff," Hannibal said, "and I'll explain."

CHAPTER TWENTY-NINE

For the first time since they left Cromwell, the fact that Joe Hannibal was a lawman came in handy. It got them some professional courtesy from Paul Fane, the sheriff in Dennison.

"So my friend was playing poker and spotted these yahoos cheating," Hannibal finished.

"*I* see," Fane said. "Well, we'll give them a oneway ticket out of town, and I'll talk to Big Mike Sideman, the man they work for. I don't think he's gonna want any card cheats workin' for him."

"Thanks for your help, Sheriff," Hannibal said, standing up and extending his hand. Sheriff Paul Fane stood up and accepted the proffered hand.

"Anything else I can do for you while you're in town?" Fane asked.

"I don't think so, Sheriff," Hannibal said. "We'll be leaving in the morning."

"Where you headin'?"

"Don't know exactly. We heard there was a town somewhere hereabouts that's been taken over by a fella name Walker Bogart, but we haven't been able to find it."

"Why are you lookin' for it?" Fane asked. "Doesn't sound like the kind of a place for a visit."

Hannibal stared at the man for a moment and then asked, "You know what town it is?"

"I do," Fane said. "Friend of mine is the sheriff there, and I'm sure he's feeling pretty helpless right about now. That's why I like bein' the sheriff in a nothin' town like this. Ain't nobody in their right minds would want to take this town over."

"But your friend's town is a different story?" Hannibal asked.

"It's a growin' town—or it was until Walker Bogart and his came along."

"Why hasn't the word gotten out more?"

"Bogart and his men got everybody scared of them," Fane said. "People are just too darn scared to pass the word."

"How did you get the word?"

"My friend, Sheriff Ben Exman, managed to get one telegraph message to me when Bogart came into town. He was askin' for help, but I just didn't have enough men to make a difference."

Fane looked a little uncomfortable about admitting that. Hannibal had a feeling that Fane wasn't immune to a little fear himself.

"I see," Hannibal said. "Well, if you'd tell me the name of the town, we'll get over there and see what the situation is."

"How many men you got?"

"We're four."

"That ain't nearly enough men, Marshal Hannibal," Sheriff Fane said. "Not nearly enough to take on Bogart and his crew. If I was you *and* your friends I'd think twice about this."

"I appreciate that, Sheriff Fane, but there's a town that is practically being held hostage, and there's a friend of ours in there," Hannibal explained. "My friend and I aim to do what we can do to change that."

"Well," Fane said, "I warned you. When you leave town, ride for about five miles and you'll come to a turnoff. Take that turnoff and you'll be on it."

"On what?" Hannibal asked.

"On the road to Ceremony."

———

WHILE HANNIBAL WENT to the sheriff's office, Maddux and Wilkes went to the hotel. Shadoweyes still had not put in an appearance since leaving the saloon that afternoon.

"What the hell happened to that Indian?" Wilkes asked when they were in their room.

"He's a big boy," Maddux said.

"What's that mean?"

"He can take care of himself."

"Okay. Then what's taking Hannibal so long?"

"Just relax, Wilkes," Maddux said. "They'll be along in time."

"Poker," Wilkes said derisively. "Three hours playing poker and what did you learn? That a couple of guys were cheating."

"I also made a few hundred dollars," Maddux said. "Not bad for three hours' work."

"A couple of hundred," Wilkes said. "We're dealing with fifteen thousand dollars here, and you're happy about a couple of hundred."

"Wilkes," Maddux said, "if we're both going to walk out of this room alive, you're going to have to change your tune."

"Is that a threat?"

"It's a suggestion, right now," Maddux said, "but I can make it a threat if you like."

They were facing each other when there was a knock on the door. Maddux walked to it, and opened it for John Shadoweyes.

"Did you find out anything?" Wilkes asked.

Shadoweyes stared at Wilkes, as if the other were speaking in a foreign language.

"Well?"

"Take it easy, Wilkes," Maddux said. "If he found out something he'll tell us."

"Yeah? And maybe he won't," Wilkes said. "Maybe he found out something and he's going to go after Bogart alone, and keep the reward. How about that?"

Maddux stared at Wilkes. "Is this the man who told me that partners should trust one another?"

"Yeah, well, it's plain that none of you want to be partners with me. Besides, he's an Indian. What's to keep him from running out on us?"

"If anyone was going to run out on the rest of us, Wilkes, my money would be on you."

"Hey, listen—"

"But I don't think any of us is going to run out," Maddux went on, "because no one of us would have a chance against Bogart alone."

Wilkes knew he was right, but wouldn't admit it.

"I found nothing," Shadoweyes said. "I asked questions and I listened to conversations, but I found nothing."

"Well," Maddux said, "maybe Hannibal has had some better luck."

On cue there was another knock at the door. Since Shadoweyes was standing in front of it, he simply turned and opened it, admitting Hannibal.

"I'm glad you're all here," Hannibal said. 'I've got the answer." He clapped his hands when he spoke, and had an excited flush on his face.

"You know the name of the town?" Wilkes asked excitedly.

Hannibal looked at Maddux and said, "I know the name of the town and how to get there."

"The sheriff knew?" Maddux asked.

"He did. He was asked for help, but he said he didn't have enough men. I think he was just too...cautious to get involved."

"Come on, come on," Wilkes implored. "What's the name of the town?"

Still looking at Maddux, Hannibal said, "The town is called Ceremony."

———

LATER MADDUX and Hannibal were sitting in the saloon. Shadoweyes was off somewhere and Wilkes in his room at the hotel. They had decided to spend the night and get an early start for Ceremony the next morning.

"I have to say something," Hannibal said.

"So, say it."

"You're taking this very well."

"Taking what well?"

"The fact that Wilkes lied to you and lured you out of your retirement."

Maddux made a face at Hannibal and said, "Joe, I learned a long time ago nobody makes a bigger fool out of you than yourself."

"What's that mean?"

"I mean, maybe I was just looking for an excuse to make this trip, and Wilkes was it. Maybe he used me, but I used him as well."

"You mean you're not angry?"

"No," Maddux said. "I guess I feel a little foolish, but I'm not angry."

"But this trip hasn't even turned out to be the one you wanted," Hannibal said. "We're going after Walker Bogart, not the Backshooter."

"Well," Maddux said, "maybe I'm thinking of that fifteen thousand dollars and what my end could mean to the ranch."

"You think if you return to Cromwell with almost four thousand dollars that Laura will forgive and forget?"

"Probably not," Maddux said. "Like we said before, Joe, there's not much we can do about the Backshooter until he claims another victim. In the meantime, we might as well go after Walker Bogart."

"Well," Hannibal said," I guess while we're in the neighborhood, it would be rude not to pay our respects, huh?"

Maddux smiled and said, "Yeah."

CHAPTER THIRTY

B en Exman didn't feel much like a sheriff in Ceremony anymore. In fact, he was surprised that Walker Bogart hadn't attempted to put his own man into his office by now. Maybe Bogart knew that the only way he'd be able to do that was over Exman's dead body. Up to now, Exman had taken his job very seriously. He'd been proud of the fact that he was the sheriff.

He wasn't so proud anymore.

He'd let Bogart and his men ride right into Ceremony, and right over everyone who lived here, including himself. That sure as well was not the action of a proud sheriff.

Exman, at thirty-five, had a combination of dedication and experience. His dedication told him to go out and face Bogart, but his experience told him that would be suicide.

Or maybe he was just frightened.

Well, sure he was frightened. He wouldn't be human if he wasn't, but he was also smart enough to know he couldn't do anything on his own. Early on he'd asked his friend, Sheriff Fane in Dennison, for help, but Fane had refused. Exman could understand that, couldn't hold it against the other man. If anyone died in defense of Ceremony it should be him, not a sheriff from somewhere else. There was no reason for the other man to volunteer to do that.

Exman had two deputies, and under normal circumstances

they were good men, but they weren't stupid enough to commit suicide either.

If and when Ben Exman made a move, the conditions were going to have to be in his favor.

When that would be was anybody's guess.

———

WALKER BOGART SAT in the saloon, thinking about Anne Redman. He had given the woman plenty of time to come around—maybe *too* much time. He knew that his men were talking about him, and he was going to have to do something before some of them started to question him.

If that happened he might have to kill those men, and he had no desire to start killing his own men.

It made it hard to demand loyalty.

He didn't understand a woman like Anne Redman. He'd treated her fairly, he thought. Except for making her dress the way he wanted her to, he hadn't forced her to do anything.

Maybe tonight he was going to have to go over to the house and show Anne Redman what she'd been missing all this time.

Maybe it was time for him to show her who was whose captive.

Maybe it was time to just go over and rape the bitch and get it over with!

CHAPTER THIRTY-ONE

"All right," Maddux said, "now that we finally know where we're going, we have to decide how we're going to play it."

"What do you mean how we're gonna play it?" Wilkes said. "We go in there and get Bogart, and collect our money."

"First of all," Maddux said, "do you know how many guns we'll be facing?"

Wilkes didn't answer.

"Do you?"

"No, I don't."

"Well, I don't either," Maddux said. "None of us do. And that's what we're going to have to find out before we do anything. Understand?"

"Sure," Wilkes said, "sure, I understand. I'm just a little...anxious."

Maddux looked at Hannibal and said, "Tell him what he gets for being a little anxious, Joe."

Hannibal looked at Wilkes and said, "Dead."

"Exactly," Maddux said. "You understand dead, don't you?"

"All right," Wilkes said, "you've made your point."

"I hope so," Maddux said. "All right, Joe or John, one of you have to ride in first. I can't because someone might recognize me, and obviously Wilkes can't because he's just not experienced enough."

"I'll go," Hannibal said.

"*I will go*," Shadoweyes said. Both men had spoken at the same time."

"We don't know how they will react to a stranger riding in, but John, I think if you ride in you might be more of a target."

"Because I am a half-breed?"

Maddux nodded. "That's like waving a red flag in front of a bull with some people. Some hardcase will see you and decide to try you just for something to do."

"So that means I go," Hannibal said.

That's the way I see it," Maddux said. "Anybody object?"

They all shook their heads.

"Anybody got a better idea?"

Again, they all indicated that they didn't.

"That's too bad," Maddux said. "I was hoping someone would."

"I'll ride on in in the morning," Hannibal said.

They had camped about an hour out of town so that whoever rode in could do so very early. The fewer people there were on the streets, the less chance there was of trouble.

"I suggest we all turn in," Maddux said. "Tomorrow's going to be a big day."

"Same watches?" Wilkes asked.

"Yeah, same watches."

Without further word Wilkes picked up his rifle and went to find himself a comfortable spot.

"Joe?"

"Yeah?"

Maddux held out his hand. "You'll have to leave the badge behind, just in case someone does challenge you. You might be searched."

Hannibal looked down at his shirt pocket, then took the badge out and held it in his hand. "I'll put it in my saddlebag."

"They might search that too," Maddux said. "Leave it with me. I'll take good care of it."

Hannibal looked down at it again and hefted it in his hand.

"All right," he said, handing it over, "but you better take good care of it. To some people it's just a piece of tin, but it means a lot more to me."

"I know it does," Maddux said, closing his hand over it. He tucked it into his own shirt pocket and said, "I'll take good care of it."

Hannibal nodded, then went to set up his bedroll.

"What about me?" Shadoweyes said.

"John, I think you should follow Hannibal to the edge of town. Keep an eye on his back trail. Wilkes and I will hang even further back. We'll have to give Hannibal enough time to ride in and get settled."

"And then what?"

"We can't all ride in," Maddux said. 'Too many strangers on the same day might tip them off. Once Hannibal's inside, we'll have to find a way into town without being seen."

"After he is in, I will circle around and see if I can find a way in," Shadoweyes said.

"All right," Maddux said.

"Do we still watch Wilkes tonight?"

Maddux looked over to where Wilkes was sitting, then said, "Yes, tonight more than ever."

CHAPTER THIRTY-TWO

In the morning they all rose and had coffee. Over the fire they went over their "plan" once again.

"This doesn't sound all that well thought out to me," Wilkes said.

"Well now, if you've got a better idea I'd like to hear it," Maddux said. "That goes for anybody."

He looked around at all of them. Hannibal and Shadoweyes were looking at Wilkes, and Wilkes was finding something else —*anything* else—to look at.

"All right, then we'll go with what we've got," Maddux said.

Hannibal and Shadoweyes saddled the horses, and Hannibal mounted up first.

"Joe, you watch yourself when you get into town. Don't look crossways at anybody. The last thing we need is somebody to challenge you."

"Right. Good luck."

"To you too."

Hannibal rode off and Maddux turned to Shadow-eyes. "Trail him, but stay well back."

"Right."

Shadoweyes mounted up.

"We'll be along behind you," Maddux told him.

"When I find a way in I will let you know."

"All right. Good luck, John."

After Shadoweyes rode off, Wilkes turned to Maddux and said, "What do *we* do now?"

Maddux turned to Wilkes and said, "Have another cup of coffee."

———

HANNIBAL RODE down the main street of Ceremony, trying not to show the tension he was feeling. Maddux's temperament was probably better suited to this kind of subterfuge. Hannibal had not come out from behind his badge for a long time, and the experience was proving to be an eye-opener—with more to come.

Ceremony was different from the other towns they had ridden through. This town had the look of a place that was progressing. The buildings were all well cared for. Some of them were obviously new, and there were a few that were still in the process of being built—only no one was working on them at the moment.

Folks were probably just flat afraid to come out onto the street because of Bogart and his boys.

When he got to the livery he handed his horse over to an old man.

"Town's pretty quiet," he commented.

"Yep," the old man said.

"Something happen?"

"Nope," the man said. It was obvious that he wasn't going to say anymore than he had to.

"How long you stayin'?" the old man asked.

"Not long," Hannibal said. "Maybe just overnight. If I change my mind I'll let you know."

"You'll have to give me some money now," the old man said.

Hannibal dug into his pocket and gave the old man what he asked for.

"Saloon open this early?" he asked.

"The saloon is always open," the old man said, and walked the horse inside.

"I'll find it myself," Hannibal said to no one. Out of habit he reached up to touch the badge on his chest but it wasn't there.

———

SHADOWEYES HAD TRAILED Hannibal right to the town limits and had stopped there. He looked for higher ground, found it, and was able to watch Hannibal ride into town. That done, he began to circle the town, looking for another way in.

Naturally, they could have entered from the other end, but that would still mean riding right down the center of the main street.

He circled the town completely twice, and could find only two other ways to enter. They could work their way down around behind the livery stable, or to an alley that ran right through from the main street to behind the general store.

He turned his horse and headed back to where Maddux and Wilkes would be waiting.

———

WHEN HANNIBAL WALKED into the saloon there was no one there but the bartender.

"You serving beer this early?" Hannibal asked.

"I am if you're drinkin' it," the bartender said.

"Well, draw me one," Hannibal said.

The bartender drew a beer and put it in front of him.

"What's wrong with this town, anyway? It's real quiet," Hannibal said.

The bartender shrugged and said, "So it's quiet. A lot of towns are quiet."

"Not towns this size," Hannibal said.

"What are you, some kind of census-taker?" the bartender asked.

Hannibal realized then that maybe he was asking too many questions.

"No," Hannibal said, "I'm just a man looking for a beer and a meal."

"Well, you'll have to go down the street for the meal," the bartender said.

"As soon as I finish this beer, I'll do just that."

When Hannibal left the saloon, the bartender took off his apron and left also.

———

"WHO IS HE?" Walker Bogart asked.

The bartender had gone to Walker Bogart's house to tell him the news.

"I don't know," the bartender said. "Just a stranger, I guess."

"So why bring him to my attention?"

The bartender shrugged. They were in the kitchen. Bogart had one of the saloon girls come in in the morning and make him breakfast, and when the food was ready he kicked her out and ate alone. He was drinking coffee now and did not offer the other man any.

"He was asking questions."

"About what?"

"About why the town was so quiet."

"What did you tell him?"

"I told him it was a quiet town."

"That satisfy him?"

"I guess."

Bogart thought a moment, then said, "All right. Go back to work."

The bartender nodded and left the house, and Bogart thought about what he'd said. From the way it sounded, the man was just a stranger riding through.

Still...

He finished his coffee and spent a moment thinking about Anne Redman. He had come back to the house last night drunk, with every intention of forcing himself on her. He'd been so drunk, however, that the flight of steps had looked miles long, so he had lain down on the sofa in the sitting room to rest.

That was where he'd awakened in the morning.

He hadn't even seen Anne Redman this morning. He'd had the girl from the saloon bring her breakfast up to her. His intention was to go up and see her after his own breakfast, but now there was this stranger to see to.

Maybe later.

CHAPTER THIRTY-THREE

Shadoweyes finished telling Maddux about the two alternate entry points he had found into town.

"Well, that's it," Wilkes said, "let's go."

"Just hold on a minute," Maddux said. "We've got to give Hannibal enough time to get the lay of things." He looked at Shadoweyes and asked, "How did the town look to you, John?"

"Quiet," Shadoweyes said, "much too quiet. I think perhaps the people are afraid to come out onto the street."

"Well, that's a possibility," Maddux said. "However, that can work for us or against us."

"How so?" Wilkes asked.

"Well, if there were people on the street we could blend in with them when we sneak into town."

"That's how it works against us," Wilkes said. "How does it work for us?"

"When the shooting starts," Maddux said, "we won't have to worry about hitting innocent bystanders."

———

HANNIBAL WAS EATING in a small cafe when two men entered. There were other diners in the cafe, and from their reaction he was sure one of the men was Walker Bogart. If he had to choose which one, he would have said the big one.

He continued eating, not looking at the two men. He didn't

look up again until the two men positioned themselves right in front of his table. Behind them Hannibal saw several people scurry out of the cafe, leaving behind partially uneaten meals.

"Can I help you?" he asked.

"Not really," the big man said. "We're sort of the welcoming committee of Ceremony. You know, we like to make strangers welcome."

"Is that a fact?"

"Mind if I sit down?"

"I like to know who I'm sitting with."

"My name's Bogart, Walker Bogart. This here's Parnell."

"My name is Hannibal. Sit down a spell."

Bogart pulled out one chair and sat down. The other man, Parnell, remained standing.

"You boys want some coffee?" Hannibal offered. "I could get another cup."

"No, thanks," Bogart said. "You just passing through?"

"That's right."

"On your way to...where?"

Hannibal shrugged and said, "No place special." As an afterthought he added, "I'll just keep drifting until I find some work."

"Work, huh?" Bogart said. "What kind of work is it you do?"

Again Hannibal shrugged. "This and that."

Bogart leaned over and glanced at Hannibal's gun, but Hannibal didn't say anything. Bogart studied Hannibal a while longer in silence.

"Well," Bogart said, "we just wanted to make you feel welcome."

"You succeeded, Mr. Bogart. I thank you."

"Don't mention it."

Bogart stood up and he and Parnell walked to the door. Hannibal watched them, then finished his coffee, wondering what Bogart was thinking.

———

OUTSIDE PARNELL SAID, "What do you think?"

"Did you see his shirt?"

"What about it?"

"On the left side, there were holes in it, small holes like a pin makes."

"So?"

"Pins," Bogart said, "the kind on the back of a badge."

"A badge?"

"Yeah," Bogart said, "what we got in there is a lawman."

"Maybe he used to be a lawman."

"Same thing," Bogart said. "Besides, that many fresh holes means that badge has been coming on and off a lot—and recently. No, he ain't no ex-lawman. He's a lawman."

"What are we gonna do?"

Bogart looked at Parnell and said, "What do we usually do with lawmen, Parnell?"

———

"ARE WE GONNA WAIT UNTIL DARK?" Wilkes asked.

"We can't," Maddux said. "I'd like to, but we can't leave Hannibal in there alone that long."

"Then when do we move?" Wilkes asked.

Maddux looked down at Ceremony, knowing that it was chock-full with Walker Bogart's men. "We might as well go now and get it over with."

"Well it's about time," Wilkes said.

"I just thought of something," Maddux said.

"What?" Shadoweyes asked.

"Look down there, both of you," Maddux said, pointing to the town.

"At what?" Wilkes asked.

"Just look at the town," Maddux said, "and imagine that you are Walker Bogart." He waited a moment, then asked, "You take what you want, right?"

"Right," Wilkes said.

"Where would you live?"

There was a moment of silence while both men thought about the question. Maddux wished he had thought of it before Hannibal had left.

"The hotel," Wilkes said.

"Use some imagination, Wilkes," Maddux said. "You can have any place you want. What would you take?"

'That saloon," Wilkes said. "I'd stay in the saloon with all the women."

'That house," Shadoweyes said, "at the far end of town."

"Why the house?" Maddux asked.

"Because it is the largest house in town."

"And would you keep a woman there, away from the other men?"

"Yes," Shadoweyes said, "if she's still alive."

"Yeah," Maddux said. "So would I. That's our first target."

"What about the saloon?"

"Forget about the saloon," Maddux said. "Shadoweyes, show us those two ways into town. We'll have to pick out the best one."

"Why don't we split up and go in both ways?" Wilkes asked.

Maddux stared at Wilkes and then said, "Wilkes, that's the first good idea you've had since we left."

Hannibal came out of the cafe and looked both ways. To his right a man stood, leaning against a post. He straightened up when Hannibal came out.

Well, they had sent a man to watch him. So much for his plan to lie back and listen like a fly on the wall.

CHAPTER THIRTY-FOUR

Maddux decided to keep Wilkes with him, and let Shadoweyes go on alone. He and Wilkes would work their way around to the back of the livery stable and Shadoweyes would come down the alley. Once they made it to the livery stable they'd be about a block away from the house they had picked out as Bogart's.

Shadoweyes was to work his way down the alley, find a place to hide and wait. It wouldn't do to have Shadoweyes walking around town, attracting attention. He was going to have to hide and wait for all hell to break loose.

Maddux and Wilkes left their horses on high ground, tied to a stand of trees, and worked their way down behind the livery stable.

"What now?" Wilkes asked.

"I'll tell you what," Maddux said. "Sit tight here, the way Shadoweyes is doing in the alley, and wait until you hear from me—or until you hear a ruckus—then come running."

"And what are you gonna do?"

"I'm going to check that house and see if there's a woman being held there."

"Look, Maddux," Wilkes said, "don't forget why we're here—"

"Your main concern is money," Maddux said, cutting him off. "Don't worry, Wilkes, you'll get what's coming to you. In fact, if everything goes right, maybe we'll both get what we want. Now stay here!"

Maddux moved away before Wilkes could argue.

———

SHADOWEYES WAS IN THE ALLEY, and there were some crates stacked against one wall. He pulled a crate away from the wall, and turned it around so that its open end fitted against the wall. He got inside the box, and inched it back against the wall so he was well hidden. He did not want to be found before the time came.

———

MADDUX WAS SURPRISED.

The town was even more deserted than it looked from outside. It seemed as if Bogart really had the entire town too scared to move.

He reached the big house and flattened himself against the wall on one side. He moved to the nearest window and peered in. He could see a sitting room, and there was a man with a rifle in the room. The excitement built inside him.

He'd found the woman. Why else would there be an armed man inside the house?

He moved around to the back of the house and looked in a window there. It was the kitchen, and there was a man sitting at a table eating. He had a rifle leaning against the table. There was no way Maddux could kick in the door, grab the rifle, and kill the man without the other man hearing it. He was going to have to find another way into the house.

He noticed that the kitchen stuck out from the rest of the house. He backed up and saw that the low roof gave access to the second floor. There was a barrel nearby, and if he stood on it he'd be able to reach the low roof and hoist himself up. He was going to have to wait for the man in the kitchen to finish and leave the room. There was no way he could walk on the roof without the man hearing him inside.

He flattened himself against the back wall of the house so that he could peek in the back window, and settled down to wait.

———

"WHAT ARE we gonna do about the lawman?" Parnell asked.

"Dutrow is watching him, isn't he?"

"Yeah."

"So he can't do anything without us knowing about it."

"Why don't we just kill him?"

"Why don't *you* kill him?"

"Alone?"

Bogart regarded Parnell across the table, then picked up his beer and sipped from it. Parnell was a good lieutenant because he did what he was told, had never had a good idea of his own, and was a coward. There was no way he'd ever turn on Bogart.

"We'll kill him when I say so," Bogart said. "Let's see what the man wants first."

"How we gonna find that out?"

"Easy," Bogart said, smiling. "We're gonna ask him."

———

HANNIBAL HAD TAKEN a turn around the whole town—the whole empty town—and his tail was still with him. He was convinced that the man wasn't there to kill him, just to keep Bogart informed about him. Apparently, Walker Bogart had noticed something about him and wanted to be sure he knew his every move. There was no way of knowing what gave him away, but he was sure he'd find out soon enough.

Hannibal decided to go and get himself a hotel room. It was as likely a place to hole up as any while waiting for the fur to fly. Before long, Bogart would be coming for him, either to kill him or talk to him, find out what he wanted.

He hoped Maddux would move before then.

Long before then.

———

MADDUX HAD one fear and that was that someone would move too soon.

He had worked with Hannibal for years now, and he knew Shadoweyes as a ranchhand, but he felt he could trust them when things got bad, and they hadn't shown him any different anywhere on the trail.

It was Wilkes he was most worried about.

If Wilkes panicked, he could get them all killed.

And Wilkes was as prime a candidate for panic as Maddux had ever seen.

As Maddux watched, the man in the kitchen finished eating, picked up his rifle, and left. Maddux waited a while to make sure the other man wouldn't come in for something to eat. When he was sure it was clear, he rolled the barrel over to the house, stood on it, reached up, grabbed the edge of the low roof, and pulled himself up onto it.

When he was on the roof he walked gingerly up to the nearest window. He looked inside the room and saw that it was a large bedroom. Best of all it was empty. He tried the window and found it unlocked. He slid it up and stepped into the room. He moved to the open door, stood still, and listened intently. He thought he could hear voices downstairs, but there was nothing up here.

He moved into the hall. Although he left his gun in his holster, he was prepared to draw it at any time. He moved quietly down the hall to a closed door and pressed his ear to it. He couldn't hear anything inside, so he turned the doorknob slowly and opened it.

The woman in the chair turned around and when she saw him her eyes widened in a mixture of shock, surprise...and utter joy.

"I don't know who you are, mister," the woman said, "but you're a dream come true."

CHAPTER THIRTY-FIVE

Anne Redman rushed into Maddux's arms and he held her tightly. He was acutely aware of how much flesh was showing from what she was wearing—or what she was almost wearing.

"Was this the way he kept you from going outside?" he asked. "By dressing you like this?"

She shocked herself by laughing.

"This is how he kept me on display for him," she said, "but now that you mention it, I *would* be too embarrassed to go out like this."

"I hope not," he said, "because we're getting out of here now."

"I knew you'd come," she said, touching his face with both hands, "I knew it. By the way, who are you?"

"My name is Maddux."

"Well, Mr. Maddux, my name is Anne Redman and I can't thank you enough—"

"You can say thank you when we get away from here," he said, cutting her off.

"Away?" she said, backing up. "I don't want to get away."

Maddux was surprised. Had he made the wrong assumption here? "You what?"

"Not without Bogart."

"I don't—"

"I came here to get Bogart, Maddux," Anne said, "and after everything I've been through, I'm not leaving without him."

"You're a bounty hunter?" Maddux asked, finally catching on.

"What's the matter?" she demanded. "You never heard of a woman bounty hunter before?"

"No."

"Well, I am one, and I want Bogart. I'm not leaving without him."

Maddux studied her face and saw how deadly serious she was.

"Well," he said, "would you settle for his head on a platter?"

She smiled and said, "Yes!"

"Then we've got to get you some clothes."

———

"HEY!"

Anne Redman waited a moment, then called again.

"Hey, down there!"

When there was no reply she looked at Maddux.

"They're deciding who should come up," he whispered.

She shushed him when she heard someone coming up the steps.

"What the hell do you want this—" the man was saying, but he stopped short when he came into the room.

Anne Redman was naked to the waist, and the sight of her just nailed him to the floor.

Maddux came out from behind the door and stuck his gun in the man's ear.

"Move and you're dead."

"I ain't movin'," the man said, and he still had not taken his eyes off Anne.

Maddux examined the man critically and said, "His clothes will never fit you."

"No," she said, "they'd be too small."

Indeed, the man was at least three or four inches shorter than she was.

Maddux screwed his gun deeper into the man's ear and relieved him of his gun.

"Call your friend," Maddux said, "and make it sound like there's something up here he's just got to see."

The man nodded. "Webb?"

No answer.

"Goddamnit, Webb! Get up here?"

"What the hell is it?" Webb called from downstairs.

"Come on up."

"What for?"

"Tell him..." Maddux said, whispering something in the man's ear.

"Webb...she's givin' it away up here."

Suddenly there was the sound of running feet on the steps. As the man called Webb ran into the room Maddux clubbed him over the head. Webb went sprawling onto the floor, and as the other man leaned over him, Maddux let him have it too.

"His clothes will fit you," Maddux said. "You might have to roll up the pants legs and the sleeves—"

"I'll roll them," Anne said. She bent over the man and said, "Help me get him undressed."

"Right."

Maddux holstered his gun and reached for the man's shirt.

"You do the pants," Anne said.

"Right."

She started to unbutton the man's shirt, then looked at Maddux and repeated, "'She's givin' it away'?"

He grinned and said, "That would bring me running."

————

"ALL RIGHT," Bogart said to Parnell, "let's go and talk to our friend the lawman."

————

HANNIBAL LOOKED out the window of his hotel room and saw Bogart and his man Parnell crossing the street from the saloon. He took out his gun and checked to make sure it was fully loaded, then opened the window.

————

WHEN SHE WAS DRESSED, Anne took one of the men's gun belts and strapped it on.

"God," she said, "I feel dressed again."

"Yeah," Maddux said, "you looked dressed again too."

"Don't look so disappointed."

"Well, I kind of liked what you had on before." The comment surprised even *him*.

She smiled at him and said, "Why do I have this feeling that you're normally shy?"

"That was before I retired."

"Well, don't be so disappointed," she said. "Remember if we get out of this, I owe you my thanks."

Maddux wasn't sure what she meant, but he didn't pursue it. "Let's tie these yahoos up nice and tight and get to it, then."

CHAPTER THIRTY-SIX

"I have a plan," Maddux said.

"I knew you would," Anne Redman said. "I'm sure it's a well-thought-out, carefully mapped plan, with a safe escape and everything?"

"Well, actually I thought it up while we were undressing that fella upstairs."

They were standing at the front window of the house, looking out.

"What was it about that that gave you a plan?"

"Well, I noticed that his cuffs were frayed."

"And?"

"Well, who pays them so they can buy new shirts?"

"Bogart."

"And if Bogart was dead, who would pay him and the other men?"

"Nobody."

"Exactly."

"And that's your plan?"

"Yep."

"Would you like to explain it?"

"If we kill Bogart maybe the others will just...go away?"

Anne stared at Maddux for a moment, and then said, "Maybe you've got something there. Why don't we go and try it out?"

"After you."

As they went out the front door she said, "Oh, I forgot to ask. Did you come alone?"

"No," he said, "I have three men with me."

"Only three?"

"Three," Maddux said again.

"Well, where are they?"

"They're strategically placed around town."

"How will they know when to move?"

"They'll know."

As they walked away from the house towards the main street—which Maddux noticed was called Front Street—Maddux said, "Oh, by the way."

"What?"

"You'll have to split the reward."

"With you?"

"With...everyone."

"Five ways?"

"I'm afraid so."

"Is the reward still fifteen thousand?"

"Last I heard."

"Well, three thousand is better than nothing."

"I hoped you'd look at it that way."

"Of course, it's top small a payment for what I've been through."

"Did he, uh..."

"No, he didn't," she said. "It was real strange. He put me in that house, dressed me, but never touched me. I couldn't figure it out."

"Maybe he just didn't know what to do with a lady," Maddux said.

"You didn't come here just to rescue me, did you?"

"No."

"You came for the reward?"

"No."

"Then...why did you come?"

"Bogart wanted me to."

"What?"

Maddux was about to make himself clearer when Anne hissed, "There he is!" She pointed. They moved out of the street and into a doorway.

Maddux saw two men crossing the street towards the hotel. "The big one?"

"Yes. What's that?"

"There?"

"Up there, on the hotel."

Maddux looked and saw a man climbing out a window. He recognized the bulk.

"That's Hannibal," Maddux said. "He's with us. Where are the rest of Bogart's men?"

"The hotel, the whorehouse—"

"How many does he have?"

"I don't know."

"I tell you what," Maddux said. "Let's go for Bogart without finding out."

"Why?"

"If we know for sure how many men he's got," Maddux said, "we might change our minds."

———

HANNIBAL WATCHED until Bogart and Parnell were out of sight and then dropped down from the low roof outside his window. The man Bogart had watching him would still be in the lobby, and the three of them were probably now going upstairs to his room.

He started down the street and stopped when he saw someone up ahead.

"Maddux," he said to himself.

Maddux waved and Hannibal quickened his pace and moved towards him.

"Who's this?" Hannibal asked.

"I'll introduce you later," Maddux said. "Get into the alley with Shadoweyes. Things are going to start jumping real soon."

"All right. Where will you be?"

Maddux looked around, saw the sheriffs office, and said, 'In there."

"That reminds me," Hannibal said. 'If I'm gonna die, I'd rather die with it on."

"Right," Maddux said, and handed Hannibal his badge.

"Luck," Hannibal said, and headed for the alley.

"Why the sheriff's office?" Anne asked.

"We can use the extra gun," Maddux said. "He'll be on our side."

———

BEN EXMAN STOOD up quickly as the door to his office slammed open.

"Who are you?" he demanded as a man and a woman entered. "Are you one of Bogart's—"

"We don't work for Bogart, Sheriff," Maddux said

"Then who are you and what do you want?"

"We're here *for* Bogart, Sheriff."

"For the bounty on his head you mean." Disdain was plain in the man's tone.

"For whatever reason we're here, it's your chance to be rid of him," Maddux said "You can either help us, or watch us fight each other. If he wins, you're still under his thumb. If we win, I'll come back and kill you. The choice is yours.""

Exman came around his desk and positioned himself in front of Maddux.

"I'll help you," Exman said, "but it's not because of any threat you made. I want my town back."

"Well then, let's go and get it."

Maddux started to turn and Exman put out his hand to stop him. "What's your name?"

"Maddux."

"How many of you are there?"

"Myself, the lady, and three others."

"When this is over, when we've taken the town back," Sheriff Ben Exman said, "I want you and your people out of it as fast as possible."

"Don't worry, Sheriff," Anne Redman said, "once I've done what I came to do, I won't be able to get out of this town fast enough."

CHAPTER THIRTY-SEVEN

Wilkes looked in the windows of the house and saw that it was empty. More than ever he felt sure that Maddux had double-crossed him—maybe even double-crossed all of them—and had already taken Bogart out of town.

He moved away from the house and started walking down Front Street.

MADDUX CAME out of the sheriff's office with the sheriff and Anne Redman.

"Sheriff, how many men does Bogart have?"

The lawman thought a moment before speaking. "You know something?" he said. "I don't know."

"How many have you ever seen at one time?"

"I always see Bogart and Parnell together, and at times I've seen Parnell with one or two other men."

"Does anybody know how many men Bogart has with him?" Maddux asked.

"I don't think so."

Maddux and Anne exchanged glances. She had only ever seen two men at a time, two pairs of them, who spelled each other staying at the house with her.

That made four men—Bogart, Parnell, and a couple of others the sheriff said he saw from time to time with Parnell.

Altogether, they had accounted for half a dozen men. Surely, Bogart had more than that with him.

"What are you thinking?" Exman asked.

"I'm thinking," Maddux said, "that Bogart may have taken this town by fear rather than by force."

"No, no," the sheriff said, "he must have an army with him."

"But no one's ever seen them," Maddux said.

"Still..."

"Look at the streets," Maddux said. "Your people are afraid to come out, but there should be some of Bogart's men around. They can't all be staying in the saloon, the hotel, and the whorehouse."

"So you're saying that there's just maybe half a dozen men?"

Maddux thought a moment, then said, "Yeah, that's what I'm saying."

"Hell, even if there's double that, we're not so outnumbered," Exman said.

"Do you have any deputies?"

"I do, but they haven't come around much since Bogart took over."

"All right, then it's the six of us," Maddux said. "Last I saw, Bogart was in the hotel."

"How do you want to handle this?" Exman asked.

"Head-on, I guess," Maddux said. "We'll face Bogart and see how many men come to his aid."

"Where are your men?"

"I've got two of them in an alley a block from here, and one back by the livery stable."

"Who's that?" Anne asked.

Maddux looked up and saw Wilkes walking down Front Street.

"He's one of mine," Maddux said. "I left him by the livery. If Bogart sees him—"

"There's Bogart," Exman said, cutting off their conversation, "coming out of the hotel with Parnell and one other man."

"They'll see him for sure," Anne said, and even as she spoke they could tell Bogart and the two men with him had seen him.

"We'd better move...now!" Maddux said.

"I swear I don't know how he got out—" the third man was telling Bogart.

"Oh, shut up!" Bogart snapped.

"Walker," Parnell said, warningly, "another stranger."

"I see him."

"How'd he get into town?"

"It don't matter how," Bogart said. "That's two strangers in one day, and I don't believe in coincidence. Come on. Let's see what this one's got to say for himself."

Bogart stepped into the street and the other two men followed.

———

WILKES SAW the three men step into the street and panicked. He had heard and read physical descriptions of Bogart, and he knew that the big man in the center was the outlaw himself.

Wilkes drew his gun and fired, missing all three.

"Scatter!" Bogart shouted, drawing his gun. He fired at Wilkes, hitting him in the shoulder. The force of the bullet spun him around and deposited him on his butt in the center of the street. From that position Wilkes fired again, missing.

———

"THAT ASS!" Maddux shouted.

"He's hit," Exman said.

"Give me some cover so I can get him."

"You've got it," Anne said.

She and the sheriff began to fire towards Bogart and his two men. Bogart, who had been taking a bead on the fallen Wilkes, turned toward the shooting, then turned again and dove for cover, as his two men had already done.

Maddux ran out into the street to grab Wilkes. At the same time three men came running from the saloon, two from the whorehouse, and two more from the hotel. They saw what was going on and drew their guns to fire at Maddux.

Hannibal and Shadoweyes came out of the alley, their guns drawn, to add cover for Maddux.

"What happened?" Wilkes asked as Maddux lifted him to his feet.

"You panicked, didn't you?" Maddux said.

"I—I—"

"Come on!"

He held the man around the waist and dragged him from the street to cover behind a horse trough.

"I'm dying!" Wilkes said.

Maddux checked his wound and saw that the bullet had struck him high on the right shoulder.

"You're not dying. Get up here, this is what you've been waiting for."

Wilkes struggled to his knees to look out over the trough.

"H-how many?" he asked.

"Near as I can figure, ten." Count the two he and Anne had left in the house, and that made a dozen. He hoped there wouldn't be more men putting in an appearance.

"That's all?" Wilkes asked.

"That's enough to take over a town," Maddux said. "Hell, two men could take a town if no one stands up to them."

The firing stopped and Maddux took stock of the situation. Down the street Bogart and his men had found cover in doorways, behind crates, inside storefronts.

Anne and the sheriff were in front of the sheriffs office, Hannibal and Shadoweyes had found some cover in doorways, and Maddux and Wilkes were behind the trough. Wilkes probably couldn't handle his rifle very well. He'd have to stay where he was and provide cover.

"Two to one odds," Maddux said. "Not bad, not nearly as bad as we expected."

"What do we do now?"

"I'd say we wait," Maddux said. "We just wait"

———

"HOW MANY YOU FIGURE?" Parnell asked Bogart.

"Looks like six," Bogart said.

"How'd they get into town?"

"They walked right in," Bogart said, "while the men were drinkin' or whorin' or whatever they were doing." He looked at Parnell and said, "How many men we got?"

"Here and now?"

Bogart nodded.

"Ten."

"The woman is out, so that means that Webb and Carnes are probably dead."

"Ten to six," Parnell said. "I'd like it if the odds were even more in our favor. What do we do now?"

"Now we just wait," Bogart said.

CHAPTER THIRTY-EIGHT

"What are they waiting for?" Wilkes said.

Maddux had torn some of Wilkes's own shirt off in order to use it to pack the shoulder wound.

"The same thing we're waiting for," Maddux said. "Someone to make the first move."

"Maybe they're waiting for the rest of their men?" Wilkes said.

"There are no more men, Wilkes," Maddux said. "If there were, they'd be here by now."

Maddux moved to the other end of the horse trough, and from there he could see Shadoweyes and Hannibal. He waved until they saw him, and then Maddux tried to convey his message through sign language. He couldn't see Anne or Exman from where he was, but he was sure Hannibal could. He hoped that he would pass on the message.

———

"What are they saying?" Exman asked. He could see Maddux's two men across the street, and one of them was waving at them.

"Up," Anne said.

"What?"

"Can I get to the roof of your office from inside?"

"No, you'd have to go to the back."

"Stay here," she said

"Wait, what's going on?"

"I'm going to try to get above them. One of our men on the other side will do the same, and then we can fire down at them."

"Wait, wait," he said, "I'll climb up. I know how."

Anne studied the man for a moment, then said, "All right, but don't fire until Maddux does."

"Right."

Exman went inside his office and Anne waved to Hannibal that she understood.

————

MADDUX WAITED until he saw Hannibal on one roof, and Hannibal waved that he saw either Anne or Exman on another roof.

"Stay here and provide cover," Maddux said.

"Where are you going?"

"I'm going to try and get closer and draw them out so we can get a better shot at them from the rooftops."

"I—I can't shoot," Wilkes said.

He'd been hit in the right shoulder, and he was right-handed.

"Shoot with the left hand."

"I can't hit anything left-handed."

"That's all right," Maddux said, "they don't know that."

Maddux got up into a crouch. "Get ready."

He took a deep breath and then ran out from behind cover.

————

"THERE HE IS!" Parnell shouted.

He stood up to fire and as he did most of the other men stood up and fired also.

"No!" Bogart shouted, but it was too late.

When the firing started Bogart saw the two people on the rooftops. From above they had a clear shot at the standing men. He heard Parnell shout as a bullet struck him, and then several other cries of pain.

The odds were getting dangerously close to even, and that wasn't Walker Bogart's idea of odds at all.

———

MADDUX FIRED ON THE RUN, striking one man. He ran diagonally across the street, his back screaming in protest, heading for a doorway. Shadoweyes came away from the buildings and fired, his bullets striking home at least once.

Maddux saw several of Bogart's men fall, and then he saw the big man shout something to his men before he started running.

Anne Redman came away from the sheriffs office firing, and also saw Bogart start to run.

He was trying to get away.

———

WHEN WALKER BOGART'S men heard him shout, "Hold them off!" and saw him start running, they were confused. Some of them didn't hear what he said, they just saw him running, and if he was running, what were they staying there for?

Maddux, Shadoweyes, and Anne were advancing on the men, firing, and Hannibal and Exman were still firing from above, pausing only to reload.

Five of Bogart's men were down, three dead and two injured, and the other four lost their taste for the fight. They tossed out their guns and stood up with their hands high.

"This is the sheriff," Exman shouted from his roof. "Just stand easy, men!"

Maddux, Shadoweyes, and Anne moved in and made sure the men were unarmed.

"Bogart," Anne said.

"I know," Maddux said, "I'll get him."

Maddux ran past everyone towards the livery. If Bogart had not bothered with a saddle he might be on a horse and out of town already.

Maddux stopped at the livery stable door and peered inside. His breathing was labored and he took a moment to close his eyes and breathe deeply. Damn, but he was too old for this.

He couldn't see Bogart, but he could hear him moving around. He was trying to saddle a horse, and the animal wouldn't stand still. It was probably spooked from all the shooting that had been going on.

"Stand still, damn it!" Bogart said.

Maddux stepped into the stable, gun in hand, and located the stall Bogart was in.

"Bogart!"

The big man turned and stared at Maddux. "Who are you?"

"I'm the man you've been waiting for," Maddux said.

"Maddux?"

"That's right."

Bogart turned away from the skittish horse and faced Maddux.

"I knew we'd end up like this," Bogart said.

"Take off your gun belt."

Bogart frowned. "This is man to man, Maddux. Holster your gun and let's get it over with."

"Don't be a fool!" Maddux said. "This is not some contest between us. I'm taking you in."

"For what? The bounty?"

"No, not the bounty."

"I didn't think so." Bogart said. "That doesn't mean anything to men like you and me."

"Don't put me in with you, Bogart. We're nothing alike."

He could tell from the look on Bogart's face that the man was disappointed.

"Maddux—"

"Come on," Maddux said, "drop the gun belt and let's go."

"You're not taking me in, Maddux."

"You're right," Maddux said. "Anne Redman is taking you in."

"The woman?"

"That's right," Maddux said. "You're her meat."

"I'm not a hunk of meat!"

"With that bounty on your head that's just what you are, a high-priced hunk of meat."

"I'll show you—" Bogart said, his hand moving for his gun.

"Don't!" Maddux said, but the man didn't stop.

Maddux ran towards Bogart, throwing the man off balance. Bogart tried to back away, his hand still clawing for his gun, and

Maddux hit him on the jaw with the butt of his gun. Bogart staggered backward, his arms windmilling as he tried to stay on his feet. Finally he fell heavily to the ground, sticking out his left hand to break his fall. Maddux heard a bone in that hand crack.

Jesus, he thought, they break the law, they kill without a thought, and when their time comes they think they're entitled to some kind of a fair fight.

If Maddux fought fair he'd have been dead long ago.

Maddux started to approach Bogart when he saw that the fight hadn't gone out of the man. Bogart, still supporting his weight with his injured hand, had drawn his gun.

"Shit!" Maddux said.

He raised his gun and fired. His bullet struck Bogart just above the right eye. The gun in Bogart's hand discharged once harmlessly, and then the man fell over, dead.

EPILOGUE

After they delivered Walker Bogart and his men to the law Maddux, Hannibal, and Shadoweyes planned to head back to Cromwell. They would leave Wilkes behind to be patched up and go his own way. Maddux handed Wilkes his share of the bounty— three thousand dollars—and then charged him fifteen hundred for the job.

"Fifteen hundred!" Wilkes screeched.

"Maybe this will teach you to be more straightforward next time you need somebody's help—and take my advice, Wilkes."

"What's that?"

"You'd better stick with what you know from now on, Wilkes," Maddux said.

"What I know is spending money," he said, "and you aren't leaving me a whole lot to spend."

Maddux smiled and said, "Spend it slowly—after you pay me my fee."

Wilkes grudgingly paid the money.

"Fifteen hundred dollars and a bullet in the shoulder," he muttered as Maddux left his room. "Don't seem near enough."

"I know," Maddux said, before going out the door, "think about it."

———

ANNE REDMAN also parted company with them in Ceremony. When Anne was saddling her horse to leave, Maddux entered the livery stable and handed her an envelope.

"What's this?" she asked.

"That's the fifteen hundred I charged Wilkes," he said. "It's yours."

"I got my share, Maddux," she said, pushing the envelope away.

"You didn't get nearly enough to make up for what you went through, Anne," he said. "Bogart was your bounty to begin with."

"The bounty is anyone's," she said. "You and others earned your shares."

"This is not my share," he said. "This is what I swindled Wilkes out of. Believe me, he had it coming."

"I don't doubt it"

She stared at the envelope, then took it and said, "All right. Thanks."

They heard footsteps approaching, and were joined by Shadoweyes and Joe Hannibal.

"I was hoping I'd be in time to say good-bye," Hannibal said to Anne. It had been clear to Maddux from the moment Hannibal met Anne Redman that he was smitten.

"You are," she said, and gave the hulking marshal a hug that made him blush.

"I don't know if I can ever thank you all for what you did," she said, looking at them all.

"You have," Maddux said.

She stepped to Maddux and surprised him by kissing him quickly on the mouth.

She mounted up, waved, and rode off without looking back.

"That's a fine woman," Hannibal said.

"Yes, she is," Maddux said, "and a good new friend to have."

"What is it about you in your old age that attracts younger women?" Hannibal asked.

Maddux ignored the remark.

"It's too bad you had to kill Bogart," Hannibal said.

"I tried not to."

"I'm sure you did," Hannibal said. "It must be hell not knowing why he chose you."

"Chose me?"

"Sure," Hannibal said. "There are other reputations he could have gone after. Why did he pick you?"

"You mean you think that the attempts on my life in Cromwell had nothing to do with Wilkes coming there?" Maddux asked.

"As much as I know you hate coincidence," Hannibal said, "that's what I think. Wilkes or no Wilkes, I think Bogart had decided to try and lure you out of retirement, one way or another. If his men had killed you, then he'd go after someone else's rep, but you killed two of them and found out from the third that Bogart had sent them. Without Wilkes's deal, wouldn't that have been enough to draw you out?"

"You know it would have," Maddux said. "You know if you're right, then I've got more of an answer than I ever thought I'd have. Thanks, Joe."

"Well," Hannibal said, "some of us are put on this earth to—"

"I have your money right here," Maddux said, interrupting his pontificating friend.

"I told you, I don't want it," Hannibal said.

"Joe-"

"Did Shadoweyes take his?"

"No," Maddux admitted. "He told me to invest it in the ranch, so now we're partners."

"Well," Hannibal said, thoughtfully, "if you can stand another partner, you can do the same with mine. Nine thousand dollars would go a long way towards putting the place on its feet."

"On its feet?" Maddux said. "For that much money we could have us one damned fine horse ranch...partner."

Hannibal grinned, and a handshake sealed the deal.

"Where do we head now?" Hannibal asked.

"Now," Maddux said, "we go home."

"What about the Backshooter?" Hannibal asked. "I mean, he's the reason you started all of this."

"No," Maddux said, "I'm the reason. I was chafing at the bit while retired, but this whole experience had shown me that retirement isn't half bad."

"Then...you're just going to forget about him? About him killing twelve people?"

"There have been a lot of killers over the years that I

couldn't do anything about, Joe," Maddux said. "This has to be just one more. This is a bad one for me to have to ignore, because of the way he kills, because I know what that feels like, but believe me, I'm going to do my best to try. Right now all I want to do is go home and see if Laura will have me back."

"Well, the man may be finished," the marshal of Cromwell said. "Twelve may have been his number."

"And now he'll disappear from sight and never be heard from again?" Maddux said.

"It's possible," Hannibal said. "I read about this killer in England who cut up a bunch of women, killing them, and then just stopped and disappeared."

Maddux took a moment to consider that possibility. He didn't like it any better than he liked walking away from the hunt. The thought that the man might get away with twelve murders didn't sit right with him.

Shadoweyes chose that moment to speak his piece. "Justice will find him," he said.

"What?" Hannibal said.

"Not your kind of justice, my friend," Shadoweyes went on, "but the kind that finds us all."

TEXAS IRON

DEADLY CROSSFIRE

Sam McCall watched the men to his right and left, until finally the one on the right moved. That move was the signal to his compadre, who was just a split second behind. Just enough time.

McCall fired as the man on his right drew. The gunsel hurried his shot and missed, but McCall's shot traveled straight and true, ventilating the man through the heart. With the side-by-side Greener in his left hand, he pointed toward the second man and let loose with both barrels. The impact of the blast picked the man up and tossed him against the saloon wall. As he fell, he left a red smear on the wall behind him.

To WWA

PROLOGUE

Clyde Wexler was stunned.

Wexler had been the telegraph key operator in Corozon, Montana, for four years. He'd never before received a message that so much as made him raise his eyebrows. At twenty-five he'd become pretty complacent about his job. He finished transposing the last clicks of the key onto paper and then stared at what he had written, his mouth agape. He was so stunned he almost forgot to acknowledge receipt of the message. He pounded the key as quickly as he could, then switched it off and ran from the office, holding the message in his hand like a banner.

Walt Keller was the sheriff of Corozon and had been for almost nine years. During that time he hadn't had to draw his gun except to ventilate the ceiling of the White Horse Saloon a time or two when the hands got rowdy. When he took office he was thirty-eight and weighed a svelte 170. Now he was forty-seven and after nine years of an easy job, with free meals and drinks, he weighed close to 250.

He was shifting his bulk in his chair, trying to fit his lard-ass more comfortably, when his office door burst open and young Clyde Wexler rushed in.

"Sheriff—" Wexler blurted, breathless.

"Take it easy, Clyde," Keller said, still shifting, "the town council ain't gonna buy me a new door if ya bust it, ya know."

"Sheriff, I gotta show you somethin'!"

"Where the hell is that deputy?" Keller complained. "I'm ready for lunch."

"Sheriff, I got a telegram today."

"That ain't so unusual, is it?" Keller asked, wondering if he should have the beef stew over at the cafe, or the meat loaf at Dillon's Restaurant. "You get 'em sometimes, don't ya?"

"This one is real important."

Keller stopped fidgeting and looked up at the young man.

"Is it for me?"

"Uh, no—"

"For you?"

"No—"

"Then what in the blue blazes are you talkin' about, boy?"

Wexler, in a gesture of exasperation, held the telegram out to Keller. "It's for Sam McCall."

Keller, who was reaching for the slip of paper, stopped short and stared at it, as if it had suddenly burst into flames.

"McCall?"

"Sam McCall."

"B—but McCall isn't in Corozon."

Wexler opened his fingers, allowing the telegram to fall, and as it fluttered to the top of the sheriff's desk he said, "You mean he ain't *yet!*"

Part One

FAMILY REUNION

Part One

FAMILY REUNION

CHAPTER ONE

McCall was feeling old.

And unwanted.

The cause of these feelings, however, was not one and the same.

He was feeling old because his keester was forty-three, and had just spent three days in the saddle. He wanted nothing more than a drink, a meal, and a soft bed, and possibly an even softer woman.

He was feeling unwanted because as he rode down the main street of Corozon, Montana, everyone was staring at him, as if they knew who he was. Now, he wouldn't have been surprised if some of them knew who he was, but all of them? That was too much coincidence for any man, let alone a man who didn't believe in coincidence.

He had the uncomfortable feeling that Corozon knew he was coming.

Deputy Sheriff Bob Collins entered his office and said to Walt Keller, "He's here, Sheriff."

Keller, seated behind his desk, looked up at Collins and wet his lips with his tongue.

For the first time in a long time, he wasn't hungry.

———

THE FIRST PERSON McCall stopped to ask directions shied away from him, as if he expected McCall to strike him. All McCall wanted was to know where the livery stable was.

He rode further down the street and tried to ask a woman this time, but she almost ran from him.

Yep, the little town of Corozon knew he was coming, all right.

But how?

He decided to try one more time before looking for it himself. He spotted a lad of about ten standing in front of the general store, eyeing some licorice candy in the window. He reined in, dismounted, and walked over to the window.

"Looks good, doesn't it?" he asked.

"Sure does," the boy said, not bothering to look up.

"I reckon you would need about a nickel to get enough, huh?

"Yeah," the boy said, "I guess so."

"Well, it just so happens," McCall said, digging into his pocket, "that I have a nickel here."

The boy looked up this time and stared at the nickel.

"If you can tell me where the livery stable is," McCall said, "this shiny nickel is yours."

"Yeah?"

"Yeah."

"Oh boy!" the boy exclaimed. "Mister, the stable is down the end of the street and to the right. Ya can't miss it!"

"I can't, huh?"

"Nope."

"Okay, here's your nickel." McCall handed the coin to the boy. "Don't eat all that candy at one time, you'll end up with a bellyache."

"No, sir!"

The boy snatched the nickel and ran into the store. McCall laughed, mounted up, and rode down toward the end of the street.

Sheriff Keller walked over to the telegraph office and found Wexler sitting at his key.

"Clyde."

Wexler looked up at Keller and read the look on the lawman's face.

"No."

"Yes," Keller said, "he's here."

"Jesus," Wexler said, "I can't, Sheriff."

"It's your job, Clyde."

"You give it to him," Wexler said, "you're the sheriff."

"You're the telegraph operator."

"I don't know where he's stayin'."

"He's not stayin' anywhere, yet."

"Then how am I supposed to know where to take the telegram?"

Keller glared at Wexler.

"I have Bob Collins watching him," Keller said. "He'll tell me where McCall is stayin', and I'll tell you, and then you deliver the telegram."

"If I give him that telegram," Wexler said, "he'll kill me."

"You give him that telegram and he'll leave Corozon," Keller said.

"And then you won't have to deal with him." Wexler's tone was accusing.

"And then none of us will have to deal with him, Clyde."

"Except me."

"Well," Keller said, "that'll make you a goddamned hero, won't it."

Wexler opened his mouth to respond, then stopped short as Keller's words hit him.

"Yeah," he said, "I guess it would."

———

McCALL FOUND the livery with no trouble. He lifted his saddlebags, bedroll, and rifle from the saddle and handed the animal over to the liveryman.

"How much?"

"A d-dollar," the man said, "uh, in advance."

"In advance," McCall said, and started to shift his saddlebags from his right hand to his left so he could dig into his pocket for the money.

The liveryman, an old timer named Jesse Dean, misread the move and thought that Sam McCall was going for his gun.

"Or not in advance!" he said, quickly. "W-whatever you want, Mr. McCall."

McCall frowned and said, "Hey, old-timer, if you want your money in advance, that's what you'll get."

He dug the dollar out and handed it to the man, who accepted it with a shaking hand.

"What the hell is wrong with this town?" Sam McCall asked.

"Huh? Oh, nothin'," the man said, "Nothin'. It's a nice town."

"Well, it sure hasn't shown me that yet. Where's the nearest hotel?"

"Three blocks, back the way you come. Only hotel we got."

"Thanks."

"S-sure, Mr. McCall, sure thing."

McCall carried his bedroll and saddlebags in his left hand, and shifted the rifle to his right. If every-damn-body in town knew who he was, he'd better have a gun in his right hand and be ready for trouble.

———

"HE'S HERE," Del Butler said.

Simon Weeks looked up from his table in the White Horse Saloon. In front of him was a drink, and he picked it up and downed it.

"Where is he?"

"He just left the livery and went to the hotel."

Weeks stood up. He was tall and rangy, dark-haired, in his late thirties. He and Butler had arrived in Corozon six days ago, and had found it a sleepy little town. They had intended to leave until they heard the news that Sam Mc-Call was on his way there, so they decided to wait.

It was the longest two days in Simon Weeks' life, but now the wait was over.

"Let's go."

———

MCCALL HAD SEEN the deputy as soon as he left the livery, and he was aware that the man followed him to the hotel. He had no problem with that.

The desk clerk, a foppish man in his early thirties with a

carefully tended mustache, exhibited the same nervousness that the liveryman had.

"A room, please."

"C-certainly, Mr. McCall."

The man reached for the key to a room, dropped it, picked it up, and then dropped it again. He looked up at McCall from his position crouched behind the desk, laughed nervously, then grabbed the key and held it tightly, standing up.

"Here you go, sir."

"How much?"

"Uh, th-three dollars a day... if that's not too much."

"No, that's fine," McCall said. "You want that in advance?"

"Uh, well, it is hotel policy...but if you'd rather pay when you leave—"

"Never mind," McCall said, "I'll pay now—here." He dropped the money on the desk.

"Will you be staying just the one day?"

"Yes."

"Well, that's, uh...too, uh...bad..."

"Yeah, ain't it!"

McCall took his key and gear and climbed the steps to the second floor. The whole damned town was so jumpy he probably should have ridden out right then and there to avoid trouble, but he was too drag-ass tired to do that.

He stopped halfway up the steps and called out to the clerk.

"Hey!"

The clerk jumped and said, "Yes, sir."

"There's a deputy outside, he followed me from the livery."

"Yes, sir, that would be B-Bob Collins."

"Yeah, well you ask Mr. Deputy Collins to come up to my room for a minute. Tell him I'd like to talk to him."

"Up to your, uh, room?"

"That's right, my room."

"I'll tell him, sir."

"Thank you."

McCall continued up the steps, found his room, opened the door, set his gear down and sat on the bed. While waiting for the deputy to arrive he yanked off his boots.

"Wait," Weeks said.

"What?"

"There, across the street."

Butler looked across the street from the hotel and saw what Weeks was talking about.

"The deputy," Butler said. "What's he want?"

"Probably just keepin' an eye on McCall," Weeks said.

"What do we do?"

"We wait," Weeks said. "We just wait."

———

"DEPUTY?"

Collins looked up at the sound of the voice and saw Anson Delacroix, the hotel clerk, crossing the street toward him.

"What is it, Anson?"

"Uh, Mr. McCall said he'd like to see you in his room... now."

"In his room?"

"That's what he said."

"How did you know I was out here?" Collins asked, frowning.

"He told me."

"McCall?"

Delacroix nodded.

"He said you followed him from the livery."

"Shit."

"You better get up there."

Collins stared at Delacroix for a few seconds, then hitched up his gunbelt and said, "Yeah, I guess I'd better. What room is he in?"

Delacroix frowned and said, "I was so nervous I forgot to look at what key I was giving him."

"Well, let's go back into the hotel and find out, then."

———

"HE'S GOIN' inside," Butler said. "What's he goin' inside for?"
"Relax," Weeks said. "We got plenty of time." "How can I relax?" Butler asked. "That's Sam McCall we're goin' after."

"I know that, Butler, but we ain't just goin' after him," Weeks said, smiling. "We're gonna kill him."

Butler's stomach churned. He wished he were as confident as Simon Weeks.

McCall was standing by the window, watching two men across the street who were watching the hotel, when there was a knock at the door.

"Come in!"

The door opened and a man stepped in. He was tall, slender, not yet out of his twenties. He was wearing a deputy's star.

"What's your name, Deputy?"

McCall was barefoot, and his gunbelt was hanging on the bedpost across the room. The deputy had to swallow hard before answering.

"Collins, B-Bob Collins." He'd almost called McCall *sir*, but he stopped himself.

"Your boss tell you to bird-dog me?"

"Yes, sir." Damn! "Yes."

"What's his name?"

"Keller," the man said, "Sheriff Walt Keller."

"Well, you go back and tell your sheriff that I'll only be in his town overnight, and I'm not lookin' for trouble. You got that?"

"I got it."

"Well, go on then... git!"

The deputy turned to leave, but McCall thought of something else.

"Deputy!"

"Yes?" The deputy turned away from the door real quick, his shoulders tensed.

"How many deputies in this town?"

"Just me, si—uh, just me."

"How'd everyone know I was comin'?"

"You, uh, would have to ask the sheriff that, si—Mr. McCall," the deputy stammered. "I don't rightly know. All I know is I was told you was coming, and then I was told to follow you."

McCall frowned. He couldn't figure out right at that moment who knew he was going to Corozon. He himself hadn't known it until he saw the road sign proclaiming Corozon five miles away.

"When were you told I was comin'?"

"Uh... two days ago."

"Two days, eh?"

"Yessss..." The "sir" almost slipped out again.

"All right," McCall said, "go and give your boss my message."

"Sure," Collins said, opening the door, "sure."

After the deputy left, McCall looked out the window again, standing to one side, not directly in front of it. He'd learned that long ago. The two men were still across the street. Now that he knew they weren't deputies, it wasn't hard to figure out what they wanted.

For a moment McCall considered just holing up in his room until sunup and then riding out, but he balked at that. For one thing, he was hungry and thirsty, and he wanted a bath.

Fuck 'em, he thought. If they want to take their chance, let 'em. He wasn't going to let some two-horse town with the willies make him dig a hole like some desert critter.

He pulled his boots back on and went looking for his comforts.

———

WEEKS AND BUTLER watched the deputy leave the hotel and hurry off down the street.

"Whataya think?" Butler asked.

"McCall just rode into town, right?" Weeks asked. "What's he gonna want?"

"A drink?" Butler said. "A meal?"

"Both," Weeks said, "and maybe a woman, too. Two of those three things he can get from the saloon."

"We just come from the saloon."

"I know," Weeks said, "and we're goin' back there to wait for McCall to show up."

"What if he don't?"

"He will," Weeks said. "He's definitely gonna want a drink, and when he comes to get it, we'll be waiting. Come on."

———

MCCALL WATCHED the two men from his window for a few moments after the deputy left. He wanted to know whether or not they'd be there when he went back out. He was about to leave when he saw them start to walk away. He kept an eye on them until they were out of sight.

Maybe they wouldn't be right outside when he left the building, but he had a feeling he'd be seeing them again, very soon.

He left the room to arrange for a bath.

––––––

AFTER COLLINS TOLD the sheriff what McCall had told him, Keller left his office and went to find Wexler at the telegraph office again.

"McCall's in the hotel," Keller said. The other choice for a place to stay might have been Mrs. McCavity's rooming house, at the other end of town. "Now that you know where he's staying you can take him his message."

"I can't do it, Sheriff," Wexler said, his voice shaking. "That kind of news—you're gonna have to take it to him."

Keller frowned at the younger man, then admitted to himself that the other man was right. He was the sheriff and it was his damned job to go and talk to McCall, no matter what the consequences might be.

It was the only time in nine years he didn't relish being sheriff of Corozon.

"All right, Clyde," he said, extending his hand, "give me the damned telegram."

Keller stuffed the piece of paper into his breast pocket, the one nearest his badge. He wanted to make sure that McCall saw the star when he took the telegram out again.

CHAPTER TWO

McCall was in the bathtub on the first floor, his gun hanging on the back of a chair that he had placed within reach. On the chair was a towel and his fresh clothes. He had a cigar in his mouth, and a bar of soap in his hands. He was lathered up good and proper when there was a knock at the door. Immediately he shifted the soap to his left hand and rinsed off the right as best he could.

"Come in," he said around the cigar.

The door opened and a fat man entered. The first thing he noticed was that the man was fast, but right after that he noticed the badge on the man's chest.

"Sheriff," he said, by way of greeting.

The sheriff opened his mouth to speak, cleared his throat, and tried again.

"McCall."

McCall once again started washing himself.

"You the one spread the word around town that I was comin' to town?"

"I, uh, knew about it, yeah."

"You mind tellin' me how you knew I was comin' here when I didn't even know?"

"Uh, we got this a few days ago," the man said.

"Got what?"

The sheriff came forward slowly, removing a slip of paper

from his shirt pocket. He held it out to McCall, but had to come even closer before the other man could reach it.

"What is it?" McCall asked, drying his right hand on the towel.

"A telegram."

"For me?"

"Yes, sir."

Curious. Not only did someone know he was coming, but they had sent him a telegram before he'd even gotten there.

"Could you unfold it for me, please?"

"Huh? Oh, sure."

Keller unfolded the paper and handed it to McCall that way. McCall held it in one hand and looked at the sheriff.

"Who's read this?"

"Oh, uh, me and the telegraph operator."

"No one else?"

"No, sir."

McCall nodded and then read the telegram.

Keller nervously watched the reaction on McCall's face. It wasn't every day that a man got a telegram telling him that both of his parents were dead, and Keller didn't know how a man like Sam McCall would react to news like that. He'd never even thought about a man like Sam McCall— a man with his reputation—even having parents!

So he watched his face closely, but from McCall's expression you couldn't tell what kind of news he was getting.

McCall took a long time, reading the telegram, reading it a second and third time, keeping his emotions off his face. Actually, he didn't know what his emotions were. He hadn't seen his parents in, what, seven years? Maybe more. Learning that they were dead should have affected him somehow. Shock? Sorrow?

Or was Sam McCall beyond those and any other emotions, after living the kind of life he'd been living all these years?

McCall put the telegram down on the chair and continued to soap himself.

"Anythin' else, Sheriff?"

"Uh, no, sir," Keller said. "I mean—uh, how long will you be stayin' in town, Mr. McCall?"

"Just long enough to get a drink, some food, and a good night's sleep. I'll be headin' out in the mornin'."

"Well, good. I mean—"

"I know what you mean, Sheriff," McCall said. "I told your deputy I'm not looking for trouble, and I'm not."

The sheriff nodded, tried to think of something else to say, and then started backing out of the room.

As the man reached the door and turned to leave, McCall called out, "Sheriff!" making the fat man jump.

"Yessir?" Keller didn't turn, he just hunched his shoulders and waited.

"Much obliged for the telegram."

Keller let out the breath he was holding and said, "Sure, Mr. McCall, sure," and hurriedly left.

WHEN MCCALL WAS FINISHED with his bath he went back to his room and read the telegram again. Still unsure about how he felt, he knew one thing: when a man's family is killed, he ought to do something about it. He figured he should find his two brothers, Evan and Jubal, head on back home to Vengeance Creek, and find out just what the hell happened.

He looked at the telegram again and saw that it had been sent by Dude Miller. He remembered Dude well, a friend of his father's who ran a business in the town of Vengeance Creek.

He was going to have to ask Dude how he knew where to find him, but of course, that question would take a back seat to the obvious question.

How had his parents been killed?

He decided that in the morning he would leave the sheriff an answer to the telegram, to have the key operator send when he opened the office. That way he could get an early start and not have to worry about letting Dude know that he and the boys were coming.

He folded up the telegram and put it in his breast pocket. Now that he was bathed and dressed in fresh clothes, his stomach and throat were demanding their satisfaction.

He left the room in search of a meal and a drink.

WHEN KELLER GOT BACK to his office he found Bob Collins and Clyde Wexler waiting there.

"Well?" Collins asked.

"Well, what?" Keller asked. He walked nonchalantly to his desk and sat down. He'd just faced Sam McCall, given him bad news, and left without a scratch. He was feeling mighty fine.

"What happened?" Collins asked.

"What did he say?" Wexler asked.

Keller looked up at both of them and said, "He said, 'much obliged.'"

"That's all?" Wexler asked.

Keller nodded.

Wexler looked at Collins and said, "Damn, I coulda done it."

————

MCCALL WALKED the street until he spotted a small cafe. He went in and got himself some steak and potatoes, some biscuits, and some good, strong coffee. It was the best meal he'd had in weeks.

Nothing special had taken him to Corozon in the first place, except the fact that he was drifting in that direction. Matter of fact, he'd been drifting for a long time, ever since he'd first left home when he was seventeen. At that age he'd fancied himself a hand with a gun and had left home to prove it. Well, he'd proved it, all right. In those days he was fast with a gun, and just mean enough to use it when the whim struck him. He didn't learn the right of it until he was in his late twenties. That was when he truly grew up, but by that time it was too late, he was already "Sam McCall."

For the past fifteen years or so he'd been trying to live down the sins of the first ten years. Unfortunately, even during that time he'd managed to find his share of trouble and add to the early reputation. He tried things like riding shotgun, and even wearing a badge for a while, to try and change his image, but all that did was add to the image. Dime novels were written about him, mentioning his days as a gunman, his days riding shotgun for Wells Fargo, his experiences as a lawman and a bounty hunter. It all mixed together to make him a real romantic figure in the eyes of some, and simply something deadly, someone to be avoided, in the eyes of others—like the people of Corozon.

The waitress who served him was as nervous as the liveryman and the clerk had been. When he left the cafe to find the saloon, men and women avoided him, and children pointed at him until their parents pulled them away.

When he reached the saloon and entered he didn't pause to acknowledge the stares of the other patrons. He simply walked to the bar and ordered a cold beer.

As he'd entered he had seen sitting at a back table the two men he'd previously seen standing outside his hotel. He was now in a position to watch them in the mirror behind the bar while he quenched his thirst with the first beer and ordered a second.

His original intention had been as he had told the deputy, to avoid trouble. His feeling now, however, was that if these two yahoos wanted trouble, all they had to do was ask.

He reckoned maybe hearing about the death of his parents had affected him to some degree after all.

He was angry and looking to take it out on someone.

———

"NOW WHAT DO WE DO?" Butler asked Weeks as McCall walked in.

"Get up real slow-like and move to the other side of the room," Weeks said. "We'll catch him in a crossfire."

"Right."

Weeks put his hand on Butler's arm.

"Do it slow. Find a table and sit down and don't move until I do."

"Right."

———

MCCALL SAW one of the men stand up and walk slowly across the room, then sit down at another table. He realized that from this position they would have him in a crossfire.

He called the bartender over.

"Yes, sir," the man said, eyeing McCall's half-finished beer. "Is something wrong?"

"You got a shotgun behind the bar?"

The man sized McCall up for a moment and then decided to answer.

"Sure."

"What kind?"

"Greener?"

"Side by side?"

"Yes."

"Where is it?"

"It's under the bar, over—"

"Don't point."

The man held his hand down by his side.

"Can I reach it from here?"

"Yes."

"Walk over and stand in front of it for a moment, then move away."

"Is—is something gonna happen?"

"I'd bet on it," McCall answered. He saw the look on the man's face and said, "Don't worry. Just stand where the shotgun is and then get ready to duck."

"O-okay."

Slowly, the bartender moved about four feet to McCall's left, stood there a moment, then walked all the way to McCall's right.

McCall slid his beer down along the bar until he reached the point where the shotgun was and waited, watching the two men in the mirror.

At one point he thought about making for the door, wondering how far he'd get, but in the end he stayed put.

The other people in the saloon slowly came to the realization that something was in the air. Some of them got up and left, others moved to tables at one side of the room or the other, until the center of the room was virtually empty. Now there would be no innocent bystanders caught in the crossfire.

McCall alternately watched the man to his right and left until finally the one on the right moved. His move was the signal to the man on the left, who was a split second behind—there was just enough time.

McCall turned to his right, and as he drew his gun with his right hand he reached over and behind the bar with his left, hoping that the bartender had been telling the truth.

He had.

McCall fired as the man on the right did. The man hurried his shot and missed, and McCall's shot traveled straight and true, ventilating the man through the heart. With the shotgun in his left hand he pointed toward the second man, who was just drawing his gun, and fired both barrels. The impact of the blast picked the man up and tossed him against the wall. As he fell he left a red smear behind him.

The bartender, who had ducked behind the bar, stood up, staring at McCall.

McCall laid the shotgun on top of the bar and said, "Thanks."

"S-sure."

He walked over to the first man to check him. That the second man was dead was obvious, but he didn't know for sure that the first man was dead until he leaned over him, his gun still in his hand. Satisfied, he stood up and looked around the room.

The attention of the onlookers was split among the three men, two dead and one standing. McCall was waiting to see if the dead men had any friends before he holstered his gun. He was still standing over the dead man when the batwing doors swung inward and Sheriff Keller walked in, trailed by Deputy Bob Collins.

"What the hell happened here?" Keller blustered, and then he saw McCall and seemed to withdraw a bit.

"Bartender," McCall said, holstering his gun, "tell the sheriff what happened."

McCall started for the door and stopped when he was alongside Keller.

"I'll be in my hotel room, Sheriff."

Keller stared at McCall, and then looked at the two dead men.

"I told you I wasn't lookin' for trouble," McCall said. "Unfortunately, these two were."

In his hotel room McCall ejected the spent shell from his .44 and loaded in a live one. That done, he removed the holster and hung the gun on the bedpost. He took the pitcher and bowl from the dresser and balanced it on the windowsill. If someone tried to enter that way, the pitcher and bowl would fall, warning him.

He removed his boots and stretched out on the bed, then removed the telegram from his pocket and read it again. No date, no details, just the briefest of messages:

SAM MCCALL,

   MOTHER AND FATHER DEAD. ADVISE YOU COME TO
VENGEANCE CREEK.

   DUDE MILLER

Obviously, Dude Miller wanted Sam McCall to come to Vengeance Creek. That could only mean that Joshua and Mary McCall had not died of natural causes.

In the morning he'd start looking for his brother Evan. Evan was a gambler, and Sam knew of just so many poker games that would attract a gambler of his brother's caliber.

After he found Evan, he and Sam, who was the older brother, would look for little brother Jubal. Then they'd go to Vengeance Creek together and find out what happened.

All he had to do was hope that he got to his brothers before they went and got themselves killed.

CHAPTER THREE

Evan McCall examined the cards on the table very carefully—not only his own, but everyone else's. In addition, he remembered the cards that had already been folded. His excellent memory was just one of the things that made him such a good gambler.

That, and his patience.

He had been sitting in this game for four hours waiting for the right hand to come along, and this was it.

The man across from him was the only one at the table who was winning more than he. That man's name was Luke Short. Also sitting at the table were Bat Masterson, Dick Stark, Jack Foxx and Carl Dekker. Of all the other men, Masterson was the only one who was even. Stark and Foxx were losing with grace, but Carl Dekker was losing and not liking it one bit.

Evan McCall had played poker with Short and Master-son before. This was the first time he'd played with the other three. He didn't mind Stark and Foxx, but Dekker's whining was getting on his nerves.

As for this hand, he and Short and Dekker were still in it. The others had folded and were watching the proceedings with great interest.

All six men had come to San Francisco for the express purpose of taking part in this game, which was now in its third day. The place was a hotel suite at the Alhambra Hotel. The management had supplied the suite at no cost, because it enjoyed having men of such caliber as guests.

Besides, whatever they won at poker some of them usually lost in the casino.

Evan sat back now and regarded his opponent's cards. Dekker was still in the game with a pair of kings on the table. Short had tens, which Evan considered more of a threat than the other man's kings. A third king had already been folded, while the other two tens were apparently still at large.

On the table directly in front of him he had a pair of threes. On the board he was low man, but he had that feeling.

"It's your bet, Dekker," Masterson said. He was the dealer.

"This is one hand I ain't losin'," Dekker said. He picked up some chips and tossed them into the pot. "Two hundred."

The next bet was Evan's. They still had one more card to come, so Evan simply called.

"I raise two hundred," Luke Short said.

"Ha!" Dekker said, "I call."

Masterson looked at Evan, who said, "Call."

"Comin' out," Masterson said, and dealt out the seventh card facedown.

"Your bet, Dekker."

"Five hundred," Dekker said, without hesitation.

All eyes turned to Evan. He took his time, looking at his hole cards even though he knew what they were.

"McCall?" Masterson said.

Evan wished that Short were betting before him, but he decided to go ahead and raise.

"I raise five hundred," he said, tossing the chips into the pot.

"With threes?" Dekker asked, incredulous. "Even if you've got three of them—"

"Can we have a little less talk?" Luke Short asked.

Dekker glared at Short, but fell silent.

"It's a thousand to you, Luke," Masterson said.

"Call the thousand," Short said, "and raise."

"A thousand?" Dekker demanded.

"That's the raise," Short said.

Dekker, sweating profusely, examined the small stacks of chips in front of him. It was quite clear to everyone that he didn't have the thousand.

"Dekker?" Masterson said.

"Gimme a minute!" Irritably, Dekker looked at his hole cards. "My credit—"

"No credit," Masterson said.

"I can get the money—"

"We play with what we have in this room," Masterson reminded him.

The only time any of them left the room was when they all took a break or suspended play for a rest period. At that time they were able to replenish their cash supply, if they had to. No one, however, left the room during the game. If they did, they were not allowed back.

"You know the rules, Dekker."

"But I don't have another thousand!"

Masterson looked away from him to Evan McCall.

"It's your bet."

"Wait a minute—" Dekker said, standing up.

"Dekker," Masterson said, "either sit down or get out."

Dekker glared and fumed, but finally sat down to watch the outcome of the hand.

Evan called and raised, and Short called. As it turned out, Short had tens full, and Evan had four threes—which he'd had through six cards. He hadn't even needed the seventh.

"Gentlemen," Masterson said, "I believe this is the end."

"And what an end!" Dick Stark said.

"I don't believe it," Carl Dekker said. "Four threes! That's the third time you've had four of a kind—"

"Luck," Evan said.

"That's what *you* call it," Dekker said.

"Don't say something you'll be sorry for, Dekker," Masterson said.

"I want a chance to get my money back."

"The game is over," Masterson said. He had been considered the host of this particular game. "Gentlemen, thank you all for coming. I suggest we go down to the bar for drinks."

Dekker leaped to his feet and said, "I won't drink with a—"

"Dekker!" Masterson snapped, cutting him off.

They all stared at Dekker, and then at Evan McCall. It was obvious that Dekker had been about to call McCall a cheater.

"Dekker, I think you'd better leave first," Masterson said.

"And if I don't?"

Masterson, not yet thirty, was the youngest man at the table, but was perhaps the most respected—and feared. He reached across the table with a gold-headed cane he'd taken to carrying when in San Francisco and tapped Dekker's chest with it.

"I'll have to make you."

Dekker looked around the table, found no support from anyone, and then turned on his heel and left.

Masterson turned to Evan McCall and said, "I'd be careful if I was you. No tellin' what a sore loser will do."

"I'll keep that in mind," Evan said. "Shall we go downstairs for those drinks?"

Evan McCall, Bat Masterson, Luke Short, and Dick Stark all repaired to the Alhambra bar for their choice of drinks. Evan and Stark chose beer, while Masterson and Short chose whiskey.

As they entered the bar they saw across the crowded room, through a haze of smoke, Carl Dekker seated at a table with three other men, who had the look of hard-cases. Dekker himself had the look of a sore loser who had been drowning his sorrows in drink. There was an empty bottle on the table, and another but half full. Even with four men sharing, Dekker had to be more than a little drunk.

"Maybe we should drink somewhere else," Stark suggested.

"You all can drink elsewhere," Masterson said, "but I have a room here, and I intend to go to it after a couple of drinks."

"We'll drink here," Evan said, and that seemed to settle that.

The four men approached the bar and advised the bartender of their choices.

"Who was it that invited Dekker, anyway?" Dick Stark asked.

The other three exchanged glances, no one answering immediately.

"Bat?" Short said. "You were the host this time, weren't you'

"I can't remember who recommended him," Masterson said, "but I wouldn't have allowed him in the game if the reference wasn't a sound one."

"Maybe you should try to remember who it was," Short said, "and mark him down as a less than reliable reference for the future."

"In the morning," Masterson said, "when I'm not so tired, it'll come to me."

Masterson and Short each had a second whiskey and then bade the other two goodnight.

"When are you leaving?" Masterson asked Evan.

"In the morning, Bat."

"See you next time, then," Masterson said, extending his hand.

They shook hands all around and then Masterson and Short left the saloon.

"They almost look alike, don't they?" Stark asked. "I mean, the way they dress, so fine and proper."

"They dress alike, all right," Evan said, "but that's where the resemblance ends."

Masterson was not yet thirty and clean shaven, while the older Luke Short had a fine mustache that he tended to expertly. Short was probably the better gambler, while Masterson's talent with a gun was probably the finer of the two. Evan McCall was willing to bet that by the time Masterson reached Short's age he would be the more famous.

"Another beer?" Stark asked.

"Why not?' Evan said.

"Masterson and Short are gone," Dekker said. "Now you lily-livered cowards can take McCall."

"You're payin' us enough to gun Evan McCall, Dekker," one of the men said, "but not nearly enough to tangle with Bat Masterson *and* Luke Short."

The others nodded their agreement.

"Well, they're gone and McCall is there," Dekker said, again.

"What about the other man?" another of the men asked.

"I doubt Stark even carries a gun," Dekker said. "Come on, get it over with."

"The man must have done you some grievous harm for you to want him dead this bad," someone said.

"Just do it," Dekker said, "and never mind my reasons."

"You gonna take a hand?"

"I might," Dekker muttered, glaring across the room at Evan McCall's back, "by golly, I just might."

Evan McCall was deep in conversation with Dick Stark about where their respective next stops would be, and he didn't see the batwing doors open to admit a tall, somewhat weary traveler. He did, however, see the three men seated with Dekker rise to their feet—by looking into the mirror behind the bar.

"Stark, are you armed?"

"Why, no," Stark replied, "why?"

"I suggest you step aside, then, before lead starts flyin'."

"What?" Stark said, turning and looking behind him. "Oh!"

He saw the three men standing, fanning out across the room, as did others in the saloon. Suddenly people began to scatter, and any hope of taking McCall by surprise was gone.

"Get 'im!" Dekker shouted, standing.

The sound of gunfire filled the room, and gunsmoke mingled with the haze already caused by cigarette and cigar smoke to almost form a fog in the room.

Through the fog the principals fired their weapons, some in haste, and some with cold deliberation.

Evan McCall produced his cutdown Colt .45 from a shoulder rig and did his firing calmly. He was facing four men, and his goal was to do as best he could before their lead took him to the floor.

His first shot drilled one man through the heart after that man's hastily fired shots went wild. As the man fell Evan turned to fire again, but before he could, a second man—who had also fired wildly—was felled by a bullet. Before Evan McCall knew what was happening, the third man fell in quick order. To Evan's mind, the rapid succession of unerring shots could only have been fired by a handful of men, one of whom was his own brother, Sam.

He looked toward the batwing doors and saw Sam standing there, a grin on his face.

"There's one left, brother," Sam said, holstering his shotgun.

Evan gave his brother a nod and then turned his attention to Carl Dekker.

"By God, Dekker, draw your gun!"

Dekker, who'd had his coat thrown back so that he could reach his weapon, had been so surprised by the turn of events that he had not been able to draw.

He wet his lips. "McCall—"

"Draw your weapon or I'll shoot you where you stand."

"You can't," Dekker said. "There's too many witnesses who'll say I didn't have my gun out."

"And there are enough witnesses who know that you and

your friend tried to backshoot me," Evan said. "They'll stand behind *my* story. Which is it to be? Will you die like a man, or a coward?"

Dekker's eyes darted about the room, searching for salvation. When he saw that none was coming he looked back at Evan McCall.

"Damn you, McCall!" he shouted, and went for his gun.

Evan McCall fired once, the bullet striking Carl Dekker on the bridge of the nose. Dekker's jaw went slack, his hand fell to his side, and he keeled over backward.

Evan shoved his gun back into his shoulder rig and walked over to where his brother was standing.

"Much obliged, Sam."

"Anytime, brother."

Before they could exchange another word the doors swung open to admit a hoard of blue-coated policemen. The officer in charge surveyed the damage before speaking.

"Who killed these men?" he demanded.

"We did, Officer." Evan told the truth because there was no hope of denying it—and no reason to.

The officer, tall, barrel chested, in his forties, gave them a stern stare and said, "You'll both turn your weapons over to me and accompany me to jail."

"Jail?" Sam McCall said. "These men tried to back-shoot my brother."

"You and you brother are still standing, my friend," the officer said loudly. "Until I can get the whole story, you two are the only ones I can take to jail—and by God, that's where you're going!"

Suddenly the other officers surrounded the brothers, giving them barely enough elbowroom. Sam and Evan McCall exchanged a helpless glance before turning their weapons over to the policeman.

At the jail they were given separate cells, but it was a simple enough thing to move the pallets over to the common set of bars and talk.

"We shouldn't be here too long," Evan said. "Enough people saw what happened."

Sam nodded..

"So tell me, brother," Evan said, "how did you happen to be in the right place at the right timer

Sam stared at his younger brother through the bars for a moment, forming the words in his mind before he spoke them.

"Ma and Pa are dead."

"What?"

Sam took the telegram from his shirt pocket and handed it through the bars. He studied his brother while Evan read it.

He hadn't seen Evan in a couple of years, not since their paths had last crossed in New Orleans. Evan was five years younger, but Sam was still struck by how much younger than that he looked. He seemed closer to Jubals twenty-four years than his own forty-three. At thirty-eight Evan McCall had none of the gray that streaked Sam's own dark hair. He was clean shaven, whereas Sam wore a heavy mustache that completely obscured his upper lip. Sam had always thought that while Evan and Jubal actually looked like brothers, he did not share very many of their attributes. He was larger and heavier, and his facial bone structure was that of their father rather than their mother. Sam had a strong, squared jaw and high cheekbones, while Evan and Jubal had their mother's finer features. Evan and Jubal also had their mother's blue eyes, while Sam's were a muddy brown.

After Evan had read the telegram several times he turned those blue eyes on Sam and said, "It doesn't say how it happened."

"I know."

"Have you sent a telegram to find out?"

"No."

"Why not?"

"Because, brother," Sam said, taking the telegram back, "you and I and Jubal are going to Vengeance Creek to find out for ourselves."

"Jubal?" There was no argument from Evan. He had already decided that he was going to go find out what happened. It pleased him that he wouldn't be going alone. "Do you know where he is?"

"All we got to do is find trouble," Sam said, "and we'll find brother Jubal."

CHAPTER FOUR

A ll his life Jubal McCall had known that he was
different from his brothers.

Sam and Evan, they had things they were good at.
With a gun Sam McCall was the best Jubal had ever seen, and
he was proud of his big brother for that.

Evan, he could do things with cards that nobody else could.
Whenever Jubal thought of his two brothers he thought of them
with pride.

When he thought about himself, it was with great disappointment, because he knew that Jubal McCall was good at only
one thing—getting himself into trouble.

Ever since he'd left home five years ago Jubal had drifted
from place to place, taking jobs where he could find them,
doing whatever he had to do to survive, but always there was a
black cloud following him around, ready to rain on whatever
good thing he managed to find.

This time, the black cloud had really done a job on him.

He stood up, climbed up on the metal bunk that was bolted
to the stone wall, and looked out through the barred window.
He could see the scaffold from there, the one the people of
Prosper, Wyoming, were building for him.

The one from which they intended to hang him without
even benefit of a trial. He was surprised that they were even
going to the bother to build a scaffold. Having been sentenced
without benefit of a trial, he'd assumed that they would take

him to the highest tree they could find and stretch his neck from there, but apparently they wanted to do the job "right and proper," as he'd heard someone say.

The men who were working on the scaffold had stopped to eat lunch, and now the hammering started up again. He turned away, stepped down, and sat on the bunk, his chin in his hands.

He knew that both of his brothers had been in similar situations at some time in their lives, and they had both managed to survive. A man couldn't live without being blamed at one time or another for something he didn't do.

Jubal McCall had not killed Ed Flanagan. He had slept with Flanagan's wife, however, and that made him the prime suspect for Ed's murder. When Flanagan's body was found with its skull bashed in, the sheriff and his men had gone directly to Jubal's hotel room to get him. It was unfortunate for Jubal that Erin Flanagan had been in his bed at the time. When the sheriff kicked in the door, Erin sat up without the benefit of a sheet, her proud, peach-sized breasts there for all to see. Jubal had used that moment to try and make the window, but his legs had gotten tangled in the bedclothes and he had fallen painfully to the floor. Moments later he was standing between two deputies, who held his arms tightly behind him while the sheriff helped Erin on with her clothes.

Of course, the fact that he was with Erin when her husband was killed should have been a perfect alibi, except for one thing —Erin Flanagan *told* the sheriff that Jubal had killed her husband.

It was only then that Jubal realized that Erin—ten years his senior, but absolutely beautiful beyond words—had used her red hair, firm breasts, and warm mouth to set him up but good.

So here he sat, waiting for the scaffold to be finished, waiting for them to come and get him and string him up for a murder he didn't commit.

Still, he *had* been stupid enough to get himself into this predicament.

Sam and Evan McCall had been released from jail the very next day. Dick Stark had gotten enough men together to back their story that the police had to let them out without charging them.

They were, however, asked to leave San Francisco as soon as possible.

Fortunately, that was not a problem.

While still in jail Evan had told Sam that he'd received a letter from Jubal just a couple of months ago, while he himself was in Sacramento. Apparently Jubal and Evan had stayed in touch much more than Sam had with either of them.

The next morning, as they bought two horses and provisions and set out for Wyoming, Sam had said, "Tell me again what the letter said."

"Jubal said that he was going to Wyoming to try and stay out of trouble."

"Well then," Sam said, "All we have to do is find the hottest spot in Wyoming, and our little brother will be there."

Of course, the hottest spot in Wyoming was definitely the town of Prosper, in the controlled Folk County. The word had gone out for miles around that a hanging was going to take place. In fact, there was so much interest that Jubal was told they were postponing the necktie party for a couple of days to accommodate certain people—highly placed people in the running of Folk County. The hanging certainly couldn't go on without them there.

And so Jubal's waiting was prolonged. Later, he'd realize what good the postponement of the hanging had done him.

The day was here, though, and Jubal was just hours from the rope. He tried to pass the night by thinking of the most pleasant thing he could. Unfortunately, the most pleasant thing he could think of was being in bed with Erin Flanagan, buried in her loving, but that just brought him full circle to being hanged again.

He wondered who was nestled between Erin's sweet thighs while he was waiting out his last night on earth.

———

THE MCCALL BROTHERS had been in Folk County only a day when they heard about the hanging, in a saloon. Apparently, some young fool had been caught in bed with the wife of Dan Flanagan, son of Darby Flanagan, who, with Seth Folk, ran Folk county. As confusing as it sounded to them, the important element was "young fool." They looked at each other and said, "Jubal." They asked a few pertinent questions, then left the saloon and rode to Prosper.

————

"LET'S GO, MCCALL," the deputy said, opening the cell door. "We kept you waitin' long enough."

"Don't rush on my account." Jubal spoke without rising from his bunk.

"Come on." The deputy entered the cell and kicked the underside of the bunk. "There are a lot of people waiting out there for you."

"Yeah," Jubal said, "we can't keep them waitin', can we?"

"No, we can't. Get up."

Jubal swung his feet to the floor and the deputy backed up, his hand on his gun.

"What are you, nervous?" he asked.

"You're Sam McCall's brother, ain't you?"

"So?"

The deputy wet his lips.

"So, that'd make anybody nervous."

Jubal laughed.

"You think big brother's gonna come ridin' in here to save me?"

"The thought had crossed my mind."

"It come to anyone else's mind?"

Now it was the deputy's turn to laugh.

"Not hardly. Folk County is so secure Folk and Flanagan aren't even worried about Sam McCall."

"So don't you worry, either," Jubal said. "I ain't seen my big brother in years, and I don't expect to."

"Let's go," the deputy said. "If you don't mind, I'll keep my hand on my gun anyway."

Jubal stood up and said, "As if that would help you against Sam McCall."

The deputy took Jubal out to the office, where the sheriff was waiting. Sheriff Ernie Watt had been hired personally by Seth Folk and Darby Flanagan, and was firmly in the Folk/Flanagan pocket. When Flanagan and Folk said to hang somebody, he hanged them. That was what he was paid to do.

"You ready, McCall?" Watt asked.

"Who's ready to be hanged?"

"Well, ready or not..." Watt said, and tied his hands behind him. "Let's go."

Both the sheriff and the deputy walked behind him as they pushed him out the door. In the center of the square stood the scaffold. Only that morning, at first light, he had heard them testing the trapdoor with sandbags. The first sound of the door opening had jerked him awake. After that the sounds merely made him wince. Even when the sounds stopped, he was still able to hear them in his head.

He wondered now if he'd be able to hear the sound of the door opening beneath his feet.

———

SAM AND EVAN MCCALL stood together on the fringe of the crowd. They had arrived early that morning, the morning of the hanging.

"As usual," Evan had said to Sam, "your timing is impeccable."

"Whatever that means," Sam said.

Now they searched the crowd, trying to match the descriptions they had obtained for Darby Flanagan and Seth Folk.

"We're makin' a mistake," Sam said, suddenly.

"How?"

"If you owned the county, would you stand out here among the... the rabble to watch a hangin'?"

"You're right."

From that point on they elevated their sights, and then they saw them. On a balcony, above a sign that said "Flanagan House Hotel," they saw a fat, bearded man who matched the description of Darby Flanagan. Standing next to him was a tall, beautiful, redheaded woman.

"At least little brother has good taste in ladies," Evan said.

There was another man with them, a tall, white-haired man wearing a derby hat and a black suit. He matched the description of Seth Folk.

"Here's what we have to do..." Sam said, and Evan listened, because this was Sam's kind of situation.

———

JUBAL FROWNED at the intense sunlight. From his cell he'd only been able to get patches of light on the floor. Now the sun beat down mercilessly on his head and shoulders. Sweat rolled down his face and dripped off his chin. It might have been the perspiration of fear, but no one would ever know that. He was grateful for the heat.

When they reached the stairway to the scaffold he stopped.

"Keep goin'," Watt said, giving him a push. Jubal stumbled, then started up the steps.

At the top Watt swung him around to face the hotel, and for the first time since his arrest Jubal saw Erin Flanagan. Jesus, she was beautiful. Even in the fix he was in he couldn't help but react to her beauty.

They stood that way for what seemed like a long time, and then Jubal saw her father, Darby, nod his head. That seemed to be the signal.

The sheriff brought the noose over and placed it around Jubal's neck. Jubal was still looking at Erin, but suddenly his attention was attracted by something behind her, and he couldn't believe his eyes.

In a hail of glass, small shards that reflected the sun like dozens of tiny fire flies, Sam McCall burst through the window behind her....

Sam McCall had made his way easily up the stairs to the room with the balcony. The security had been lax because Flanagan and Folk never expected anyone to try and stop the hanging.

He entered the room and saw the backs of the people on the balcony. As he approached the window, beyond them, he could see Jubal on the scaffold. The sheriff was putting the noose around his neck.

Sam ran the rest of the way and hurled himself through the window. His momentum carried him into Seth Folk, knocking the man over the railing. McCall slipped his left arm around the throat of the fat man, Darby Flanagan, and pressed the barrel of the gun to the man's head. He was taller than Flanagan and had no problem holding the man fast.

"That's enough!" he shouted.

Everyone froze, including the sheriff on the scaffold.

"Tell the sheriff to let him go."

"Who are you?" Flanagan demanded. "You'll never get away with this."

"The name's Sam McCall, Flanagan, and that's my brother down there."

"McCall—" Flanagan started, but Sam tightened his arm on the man's windpipe, causing him to choke, and then eased the pressure. As fat men will, Flanagan was sweating profusely, and Sam could smell the sour scent of him.

"Tell the sheriff to let him go."

"No," Flanagan said.

"Your friend is lyin' on the ground, Flanagan. You want to be next?"

He felt the big man shake, and then heard the rumble of laughter that rose up out of him.

"It was time to dissolve the partnership, anyway. I think I'll change the name to Flanagan County."

"You're as good as dead, Flanagan."

"And then you will be, too, McCall," Flanagan said. "It sounds like a mexican standoff, to me."

On the scaffold, and on the street, everyone was watching the tableau, waiting for it to be resolved.

Sam McCall did some fast thinking. It didn't look as if Darby Flanagan was not afraid for his life. Sam was going to have to try another tack. He turned his head to his left and saw Erin Flanagan watching him. Up close her beauty was stunning, and she was presently rather excited by the turn of events, her nostrils flaring, her white teeth biting her lush lower lip.

Abruptly, Sam pushed the fat man away from him, took a step to his left, and pressed the barrel of his gun against Erin Flanagan's head. As an afterthought, he slid his left arm around her chest, feeling the firmness of her breasts.

She was sweating, but her scent was hardly as offensive as her father's.

"Now tell him to let Jubal go."

Flanagan studied Sam for a few moments, obviously trying to figure out how willing the man was to shoot a woman if he didn't get his way.

"I think you're bluffing," the fat man finally said.

"That's my little brother down there, Flanagan," Mc-Call said. "My family against your family. Where do you think my concerns lie?"

Flanagan chewed on the end of his mustache while he tried to make up his mind.

"Come on, Flanagan," Sam said, "it's gettin' hotter and hotter out here." To bring his point across, Sam cocked the hammer on his gun. He felt Erin flinch.

'Tather..." she said in a tiny voice, and that seemed to make Flanagan's mind up for him.

"All right," the fat man said to Sam McCall, "all right, don't hurt her."

"Tell'em!" Sam said.

"Sheriff!" Flanagan shouted. "Let him go."

There was a moan of disappointment from the crowd, but they fell silent when Sam pointed his gun into the air and fired it. Erin Flanagan closed her eyes and screamed, and Darby Flanagan started, jumping almost a foot and shaking the balcony.

"You heard the man," Sam shouted into the silence, "let him go."

Sheriff Watt hurriedly untied Jubal McCall's hands, and Jubal removed the noose from his neck himself.

At the sound of horses the onlookers turned and looked down the street. Evan McCall was riding toward them, trailing two horses behind him, and it was clear he wasn't about to stop for anyone. Men and women scattered, lest they be trampled, and Evan rode right up to the scaffold with the horses. Sam's shot had served not only to silence everyone, but to signal Evan to come with the horses.

"Jubal!" Evan shouted, and tossed his brother a rifle. Jubal caught the weapon and covered the sheriff while he removed the man's gun and tucked it into his belt.

"Watt, tell your deputy to drop his gun. He's about to get himself killed," Jubal said.

"Drop the gun, Willie."

"But sheriff—"

"Drop it, damn you!"

Reluctantly the deputy slid his gun from his holster and dropped it.

"Kick it under the scaffold," Jubal instructed, and the man did so.

"If there are any heroes in the crowd," Sam called out, "I'd advise you to think twice."

Sam turned Erin around to face him and kissed her fully on the mouth. He held her tightly to him, her breasts flattened against his chest. Startled, she was just beginning to return the kiss when he broke away.

"Ma'am, it's been a pleasure."

Jubal kept the crowd covered while Evan brought Sam's horse closer to the hotel. Sam stepped over the railing and dropped down into his saddle. That done, he covered the crowd with Evan while Jubal descended from the scaffold and mounted up.

"Let's go," Sam said, and the McCall brothers spurred their horses into a full gallop before someone decided to go ahead and play hero.

They rode hard for several hours and then stopped and checked their back trail. Even a hastily formed posse would have been left far behind, and they took a moment to catch their breaths and rest their horses.

"Not that I ain't glad to see you fellas," Jubal said, "but just how did you manage to ride into Prosper right on time?"

"We were looking for you," Evan said.

"When we heard that some young fool was about to get himself hanged," Sam chimed in, "we figured it had to be you."

"Well, thanks... I think," Jubal said. "Now maybe you can tell me why were you lookin' for me. Time for a family reunion all of a sudden?"

"Sort of," Sam said, and handed Jubal the telegram. Sam and Evan waited silently while their younger brother read the news.

"What the hell—" Jubal said, looking up at both of them.

"That's what we intend to find out," Sam said. "Are you with us, little brother?"

"You know I am, Sam," Jubal said, handing the telegram back. "We're all gonna be wanted in Wyoming after this, you know. I think old Seth Folk was killed when he fell off that balcony."

"That's unfortunate," Sam said, "but that's something we can worry about after we find out what happened in Vengeance Creek. Agreed?"

"Agreed," Jubal said, and they both looked at Evan.

"Well," Evan McCall said to his brothers, "sitting here isn't getting it done, is it?"

Part Two

VENGEANCE CREEK

CHAPTER FIVE

Dude Miller stared out the front window of his store at the dusty main street of Vengeance Creek, Texas. It had been two months since he had sent all those telegrams, hoping that one of them would find their way into the hands of Sam McCall. Each day Dude spent a few hours watching the street, waiting for the tall figure of McCall to ride down Main Street, with or without his brothers. Dude had the feeling that if Sam McCall did come back to Vengeance Creek, it would definitely be in the company of his two brothers, Evan and Jubal.

Although the McCall boys were spread far and wide through the west—and sometimes the east—Dude Miller knew that their sense of family would remain intact. Up until their deaths Joshua McCall and his wife remained proud of all three of their sons, speaking of them often to anyone who would listen.

The boys all decided to travel, led by the exploits of older brother Sam. Soon after Sam left Vengeance Creek, Evan followed, to make his own name. Later, when he was old enough, Jubal followed in the footsteps of his brothers—or tried to. Jubal was not the man Sam or Evan was; he had spent too much time in their shadows, trying to be like them, to develop his own personality. Perhaps by this time he had.

Dude Miller'd had several motives for sending the telegrams. For one, he did not believe that the real solution to the deaths of the McCalls had been found. Second, he was curious about what had become of the McCall boys.

Sam, of course, had become the stuff of legend, and Dude wondered just how much of it was true. He had heard less of Evan and nothing of Jubal over the years. He had known them all as boys, and he'd known none of them as men—and he wanted to.

Miller's business was on the order of a general store, except that he carried a wider array of goods. For that reason he was often interrupted from his reverie about the Mc-Calls to service a customer. The time he spent looking out the window, however, *did* eventually add up to hours.

Looking out the window now he saw Lincoln Burkett step from the bank. Over the past nine months Burkett had become the most powerful man in Vengeance Creek. Just before the deaths of the McCalls he had purchased Joshua McCall's ranch. Knowing how much it meant to the McCalls to keep the ranch so that their sons would have a home to come back to, Dude Miller had been suspicious of the sale ever since. He had been unable, however, to wrest the truth from Joshua McCall about the reason for the sale. A month later, the McCalls were dead, under what Miller considered suspicious circumstances. The powers that were in Vengeance Creek, however, led by Lincoln Burkett, had come to their decision fairly quickly, and there had been no investigation into the matter.

That would change when Sam and his brothers arrived.

And they would arrive.

Eventually.

Lincoln Burkett stepped from the bank and took a moment to slip his wallet into his jacket pocket. As he did so he looked across the street and saw Dude Miller watching him from the window of his store. Burkett frowned, staring back at the man, but that did not deter Miller, who stared back boldly.

Dude Miller was one of the few people in Vengeance Creek who resisted what Lincoln Burkett could do for this town. The man didn't realize that the more powerful Burkett became, the more he could do for the town, and the faster the town would grow.

Burkett knew that Miller was one of those people who worried about how to get there, while Lincoln Burkett merely worried about getting there, period. That was why Dude Miller would always be a storekeeper, and why Lincoln Burkett would eventually become one of the most powerful people in Texas—and maybe in the whole damned country.

Burkett stepped down from the boardwalk in front of the bank and started walking toward the saloon, where he was to meet his son, John.

Lincoln Burkett was a big man, still robust enough at sixty-three to give the town whores a ride or two. It was to his everlasting consternation that his twenty-two-year-old son seemed to be most interested in those same whores than in following in his father's wake.

John Burkett was Lincoln Burkett's only child, a child who came along late in life to Burkett and his wife. The birth had been very hard on the forty-year-old Virginia Burkett. She had survived it, but had never been the same after it, and eventually died when the boy was four. At that time the Burketts had a ranch in the Dakotas, and Lincoln had too much to do building his empire to spend much time with his son. The task of raising the boy had fallen to a governess, and too late Burkett realized his error. A boy raised solely by a woman would have a woman's values. When the boy was fourteen Burkett dismissed the governess and took charge of the boy himself. Unfortunately, in his efforts to make up for his earlier error, he rode the boy too hard, and ended up with a defiant young man who resisted his father's ideas of what constituted manhood.

The Burketts eventually were forced by circumstances to leave the Dakotas—through no fault of their own, of course—and had come to Texas. Here, Burkett hoped to build himself a more lasting empire. He also hoped that his son, in this new environment, would come around and realize where his future lay.

So far, all the boy was interested in was what lay between the thighs of the whores in the town cathouse.

Of late, though, Burkett had decided that he could reverse that by buying the cathouse, and that was the deal he had just completed in the bank.

Of course, the madame, Louise Simon, had resisted his offers to buy, but he had finally made her an offer she found impossible to resist: sell, or be burned out.

Burkett magnanimously allowed the woman to retain ten percent of the business, and was also allowing her to continue to run it, on the condition that she turn John Burkett away each time he tried to make use of the establishment.

To aide her in this he had hired two bouncers who ostensibly worked for Louise, keeping her girls safe.

Lincoln Burkett smiled. He wished he could be on hand the first time young John met those bouncers.

That night Dude Miller locked up early and walked to the home of his friend Ed Collins. There was a bite in the air and he pulled the collar of his topcoat close around his neck.

Miller and Collins were trying to find more people to oppose Lincoln Burkett and his attempt to own everything he could see. They had some supporters, but not enough to make a difference. Burkett seemed to have won over the people who counted in Vengeance Creek, including the mayor and the president of the bank. Three months ago a new sheriff had been appointed, and it was the opinion of both Miller and Collins that the man had been handpicked by Lincoln Burkett.

When Ed Collins admitted Dude Miller to his house he offered his friend a drink, and Miller accepted.

"Have you had dinner? Collins asked.

"Serena is waiting dinner for me, I'm sure."

"She's a good girl, your daughter," Collins said, handing Miller a glass of sherry. "I wish Ada and I had been able to have children."

Miller and Collins were roughly the same age, early sixties, and had been widowed within the past ten years. Both men sorely missed their wives, but Miller had his daughter, Serena, to keep him company. At twenty-eight she was the spitting image of her mother, a true beauty. Collins envied Miller unabashedly, and Miller felt sorry for Collins. All he had was his gunsmith shop, and he spent as much time there as possible.

Sitting together on the sofa Collins asked, "So, how do we stand?"

"As we did yesterday, last week, and last month," Miller said.

"Then Burkett will go on," Collins said, "and absorb everything around him, until he owns everything... and there's nothing we can do about it."

"I've done something about it, don't forget."

Collins made a face.

"Those damned telegrams. Do you really expect Sam McCall to ride in here to the rescue?"

"I expect Sam and his brothers to ride in here to find out what happened to their parents," Miller said.

"Those boys have long ago forgotten they even had parents." Collins' distaste for such sons was plain in his voice.

"You're wrong, Ed," Miller said. "They'll be here, all right."

"It's been months..."

"Two months," Miller said, "but don't forget, Sam would have to find both Evan and Jubal and then they'd all have to find their way back here. They'll be here, don't you worry."

"Come on, Dude," Collins said, "give it up. What makes you so sure they'll come?"

"Serena."

"What? What about Serena?"

"She says that no child could let the death of their parents go uninvestigated," Miller said. "She says the bond between child and parent is too strong, too deep to ignore even if the child wanted to—in this case, *three* children."

"That may be," Collins said, "but the McCall boys are not children any longer, Dude—especially Sam."

"Serena says they'll be here," Miller said, "and I believe her."

"Well," Ed Collins said, grudgingly, "both you and she would know more about this subject than I would, wouldn't you?"

Dude Miller laid his empty glass aside and stood up. His friend was about to descend into a well of self pity, and he had no desire to stay and watch.

"I've got to get home to Serena, Ed," Miller said. "We'll talk again."

"Sure," Collins said, "when the McCall boys get here."

"Goodnight, Ed."

Dude Miller left the Collins house. Even though he knew Ed Collins was inside, he felt as if he were leaving an empty house behind.

He wondered how it must feel from the inside.

———

As Dude Miller entered the wood-frame, two-story house he shared with his daughter Serena his nostrils were assailed— no, *rewarded*—With the smells of Serena's wonderful cooking. If she had succeeded in replacing her dead mother in no other way, Serena was almost as fine a cook as her mother was.

Actually, Miller wished that Serena would stop trying to replace her mother. At twenty-eight she was much too old to be living at home with her father. True, at that age she was considered something of an old maid in Vengeance Creek, but to Miller she was still a beautiful young woman who should be married and giving him grandchildren.

"Father?" Her voice came from the kitchen.

"It's me," Miller said, removing his top coat and hanging it on a wall rack that he had built.

Serena came from the kitchen, wiping her hands on her apron. A tall woman, she needed only to lift her chin slightly to kiss her father, who was six feet tall. Along with being tall she was slender, almost rangy. To his prejudiced father's eye she was a beauty, with hair the color of corn, smooth, unblemished skin, naturally rosy lips and very white, even teeth. He was glad that he made enough money at the store that she didn't have to work unless she wanted to, and then it was not work that would weather her skins or her hands, or give her a weary look. Her mother, God rest her, as beautiful as she was, had to work hard almost all her life, and paid for it. When she died she was tired looking, and slightly stooped; her hair had lost its natural luster and her flesh its resiliency. A finer woman had never lived, though, and Miller loved her with all his heart to the day she died—and more that day than ever before.

"What smells so wonderful?"

"You should be able to tell," she said, smiling. "It's your favorite."

"Yes," he said, sniffing the air, "it is—meat loaf!"

"It's ready," she said. "Just go upstairs and clean up and I'll put dinner on the table."

"Have you eaten?"

"Not yet."

"You should have."

"I knew you'd be home soon. Go and clean up."

"All right, all right," he said. "Next you'll want to check behind my ears."

"I'm not trying to be your mother."

"No," he said, "you're trying to be yours."

Her smile disappeared and she said, "Let's not go through that again, please?"

"You're right," he said, raising his hands in a gesture of supplication. "I'm sorry. I'll wash up."

While cleaning up he chided himself for the remark. They had had many hours of arguments over her staying to live with him, and he should have known by this time that further argument was futile. Just like her mother, Serena was doggedly stubborn when she set her mind to something.

At sixty-three Miller felt he still had many years on this earth. He despaired at the thought of Serena staying with him for every one of them. Once he was gone she'd be in her late forties or early fifties, and it would be she who was alone. The thought of his beautiful daughter wasting her youth and then living the final thirty or forty years of her life alone made him shake his head. If only he could think of a convincing argument.

If only she'd fall in love... and all right, old man, he told himself, that's another reason you want the McCall boys to come home. None of them would remember Serena as anything but a little girl. Maybe when they met her now, all grown up, she'd fall in love with one of them. Lord knew they were strong men and would certainly not be unattractive at this point in their lives. Sam had to be in his early forties, Evan in his late thirties. Jubal, the youngest, would only be several years younger than Serena; it was certainly not an insurmountable age difference.

Miller could imagine the kind of grandchildren a union between Serena and Sam McCall would produce.

"Father," her voice called from the kitchen. "Dinner is on the table."

"I'm coming," he called out.

Drying his hands, he thought, *and so are the McCall boys...I hope.*

The taste of the steel gun barrel frightened him, but he left it there, in his mouth, lying on his tongue. His finger tightened on the trigger, and even as it did he knew he would not have the nerve to give it the last, final twitch that would fire the gun, ending his life.

Because he could not shoot himself lid Collins considered

himself a coward. With a sob he jerked the gun from his mouth, catching a tooth on the raised sight and almost snapping it. The pain brought tears to his eyes, tears of pain and of humiliation.

On the one hand he enjoyed the visits of his friend Dude Miller. They had been friends for a very long time, and he now counted Miller as perhaps his only friend.

He knew that since his wife's death he had become a sour, bitter, unfriendly old man, and Dude Miller was the only one who still came around. True, they were allied together against the onslaught of Lincoln Burkett, but beyond that was something deeper and more important—friendship.

And yet every time his friend left, Collins would pick up his gun and lay it upon his tongue. Miller had also lost his wife, but he'd had the courage to go on with his life, aided by his daughter. If only Ada had been able to give them a son or a daughter, things might be different today.

Ed Collins wouldn't feel so utterly alone.

He eased the hammer of the gun down and replaced it in his desk drawer. As always, after just a few minutes of trying to pull the trigger, he felt exhausted.

As he dragged his worthless carcass to his bedroom he wondered what took more courage, to kill himself, or to go on living.

————

"DID YOU SEE MR. COLLINS?" Serena asked at the dinner table.

"I did."

"And?"

Miller chewed the food in his mouth, taking the time to choose his words carefully.

"He is a sad, sad man, Serena," he finally said. "Every time I visit him I thank God for you, for without you I would probably be as sad and pitiful as he is."

He closed his eyes and spitefully bit his tongue. Even taking a few moments to form his words he had said the wrong thing. For every argument he had ever given Serena for leaving and going out on her own, he had given a powerful one for her staying with him.

Stupid old man, he chided himself.

"This meat loaf is like heaven," he said, to cover the annoyance he felt with himself.

"Perhaps tomorrow I will take some to Mr. Collins," Serena said. "Do you think he'd like that?"

"He'd like that, and a visit from you, very much, my girl," Miller said, feeling a great pride in her.

"Well, if that's the case," she said, taking the meat loaf pan up from the center of the table, "don't eat it all."

"Hey," he protested, "I'm not finished."

"Yes, you are," she said, walking to the stove. "You don't want to get fat, do you?"

"What does it matter?"

She turned and stared at him with mock severity.

"Don't think I don't see you when you're looking at the widow Jones, Papa."

"Ah," Miller said, "the widow Jones is an old woman."

"She's fifty-eight," Serena said, "and five years younger than you."

"If I ever took up with another woman," he said, "it would be one much younger than the widow Jones."

"Like who?"

"Oh..."

"Never mind," Serena said, turning to face the oven again, "I don't want to hear it."

"Is there coffee?"

"It's coming."

Whenever they even joked about Miller and women Serena ended up embarrassed by it—or maybe she was thinking about her own social life.

Where the hell were those McCalls, Miller thought to himself, and in the next moment voiced his thought.

"They'll come," she said, her back still turned.

"How can you be so sure?" He asked the question, even though only hours before he had been explaining her logic to Ed Collins.

She carried a cup of coffee to the table. She placed it in front of him and leaned her elbow on his left shoulder.

"No child can ignore the death of a parent, let alone two parents, Pa," she said. "It cannot be done. They will come, if only to stand at the graves."

"When they do come," Miller said, "they're not going to like what they find... not at all."

"Well," Serena said, her voice firm, "that's as it should be."

———

LINCOLN BURKETT LOOKED up as his foreman, Chuck Conners, entered his office. "Well?"

"Me and the boys got him bedded down, Mr. Burkett," Conners said. "He was real upset when he couldn't get into Louise's and went right to the saloon. He got real drunk and tried to pick a couple of fights, but the boys got him out of there."

"Who was with him?"

"Earl Murray, Mike Gear, and Greg Tobin."

"And they kept him out of a fight?"

"Yessir."

"See to it that they each get a bonus."

"I'll take care of it, sir."

Burkett sat back in his leather chair and stroked his chin thoughtfully.

"Is there anything else, sir?"

"Yes," Burkett said, sitting forward again. "That storekeeper, Miller?"

"Dude Miller."

"He's starting to get on my nerves," Burkett said. "Every time I pass his store he's staring out that damned window."

"Why is that annoying, sir?"

Burkett slammed his hand down on the desk. The noise it made was so loud it made Conners flinch.

"He's watching for that damned Sam McCall."

"Sir," Conners said, "if McCall does show up, me and the boys can handle him."

"I wouldn't bet my life on that, Chuck," Burkett said. "We all know McCall's reputation—and if he does show up, he's likely to have his brothers with him. No, I think maybe we'd better import some talent."

"Who?"

"I'll let you know in the morning," Burkett said. "Meanwhile, I don't want that storekeeper looking out his window for a while."

"What would you like—"

"Just handle it, Chuck," Burkett said, clearly dismissing the man, "tonight."

———

WHEN THE FRONT door of his house slammed open Dude Miller was sitting in the living room reading a book. He turned his head and saw the three men burst through the door, their faces masked. The nearest gun was in his desk in the den and he knew he'd never get to it, but he rose anyway.

As he turned to face them the first man hit him flush in the face with a massive fist. Miller went down, smashing against a coffee table.

"Pa!"

The three masked men looked up toward the voice and saw Serena Miller on the staircase. When she saw them she started to pull the front of her housecoat tightly closed, but when she saw her father on the floor she forgot about that.

"Pa!"

As she hurried down the steps two of the men hauled Dude Miller to his feet and one of them stepped into Serena's path.

"Let me by!" she screamed. "What are you doing?"

"Just teachin' the old gent a lesson," one of the men said.

"Let me by!"

She tried to shoulder past him but he grabbed her by the upper arms, squeezing them hard. The smell of his sweat made her wrinkle her nose in disgust.

"You wanna watch?" he asked. "Be my guest."

He turned and walked to the door, pulling her with him.

When they stepped out onto the porch she saw what the other two men were doing to her father. One of them was holding him with his arms pinned behind him, and the other man was hitting him, methodically, first a left, then a right, with no passion whatsoever. It was then that she knew they were doing a job, and it wasn't hard to figure out who for.

"That's enough," she shouted. "You'll kill him."

The man doing the hitting had been alternating his punches between the body and the head, and Dude Miller's face was livid with bruises and blood.

"She's right," the man holding her said. "We weren't told to kill him."

The man doing the hitting looked at the man on the porch, then gave Dude Miller one more punch in the face. The man who was holding Miller released him, and he sprawled into the dirt face first, lying as still as death.

"What about her?" the other man asked.

"We weren't told anything about her," his friend said. "Why, you wanna punch her?"

"Yeah," the man said. "I wanna punch her with this." He grabbed his crotch.

Suddenly the pit of Serena's stomach went icy cold and she started to shiver in fear. As the man advanced on her she realized that she had never felt terror like this before.

"No..." she said, and she was dismayed to hear that it came out as a whimper.

"Forget it," the man holding her said. Abruptly he released her arms. "We wasn't told to touch the girl. Let's go. We're finished here."

The man who had grabbed his crotch stared at Serena for a few moments and then said, "That's too bad, Missy. You woulda liked what I got for you. Maybe another time, huh?"

The other two men were walking away and now the third one turned and followed.

Serena stood there for a few moments, struck motionless by the fear she'd experienced, and then suddenly she leaped from the porch to her father's side, feeling ashamed.

Where the hell are you, Sam McCall? she thought viciously. The intensity of her anger was as foreign to her as had been the intensity of the fear she'd felt a moment ago.

Come and kill these bastards!

CHAPTER SIX

"Well, there it is," Evan McCall said. "Vengeance Creek."

They were on a steep hill from which they could look down at the town. Vengeance Creek had a wide radius because it had been laid out in such a sprawling fashion. There were two main streets which contained the bank, the general store, the hotel, the saloon, other shops, and the sheriff's office, but the livery, the feed and grain, the undertaker's, and the whorehouse were all spread about with a decent amount of elbow room between them.

Sam, Evan, and Jubal McCall sat atop the hill, with black chaparral spread about them, and a single Joshua tree, taking their first look at the town of their birth in a long time.

Sam McCall was riding a seven-year-old black coyote dun, a dun with a black stripe running down its back, and distinctive markings on its legs.

True to the McCall predilection for individuality, Evan's horse was a four-year-old claybank, a yellowish breed achieved by breeding a sorrel and a dun.

Jubal, as if it were a symbol of his lifelong efforts to be like one or both of his brothers, was riding a sorrel.

"Yep," Jubal said, "there it is."

"Looks the same, don't it?" Evan asked.

"When was the last time you were here?" Jubal asked his brothers.

"Jeez," Evan said, "I don't—probably seven, eight years, something like that. What about you?"

"Less," Jubal said, "about five."

"Did you ever write?" Evan asked.

"Some," the younger brother answered.

Evan and Jubal looked over at Sam, who had remained silent throughout their exchange.

"Sam?" Evan said.

Sam McCall looked at them.

"I don't like being here."

"Why not?" Jubal asked.

"Didn't I ever tell your Sam asked. "I hate this place."

McCall kicked his horse's ribs and sent him jogging down the hill.

"When was the last time he was here?" Jubal asked.

Evan looked at Jubal, said, "When did he leave?" and sent his horse down the hill after Sam. Jubal thought a moment, shrugged, and followed.

————

DUDE MILLER WAS NOT STANDING at his shop window when the McCall brothers rode into town. He was lying in his bed, where he had been confined by the doctor following the beating he'd received several days before. He had several cracked ribs, and one eye had only recently reappeared from behind a huge swelling.

Serena entered her father's bedroom with lunch on a tray.

"Papa?"

Miller stirred and opened his eyes.

"Serena..." He frowned at her and asked, "Is that breakfast?"

"No," she said, smiling, "lunch."

"Is it that late?" he demanded. "Why did you let me sleep so late, girl?"

"Because you need your rest." She set the tray down on the night table next to the bed. "Let me help you sit up."

"I can sit up!"

She stood back and watched as he struggled to do so, without success.

"Well, don't just stand there, girl," he said, impatiently, "help me sit up."

She assisted him into a seated position, propped a couple of pillows behind him, and set the tray of food on his lap.

"Are they here?" Miller asked.

"I don't know," she said. "I haven't been spending half my time at the window watching for them."

"Have you changed your mind?"

"No," she said. "I'm sure they'll come, but I'm not prepared to sit around and wait for them. They'll come. Now eat your lunch. I made you some soup."

"How about something solid?

"For dinner," she said. "Oh, and the doctor will be by later. I'll check back in about twenty minutes, and all that soup better be gone."

"Yes ma'am," he said, wryly.

The McCall brothers rode to the livery and dismounted.

"In the old days this place was run by old Charlie Run-yon," Evan said.

"It was Charlie who caught you when you fell from the hayloft," Sam said.

"You fell from the hayloft?"

"I didn't fall," Evan said.

"I never pushed you," Sam said.

"I never said you pushed me from the loft deliberately," Evan said, "but we were horsing around, and you did push me. If it wasn't for old Charlie catching me, I would have broken a leg for sure."

"Maybe you should have landed on your head."

"Ha, ha."

"When I left, the place was owned by Swede Hanson," Jubal said. "It's only five years, maybe he's still here."

As if on cue a tall, well-muscled blond man came out of the livery.

"Swede?" Jubal called.

The man stopped and narrowed his eyes, peering at the three men in front of him.

"Is dat you, Jubal McCall?"

"It's me, Swede."

Jubal moved closer and Swede Hanson said, "You've grown, boy. *Ja*, you have grown a great deal."

"It's good to see you, Swede."

"What brings you—ah, I see," Swede Hanson said, suddenly. "You have my sympathy for the death of your parents."

"Thank you. Oh, Swede, I don't think you ever met my brothers, Evan and Sam McCall."

"Evan," Swede said as Evan stepped forward to shake hands. "And Sam McCall? I know you by reputation, of course."

"Of course," Sam said, shaking the big man's hand. Swede was about two inches taller than McCall's six-four, and probably outweighed him by twenty pounds, most of it shoulders and upper arms.

"You all have my sympathy."

"Thank you," Sam said. "Will you put our horses up for a few hours?"

"Ja, of course... but only for a few hours?"

"We want to talk to the sheriff here about our parents," Evan said, "and then we'll probably be riding out to their— our —ranch."

"Well, your horses will be here," Swede said. "That's a coyote dun, isn't it?"

"It is," Sam said.

"And a claybank?"

"Yes," Evan said.

"I'll take good care of them, you can be sure," Swede said, and then to Jubal he added, "Of course, that includes your sorrel."

"Of course."

"Who's the sheriff here, Swede?" Sam asked.

"Fella named Tom Kelly."

"Has he been sheriff long?"

"No, maybe three months."

"What happened to Mel Champlin?" Jubal asked.

"Mel?" Sam said, surprised. "Was he still sheriff when you left?"

"Yes."

"Jesus," Evan said, "he was the law when I left."

"And when I did," Sam said.

"That was part of the problem," Swede said, "the Town Council felt they needed a younger man."

"What can you tell us about this Sheriff Kelly?" Jubal asked.

"Not much," Swede said, "except that he has not impressed me yet."

"Well," Sam said, "I guess we'll form our own opinions. We'll be back in a few hours, Swede."

"The horses will be ready," Swede said, "*Ja*, you can count on it."

"Thanks," Jubal said, patting the big Swede on the shoulder.

The McCalls removed their rifles, war bags, and sugans— and, in Evan's case, a carpetbag—from their saddles and allowed the Swede to lead their animals inside.

"Let's go," Sam said, and they started toward the sheriff's office, assuming correctly that it would be in the same place.

———

As THEY ENTERED the sheriff's office they found it empty. There was a coffeepot on a pot-bellied stove and Sam went over to feel it.

"Still hot." He opened it and sniffed it. "It's fresh, and more than half full."

"Good," Evan said, "we might as well help ourselves while we wait."

Evan McCall had more patience than his brother Sam. By nature they had different attitudes toward things like waiting.

"Come on," Evan said, handing Sam a cup of coffee in a tin cup, "there's nothing else we can do until we talk to the law."

Evan looked around, found two more tin cups— swamped one out with his fingers—and then poured two more cups and handed one to Jubal.

They laid their belongings down on a chair and settled in to wait. Only fifteen minutes or so had gone by— the wink of an eye for Evan, a lifetime for Sam—before the door opened and a man entered. He was tall and dark-haired, in his thirties, with a sheriff's star on his chest. He stopped short when he saw that his office was full.

"What do you people want?"

"Sheriff Kelly?" Evan asked.

"That's right." Kelly walked across the room to the coffee pot. "Did you leave me any?"

"There's plenty," Sam said. He drained his cup and said, "Here."

Kelly looked at Sam, then took the cup, cleaned it out with a rag, and poured some coffee. That done, he carried it to his desk and sat down.

"What can I do for you gents?"

"We're the sons of Joshua and Miriam McCall," Evan said.

"The McCalls," Kelly said, "Of course. A sad thing, that."

The sheriff looked them over, then directed his attention to Sam, looking him over, fastening his eyes for a moment on the .44 on Sam's hip.

"That would make you Sam McCall."

"Yes, it would."

They matched stares for a few moments, and then the lawman looked at the younger McCall.

"And you?"

"Jubal."

"Uh-huh. Well, I'm new here and I didn't know your parents all that well."

"Tell us what happened," Sam said.

Kelly hesitated a moment, then said, "*Well*. It was a fairly simple conclusion to come to. You see... I'm sorry to have to tell you this, but apparently your father shot your mother, and then himself."

There was a moment of stunned silence in the room. Kelly suddenly tensed and put his coffee cup down. He lowered his right hand so that it hovered near his gun, but he knew that if Sam McCall wanted to kill him, there wouldn't be much that he could do to stop it.

"That's crazy."

"It can't be," Jubal said.

They both looked at Sam, who hadn't said a word yet.

"Sam?" Evan said.

Sam's eye flicked to Evan's and held them.

"We'll ask around," Sam said, "talk to the doctor." He looked at the sheriff and asked, "Who is the doctor hereabouts now?"

"Doc Leader," Kelly said.

"Doc Leader?" Sam said, surprised. "He's the sawbones who delivered us—all three of us. He must be close to eighty by now."

"That may be," Kelly said, "but he's the only doctor we've got."

"Then we'll talk to him," Sam said, picking up his belongings. "I assume he's the one who looked at the bodies?"

"He is."

"And signed the death certificates?"

"Like I said," Kelly said, "he's the only doctor we've got."

"You could have brought another one in from somewhere else."

"We didn't."

Sam looked at his brothers and said, "We'll talk to Doc Leader."

"But Sam," Jubal said, "Pa wouldn't—"

"Thanks for your help, Sheriff," Sam said, cutting Jubal off. To his brothers he said, "Let's go."

He went to the door, opened it and walked out. Evan and Jubal exchanged a glance, then gathered their things and went outside. Sam was standing on the boardwalk, waiting for them.

"What was that all about?" Jubal demanded.

"Take it easy."

"Take it easy? You heard the things he was saying about Pa."

"I heard them."

"So?"

"There's no point in arguing with the sheriff, Jubal," Sam said. "He didn't have anything to do with it."

"How do we know that?"

"I mean, he isn't the one who came to the conclusion."

"He's a sheriff."

"But," Evan said, "the doctor is the one who would come to the conclusion about the manner of death—isn't that what you're getting at, Sam?"

"That's it."

"Then let's talk to Doc Leader," Evan said.

"And after that," Sam added, "Dude Miller. After all, it was Dude who sent the telegram."

They walked to where they all remembered Doc Leader's office as being, above the general store—and it was still there.

They stopped at the stairway that went up the side of the building and Sam said, "Same damned stairway."

"How does he get up and down it every day, if he's as old as you figured?" Evan wondered.

"Well, maybe I overstated it," Sam said, "but he's gotta be at least in his sixties."

"Why are we standing down here guessing?" Jubal asked.

"Good point, little brother," Sam said.

"Don't call me that!" Jubal said. "I don't like the sound of it."

"Sure, Jube," Sam said, "whatever you say."

Sam felt his brother's anger. Jubal was still fuming at having been cut off in the sheriff's office.

They ascended the steps, not enjoying the creaking sound they made.

"When we go back down," Evan said, "I suggest we go one at a time."

When they reached the door Sam knocked and waited. When the door opened there was a short man in his sixties standing there, squinting up at Sam and shading his eyes against the sun with hands stained from years of nicotine.

"Still smoking, huh, Doc?" Sam asked. "For a sawbones, that ain't exactly smart."

"Jesus," Leader said, "I hate that word, sawbones. What the hell are you doing here, Sam McCall?"

"We're all here, Doc," Sam said.

Leader leaned out to spot Evan and Jubal and said, "So you are."

"Can we come in? We've got some things to talk about, haven't we?"

Leader scowled and said, "I suppose we have. Yeah, come in, all of you."

They entered the office and the doctor closed the door behind them. The office looked the same to Sam, with furnishings as ancient as the doctor himself.

"I suppose you're here about Joshua and Miriam."

"That's right, Doc," Sam said.

The doctor turned his head and looked directly at Jubal.

"Jubal, you've grown."

Jubal said to the room at large, "Why is everyone saying that?"

"Well," the doctor said, looking at them each in turn, "what do you want to know?"

"Doc," Sam said, "we want to know how our Ma and Pa died."

"I suspect you've already heard that from Sheriff Kelly."

"We want to hear it from you."

"All right," Doc Leader said, "near as I can figure, Joshua shot Miriam, and then turned the gun on himself."

"That's a lie!" Jubal said.

"Easy, boy," Sam said.

"It can't be true, Sam," Evan said. "Pa wouldn't do that."

"And when's the last time you saw Pa, or talked to him?" Sam asked.

"Well...seven years or so—"

"And more for me," Sam said, "and how do we know how he might have changed between now and then?"

"You boys have a lot of gall," Doc Leader said.

"What do you mean, Doc?'

"Your Ma and Pa were proud as hell of you boys, but did any of you ever come to see them? And now that they're dead you want me to point the lot of you like loaded guns at someone and say, there, he killed your father and mother, after which you'd get your revenge. Well, there's no revenge to be gotten, boys... not unless you want to go and piss on your father's grave."

"You old—" Jubal snapped, rushing at him. Sam turned half to his left and caught Jubal with one sweep of his arm.

"Easy, boy."

"Don't call me 'boy'!" Jubal shouted. "I don't like that any better than 'little brother,'...and let me go!"

"Evan," Sam said, "take Jubal outside and calm him down, will you?"

Evan walked over to where Sam was holding Jubal and stared at Sam for a long moment.

"Go ahead," Sam said.

Evan took hold of Jubal and ushered him toward the door.

"But he can't say that—" Jubal was protesting.

"Shut up, Jube," Evan said, and pulled the door shut behind them.

"You've got a burr under your saddle, Doc," Sam said when they were alone. "Do you want to tell me what it's about?"

Doc Leader glared at Sam for a moment or two, then turned and reached for a half full bottle of whiskey on his desk. He uncorked the bottle and tilted it to his lips.

"You want some?"

"No, I don't want a drink, Doc, I want answers."

"I can't give you any," Leader said, putting the bottle down.

"The burr under my saddle? I don't know where you get off playing the outraged son, Sam McCall, that's what's rubbing me the wrong way."

"I'm not outraged," Sam said. "That's Jubal."

"Any of you!" Leader said. "You all broke your mother's heart when you left."

"Children leave home, Doc."

"And they come back once in a while to visit."

"I been busy—"

"Oh, I know how busy you been, Sam McCall," Leader said. "Big man, big rep, we all read all about it, me, Dude Miller, your mother and father—"

"I'm gonna talk to Dude next."

"If he's in any shape to talk."

"What's that mean?"

"Dude was beat up a few nights ago."

"By who?"

"I don't know," Leader said. "Three masked men broke into his house, dragged him outside, and gave him a sound beating."

"How bad?"

"Bad enough to put him in bed."

"Dude's a tough old bird."

"Now how would you know that? You ain't seen him for years."

Sam frowned.

"I can see we're not gonna get anywhere, Doc," Sam said, moving toward the door. "Something's eatin' at you. I don't know what it is, but if I find out that it's somethin' that I should have known, then this loaded gun just might end up pointin' at you. Remember that."

Evan and Jubal were waiting at the base of the steps when Sam came down.

"Well?" Evan asked.

"Pa didn't do it."

"Well, why didn't you say that in the sheriff's office?" Jubal demanded. "Or upstairs?"

"Because I wasn't sure then."

"And you are now?" Evan asked.

"Yes."

"Why?"

"Because that old man is hiding something" Sam said.

"I can feel it, and if he's got something to hide, then somethin' is goin' on here."

"And we're gonna find out what it is, right?" Jubal asked. "That's right, kid," Sam said. "We're gonna find out." "Well, good!" Jubal said, and then as Sam and Evan

started walking away he shouted, "And don't call me 'kid.'"

CHAPTER SEVEN

"Do you remember Dude's daughter?" Sam asked Evan as they walked from the doctor's office to Dude Miller's house.

Before Evan could reply, Jubal said, "I remember her. Yellow-haired gal, right?"

"Yellow-haired child, by my remembrance," Sam said. "I don't think she was more than seven or eight when I left."

"She was a little older than that when I saw her last," Evan said, "and she was pretty."

"When I left she was over twenty," Jubal said, "and she was still pretty."

"Look at the gleam in the kid's eye, Evan."

"I said, don't call me—"

"Well what the hell do you want us to call you?" Evan asked.

"Jubal," the younger brother said. "My name's Jubal, ain't it?"

"It sure is, kid," Sam said.

"Jesus..." Jubal said.

Walking through town they found themselves the center of attention. Men and woman stopped on the street to stare, or to point. There go the McCall boys, they were saying, or, There goes Sam McCall.

"You recognize any of these people?" Sam asked.

"Not many," Evan said.

"Some were children when I left," Sam said, "and are hard to recognize now."

"Some were not so elderly," Evan said, "and are also hard to recognize."

"I know some of them," Jubal said, "but it ain't me they're pointing at."

"Oh?" Evan said.

"It's him," Jubal said, jerking his thumb at his older brother. "Big Sam McCall. They're afraid of him."

"Are they?" Evan asked.

"Well, sure they are," Jubal said. "They know how many men he's killed, just as I do."

"Do you?" Sam asked. "How do you know how many men I've killed?"

"Well...I heard, and I read the papers—"

"And you believe all of that?"

"Well, ain't it true?"

"Some of it, yes."

"What do you mean, some of it?"

"I mean just that," Sam said. "It ain't all true. I've killed men, yes, but only if they were tryin' to kill me."

"You mean you ain't killed all those men they say you killed?" Jubal sounded betrayed.

"Jubal," Sam said, "grow up."

Jubal looked at Evan.

"What's he mean by that?"

"He means you shouldn't always believe what you hear, or what you read."

"What are you supposed to believe, then?"

"You believe what you see, Jube," Sam said. "That's the best rule to follow."

Jubal was thinking that over when they reached the Miller house.

"He's kept it up well," Sam said, as they opened the gate and entered the yard.

They mounted the steps and knocked on the door. After a moment Jubal reached to knock again.

"Easy," Evan said, intercepting his hand. "Give them a chance to answer."

They waited a few minutes and then the door swung inward.

The woman who was standing there was so much more than just pretty that they were all struck momentarily dumb.

"Yes?" she said, and then suddenly recognition dawned in her eyes. It wasn't so much that she recognized them as that she *knew* that the three of them could only he the McCall brothers.

"I knew you'd come."

Sam was the first to speak.

"Tell me, ma'am, how you knew that?"

"I just knew," she said. "I felt it. You're Sam, aren't you?"

"Yes."

"And Evan? And, of course, Jubal. I recognize you now. You've grown."

Jubal looked annoyed at the comment, but said nothing.

"Well, come in," she said, stepping back from the door. "Did you only just arrive?"

"Yes," Sam said, "only a couple of hours ago."

She closed the door and turned to face them. They had all removed their hats and were holding them in their hands.

"Do you want to take off your coats?"

"We'll keep them if you don't mind, ma'am," Sam said.

"Oh God, don't call me that," Serena said. "You boys know my name."

"I reckon we do, Serena," Sam said.

"Who have you spoken to so far?"

"The Swede," Jubal said, "the sheriff and Doc Leader."

"So you've heard the verdict, then."

"It's all lies," Jubal said.

"That's what we think, too."

Jubal gave his brothers a triumphant look.

"We heard about your father," Sam said. "How is he?"

"Sore, but he wants to get out of bed."

"Can we see him?"

"Of course," she said. "I'll take you to him."

They followed Serena Miller through the living room and up the stairs to the second floor.

"Let me see if he's awake."

"I'm awake," her father's voice called. "How could I not be with so many people traipsing through the hall? Is that you, Sam McCall?"

"It's me, Dude," Sam said.

"Go on in," she said, stepping aside. "I'll get you some coffee."

"Thanks," Evan said.

They stepped into the room and Sam was shocked when he saw Dude Miller. The man had aged so. His hair was white, the bones of his face looked as if they were trying to push out through his flesh. Sam wondered... if his father were still alive, would he look like this as well?

"Dude."

"Sam," Miller said. "Boys, how are you?"

"We're fine, Mr. Miller."

"Jubal, is that you?" Miller said, peering at Jubal. "You've—"

"Yeah, I know, I've grown."

"I wish I could get up and greet you proper but Doc insists I stay in bed. Got some cracked ribs."

"Do you know who it was did this to you, Dude?" Sam asked.

"Didn't see anyone's face, if that's what you mean," Miller said. "Can't describe anyone to the sheriff, not that it would matter."

"What do you mean?"

"He means we know who did it," Serena said from behind them. "We can't prove it, but even if we could, the sheriff wouldn't do anything about it."

She entered the room carrying a tray with three steaming cups of coffee on it. Sam knew from the smell it would be better coffee than the sheriff's.

"Thank you," he said, taking one. "You want to explain that to me a little better?"

"They had to be Lincoln Burkett's men," Miller said from the bed.

"Burkett," Sam said. "I don't know the name."

"I do," Evan said.

They all looked at him.

"I was in the Dakotas when he had a spread up there. That was several years ago. What's he doing down here?"

"Who knows?" Miller said. "All we know is that he arrived with a lot of money, and a lot of men, and started taking over the county, and the town. He owns a big spread, some businesses here, he's got the town council buffaloed, and the sheriff is his."

"That's an awful lot for one man to bite off," Sam said.

"Well, he's bitten it off, chewed it, and swallowed it, and he's still hungry."

"Why would he send men to beat up on you?"

"Because I'm opposed to him," Miller said. "He's got most of the people hereabouts thinking that he's good for the town, but the only thing he's good for is Lincoln Burkett."

"Sounds like you've got your work cut out for you, opposin' him," Sam said.

"Us?" Serena asked. "What about you?"

Sam looked at her.

"Well, ma'am—Serena, what Burkett does ain't none of our business. We just came to find out what happened to our Ma and Pa."

"They were killed, that's what happened."

"Well, we know that, but by who and why? That's our business."

"Then your business and our business is the same," she said.

"Serena—"

"Papa, come on. You know that Burkett killed their parents."

Sam gave Miller a sharp look.

"What about that, Dude?"

"That's something else we can't prove," Miller said.

"But do you believe it?"

"I...suspect it."

"Why? Did the death of our parents benefit Lincoln Burkett?"

"Actually, if you look at it that way, no."

"He owns your father's spread!" Serena said.

"What?" Evan said.

"He bought it," Miller said. He looked at Sam and said, "He already owned it when your parents were killed. Killing them didn't benefit him that I can see."

"Unless our Pa was opposing him, too," Evan said. "Was he?"

Miller looked away.

"Dude?" Sam said. "There's somethin' stickin' in Doc Leader's craw. Do you know what it is?"

"Again," Miller said, "I suspect..."

"Suspect what?" Evan asked.

"Doc examined your parents," Serena said quickly. "He knows your father didn't kill himself."

Sam started to look annoyed.

"There seems to be a lot of suspectin' and supposin' goin' on here."

"Then maybe you'd better start trying to find out the facts," Serena suggested.

"That's what we came here to do."

"Then the quicker you do, the quicker you'll see that your fight and our fight are the same."

Sam looked away from Serena toward her father.

"Dude, where were Ma and Pa livin?'

"A small adobe house about three miles out of town," Miller said. "They moved there after your father sold the spread."

"I don't understand this!" Jubal said. "Pa would never sell that ranch."

"Well, he did," Miller said. "The sale is on record at the courthouse."

"Well, we'll look into that as well," Sam said. He put his coffee cup, barely touched, down on the end table. When Evan and Jubal put theirs down they were empty.

"Dude, we'll look in on you again."

"I'll show you out," Serena said.

She led Evan and Jubal out into the hall, but Miller said, "Sam? Stay a minute."

"I'll be right out," Sam said to the others. He turned to Miller and asked, "What is it?"

"Serena's a little bull-necked about this, Sam," Miller said. "Being on my back and all, I can't protect her if Burkett decides to send some more men—"

"Don't worry, Dude," Sam said. "We'll keep an eye on her."

"I'd be much obliged for that, Sam."

"It's the least we can do, Dude, you sendin' that telegram and all. Speakin' of that, how the hell did you know where I was?"

"I didn't," Miller said. "I heard tell you were in Montana, and I must've sent out dozens of those telegrams to different towns."

Sam thought that over a moment and then started laughing.

"What's so funny?" Miller asked.

"Well, if you knew how that telegram affected the people in

Corozon, Montana, you'd laugh too at the thought that there were dozens of towns in Montana waitin' for me to show up."

"I hope I didn't cause you any trouble."

"No trouble, Dude," Sam assured him. "I'm obliged to you for sendin' it, or we might never have known."

"There's some shame in that, Sam," Miller said. "You probably never would have known because you boys never came around."

"Now Dude, I heard enough of that from Doc."

Miller raised his hand and waggled it, saying, "I ain't gonna judge you, Sam. It's just a shame, is all."

"I agree with you, Dude," Sam said, "there just ain't a whole hell of a lot I can do about it now."

Sam left the room and went downstairs, where Evan and Jubal were talking to Serena.

"Serena, would you be so kind as to tell us where our parents are buried?"

"Near the house."

"The ranch house?"

"No," she said, "the adobe house they... they died in."

"Pa always talked about him and Ma being buried on the ranch," Jubal said.

"I know," Sam said. "Jubal, you know how to use that gun you're wearin'?"

"Well enough, I reckon. Why?"

"You're stayin' here with Serena."

"I am not!"

"Yes, you are."

"That's not necessary—" Serena started.

"I promised your Pa we'd look out for you until he got back on his feet. It's the least we can do. Jubal? You gonna make a liar out of me?"

"Are you and Evan gonna spell me here?"

"We are."

"Well, then... all right, but don't take too long."

"Well be back soon enough," Sam said. "Evan?"

Sam and Evan left the yard, closing the gate behind them.

"Where to now?" Evan asked.

"Well, we can go to the bank and see if Pa left behind any unsettled accounts, then we can go over to the courthouse and check on the sale of the ranch. After that we'll collect Jubal and go out to the gravesite, and look at the house where they died."

"What about Serena?"

"Maybe we'll just take her with us. After that, one of us will come back here with her."

"And the other two?"

"By that time," Sam said, "A visit to Mr. Lincoln Burkett will be in order."

Soon after the McCalls had left his office Sheriff Tom Kelly left, went to the livery, saddled his horse, and rode out to what was once the McCall ranch and was now the Burkett place.

As he rode up to the house and reigned his horse in off a gallop, he attracted a lot of attention, including that of Chuck Conners, the foreman.

As Kelly dismounted and started for the house Conners intercepted him.

"Whoa, there, Sheriff," Conners said. "What's the hurry?"

"I got something to tell Mr. Burkett."

"Well, you tell me and I'll tell him."

Kelly considered this for a moment, then nodded.

"They're in town."

"Who's in town?"

"The McCalls?"

Conner's eyes widened with interest.

"Sam McCall??"

"And his brothers," Kelly said, and then added, "and they're asking questions."

"Well, of course they are," Conners said, rubbing his lantern jaw. "Wouldn't you if you found out your parents were dead?"

"Mr. Burkett's got to know—"

"Don't you worry, Sheriff," Conners said. "I'll let Mr. Burkett know, and I'll tell him it was you who brought the information. He'll be grateful."

"Well...all right."

"Now... what did you tell them?"

"What everybody knows, that their Pa shot their Ma and then himself."

"Nothing else?"

"What else would I tell them, Conners?"

"I'm just asking to make sure, Sheriff. See, Mr. Burkett's going to ask me."

"Well, I didn't tell them nothing else."

"Good. And who else have they talked to?"

"They said they was gonna talk to Doc, and to Dude Miller."

"Miller," Conners said, nodding. "We know what he'll tell them."

"What should I do?"

"Just go back to town and keep an eye on them, Sheriff," Conners said, clapping the man on the back. "That's all you have to do—for now."

CHAPTER EIGHT

As Sam and Evan McCall entered the small Bank of Vengeance Creek the bank president, James Boland, stood up behind his desk, but did not come around. He fidgeted from one foot to the other as the two brothers approached his desk.

"You the bank president?" Sam asked.

"That's right," Boland said. "What can I do for you gentlemen?"

There was only one other person in the bank, a bored-looking clerk standing behind a caged window.

"We're the sons of Joshua and Miriam McCall."

"I see. Terrible thing. You have my sympathy."

"Thank you," Evan said. "We're here to see if our parents left any unsettled accounts behind. If so, we'd like to settle them."

"Unsettled accounts?" the bank president said. "No, no unsettled accounts."

"You know that without looking it up?" Sam asked.

"Oh, yes, yes indeed," Boland said. "I am, after all, the president of the bank. I look at every account personally."

"I see," Evan said. "What about the house they were living in?"

"It was theirs."

"Theirs?"

"Yes, they owned it outright. I believe it was included in the sale of their ranch."

Evan looked at Sam, who shrugged.

"All right," Evan said. "What about the estate? Did my father have a lawyer in town?"

"No, no lawyer," Mr. Boland said, "and there was no estate."

"What do you mean, no estate?" Sam asked. "What about the money from the sale of the ranch?"

"I don't know anything about that," Boland said. "All I can tell you is that there is no estate."

"Did my father have an account here?"

"He did," Boland said, "and he still does, but it's empty."

"Empty?"

"Completely."

"I don't understand."

"I'm afraid I don't have anything else to tell you, uh, sir."

"It's all right," Evan said, cutting Sam off. "Thank you."

"You're welcome."

As Sam and Evan McCall left, John Boland sat down heavily behind his desk and heaved a sigh of relief.

Outside Sam said, "What the hell—"

"Let's go to the courthouse and check on the sale," Evan said. "I don't like the way this smells."

They stopped at the courthouse next and told the clerk they wanted to look at some sale records.

"Which one?"

"The McCall ranch."

"When was the sale completed?" the man asked.

Evan was about to answer when Sam reached past him and grabbed the front of the clerk's shirt. He jerked him forward across the counter so hard that his wire-framed glasses fell off.

"Look," Sam said, "Lincoln Burkett bought the property. I'm sure you know where all the records of Burkett's purchases are."

"Oh, Mr. Burkett?" the clerk said. "Why didn't you say so?"

"I'm saying so now."

"Of course," the man said, "I'll get it for you."

Sam released the man, who grabbed for his glasses and backed away from them.

"Sometimes it doesn't pay to be too patient," Sam said.

"I guess not."

"First Doc acts like he doesn't know nothin', and then the bank president acts like he knows everythin'," Sam said. "I didn't feel like playin' games with this one."

"You don't have to explain anything to me, Sam."

"Good."

The clerk returned with a large book with a black hard cover.

"All sales are recorded here."

"Thanks," Evan said. He took the book and reversed it so he could read it.

"What?" Evan said suddenly.

"What is it?"

"Wait."

Evan read the book again, and then closed it, shaking his head. He pushed it across to the clerk and said, "Thanks." He turned to Sam and said, "Let's go outside, Sam."

They walked outside and Sam stopped and put his hand on his brother's arm.

"Well?"

"I don't get it."

"Get what?"

"The conditions of the sale."

"Are you gonna make me drag it out of you?"

"Sam," Evan said, "according to the records, the condition of the deal was an even swap."

"A swap? Of what?"

"The ranch for the house they...they died in."

Sam started to say something, then stopped and put his hands on his hips. He stared at the sky for a few moments before speaking.

"Let's get Jubal," Sam said. "I think it's time to take a look at the house."

Before leaving the Miller house Sam made sure Dude Miller had a gun by his bed.

"What about Serena?" Miller asked.

"She's gonna show us where the house is," Sam said, "and the markers."

They went to the livery for their horses, rented one for Serena—who insisted she'd rather ride than take a buggy—and rode out to the adobe house where their parents had died.

"We can go to the markers first," Serena said after they'd ridden a couple of miles. "They're not right near the house."

"All right?" Evan said to Sam.

After a moment Sam said, "All right."

She lead them to the grave markers, which were about a half mile from the house. They were plain wooden markers on which someone had scrawled their names. Obviously whoever had done it did not know their birth-dates, so only the dates of their deaths were recorded.

Evan and Jubal dismounted and walked to the markers. Serena remained mounted and stared at Sam, who did the same.

Sam felt her looking at him, and did not look at her. Instead he stared not at the gravesites, but at his brother's backs.

After a few minutes Evan and Jubal turned and remounted.

"We'll have to get them something better," Evan said.

"Sure," Sam said, "but first let's make sure they're buried in the right place."

A stranger rode into Vengeance Creek while the Mc-Call boys were out of town. He rode directly to the livery and asked the Swede for directions to the Burkett spread, and then immediately left town and headed for the ranch.

From the gravesites they rode to the house, where they all dismounted. They went into the house together, a small two-room house with a hard-packed dirt floor and flimsy wooden doors and shutters.

"They lived here?" Evan said in disbelief.

Sam looked down at the dirt floor. There were stains in some places, which made the floor darker. He knew they were bloodstains.

"No," Sam said, "they died here."

There was some furniture, but it was all old, dusty and in various stages of disrepair. Evan walked over to the wooden chair, shook it, and then lifted his foot and easily smashed it.

"They traded the ranch for this?" he said, angrily.

"What?" Jubal asked. "Traded?"

"Even up," Sam said. "The ranch for this."

"They didn't get any money for the ranch?" Serena asked in disbelief.

"Not a penny."

"I don't believe it," Jubal said.

"It's on file at the courthouse," Evan said.

"I mean, why would Pa do that? It doesn't make any damn sense."

"I agree with Jubal," Serena said. "We all heard that Burkett had bought the ranch. We never suspected...this."

"Well," Evan said, looking around in disgust, "it's plain that the answers are not going to be found here."

"Jubal," Sam said, "take Serena back to town."

"Where are you going?" Jubal demanded.

"Out to see Lincoln Burkett."

"I wanna go with you!"

"As a matter of fact," Serena said, "so do I."

"Sam," Evan said, "I have a suggestion."

"What's that?"

"Since I'm just a little less excitable than you, I think I'd better go and see Mr. Burkett alone."

"I don't like that suggestion," Sam said.

"I like it better than yours," Jubal said, with a smile.

"Besides," Evan said, "someone has to register us in the hotel. It's plain that we can't stay here."

"Evan—"

"Sam," Evan said, "I'm just going out there to talk. That won't take all three, or even two of us. Come on, see it my way."

Sam frowned, obviously not happy. Jubal was smiling because Sam was getting some of his own medicine.

"I can go with you and introduce you, Evan," Serena said.

Evan smiled.

"Don't worry, Serena, I know how to introduce myself. You go home with Jubal." Evan looked at Sam and said, "All right?"

Sam's jaw was tight but he nodded and said, "Yeah, all right...but watch your step."

"I'll watch it, brother," Evan said. "I've had a lot of practice doing just that."

The stranger rode up to the Burkett house and dismounted. As a ranch hand approached him to ask if he could help him, the stranger tossed him his horse's reins and said, "See to my horse, boy."

The hand tossed the reins right back and said, "I ain't your boy. Whataya want here?"

The stranger ignored the reins, which struck his chest and fell to the ground.

"I have business with Mr. Burkett."

"Is that so?" the hand said. "Well, maybe Mr. Burkett doesn't have business with you."

The stranger's face split into a humorless smile. He was very tall, and clad in black, which made his dark eyes seem black, as well—as black as two small holes which now bore into the hand's own eyes, chilling him.

"Why don't I go and ask him?" he said, and started for the front steps.

"Hold it—" the hand said, putting his hand on the stranger's arm. The stranger turned and rammed the heel of his other hand into the man's jaw. The man's head snapped back and he fell to the ground, blood from his severely bitten tongue seeping out from between his lips.

As the stranger turned to approach the steps he heard some more men running up behind him. At that moment the front door opened and a man stepped out.

"Are you Coffin?" Lincoln Burkett asked.

"That's me," Coffin said. "You Burkett?"

"Yes."

"You want to call off your dogs before I have to kill some of them?"

"Hold up, men!" Burkett said.

Seven or eight hands had been rushing to the aide of their friend, and Burkett's voice stopped them in their tracks.

"This man works for me," Burkett said. "Gear, have some men pick up Adams and take him to the doctor. Coffin, come inside."

"Sure," Coffin said.

He climbed the steps without looking back.

———

As Evan McCall rode up to the Burkett house—what used to be his father's house—he saw a man being helped to his feet by several others. There was blood on the man's chin and chest. It seemed to be pouring from his mouth.

He reined in as the men helped the injured party away, and another man turned to face him.

"Help ya?" Mike Gear asked.

"I'd like to see Mr. Burkett."

"About what?"

"Tell him Evan McCall is here. I'd like to talk to him about my father."

"McCall?" the man asked.

"That's right."

"You Sam McCall's brother?"

"Right again."

"Is Mr. Burkett expecting you?"

Evan opened his mouth to say no, then thought better of it and said, "I believe he is."

He looked at Evan as if he didn't believe him and said, "Wait here."

The man was gone five or six minutes, and during that time Evan looked over the house. Several improvements had been made since the last time he was there. They could have been made by his father, but he suspected that they had been made recently, by Lincoln Burkett. For one thing, the wood of the front steps looked rather new. There also seemed to have been some work done on the roof. Off to one side of the house, on the second floor, a new room was under construction.

To his left he saw another horse, a gelding as black as night, tied off. From the look of it, it had just recently been ridden in. Evan was not Burkett's only visitor.

When the man returned he simply motioned to Evan from the top of the steps.

Evan tied his horse off on a post in front of the house and followed the man inside. Without saying a word the man led him to a room that was either an office or a library. When he and his brothers had lived there with their parents it had simply been a spare room. Somehow Evan doubted that Lincoln Burkett would have any spare rooms in the house when he was finished.

This room had been lined with bookshelves, which were now only half filled.

"Mr. McCall," Burkett said. At least, he assumed the man behind the desk was Burkett. He was a big man in his sixties who, in his youth, might have rivaled Sam McCall in size and girth. Now there seemed to be more belly than the man would have liked. "Evan McCall, I presume."

"That's right."

"You can leave, Gear," Burkett said to the other man. To Evan he said, "Please, sit down."

Evan moved to a cushioned chair and sat in it, his hat in his hand.

"I'm Lincoln Burkett," Burkett said, somewhat unnecessarily, at this point. "May I offer you a drink?"

"Some good sherry, if you have it."

"Of course I have it," Burkett said, and Evan thought, I knew you would.

Burkett poured two snifters of sherry and handed one to Evan over the desk. He then sat in his leather chair with the other glass in his hands.

"Your brothers are not with you?"

"No."

"You are the spokesman, then?"

"You could say that."

"Well, tell me how I can help you."

"You can tell me about the... sale of this house."

"What is there to tell?" Burkett said. "I made your father an offer and he took it."

"An offer?" Evan said, leaning forward. In spite of himself he was growing angry. "That broken-down adobe hut for this ranch?"

Burkett laughed, which raised Evan's temperature even higher.

"I assure you, Mr. McCall, it was not broken down when I made the deal. It was a fine-looking house. Your father expressed an interest in moving to a smaller house. If it is broken down now, well. . ."

"Still, I don't see how anyone could have exchanged this ranch for any house, even-up."

Burkett put his glass down on his desk and spread his hands helplessly.

"What can I tell you, Mr. McCall? That was the deal your father and I made."

Evan put his glass down so hard on Burkett's desk that some of the sherry spilled.

"Bullshit!"

"Now look—" Burkett started, but Evan stood and cut the man off.

"Nobody can tell me my father agreed to a deal like that...not of his own free will!"

"Are you suggesting that my purchase of this house and this land was not legal, sir?"

"I'm saying it wasn't on the up and up," Evan said. "It couldn't have been."

"I don't know who you've been talking to, Mr. McCall, but someone must be giving you bad information—"

"I suppose it wasn't you who had some of your men beat up Dude Miller the other night?"

"Mr. Miller was beaten up?" Burkett said, looking surprised. "I hadn't heard that. I hope he wasn't severely injured."

"As if you really care."

"Now, Mr. McCall," Burkett said, standing, "if you're going to become abusive I'm going to have to ask you to leave my house."

"Your house!" Evan said, rising to his feet in disgust. "You stole this house, Burkett, and my brothers and I intend to prove it."

Burkett's hand came up and he was holding a Navy Colt in it that must have come out of his desk. It was a pretty big gun to keep in a desk drawer. Evan assumed that when Burkett produced it he intended to impress someone.

Evan was impressed, and he was angrier than before, this time at himself for being caught flatfooted like that. Sam wouldn't have allowed that to happen....

"Please," Burkett said, "leave."

"I'm leaving," Evan said, moving toward the door, "but you haven't seen the last of me."

"Don't make threats, McCall," Burkett said, dropping his polite act. "You're in no position."

"I'm not making threats, Burkett, I'm making a promise. If my brothers and I find out you had anything to do with my father's death—"

"Oh, so now I'm a murderer?" Burkett demanded, cocking the hammer on the Colt.

Evan stared at the barrel of the Colt and said, "I don't know —suppose you tell me."

There was a tense moment as the two men stood that way, and then Burkett slowly let the hammer on the Colt down.

"I haven't had anyone beaten up, I didn't have anyone killed, and I bought this house legally. If you want to prove otherwise, be my guest."

Evan put his hat on and left, too angry for words.

Riding back he thought maybe he should have let Sam come. Maybe when Burkett went for the Navy Colt, Sam would've seen the move and killed him.

Maybe, if Burkett had been facing Sam McCall instead of Evan, he never would have gone for the gun.

As the front door closed on Evan McCall, Burkett put the Navy Colt away and left the room. He walked down the hall and opened the first door he came to.

"Could you hear all that?" he asked Coffin.

"I heard."

"That was Evan McCall."

"I said I heard. What do you want me to do?"

"Eventually, I'll want you to kill Sam McCall—maybe even all the McCalls."

"Eventually?"

"I don't want to jeopardize my standing in this community, Burkett said, "not just yet. I want to watch them for a while."

"I get paid, whether I kill them or not."

"Of course," Burkett said. "For now take a room at the hotel and keep yourself ready."

"That's it?"

"That's all...for now."

Coffin shrugged.

"It's your money."

"It's my money," Burkett said, "my ranch, and my town. Soon everyone will know that."

When Evan returned to town he found Sam and Jubal waiting for him at the Miller house.

"What happened?" Jubal asked as Serena led Evan into the parlor.

"You don't look like it went real well," Sam said.

"Remember what a good idea I thought it was if I went alone?"

"Yes?"

Evan related his conversation with Burkett word for word, then watched his brothers and waited.

"So?" Sam finally said. "*Was* it good sherry?"

"Is that all you can say?"

Sam shrugged.

"So you made an ass out of yourself. It happens to us all at some time or another. I'm sure this wasn't your first time?"

"And it won't be your last," Serena said.

"I woulda killed him," Jubal said.

"You probably would have got yourself killed," Sam said. "Evan did fine."

"I started airing my lungs and got caught flatfooted," Evan said. "That wouldn't have happened to you."

"I've been known to cuss my head off a time or two," Sam said.

"He was lying, you know," Serena said. "About everything."

"He probably was," Sam said, "but we still can't prove it."

"We should just kill him," Jubal said.

"That's real smart thinkin', kid," Sam said.

Jubal stuck his jaw out and said, "Don't tell me you ain't never killed anybody."

"Sure I did, when they needed killin'—and when they were tryin' to kill me. Now shut up and let the adults think."

"I ain't an adult?" Jubal asked, belligerently.

"You ain't actin' like one."

"I'll show you who ain't an adult."

"Pshh." Sam made a sound that meant "Don't bother me," and Jubal stepped up, swung and hit his older brother right in the jaw.

Sam's head jerked a bit, certainly not the reaction Jubal was looking for. On top of that, Jubal had hurt his hand.

"Ow," he said, and then his eyes widened as he saw Sam swing backhanded. He couldn't avoid the blow, which struck him on the jaw and knocked him over the sofa.

"Stop it!" Serena shouted.

"I'll stop them," Evan said.

He went over to Jubal and hauled him to his feet.

"That's enough, kid."

"I told you not to call me kid," Jubal said, and he hit Evan. "Damn!" he said, because he used his already bruised hand.

"Why, you—" Evan said, and hit Jubal in the stomach. Jubal grabbed himself and fell onto his butt. He sat there, gasping, trying to get his air.

"Stop it!" Serena said again.

"It's stopped," Sam said, scowling down at Jubal. "You wanna hit anyone else?"

Jubal looked up, his eyes wide, and shook his head.

"All right," Sam said, "so we've all let off a little steam and we didn't break any furniture, or any bones..." He looked down at Jubal and said, "Did we?"

Jubal was breathing a bit easier, but he wasn't yet able to speak, so he just shook his head.

"Serena, why don't you make some coffee and we'll sit down and see if we can't figure out what our next move should be."

"If I leave the room you won't start hitting each other again, will you?"

"No," Sam said. "In fact, we'll even help Jubal up."

She gave them all a dubious look, as if she expected them all to start swinging as soon as she was gone, and then turned and went into the kitchen. She listened for a moment, didn't hear anything that would indicate a fight had broken out, and then proceeded to make coffee.

CHAPTER NINE

Mike Gear watched Coffin mount his horse and leave and then went to tell Chuck Conners that the man was gone. Conners was standing by the bunkhouse with Earl Murray and Greg Tobin. Gear, Murray, and Tobin were the three men who had beaten up Dude Miller.

"Coffin's gone, Chuck," Gear said.

"I don't understand why the boss thinks he needs Coffin," Murray said. "We can take care of the McCall brothers."

"You think so?" Conners asked. He was also stung by the fact that Burkett thought he had to go outside his own men to handle the McCall brothers—specifically, Sam McCall.

"I know so," Murray said.

"What about you guys?"

Gear and Tobin exchanged glances, and then Gear said, "Yeah, we can handle them."

"All right, then," Conners said. "Maybe we should try and save the boss some money. Whataya say?"

"I say let's do it," Gear said, and the others nodded enthusiastically.

"Of course," Conners said, "it wouldn't hurt us any if we were known as the men who killed Sam McCall, huh?"

The other three men grinned widely and nodded their agreement.

"All right, then," Conners said, again, "let's decide how we're gonna do this."

"We need someone who knows that the whole deal was phony," Sam said.

"Who would that be?" Serena asked. "I mean, *we* know the deal was phony."

"But we can't prove it," Sam said. "We need someone who will testify."

"To who?" Evan asked.

"We'll have to bring in some outside law," Sam said. "A federal marshal."

"You know anybody?"

"I have a friend," Sam said, thinking of his friend, a man named Murdock, who was a federal marshal up north. "He might be able to recommend someone we can work with."

"Why not him?"

"He usually works further north," Sam said, "but I'll send him a telegram."

"How do we know that Burkett doesn't control the telegraph office?" Jubal asked.

"That's a good point, little brother," Sam said, "but remember, Dude sent over a dozen telegrams out to me in Montana. If Burkett controlled the telegraph key in town, those messages never would have gotten out and I never would have gotten the one I did."

"All right," Evan said, "so we send a telegram to your friend Murdock and he sends one back with a name. We still aren't going to get a marshal here without proof."

"Then that's our next order of business," Sam said. "We're gonna have to split up and start askin' questions."

"Burkett's not going to like that," Serena said, "and he will find out about it."

"We'll just have to be alert," Sam said. "Evan, one of us will have to stay with Serena at all times, instead of switching off."

"Am I volunteering?" Evan asked with a smile.

"I thought you never would."

"Wait a minute," Serena said, "don't I have anything to say about who my bodyguard is?"

"No," Sam said.

"Why not?" she asked, bristling.

"Because if you picked one of us," Sam said, "the other two would feel slighted. You wouldn't want that to happen, would you?"

She glared at Sam for a moment, and then had to laugh in spite of herself.

"Why Sam McCall," she said, "you could become a politician."

"Bite your tongue."

"Very well," she said, "I accept Evan as my bodyguard."

Evan executed as gracious a bow as he could manage while seated at the table.

"When do we get started?" Jubal asked. "I'm gettin' tired of all this talk."

"We get started right now," Sam said, standing up. "Right now."

As Coffin rode into town he saw three men and a woman standing on the boardwalk just at the point where the main street started. He knew Sam McCall on sight, and assumed that the other two men were his brothers. He didn't know who the woman was, and he didn't care. If he wanted a woman he'd go to the whorehouse. They weren't worth much more effort than that.

Coffin rode past them, keeping his head straight but studying Sam McCall as well as he could peripherally. He'd heard and read all the stories about Sam McCall, but he'd also read and heard all the stories about his own exploits, so he knew how much they were worth. What worked in his favor was that he had seen Sam McCall in action on two occasions, once in St. Louis, and once in Mexico. Neither time had he allowed McCall to see him, although if the man was as good as Coffin thought he was, he might have noticed that he was being watched.

Coffin was thirty-five, but he felt old beyond his years. By the time he picked up his first gun Sam McCall had already earned himself a reputation. He made up for lost time, though, killing four men before he was twenty and earning a rep of his own by his twenty-first birthday.

Coffin had always operated on the fringe of the law, hiring his gun out, hunting for bounty. He had never killed just for the sake of killing. He thought men who did that were fools. Eventually they'd end up being killed for nothing. Men like him and McCall killed when they had to, and that was often enough. Trouble followed them around like a black cloud, and they dealt with it. Men who succumbed to it didn't built reps because they died at an early age. The fact that McCall had lived past forty was testimony to just how good he really was.

Coffin left his horse at the livery with the Swede and went over to register at the hotel. He wanted a nap. One of the reasons he had lasted so long was that he took care of his body and never pushed it beyond its limits. He needed some sleep, and then some food, and then some recreation. Tomorrow, he'd start watching McCall, and McCall would know he was being watched. Coffin would not approach McCall unless Burkett told him to. There was no percentage in it unless he was being paid.

Of course, he wondered which of them was best, but that was a shit-poor reason to call a man out.

Money was the only driving force in Coffin's life. He had no ego, and that was a major reason why he was still alive.

"Sam," Evan said. "Yeah?"

"The man who just rode in."

"His name is Coffin."

"You know him?"

"I know of him."

"The man all in black?" Serena said. "He's frightening."

"He should be," Sam said.

"Wait a minute," Evan said. "Coffin...I know that name."

"Sure you do," Sam said, "a lot of people do."

"The way they know yours, Sam?" Jubal asked.

Sam looked at Jubal and said, "Sure, ki—sure, the way they know mine."

"Think he's here for you?" Jubal asked.

Sam shrugged.

"He's here," he said. "We'll deal with that fact if the need arrives. For now let's get to doin' what we're supposed to be doin'."

"Right," Jubal said. "I'll work the other side of the street."

"Don't push too hard, Jube," Evan said. "Just ask a few questions, and most important, keep your ears open."

"Right."

"And stay out of trouble," Sam said.

Jubal was already crossing the street, and he turned, spread his arms and said, "Of course."

"Evan, I'll work the side streets."

"All right, Sam. Serena and I will work this side of Main Street."

"Serena, where's the telegraph office?'

"Two streets down, on your right."

"I'll work my way over to it."

"Serena," Evan said, "why don't you wait over by the gunsmith shop for a minute."

"Why?"

"I just want to talk to Sam for a second."

Her mouth tightened at her dismissal, but she did as she was asked.

"What's wrong?" Sam asked.

"When I was out at Burkett's, Coffin was there, too."

"Are you sure?"

"I saw his horse. That big black is not easy to mistake."

"No, it's not," Sam said. "I guess that means there's a good chance he is workin' for Burkett."

"A good chance? Doesn't that cinch it?"

"No," Sam said. "He could have been there to hear an offer from Burkett, and he might have turned it down."

"Do you think there's an offer from Burkett that a man like Coffin could turn down?"

"Probably not," Sam said. "Coffin does what he does for money, I know that much about him."

"Can you take him, Sam?" Evan asked. "I mean, if it comes to it, can you take him?"

Sam hesitated a moment and then said, "I don't know, Evan. I don't know that much about him."

———

"HELLO, MR. COLLINS?"

Ed Collins turned and saw Serena standing at his counter with a well-dressed, handsome man.

"Serena," he said. "How nice to see you."

"Mr. Collins, this is Evan McCall."

"Mr. McCall," Collins said, extending his hand. "I'm sorry for your loss."

"Thank you, Mr. Collins," Evan said, shaking his hand. "Serena tells me you're one of her father's supporters."

"If by that you mean I don't like what Lincoln Burkett is doing, then you're right. I wish I'd been there the other night when they dragged Dude from his house. It wouldn't have been so—"

"Mr. Collins," Serena said, putting her hand on his arm, "I appreciate what you're saying, but you might have gotten the same—or worse than—my father did. I'm glad you weren't there."

Collins took her hand and said, "You're a treasure, Serena, did you know that?"

"Yes, Mr. Collins," she said, laughing, "I know that."

"What can I do for you, Mr. McCall? Do you need a gun? You can have the best in my store."

"I have a gun, Mr. Collins. What we need is someone who knows something about the so-called 'sale' of my father's ranch to Lincoln Burkett."

"That shocked the hell out of me," Collins said. "I didn't know your father well, Mr. McCall—"

"Please," Evan said, "call me Evan."

"I didn't know him well, Evan, but I'd done some business with him. He loved that ranch, I know that. I don't understand why he sold it."

"Did you know the terms of the sale?"

"I did not. Why? Were they unusual?"

Evan related to Collins the exact terms, and Collins' mouth fell open.

"Well, now I'm even more confused."

"We need someone who knows more than that, Mr. Collins. I assume from our conversation that you do not."

"I'm sorry, Evan, but I don't," Collins said. "I wish I could help you."

"I appreciate that, Mr. Collins. Thanks for your time."

"Thank you, Mr. Collins," Serena said. She leaned over the counter and kissed the old man on the cheek.

As they were leaving Collins called out, "If there's anything else I can do... if you or your brother need any guns..."

"We'll be sure to call on you, Mr. Collins," Evan said. "Thanks again."

Outside Serena said, "I was sure he didn't know anything. If he did he would have told my father long ago."

"Sometimes," Evan said, "people don't know they know something until they're asked."

"Well, if that's the case," Serena said, "let's keep asking."

While the McCall brothers and Serena were asking their questions Mike Gear, Greg Tobin and Earl Murray rode into town with four other men from the ranch. The extra four men were loyal to the foreman, Chuck Conners, and were willing to do whatever they could for him.

As they rode in Gear spotted Serena and Evan McCall walking from one store to another on the left side of the street.

"That's one of 'em," he said to Murray, who nudged Tobin and repeated the words.

"Which one?" Tobin asked.

"Evan, the one who came out to see Mr. Burkett."

"He don't look so tough," Tobin said.

"He's a gambler," Gear said, "not a gunman. Sam Mc-Call's the one we want. With him gone the others will be easy."

"How are we gonna justify gunnin' down Sam McCall?" Murray asked.

Gear answered, "He's Sam McCall, ain't he? Besides, what's the sheriff gonna do about it? Nothin'."

"What about outside law?" Tobin asked.

"Forget about it," Gear said. "A man like Sam McCall gets killed, people just naturally assume he was lookin' for it—and we're gonna make sure he finds it."

Evan saw the men riding in and recognized the brand on the horses.

"What is it?" Serena asked.

"Those are Burkett's men, aren't they?"

She looked at the men and said, "Yes. I recognize two of them. In fact," she added, squinting her eyes for a better look, "one of them looks like one of the men who beat up my father."

"How can you tell? I thought you said they wore masks over their faces."

"They did," she said, "but one of them was squat, and thickly built, like that fellow in the center."

"What are they doing in town now, I wonder?" Evan asked.

"Maybe they're looking for someone else to beat up," she suggested.

Evan nodded thoughtfully and then said, "Or worse."

Sam worked his way up and down side streets until he reached the telegraph office. As he was entering he saw a group of men riding by on Main Street. They paused and looked down the street at him, and then continued on. He went inside.

Jubal came out of a store just as the seven men paused on their horses. They were apparently peering down a side street. Jubal didn't know who they were, but he moved over to the side so he could look down the same street, and he saw Sam. It looked as if they were watching Sam, but he couldn't be sure. Jubal looked around and spotted a straight-backed wooden chair in front of a store. He went over to the chair, moved it so he could see who was coming, and sat down.

"That was Sam McCall," Gear said. "I'm sure of it." "Looked like he was goin' into the telegraph office,"

Tobin said. "Who do you suppose he's sendin' a telegram to?" "I don't know," Gear said, "but we can get 'im when he comes out, and then find out. Come on, we'll leave the horses by the saloon and then walk back."

Coffin couldn't sleep. He was tired but he had the feeling that some kind of trouble was brewing. He could smell it in the air. He got up off the bed and walked to his window, which overlooked Main Street. He saw the seven men tying their horses off in front of the saloon, and he recognized one of them from the Burkett place. Suddenly, he had an overwhelming urge for a drink.

Jubal saw the seven men walking back and knew that they were after Sam. He didn't have time to warn Sam, or to find Evan. He was just going to have to watch and wait, and be ready.

Evan and Serena were in the hardware store, and Serena was talking to the owner, telling him what Evan had told Ed Collins. Evan walked to the front window and looked out from behind the farm tools that hung there. He saw Jubal sitting in a chair across and up the street, and he seemed to be watching something.

"Serena."

She turned and said, "What is it?"

"Stay here," Evan said, putting his hand on his gun and moving toward the door.

"Evan, what is it?"

He turned, pointed a finger at her and said forcefully, "Stay in here. Mr. Norris, keep her here!"

Norris, the owner of the store, knew trouble when he saw it, and nodded.

"Just stay here, Miss Miller," he said. "Whatever happens in the street is better off happening with you in here."

They were about a hundred yards from the telegraph office when Gear called a halt to their progress.

"Tobin, take two men and cross over to the other side of the street, across from the telegraph office."

"All right." Tobin called two names and the three of them hurried ahead.

"Earl, you and Roberts walk past the telegraph office and find some cover. When he comes out we'll catch him in the crossfire."

"Right."

Murray and Roberts moved on ahead.

"Gary, you and I will set up on this side of the office."

"You sure this is what Chuck wants done, Mike?" Gary asked.

"Believe me, Gary," Mike Gear said, "this is what's best for everyone."

Evan came out of the hardware store and looked down the block. Further down, on his side, he saw the men who appeared to be splitting up. He counted as they did, making them out to be seven.

After they had all moved into the side street he stepped out into the open, trying to catch Jubal's attention. Finally, Jubal looked over at him, waved, and pointed. Evan nodded, and waved at Jubal to join him.

Jubal left his chair and trotted across the street.

"What's going on?" Evan asked.

"Sam's in the telegraph office, down that street," Jubal said. "I don't know who those men are, but they look like their getting ready to bushwack him."

"They work for Burkett."

"And they're gonna kill Sam!"

"Not if we can help it," Evan said. "Jubal, try and cross over without being seen, and I'll be on this side. We'll try to work our way down to the telegraph office. When Sam comes out we're going to have to start shooting first. It's the only way to warn him. Got it?"

"I understand."

"And if we're going to shoot," Evan added, putting his hand on Jubal's shoulder, "we might as well shoot to kill."

"All right."

"Have you ever killed a man?"

Jubal looked at Evan. "No, but this looks like a good time to start."

"To save your brother's life," Evan said, "it's the best time."

———

COFFIN COULD SEE everything from in front of the saloon, where he stood with a beer. He saw the seven men split up and work their way into the side street. He saw Evan and Jubal come together and then work their way to that same side street.

Without even being told, Coffin knew that Sam Mc-Call was already somewhere on that street, and that he was probably the focal point of all this activity.

He could even see McCall's dark cloud, just hovering up there over that street, getting ready to rain down its dose of trouble.

This, he thought, sure had the makings of something interesting.

CHAPTER TEN

S am waited while the clerk sent his telegram. It had taken him a few moments to compose a message, saying as much as he could in as few words as he could. Basically, he asked his friend Murdock for the name of a marshal who might be willing to come to Vengeance Creek, in southern Texas, to mediate a dispute. Sam knew that Murdock had once mediated a dispute, and that was what gave him the idea. Under those circumstances they'd be able to get a marshal here without having to produce too much evidence. Maybe the presence of a federal marshal would bring the truth to the surface.

"All right, sir," the clerk said. "It's been acknowledged as received."

Sam had already paid the man for the message, so he simply thanked him.

"I have a room at the hotel. Would you bring over the reply as soon as it comes in?"

"Sure."

"Thanks again."

The clerk nodded, and Sam turned and walked to the door. He was about three steps from it when he stopped short. He remembered the men he had seen riding by as he was entering the office, six or seven of them. It was odd for that many men to ride into a town at one time unless they had a job to do.

He moved to his left so that he could look out the window of the office. The window was dusty and he had to squint to try to see through it. He thought he saw a couple of men across the street in a doorway, but he had no way of knowing if they were some of the same men.

He chose to believe that they were, and acted accordingly.

"What's taking him so long?" Gary asked.

"I don't know," Gear said. He caught Tobin's attention and tried to ask the same question with sign language, but Tobin shrugged.

"I don't like this," Gear said. "He's caught on."

"How?"

"How has he stayed alive this long?" Gear asked. He caught Tobin's attention then and waved his gun frantically.

Tobin and his men started firing.

The first volley of shots shattered the dusty plate glass window, and suddenly everything was clear.

"Down!" Sam shouted to the clerk as he threw himself to the floor.

Lead continued to rain on the office, chewing large chunks from the desk and the wall, and shattering glass and other breakables.

Sam had his gun in his hand, but there was no way he could lift his head until there was a lull in the firing—if there was. If there were six or seven men out there they could take turns firing and never let up.

He scrambled across the floor so that he was beneath the shattered window. When his chance came he was going to have to seize it immediately, for it might be the only one he got.

"Jesus," Jubal said to himself, "they're not waiting—"

"Fire!" Evan shouted from across the street. They could both see the men who were doing the firing, three of them across from the office. They started firing at them, and when the men became aware of the fact that they were being fired at, they stopped and threw themselves to the ground.

Sam McCall had heard gunfire for most of his life. For the past ten seconds or so someone had been firing into the office, but suddenly he heard other guns join in, and then the lead stopped pouring in on him. He risked a look and saw that the men across the street were being fired upon. He did not join the fray, but rather remained content to wait until he had something—or someone—to fire at. Whoever was firing now—most likely Evan and Jubal— were keeping the men pinned down.

Sam moved over to the door and cautiously stuck his head out. Suddenly, lead came in on him from left and right, and it was clear that a crossfire had been set up to ambush him. His own caution had saved him from walking right into it, and now his brothers were involved.

There had to be six or seven adversaries, but with his brothers on his side, Sam felt as if the sides were almost even.

He had to get out into the street in order to do any good.

"Damn!" Evan said.

Now there were two men to either side of the office and they were firing, keeping Sam pinned inside. He and Jubal had only their six-shooters with them, not having had time to get rifles. Evan paused to load, and heard Jubal fire his last two shots. Suddenly it was quiet as both sides took stock of the situation.

The McCalls, to Evan's thinking, were three guns against seven—and some of the men had rifles, so that increased the odds against them.

Evan caught Jubal's attention and tried to convey his intentions with an age-old method—sign language. He wanted Jubal to come across to his side, and tried to tell his brother to start moving when he started firing.

Evan had taken cover behind some crates, and now he looked over them and began to fire. Immediately Jubal ran across the street, firing to cover himself as he did so.

When Jubal was on his side they both ducked down behind the crates. They could still hear gunfire, and apparently Sam was trading shots now.

"Jubal, a couple of blocks down, there's a gunsmith's shop. The man's name is Miller. Run back there, tell him who you are, and get us a couple of rifles."

"Good thinking."

"Reload and leave me your gun. I'll try and keep them from rushing Sam until you get back."

Jubal reloaded his gun and handed it to Evan.

"Don't worry," he said, "I'll be right back."

Sam abandoned the idea of moving outside the office. He'd be much too vulnerable out there. Of course, remaining in here had its problems, too. Eventually they might get brave enough to rush him. Sam was going to have to count on his brothers doing something out there that would prevent that.

"W-what's going on?"

The clerk's voice came from behind the counter.

"Just stay down," Sam said. "It'll be over in no time."

He hoped.

This was not going the way it had been planned, Mike Gear thought. Still, even if McCall's brother were at the other end of the street, they were still outnumbered.

"What are we gonna do?" Gary asked.

"Tobin and his men are gonna have to rush him," Gear said. "We'll cover them."

Gear tried to convey this to Tobin, across the street, but Tobin either couldn't or wouldn't understand.

"Damn it!" Gear said. He stood up and shouted, "Rush him!"

Gear felt the slug punch him in the back, and then he was falling forward...

"Jesus," Gary said, looking around.

"Here!" Jubal said, handing Evan a rifle. "What'd I miss?"

"Nothing," Evan said. "I think they're trying to make up their minds what do to."

"Look," Jubal said.

A man on the other side of the street, between them and the telegraph office, stood up and shouted across the street, "Rush him!"

"They're gonna rush him!" Jubal said.

"Not if we can help it."

Evan stood up, raised the rifle and fired.

After that, everyone started firing....

Sam was looking out the door when he saw the three men across the street stand up and prepare to rush him. He fired once, and one of the men was pushed back by the impact of the bullet. The other two seemed uncertain about what to do next.

Sam chose that moment to step out of the store.

"He's coming out," Jubal said. "Let's cover him!"

"He's comin' out," one of the men with Earl Murray said. "What do we do?"

Murray had seen Gear go down, and one of the men with Tobin.

"Fire, damn it," he said, "fire!"

Sam ducked down behind a horse trough and heard the lead

slapping into the wood from across the street. He felt something tug at his foot, and when he looked down he saw that a bullet had sheared off his left bootheel. The bullet had come from his right. If he turned that way he'd be leaving himself vulnerable from the left, but he decided to leave his back to his brothers.

When he turned he saw two men standing up preparing to fire at him. He fired once, catching one man high in the chest. When he move his gun to fire at the second man, he was already falling forward. He couldn't explain that, but he didn't have time to ponder it.

When he turned left he saw both his brothers running toward him. Evan was across the street, and Jubal was running across to his side...

"Let's move!" Evan said. "You cross over."

"Right."

Evan ran along the boardwalk toward the two remaining men across from the telegraph office. Both men stood up to face him. Evan had the rifle in his left hand and his handgun in his right. He fired his pistol, the bullet striking one man in the stomach. When he moved to fire at the second man, he was already falling forward.

He turned and looked across the street....

———

As Jubal approached the last man he turned on him, raising his gun. Jubal fired at the same time the man did. His bullet hit the man in the throat, while the man's bullet tugged at his sleeve. Jubal kept moving until he reached the body. He leaned over both men and saw that they were both dead. He stood up and waved to Evan across the street.

Evan checked the three men and found that they were all dead, one having been shot in the back. He stood up, waved to Jubal across the street, and then looked for Sam. Sam McCall was across the street checking on the other two men.

———

Sam checked both men and saw that one of them had been shot in the back. He couldn't figure that. They were both dead, though, so he turned to check on his brothers. He saw Evan across the street and waved.

The McCall brothers came together in front of the telegraph office.

"Looks like you boys got here just in time," Sam said.

"Jubal spotted it," Evan said.

"Just by accident," Jubal said.

"Thanks, Jube." Sam put his hand behind his younger brother's neck. "Thanks."

"Sure."

"They all dead?" Sam asked.

"All of'em," Jubal said.

"You know, there's something funny about one of the men across the street," Evan said.

"What?" Sam asked.

"He was shot in the back."

Sam looked at his brother.

"You know, one of the others was shot in the back, too."

"One of those two was shot in the back," Jubal said, pointing behind him, "but Evan shot that one."

"Who shot the other two in the back?" Evan asked.

"I don't know," Sam said, "but I think someone else might have some questions for us."

"Who?" Evan asked.

Sam pointed behind his brothers, and they turned and saw Sheriff Kelly hurrying toward them.

———

COFFIN SAW the sheriff and slipped out of sight, into an alley. It was the same alley he had used to slip up behind the bushwackers. He paused a moment to eject the two spent shells from his .45 and lay in two live shells.

He wasn't all that sure why he had decided to help the McCalls, unless it was to keep Sam McCall alive until...

He retraced his steps down the alley. He had left a beer on the bar in the saloon.

Sam sat in a chair in the sheriff's office, picking at the bottom of his left boot, which now had no heel.

In two other chairs sat Evan and Jubal. All of their rifles and pistols were on the sheriff's desk.

The sheriff was seated behind his desk, wearing a hangdog expression.

"You know, this is a hell of a mess," Sheriff Kelly said, shaking his head.

"Not of our making," Evan said.

"No? Then whose?"

"Why don't you talk to Lincoln Burkett?"

"Mr. Burkett? Why should I talk to him?"

"Those were his men, weren't they?"

"Maybe, but that don't mean that he was involved."

"It doesn't mean he wasn't, either," Evan said. "I think you should talk to the man. Hell, we'll even go with you, if you like."

The sheriff bristled.

"I don't need help doing my job."

"You could have fooled us," Sam said.

"Look, McCall," he said, speaking to Sam, "if anyone's to blame for this it's you."

"Me?"

"You and your reputation, you invite things like this to happen."

"I was minding my own business, Sheriff, sending a telegram. You tell me how I invited this."

"Come on, you know how many men would like to be the man who killed Sam McCall."

"Or the *seven* men who killed Sam McCall," Jubal said. "You're saying that seven men tried to bushwack my brother and it's his fault?"

"He ought to leave town," Kelly said, glumly. "You all should leave town."

"Oh?" Evan said. "Are my brother Jubal and I inviting some sort of attack by being here, Sheriff?"

"We're not leaving until we find out who killed our parents," Jubal said.

Kelly stared at him.

"Your father killed your mother and then himself."

"That's what we hear," Evan said, "but we're not accepting that."

"I think we should leave now," Sam said. He stood up and took his gun off the desk, fitting it into his holster.

"I didn't say you could have your gun," Kelly said.

"You want to take it away from me again?" Sam asked. "It ain't gonna be so easy this time."

"Easy, Sam," Evan said.

"You're the one who said I invite these attacks," Sam went on. "Well, if that's the case, I'm not about to walk around unarmed. Boys, pick up your guns."

Jubal didn't have to be told twice. He stood up, picked up his handgun, put it in his holster, and then took a rifle from the desk.

"Sheriff," Evan said, "my advice to you would be to talk to Burkett. Tell him his men missed this time. Maybe next time he should send more."

"I'm sure Mr. Burkett had nothing to do with this."

"Well then maybe he'd appreciate a visit from you and the information that he's got seven dead men."

Evan picked up his guns and started for the door, followed closely by Sam and Jubal.

Before leaving Sam turned and said, "Much obliged for your understanding, Sheriff."

———

FROM THE SHERIFF'S office they went back to the hardware store, where Serena had waited all this time.

"At last!" she said when they entered. "I was so worried. Jubal, are you hurt?"

Jubal looked down at his left arm. The shirt had been torn by the bullet, and his flesh inside creased. Whatever bleeding it had done had long dried.

"Are you all right, Jube?" Sam asked.

"I'm fine," Jubal said. "Don't make a fuss."

"Are you all okay?" Serena asked. "It sounded like a war."

"It wasn't a war," Sam said, "just a battle."

"And we won it," Jubal was quick to point out. "Seven men were waiting to bushwack Sam when he came out of the tele-graph office."

"Seven?" That someone would think it would take so many men to do it seemed to shock Serena. It was as if she was just beginning to believe the stories she had heard about Sam McCall.

"Don't worry," Jubal said. "We got them all. In fact, I think if we hadn't come along Sam would have gotten them all anyway. They were amateurs, weren't they, Sam?"

Sam seemed deep in thought and appeared not to have heard a word Jubal said.

"Be still, Jubal," Evan said. "If we hadn't gotten there Sam would be dead."

"He coulda taken them all, I tell ya," Jubal said. "Couldn't you, Sam?"

"You're right about one thing, Jubal," Sam said.

"What's that?"

"They *were* amateurs, or we'd all be dead."

"What are you getting at?" Evan asked. "You don't think they were sent by Burkett?"

"I don't know," Sam said. "The sheriff was right about that. Just because they were Burkett's men doesn't mean he sent them. I think if Burkett wanted me dead he would have sent a hired gun."

"You mean, someone like Coffin?" Evan asked.

"Coffin?" Jubal said. "Who's Coffin?"

"A gun for hire," Evan said.

"And he's here?"

"Yes."

"Why didn't you tell us?" Serena asked.

"We just found out today."

"So if Burkett hired Coffin," Evan said, "why would he send seven of his hands after you?"

"That's what I'm thinkin'."

"Look," Serena said, "you boys haven't eaten since breakfast—"

"We didn't have breakfast," Jubal said. "You know what? I just realized how hungry I am."

"I have to make dinner for Papa," she said. "Come back to the house and I'll cook for all of you."

"Sounds good to me," Jubal said.

"I'd like to go to the hotel and clean up first," Sam said.

"So would I," Evan said.

"Evan, you can clean up at Dude's house," Sam said. "Why don't you go back there with Serena?"

"All right. Jube, why don't you go with your big brother and keep him out of trouble?"

"I'll do my best," Jubal said, "but you know what the sheriff said."

"What did the sheriff say?" Serena asked.

Evan patted her on the shoulder and said, "I'll tell you when we get back to the house."

CHAPTER ELEVEN

Sheriff Kelly hated to be the one to tell Lincoln Burkett about his men, but since all of his men were dead, there was no one else. As soon as the McCall brothers left his office he went to the livery for his horse and rode out there. He was met at the front of the house by the foreman, Chuck Conners.

Conners had been expecting his men back from town with news about Sam McCall. When he saw Sheriff Kelly riding hell bent for leather through the gate and toward the house, he had a bad feeling.

"What can I do for you, Sheriff? Second visit today," Conners said.

"I'm afraid I have bad news, Mr. Conners," Kelly said. He saw his chance to avoid talking to Burkett himself.

"What kind of bad news?"

"Well, it seems that some of your men got into a shootout with Sam McCall."

"Is that right? Kill him, did they? Are they in your jail?"

"Uh, no sir, they're at the undertaker's."

"All of them?" Conners asked. "McCall killed all of them?"

"Well, he had some help from his brothers."

"Damn."

"I know, it's a terrible shame," Kelly said. "I don't know what got into those men, but Sam McCall is the kind of man who—"

"I'll tell Mr. Burkett about this, Sheriff," Conners said, interrupting him.

"Would you? I'd really appreciate—"

"Tell me something, Sheriff."

"What?"

"How did you find out about this?"

"I, uh, heard the shooting—"

"I thought you were supposed to be watching the Mc-Calls."

"Uh, yeah, well, there *is* three of them, and I was watchin' one of the others, see—"

"All right, forget it," Conners said. "You can go back to town."

"Will you, uh, arrange for burial for your men?"

"I'm sure Mr. Burkett will want to take care of it," Conners said.

"Uh, Mr. Conners, you wouldn't know why your men went after Sam McCall, would you?"

"No, I wouldn't," Conners said, "and neither would Mr. Burkett. Like you said, Sam McCall does bring that out in some men."

"Yeah, that he does," Kelly said. "Well, I'll be gettin' back."

"Sure."

Conners watched Kelly ride back toward town, then took a few moments to formulate his story before he went in to see Burkett.

———

LINCOLN BURKETT LISTENED CAREFULLY to Chuck Conners' news about the men who had been killed by Sam McCall.

"How many did we lose?" he asked when Conners stopped talking.

"Seven, sir."

"Who?"

"Gear, Murray, Tobin, Gary, three others. I'll have to find out who they all were."

Burkett slammed his hand down on the top of his desk.

"What the hell did they think they were doing?"

"I don't know, sir. I guess they just saw Sam McCall, knew his reputation—"

"I don't want this repeated, Conners," Burkett said. "I want you to tell all the other men they are to stay away from Sam McCall and his brothers unless they are told otherwise. Understand?"

"I understand, sir."

"Son-of-a-bitch!" Burkett said. "Dude Miller and his cronies are going to jump on this with both feet. Did you tell the sheriff we knew nothing about it?"

"I did."

Burkett sat behind his desk quietly for a moment, then said, "Chuck, I want the editor of the newspaper out here."

Vengeance Creek's newspaper, the Eagle, was a four-page publication that appeared three times a week.

"The editor of the Eagle? Why is that?"

"I want him to interview me about this attempt on Sam McCall's life. I want to make it clear in the newspaper that I knew nothing about it. Get him for me."

"It'll be dark in half an hour—"

"All right, then, tomorrow, first thing, get him here."

"I'll send someone—"

"No, don't send someone. Get him here yourself."

"All right, Mr. Burkett," Conners said.

"Now get out. I've got to think about what I'm going to say."

"Yes, sir."

Conners left the office, closed the door behind him, and breathed a sigh of relief. From now on he'd leave the thinking to Burkett and did what he did best—take orders. It was good for a man to find his niche in life.

ON THE WAY back to the hotel Sam and Jubal passed the saloon.

"How about a drink before we go to the hotel?" Sam asked.

"Sure, I could use one."

"You do drink, don't you?"

"Sam," Jubal said, "I'm twenty-four, remember. I'm not a kid."

"Oh, yeah, I keep forgettin'."

They went into the saloon, which was doing a brisk business

as darkness fell. More than a few men knew who Sam was and stared at him. Already word of the shootout had spread, and the stories had conveniently left out the fact that Evan and Jubal McCall were also involved. That was the way legends grew.

They went to the bar, and Sam ordered two beers. In the mirror he could see Coffin sitting at a back table by himself, nursing a beer.

"Make that three," he told the bartender.

"Who's the third one for?" Jubal asked.

"A new acquaintance."

"Who?"

As the bartender laid the beers in front of them Sam picked up two of them and said, "Wait here and watch my back, all right?"

"All right, Sam, but—"

"Just stay here."

Sam turned and walked with two beers to Coffin's table.

"Need a fresh one?"

Coffin looked up at him for a moment, then shrugged and said, "Why not?"

Sam laid the fresh beer down in front of Coffin, and then pulled out the chair across from him and sat down.

"I didn't know the price for the beer would be your company."

"Let's cut the shit, Coffin," Sam said. "I don't know why, and I don't know where, but I do know you were out on that street today, and you backshot two of those men."

"What men are you talking about, McCall?"

"The beer is my way of sayin' thanks," Sam went on, "but I have a feeling that you weren't helpin' me out of the goodness of your heart. What was in it for you, Coffin?"

"I suppose you're talking about this already famous telegraph office shootout where you outshot seven men and killed them all?"

"You know as well as I do how reputations are built, Coffin."

Coffin smiled tightly and said, "Yeah, I know, Sam."

"Are you workin' for Burkett?"

"Burkett who?"

"All right," Sam said, "you had your reasons for what you did. If you *are* workin' for Burkett, then maybe you and I will meet, maybe that's why you helped me out there today, I don't know. What I do know is that I have enough to do without having to worry about you."

"You don't have to worry about me, Sam," Coffin said. "If I come for you, for whatever reason, you know I'll come straight at you."

"That's what I figured," Sam said. "I just wanted to hear you say it. Enjoy the beer."

"Thanks," Coffin said, raising the mug to Sam, "I will."

Sam walked back to the bar and stood next to Jubal.

"Is that Coffin?"

"That's him."

"What was that all about?"

Sam sipped his beer and said, "Just establishing the rules, that's all."

"Rules?"

"Yeah," Sam said, "remember that, Jube. Every game has rules, you just have to establish them."

"I'll remember."

"And," he added, "remember that there's always somebody around to break them."

"Coffin?"

"No, Coffin's a pro and will go by the rules," Sam said. "It's usually the goddamned amateurs who muck everythin' up."

"Like today?"

"Exactly like today."

At Dude Miller's house Evan was watching Serena prepare dinner. Actually, he was helping her.

"I'm not used to doing this," he said, trying desperately to peel potatoes.

"You're doing fine."

She was cutting several chickens into pieces and when she finished that she sat down and helped him peel the potatoes.

"I'm not used to cooking for so many men," she said.

"We all eat the same way."

"But not the same amount."

She fell silent and looked pensive, so he left her alone with her thoughts. Eventually she would speak her mind.

"Tell me about Sam," she finally said.

"I'm here and you want to talk about Sam?" he asked. "You really know how to flatter a guy."

"I'm just interested."

"All right," he said, "What do you want to know about him?"

"His reputation."

"Serena," Evan said, "you're going to have to be more specific."

"Is he really a killer?" she blurted.

He stared at her for a few moments, then said, "We all killed someone today, Sam, Jube, and me."

"You know what I mean," she said. "Is his reputation so...so fearsome that seven men—*seven men*—had to try and kill him today?"

"There isn't one of those men who would have had the courage to face him alone," Evan explained. "That's their problem, Serena."

"But his reputation—"

"A reputation is like gossip," he said. "It starts at one end of town and by the time it gets to the other end it's grown into something entirely different."

"Is that true of Sam?"

"Look," Evan said, "I've seen Sam maybe three or four times in the last I don't know how many years. I know as much about him as you do, because I've read and heard the same stories."

"But you're his brother," Serena said. "You know him— the real him."

"The real Sam McCall is what you see, Serena. Judge him on that, not on anything else."

"I suppose you're right."

"Satisfied?"

She smiled and said, "Yes."

"Good," he said, smiling, "now maybe we can talk about me."

———

DUDE MILLER INSISTED on coming downstairs to dinner and was assisted by Evan and Jubal. Serena had also invited Ed Collins to come by and eat with them.

"I heard what happened today," Collins said.

"Who could help but hear?" Miller said. "It sounded like a war."

"So what do you boys plan to do now?" Collins asked over dinner.

The McCalls exchanged glances and in that moment silently chose Evan as the spokesman.

"We plan on rinding out who killed our parents."

"You don't believe that your father did it himself?"

"No," Evan said.

"You boys hadn't seen your father in a long time," Miller said. He seemed intent on playing the devil's advocate.

"That don't matter," Jubal said. He couldn't restrain himself. "Pa wouldn'ta done that."

"I agree," Dude Miller said.

"Well, so do I," Collins said. "How do you plan to go about it?"

"We don't rightly know that, Mr. Collins," Evan said.

"Please, call me Ed. Anybody who's planning on making a move on Lincoln Burkett is a friend of mine."

"We didn't say we were moving on Burkett."

"You don't have to," Collins said. "Anything dirty that's happening in this town, Lincoln Burkett is behind it, take my word for it."

"You fellas haven't been able to convince the Town Council of that, have you?" Sam asked.

"Not a chance," Miller said. "They're blinded by what they think Burkett can do for this town."

"They don't realize what he's going to do to it," Collins said.

"And what's that?" Evan asked.

Collins sat forward and momentarily forgot about Serena's delicious chicken and potatoes dinner.

"He wants to put this town right under his thumb," he said, his face reddening, "and once he's done that he'll set himself to grinding it under his heel. Before long, he'll want to change the name of the town."

"Well," Jubal said, "hopefully not until we've made it live up to its old name."

"Well," Collins said, "take my advice and concentrate your efforts on Lincoln Burkett."

Later, in his hotel room, Evan wished that Collins was basing his opinion on more than just a personal dislike for the man. Still, he tended to agree with the man, moreso because of the attempt on Sam's life. Even if Burkett hadn't sent them after Sam, Burkett's men must have thought they'd be doing their boss some good by killing him, and since Sam and Jube and Evan himself were only in Vengeance Creek to look for their parents' killer, there had to be a connection.

The presence of Coffin only underscored Burkett's involvement in his parents' death. If Burkett had nothing to do with it, there wouldn't be any reason for him to worry, and there wouldn't be any reason for him to import a professional gun. He certainly didn't need Coffin to strengthen his hold on the town. His only obstacles were Miller and Collins, and he'd already demonstrated that he had the right kind of men to handle them.

He decided to go to sleep. All the thinking was giving him a headache. What he had to do tomorrow was find himself a poker game. He was always able to think clearest with a deck of cards in his hand.

IN HIS ROOM Sam was also thinking about Burkett's possible involvement in the death of his parents. What he couldn't figure out was why Burkett would need to kill his parents after he'd already taken their ranch from them. What possible harm could they have done him then?

Sam knew that Evan had already talked to Burkett but figured maybe he should take a ride out there himself tomorrow and pay his respects.

In his room Jubal McCall was just plain restless. He thought their best bet to settle this was just to ride out to Burkett's—to his *parents'* ranch—and kill the man.

He knew his brothers would never agree to that, but maybe he ought to surprise them and just go and do it himself.

Serena Miller couldn't sleep. Something had happened that she had never expected. With the arrival of the McCall brothers she found herself attracted to two of them. Actually, she was attracted to Evan, but she was intrigued by Sam. After the attempt on his life today there was an aura of danger about him. She still could not believe that someone thought it would take seven men to kill him. How could one man command that much respect—or that much fear?

She wished she knew him better, but she doubted that there would be enough time.

Dude Miller was excited.

He believed that the attempt on Sam McCall's life had set in motion a series of events that would result in the end of Lincoln Burkett. There was no way Burkett was going to come out on top of the McCall brothers—not all three of them. Sam McCall was, of course, the most dangerous of the three, as evidenced by the fact that seven men had been sent by somebody to kill him. The fact that his brothers had saved him just proved how tough the three of them would be to beat.

He didn't know how long it would take, but Dude Miller was sure the McCalls would defeat Lincoln Burkett, and then Vengeance Creek could get back to the task of growing on its own.

Ed Collins sat with the gun in his lap and stared down at it. Tonight he had not laid the barrel on his tongue. He had taken it out and held it, and now he was ready to put it away.

He wasn't about to kill himself before he saw the outcome of the McCall-Burkett fight.

Part Three

SEARCH FOR VENGEANCE

CHAPTER TWELVE

Nothing happened for several days.

The McCalls, with Serena, continued to ask questions and keep their ears open around town. At the end of each day they had dinner at Dude Miller's house and compared notes. They were all getting used to Serena Miller's fine cooking.

Jubal started teasing Evan about Serena whenever he got the chance. It was obvious, he said, that Serena was sweet on Evan.

It was obvious to Evan that although he and Serena got along quite well, it was Sam who interested her the most. What he couldn't figure out was whether or not her interest was romantic. He rarely saw her speak to Sam, unless they were all together. She also looked at Sam with a degree of interest, and awe. Sometimes, Evan wished she would look at him that way.

Over the course of the next several days Dude Miller improved to the point where he was no longer confined to bed. He took all his meals in the kitchen and spent most of his day in the living room.

In the evening Evan had taken to playing poker in the saloon. If he was going to hear anything worth hearing, it would be in there.

They decided that during the poker games Jubal and Sam would take turns standing at the bar, watching Evan's back. Whichever one was at the bar, the other would be with Serena and Dude Miller at the house.

———

Evan and Jubal left the house to go to the saloon, which left Sam to help Serena clean up after dinner.

"You don't have to do that," she said, as he cleared the table and carried the plates and utensils to the sink.

"It's all right," Sam said. "I have nothin' better to do."

"Why don't you go out into the living room with Pa and have a drink?"

He stopped and looked at her. He was so big that standing, he dwarfed the kitchen. When he was there with her she felt crowded—and he always wore his gun. Evan and Jubal, when they were there with her, kept their guns close, but they didn't always wear them. Sam never took his off.

"Is there some reason you don't want me in the kitchen with you?"

She stopped what she was doing and turned to look at him. She was drying her hands on a towel. Her hair was caught back above her nape, but some strands had come loose and were flying around her head. He thought he'd never seen anything prettier.

"You make me nervous."

"I do?" he asked, surprised.

"Maybe I should say you... intimidate me."

"Why?"

She didn't answer, but her eyes went to the gun on his hip.

"Oh."

"Do you ever take it off?"

"Sometimes," he said, "when I sleep."

"Sometimes?"

"It's not always wise to take it off, even when I'm asleep."

"Must you..." she started, then shook her head and stopped.

"Go ahead," he said. "If you want to ask me something, ask me."

"Could you sit down? You're... very big."

"I'll sit if you'll' give me a cup of coffee."

"All right."

"And have one with me."

"A-all right."

She poured two cups of coffee, came to the table with them, and sat down.

"Must you always be afraid that someone will...will try to kill you?"

"I guess I must."

"That must be a horrible way to live," she said. "How do you stand it?"

"The way I live is of my own choosing."

"Really?"

"Well," he said, "it's a result of the way I chose to live my life when I was younger."

"Is that when you made most of your...reputation?"

He scratched his jaw.

"That's hard to say," he said. "Let's say it's when I set the tone for the rest of my life."

"I'm afraid I don't understand..."

"What do you know about me?"

"Only what I've read, and heard."

"How much of that do you believe?"

"I...I guess I believed most of it, until..."

"Until what?"

"Until I met you...again."

"And now?"

"Now, I guess I'm confused."

"I had a wild youth."

"Unfortunately," he said. "Some of the things I did caused me to gain a reputation."

"And you have to pay for that for the rest of your life?"

He shrugged and said, "Yes."

"And you accept that?"

"I have no choice."

"You could take your gun off."

"What would have happened to me if I hadn't had my gun on a few days ago, when those men tried to ambush me?"

"I—I suppose you would have been killed."

"That fate doesn't appeal to me, Serena."

"What if you stayed here, lived here?"

"Here, in your house?"

She blushed and said, "I mean, what if you took up residence somewhere and took off your gun. Wouldn't your reputation... uh, go away after a while?"

"That kind of a reputation never goes away, Serena," he said.

"At some time someone would recognize me and decide to try me. It's happened before."

She looked interested.

"You tried to do this before?"

"Once," he said, "in Mexico. I thought I could settle down there and not be bothered."

"Settle?" she asked. "Uh, did you have a woman?"

"I had a wife."

"A wife?"

"Yes," he said. "A beautiful Mexican girl."

"What happened?"

"I was recognized by a man who wanted me to face him with my gun."

"And what happened?"

"I refused."

"And?"

"And he and his three friends raped and killed my wife when I was away from my house."

"Oh my God," she said, going pale. "W-what did you do?"

"I killed them."

She swallowed and asked, "All of them?"

"Yes, all of them."

"T-thereby adding to your reputation."

He nodded and said, "Through no fault of my own, right?"

"Of course."

"Wrong," he said. "What happened was a result of the way I chose to live my life when I was younger. You see, I can't escape it, Serena. I've tried."

She stared at him for a few moments, her eyes moist, and then she said, "I'm sorry, Sam."

"Don't be," Sam said. "It was a long time ago. Would you like me to help you wash these cups?"

"No," she said, "no..."

He stood up and said, "Do I still make you nervous?"

She looked up at him and said, "Yes."

He smiled and said, "Don't worry, it'll pass."

Sam left the kitchen and went into the living room with Dude Miller.

EVAN MCCALL LOOKED DOWN at his cards. It was the best hand he'd had all night, and he wanted to be careful not to tip it.

They were playing seven-card stud, and he had all but one card. He already had a flush, with two of the flush cards in the hole and three on the table. He still had a shot at a straight flush to the queen, if his seventh card was a jack of spades.

He looked up at Jubal, who was standing at the bar with a beer in his hand. Jubal raised his mug a half inch, just to tell his brother everything looked all right.

At that moment the batwing doors opened and four men entered. They were all Burkett's men and, in fact, one of them was John Burkett, Lincoln Burkett's son.

Evan and Jubal didn't know that, because they had never seen him before.

The Burkett men walked to the bar, and it was plain that they had already been doing some drinking elsewhere.

"What'll it be John?" Jubal heard the bartender ask.

"A bottle for me and my friends," John Burkett said. He resembled his father slightly, but since Jubal had still not seen Lincoln Burkett, he didn't notice that. All he saw was a man about his own age, slighter than he was, pale, with a poor growth of beard. It was clear to Jubal that the others were with him, and he was in charge.

He leaned over to the bartender and asked, "Who is that fella?"

"Why, that's Lincoln Burkett's son, John," the barkeep said.

"Thanks," Jubal said, and proceeded to listen very carefully...

"When is this geologist supposed to be getting in, John?" one of the other men asked.

"He was supposed to have been here already," John Burkett said.

"We just gonna wait for him?"

"For as long as it takes," John Burkett said.

"I can't think of a better place to wait," one of the others said.

"You can't?" Burkett asked. "I can."

"Where?"

"Louise's."

"Johnny, you know you been gettin' kicked out of there."

"Yeah, but now I know why."

"Why?"

"My old man," John Burkett said, "he bought the place."

"And he wants to keep you out?"

"Yeah," John Burkett said, "he's trying to save me from myself."

"So what're we gonna do?"

"Tonight, we're going in there and we're gonna get us Louise's best girls—for free."

"All right," one of the other men said, and they all laughed.

"Except for you, Truck."

"Why?" the man called Truck asked.

"You gotta stay outside and wait for the geologist."

"That ain't fair!"

"I never said it was. Come on, drink up—the girls are waiting."

The men drank up and followed John Burkett out of the saloon.

At the poker table Evan raked in his chips. He had filled in for the straight flush, which was fortunate because one of the other men had had a higher flush than his.

"You got to be the luckiest man alive," the disgruntled loser said.

"It isn't luck," Evan said.

"What do you call it, then?"

"You wait for the right hand," Evan said, "and you play it right. That's all for me, gentlemen."

"Whataya mean?" the loser asked. "You ain't gonna give me a chance to win my money back?"

"I'll be here tomorrow night."

"Well, I won't," the man said. "I'm leavin' in the mornin', and you ain't leavin' this table with my money."

The table went quiet and everyone around it sensed the tension. Jubal straightened up at the bar and picked up his rifle. It was one of the ones he'd gotten from the gunsmith shop the day of the ambush on Sam. Ed Collins had insisted that they keep the rifles.

"I say I am, friend," Evan said. "If you can't make it back in this game, you can make it back somewhere down the road."

"I wanna make it back tonight, friend," the man said. "The only way you're leavin' this table is dead."

Evan eyed the man coldly and said, "Then the next play is all yours."

One of the other players leaned over and said, "Don't you know who that is?"

The loser's eyes flickered and he said, "I don't care who he is. He ain't leavin' the table with my money."

"His name is McCall," the other man said urgently. "He's Sam McCall's brother."

"Sam McCall?" the loser said.

The helpful player said out of the side of his mouth, "And Sam McCall is in town."

The loser's eyes flickered again and his shoulders slumped as he relaxed.

"Come on," Evan said. "Am I leaving or not?"

"Sure, friend," the loser said, "sure. You won, you can leave if you want to. I don't want no trouble."

Evan picked up his money and walked over to the bar, to stand next to Jubal.

"Everything all right?" Jubal asked.

"Sure," Evan said. "I'm Sam McCall's brother, ain't I? Why wouldn't everything be all right?"

"You need a drink."

"Yeah."

"Beer?"

"Whiskey."

Jubal called the bartender over and asked for a whiskey.

"Guess who I just saw," Jubal asked when Evan had his drink.

"Who?"

"Burkett."

"Lincoln Burkett was here?" Evan asked, looking at his brother.

"No, not Lincoln," Jubal said, "John, his son."

"Oh, so?"

"He and some of his friend went over to the whorehouse. It seems Lincoln Burkett owns it and has been keeping his kid out."

"I wonder what else Lincoln Burkett owns that nobody knows about."

"Maybe we should find out."

"How?"

"Well," Jubal said, "we could ask his son."

"Bracing Burkett's son is looking for trouble."

"Ain't that why we're here?"

Evan finished his drink and put his glass on the bar. He was still seething over what had happened at the table. He wasn't angry that he'd been braced so much as by how it had been resolved. He'd always solved his own problems and had never before depended on being Sam McCall's brother.

"Evan?"

"Are you interested in a whore tonight, Jube?"

"What?"

"Share a girl with a fella, buy him a few drinks, and he might talk to you."

"Share a girl..."

"Well," Evan said, "maybe you won't have to go that far."

Jubal still wasn't quite sure what his brother was talking about, but when Evan said, "Come on," he followed him out of the saloon.

————

Although Evan and Jubal had not been to Louise's before they knew where it was from passing it on the street. It was a building the size of the hotel, but there was no sign over the door proclaiming it a whorehouse. Still, everyone in town knew what it was.

The front door was locked, so they had to knock to gain entry. The man who opened the door was almost as big as Sam, and uglier.

"Whataya want?" he asked.

"What do you think we want?" Evan asked. "You serve food here?"

"Hell, no," the man said. "Just whiskey and women."

"We'll settle for that," Evan said.

"Come on in," the man said, stepping back.

When they entered they were almost blinded by the crystal in the chandeliers. In a room filled with overstuffed sofas and brocade curtains, men and women sat around, relaxed, drinking, the women in various stages of undress. The men were comfortable, but they still had their pants on.

Someone was playing a piano in one corner, and some men and women were standing by the piano, dancing.

"Would you look at this place?" Jubal asked. "What's a place like this doing in Vengeance Creek?"

"I don't know," Evan said, still looking around in wonderment.

"Well, well, new blood," a woman said, approaching them. She was in her thirties, heavily made up, with lips as red as blood and hair as black as night. She was wearing a black nightgown that left little to a man's imagination.

"Hello, boys, my name is Louise. I run this place. I can see you're impressed, and this is just the downstairs. You should see what happens upstairs."

Jubal was dumbstruck. He'd been in whorehouses before, but he'd never seen a place like this. Evan had, but only in Portsmouth Square, in San Francisco.

"You boys want to start with a drink?"

"Uh, sure," Evan said.

"Well, come on then," she said, linking her arms in theirs. "The whiskey is included in the price."

She took them into the sitting room and turned them over to two girls. One was a tall, lank blonde with small breasts, the other a slightly chubby redhead with a very pretty face. They gave each man a drink and sat with them on a sofa. Evan and Jubal were between the two women, who were pressing their thighs tightly against the brothers'.

Jubal looked up and saw John Burkett and two of his friends pushing past the big man at the door.

"Uh-oh," the blonde said. "Looks like trouble."

Evan and Jubal watched as the big bouncer tried to bar the three men from entering.

"Look, fat boy," they heard John Burkett say, "if you want to keep your job you'll get out of the way."

"You are not allowed in here," the big man said.

"If you don't move," Burkett said, "we're gonna move you."

At that moment Louise appeared with another big man in tow. The second man joined the first man in blocking the door.

"Please, John," Louise said, pleading, "you know your father doesn't want you in here."

"Tell these two to step aside, Louise," John Burkett said.

"John—"

She didn't get any further before John Burkett threw a punch at one of the men. The big man caught the punch easily and pushed it aside.

"Don't hurt him," Louise said loudly.

"Move on, cowboy," the bouncer said.

"To hell with you," Burkett said, and threw another punch. This one bounced off the man's nose, angering him. He drew back a massive fist.

"Don't hurt him!" Louise shouted, but the man was beyond hearing her.

John Burkett ducked and the punch hit the man behind him, knocking him out. The third man with Burkett turned to leave, but the second bouncer caught him by the collar, turned him around, and knocked him to the floor with one punch.

"Now's your chance," Evan said to Jubal.

"For what?"

"Get in there," Evan said, pushing Jubal up off the sofa.

The girls moved so that they were sandwiching Evan between them, and he threw an arm around each of them and settled back to watch.

Both bouncers had now cornered John Burkett, and there was no way he was going to be able to duck a punch this time.

As one of the bouncers drew back his fist Jubal launched himself and landed on the man's back. Burkett, seeing a reprieve, lowered his head and drove it into the other man's belly, staggering him back. As the man straightened up Burkett hit him with a punch. The man rocked back on his heels, but refused to go down.

Meanwhile, Jubal was riding the other man like he was a bucking bronco, holding on for dear life as the people in Louise's came to life and began shouting encouragement to the two young men.

Jubal slid his forearm down across the man's throat and began to throttle him. Meanwhile, Burkett had hit his opponent again, and then fell back a step and launched a kick that landed right between the big man's legs. The bouncer gagged and slowly fell to his knees. From that position it was easy for Burkett to kick him in the chin, finally felling the man like a huge tree.

Jubal's man was blue in the face by this time and had gone to his knees. This allowed Jubal to plant his feet on the floor for better leverage, and before long the big man was unconscious. Jubal released his hold before he killed him, and the bigger man fell to the floor.

The place went crazy, cheering and yelling and stomping their feet.

Burkett and Jubal, both huffing and puffing, looked at each other across the two fallen men, and John Burkett smiled.

"Much obliged for the help," he said.

"Couldn't see letting them pound on you. Two-to-one odds just ain't fair."

"You two better get out of here," Louise said.

Jubal looked at Burkett, raising his eyebrows.

"Now that you're in, what do you want to do?"

"I proved my point," John Burkett said. "How about I buy you a drink someplace else, by way of thanks?"

"Sure."

They started for the door and Louise said, "What about them?" She was pointing to the two men who had come in with Burkett.

"When they wake up, tell them to meet me at the saloon," Burkett said. "I'll be buying my friend a drink."

Burkett went out the door and before following him Jubal looked over at Evan and smiled.

Evan pulled the two girls to him tightly and said, "Now, which one of you ladies is going to offer to show me the upstairs?"

The blonde leaned over, put her tongue in his ear, and said huskily, "Why not both of us?"

Evan smiled and said, "Sure, why not?"

CHAPTER THIRTEEN

S am was awakened by an insistent pounding on the door. He got out of bed and staggered naked to answer it. When he swung it open he saw his brothers standing in the hallway.

"Jesus," Evan said, "is that the way you always answer the door?"

"When I'm awakened at an ungodly hour, yes," Sam said. "What the hell is it?"

"We want to have coffee in the hotel dining room," Evan said.

"Coffee here?" Sam said. "But we're gonna have breakfast at Serena's."

"We won't ruin our breakfast," Evan said. "There are some things we have to talk about without Serena listening."

Sam ran his hand over his face and said wearily, "What things?"

"Get dressed and we'll talk downstairs. We'll wait for you there."

"All right, all right," Sam said. "Just gimme five minutes."

He closed the door, splashed some water on his face, got dressed, and strapped on his gun. He couldn't imagine what his brothers had found out that they wouldn't want Serena to hear. But if they were so eager to talk to him about it that they'd awakened him early, it must have been important.

He left his room and went down to the dining room.

———

"IT'S NOT SO MUCH what we found out that we don't want Serena to hear," Evan said, "but where."

Jubal laughed.

"We followed John Burkett to the whorehouse last night," he said. "I made friends with him by keeping him from getting his head bashed in. I left and went to the saloon with him for a drink, and Evan stayed at the whorehouse. That's what he doesn't want Serena to find out about."

Amused, Sam looked at his middle brother.

Evan shrugged and said, "It would have been impolite for both of us to leave."

"Of course," Sam said. "John Burkett is Lincoln's son, right? Why would he talk to you, Jube?"

"He's never seen me. In fact, I'd never seen him before last night. A couple of bouncers were going to take him apart at the whorehouse. I helped him."

"And became his friend."

"Right."

"Why?"

"To see what I could find out from him."

"And? Did you find out anythin'?"

Jubal looked at Evan, and then back at Sam.

"Yes, I did. John and three other men were sent to town to await the arrival of another man, a man his father has been waiting impatiently for for over three months, since he first sent for him. The man's name is Jason Cord."

"What's so important about this Cord?"

"He's a geologist, Sam," Evan said.

Sam looked at Evan and said, "A geologist?"

"Interesting, huh?"

"Now what would Lincoln Burkett need with a geologist?" Sam wondered aloud.

"That's what we were wondering," Evan said.

"Gold," Jubal said. "It's got to be, and I'll bet it was on Pa's land."

"Gold?" Sam said. "On the ranch? If that's the case, why would Pa sell it?"

"Maybe he didn't know," Evan said. "Maybe Burkett did."

"This might tell us why Burkett wanted the ranch," Sam

said, "but it still doesn't tell us why Pa made the deal he made with Burkett. Did John Burkett have anythin' to say about that?"

"No," Jubal said. "He was pretty drunk to start with, and got drunker still. All he did most of the night was complain about the way his father treats him. His old man owns the whorehouse, Sam, and he keeps John out of it."

"Is Burkett the owner of record?" Sam asked.

"I doubt it," Evan said, "but we can check that today, at the courthouse. It would be interesting to know what businesses Burkett has bought out, and what deals he made with the owners."

"My guess," Sam said, "would be that whatever he's bought he hasn't done it openly. His name won't be on the record of the sale. He's not gonna want the town to know he's buyin' it up. Not yet."

"Maybe if they did find out," Evan said, "they wouldn't be so eager to have him as a citizen."

"Maybe somebody should let them know," Jubal said.

"Yeah, but we need proof first," Sam said. "After breakfast why don't you go and look it up, Evan. Jube, you can stay with Serena until Evan comes back."

"And what are you gonna do?"

"I thought I might go out and ride around the ranch a bit."

"If Burkett's men see you—" Evan started.

"That'll be their hard luck," Sam said.

"You think you're gonna find gold on the ground, just like that?" Jubal asked.

"I don't know what I'm gonna find," Sam said. "I won't know until I get out there."

"You're not going to see Burkett, are you?" Evan asked.

"I've thought about it," Sam said. "I think I'll play it by ear for a while, though. I'll try to be back before dinner."

"All right," Evan said, "we'd better get over to Serena's for breakfast."

As they left Sam wondered when they had started referring to the Miller house as "Serena's" and not "Dude's."

Serena wondered why Sam, Evan, and Jubal were so quiet at breakfast. She thought that they were probably planning something, but she didn't want to ask them yet. They were talking mostly to her father, but it was all small talk, about the past, about their parents.

After breakfast they went into the living room with her father while she cleaned up the kitchen.

There Evan said to Miller, "Dude, has there ever been a gold strike around here?"

"Here? Hell, no. What makes you ask that?"

The three brothers exchanged glances and then Evan said, "Burkett's brought in a geologist."

"A geologist? What would he need a geologist for?"

"We figure there's something on Pa's land that Burkett knew about. Gold seems the most likely thing."

"But why would your father—"

"We've already asked those questions, Dude," Evan said. "Sam's gonna ride out today and take a look around the ranch. Maybe he'll find something."

"Yeah, trouble," Miller said. "You can't let him go out there alone."

"We don't have a choice," Evan said. "I have something else to do. Jubal's going to stay here with Serena."

"There's no need for that," Miller said. "I'm fine now. Serena and I can go and open the store and stay there. I can take care of her."

"Just the same," Evan said, "Jubal'll go with you."

"Evan—"

"Do this our way, Dude," Sam said.

Miller looked at Sam and then said, "All right."

"I'm gonna leave now," Sam said. "I'll see you all later."

"Be careful," Jubal said.

"Always."

Just as Sam went out the front door Serena came into the room.

"Where's Sam?" she asked, looking at all of them in turn. "What's going on? You all look like you got caught with your hand in the cookie jar."

"I've got to go to the courthouse," Evan said. "Jube, explain it to her."

"Sure," Jubal said as Evan headed for the door, "thanks."

Sam went to the livery and told Swede he needed his horse.

"I'll get him for you, Sam," Swede said.

While Sam waited for his horse he thought back to his

prospecting days in Shasta County, California. That was another time when he'd thought he could put his gun down. It didn't work out any better than his marriage had, but he had learned about what to look for when searching for gold.

The Swede walked his horse out to him and handed him the reins.

"Are you going riding alone?"

"Yes."

"After what happened near the telegraph office—"

"The telegraph office!" Sam said.

"What about it?" Swede asked, but Sam had already mounted up and was riding to the hotel. The incident at the telegraph office had been several days ago, and Sam had completely forgotten to check for his reply.

He stopped at the hotel and went inside to the desk clerk.

"Is there a telegraph message for me?"

"I'll check, sir." The clerk turned and looked in Sam's box, then came out with a yellow slip of paper. He handed it to Sam.

"Thanks."

Sam took it outside and read it there. It was from Mur-dock, who said that while he was too far away to be of any use there was a man who might be able to help them out. His name was Carson, Frank Carson. Murdock further stated that he would have Carson ride into Vengeance Creek as soon as he could.

Good ol' Page, Sam thought. Came through, as always.

He put the message in his pocket to show to his brothers later, mounted up and rode out.

At the courthouse Evan McCall looked up the ownership of Louise's, which was on the records as a saloon. Louise Simon was the only owner of record. If Burkett did own a piece of the business—or the business as a whole—it was through a private deal he made with Louise.

That made sense to Evan. It fit with what he and his brothers figured, that Burkett would be keeping his movements to himself as long as possible.

There was no point in looking up any other records. If Burkett owned any other business it would not be reflected in any records that were available to the public.

Since he finished at the courthouse so early, Evan decided to ride after Sam, just in case his older brother found more trouble than he'd anticipated.

Jason Cord came down to breakfast at the Burkett house and found his host and his son waiting there for him. The breakfast that was laid out on the long dining room table was impressive: eggs, potatoes, ham and biscuits, flapjacks, coffee and milk.

"Well," Cord said, "this is quite a feast, gentlemen. Do you eat like this all the time?"

"Never mind that," Lincoln Burkett said. "Sit your skinny ass down and answer some questions, Cord."

Jason Cord was a rather timid man in his late twenties, sandy-haired, tall and thin. Violent language and violence had never been part of his life. He had thought twice about coming west, but the offer of payment was so good that he couldn't resist. And if he managed to find what Burkett thought he'd find, it would mean even more money.

"Urn, yes, sir," he said, sitting down. "What kind of questions?"

"Like where the hell you been for the past three months?" Burkett asked. "It shouldn't have taken you this long to get here from Chicago."

"Well, sir," Cord said, helping himself to the food on the table, "there were matters which had to be put to rest before I could leave Chicago. I had business dealings there which had to be transferred, and then there was the matter of my fiancee, Abigail. She was not very happy about my coming out here, but when I explained to her the possibilities—"

"You told her what you were coming out here to look for?" Burkett said, exploding. "I thought I made it clear in my letter that no one was to know—"

"No, no, Mr. Burkett," Cord was quick to say, "I did not tell her exactly what I was coming out to do, but I did tell her that very soon I would have the money to send for her—"

"All right, all right," Burkett said, "I don't want to hear about your goddamned woman. Just eat your breakfast and we'll get started."

"Yes, sir."

"And you?" Burkett said to his son.

"Yes, Pa?"

"You were at Louise's last night, weren't you? Causing a ruckus."

"Aw, Pa, we was just havin' some fun—"

"Never mind," Burkett said. "At your age you should be thinking less about fun and more about business."

"The business is yours, Pa, not mine."

"But it will be yours someday, God damn it!" Burkett said, slamming his hand down hard on the table. "I wish you'd stop getting drunk all the time—"

"I don't get drunk all the time—"

"I heard those bouncers at Louise's would have taken your head off if some fella hadn't helped you out."

"And it would have been your fault."

"My fault?"

"Sure, they work for you, don't they?" John Burkett said. "I mean, you own Louise's, don't you?"

"Where did you hear that?"

"Never mind where. You bought it and instructed her to keep me out. Why'd you do that?"

"Son," Burkett said, "if you want a woman I'll get you a woman. But if you keep mixing with those kind of women you're gonna end up with some goddamned disease or other. You want a wife, I'll get you one, but—"

"I'll get my own women, thank you," John said. "Jesus, Pa, I don't want you giving me everything."

"Then how do you expect to get it?" Lincoln Burkett demanded. "You don't do a lick of work!"

John was about to answer when Chuck Conners entered the room.

"Chuck," Burkett said, "come and fall to and have some breakfast. Meet Jason Cord, the geologist I sent for from the east."

"Mr. Cord."

"Cord, Conners is my foreman. You'll be taking orders from him as well as from me."

"Very good, sir."

As an afterthought Lincoln Burkett added, "And from my son."

John Burkett looked at his father in surprise.

"Your orders will come from one of the three of us and no one else. Do you understand?"

"I understand, Mr. Burkett."

"Johnny," Burkett said, "after dinner you and Chuck take Mr. Cord out and show him what we found. All right?"

"Sure, Pa," John Burkett said, "sure."

Sam knew the land that had been his father's very well. The land didn't change, and after all these years he still knew where everything was. For what he was looking for, he chose to check the streams and water holes that were on Burkett's land.

He rode the streams, dismounting every so often to stick his hand in the water and bring up some of the bottom. He was riding along the edge of a wide stream when he noticed something he hadn't noticed elsewhere: the soil here seemed blacker, and deeper, than in other places. He dismounted, grounded his horse's reins, and hunkered down on his heels.

He stuck his hand into the soil, which was like black mud, and lifted it to his nose. He sniffed it, then touched it to his lips so he could taste it. He rubbed it between his fingers and then between his palms and then fell deep into thought.

He stayed that way until he heard the sound of approaching horses. There was a stand of Joshua trees nearby, and he grabbed up his horse's reins and walked him over to it. He had just secreted himself there when he saw three riders coming from the other side of the stream. He had seen John Burkett around town a few times and recognized him. The same went to Chuck Conners, Burkett's foreman. The other man he didn't know, but from the way he was dressed and the way he sat his horse, it wasn't hard to peg him for an Easterner. He was probably the geologist Burkett had sent for.

Sam stood right next to his horse, keeping his hand on the animal's nose, wanting to keep him as quiet as possible until the three men had passed. They weren't passing, however. Instead they stopped several yards further down the stream from where he had stopped. That was good; they wouldn't notice his horse's tracks.

He watched as all three men dismounted. The geologist was the only one who hunkered down and examined the mud the way he had, but the man went further: he had some supplies and tools with him, and he was apparently going to run some tests.

Sam watched with great interest as the minutes passed and finally, after an hour or so, the geologist was apparently ready to leave. Sam watched the man take some samples of the mud and then all three men mounted up and rode off.

Sam walked his horse back down to the stream, over to where the geologist had been.

Suddenly, Sam was convinced that there was no gold here, but that there was something here that was almost as valuable.

He mounted up and headed back to town. He had a lot to tell his brothers.

――――

EVAN WAS BEGINNING to think he'd made a mistake. Although he knew the land almost as well as Sam, he didn't quite know what Sam would be looking for, or where. The ranch was large enough that they could ride around all day and never run into one another.

And then, of course, you could always run into someone just by accident.

When Evan saw the three riders approaching him he recognized two of them immediately. He could have turned and rode off, but he decided to brazen it out. For one thing, the third rider didn't look like he'd be any harm to anyone, and Evan doubted if there would be any violence.

As the three reached him they reined in.

"What are you doing here, fella?" Chuck Conners asked.

"Just riding around."

"You're on private property, you know."

"I know," Evan said, "but I'm not harming anything."

"That don't make no never mind, mister," John Burkett said. "I'd advise you to ride out of here right now, hear?"

"I hear you, boy."

John Burkett didn't seem to like being called "boy" anymore than Jubal McCall did.

"Mister, I don't know who you are—"

"The name's McCall."

"McCall?" Burkett said.

"Now I remember you," Conners said. "You're Evan McCall."

"That's right."

"I didn't recognize you without your fancy gambler's suit."

Before leaving town Evan had gone to his room to change from his dark suit into something more suitable for riding.

"What are you doing out here, McCall?"

"Just riding around, thinking back," Evan said, feigning interest in his surroundings. "You know, bringing back some memories."

"Look," Burkett said, "this land may have been yours once, but now it's mine—my father's and mine—and you don't belong here. I told you once and I'll tell you again. Haul ass!"

"Your father know what a bite you have when you have Conners to back you up?"

John Burkett's hand went for his gun, but Chuck Conner's hand got there first, blocking the move.

"Take it easy, kid," he said. "Remember who his brother is."

"I'm looking at him, not his damned brother," John Burkett said.

"I agree with the lad."

"Get going, McCall," Conner said, "before I see if you can take the two of us at once."

"I'm going, young Mr. Burkett, I'm going," Evan said, turning his horse.

"And don't come back!"

Evan waved at the men and started off at a leisurely pace. He wanted to avoid trouble, but he didn't want them to think they had run him off.

Although, of course, that was exactly what they had done.

CHAPTER FOURTEEN

E van McCall returned to the Miller house before Sam did.

"Sam back yet?" he asked Jubal as he entered.

"No. Anything wrong?"

"No," Evan said. "I finished at the courthouse early and rode out to find him. It was a bad idea."

"What happened?"

"I ran into John Burkett, Chuck Conners, and another man I took to be the geologist."

"Anything happen?"

"Not much," Evan said. "We all acted tough—except for the geologist. He just sat on his horse and looked scared."

"And you didn't see Sam?"

"No," Evan said. "It was a bad idea to go looking for him. He always knew the ranch better than I did."

"He should be back soon, shouldn't he?" Serena asked. Neither of the brothers had seen her enter from the kitchen.

"He should," Evan agreed, "depending on what he found."

Or, Evan thought to himself, *cm who found him.*

Sam's original intention after he left the stream was to ride back to town, but he decided to continue looking around. He figured he might find some more locations where there was black mud. He searched until early evening and found only one more place, not far from the first one. This one was at a water hole, a small basin of water where the black mud seemed to bubble up from below. Finally, he gave up, washed the mud off his hands in another stream, and headed back toward town.

When Burkett, Conners, and Cord returned to the ranch, Cord went off to do his tests while John Burkett and Conners sought out the elder Burkett. They found him out by the corral, where he had been talking to a couple of hands. He walked away from those men to talk to his son and his foreman.

"Did Cord get what he needed?" Lincoln Burkett asked.

"I guess he did," John said. "He poked around in the mud for an hour and then brought some back with him."

"Good," Lincoln Burkett said. "Before long we should know what we have. Now tell me what else happened."

"We ran across one of the McCalls," Conners said.

"Sam?"

"No, Evan, the gambler."

"And?"

"I would have taken him if Chuck hadn't stopped me," John Burkett said.

"Don't be a fool, boy," Lincoln Burkett said. "The man would have killed you."

"We're talking about Evan McCall, not Big Sam," John Burkett said.

"Evan McCall is no slouch with a gun," Chuck Conners said.

"And what if you had killed him?" the elder Burkett asked. "Sam McCall would track you down and shoot you like a dog."

"I'm not afraid of Sam McCall."

"You should be," Lincoln Burkett said.

"Are you?"

"Damn right."

"You're not afraid of anyone."

"Don't get me wrong, boy," Lincoln Burkett said. "If I had to face him I would, and if I could kill him I would, but that doesn't mean I'm not afraid of him. You should always fear *and* respect men like Sam McCall, and men like Coffin."

"What are we paying Coffin for?" the younger Burkett demanded. "So far all he's done is sit in town eating and drinking and whoring."

"So far that's all I'm paying him for."

"Why don't we send him after Sam McCall?"

"I will," Burkett said, "eventually, but the time's not right yet." The older man looked at his foreman and said, "What was Evan McCall doing on my land?"

"He said he was just riding around, thinking of old memories."

Lincoln Burkett rubbed his jaw thoughtfully.

"You think they know what's on this land?"

"I don't know—"

"If old man Joshua knew and wrote it down somewhere, they may know, too."

"And if they do?"

"If they do," Lincoln Burkett said, "I'll have to move my timetable up."

"Meaning what?"

"Meaning I may have to use Coffin sooner than I'd planned. Chuck, get some of the men together, send them out in groups of four or five."

"What do you want them to do?"

"I want anyone who doesn't belong on our land chased off."

"That include Sam McCall?"

"Yes," Burkett said, "that includes Sam McCall."

"You want McCall killed?"

Burkett took a moment to ruminate over that.

"I don't want to lose any more men, but this would be different from an ambush in town. He'd be trespassing, and we'd have a right to shoot him."

"Tell me what you want them to do, Mr. Burkett, and they'll do it."

"I'll ride out, too, Pa," John Burkett said. "If we see Sam McCall, we'll kill him."

"You stay here. I don't want to take a chance on you getting killed."

"Pa—"

"Do as I say!"

John Burkett gave his father a murderous glare and then stalked away.

"You hurt his pride," Conners said.

"I'd rather have that than have him get killed. Look, Chuck, talk to the men, make them understand that I don't want them going after Sam McCall unless they're absolutely sure they've got him outnumbered and out in the open. Once he gets himself in a position to shoot back, I want them to lightout. Understand?"

"I understand."

"Well, make sure *they* understand. I'll settle for them just chasing him off the property, if that's all they can accomplish."

"I'll make sure they know."

"All right," Lincoln Burkett said. "I'd better talk to Cord, and then I'll talk to the boy."

"He's not a boy anymore, Mr. Burkett."

"Maybe not," Lincoln Burkett said, "but he's certainly not thinking like a man yet, either. If he's somewhere in the middle I'll settle for that, because that's more than I've gotten from him in a long time."

———

"THAT'S HIM."

Jim Priest was pointing down at a lone rider. He and his men had topped a rise and spotted the rider immediately.

"How do you know?" Len Unger asked.

"He's riding a coyote dun," Priest said. "I heard in town that Sam McCall rides a coyote dun."

He turned and looked at Unger and the two men with him.

"What do we do?" Unger asked. "Take him?"

"Well," Priest said, "he is out in the open, and we do out-number him."

"So did Mike Gear and six other men in town," Unger reminded him.

"You have a point."

"Dan Hitchcock and his group are about ten miles east of here," Bill Granger said.

"And McCall is riding that way," Unger said.

"Good idea," Priest said. "We'll hook up with Hitchcock and his men, and then we'll take him."

The others agreed, and so the four began to ride parallel to Sam McCall.

———

SAM SPOTTED THEM IMMEDIATELY. If they hadn't been trying so hard not to be seen, he probably wouldn't have seen them.

At first he expected them to come riding down the hill, most likely shooting at him. When they didn't, he figured they were just there to watch him. He didn't mind if they watched him because he wasn't doing anything—now. He was simply riding back to town.

Suddenly he became aware that there were eight men instead of four. That meant that they would be twice as brave as before.

He was already spurring his horse on when he heard the first shot.

The fact that Big Sam McCall was running from them and not turning to fight them made the eight men, led by Jim Priest and Dan Hitchcock, even braver than before.

This caused several of them to ride faster, leaving behind others whose horses couldn't keep up. As they stretched out behind Sam McCall they didn't realize that this made them somewhat less menacing.

The man in front was Len Unger. His horse, a strapping mahogany bay, was the fastest of the eight. It was even starting to cut into the distance between Unger and Mc-Call's dun.

Sam guessed that they would probably chase him until he was off Burkett property. However, they were so filled with false courage that he could smell it. In such a condition they might chase him to the ends of the earth. He had to do something to deflate their courage.

Without warning Sam reined his dun around to stand sideways. He drew his gun, pointed at the lead man, who by this time was far ahead of the others, and fired. The man fired just a split second before Sam did. His bullet smacked into Sam's thigh just before Sam's bullet hit him in the center of his chest.

The impact of the bullet almost made Sam drop his gun. He holstered the weapon and grabbed his saddle pommel with both hands. Actually, he was glad the bullet had hit his thigh. A little to the right or left and the horse would have bought it. With a dead horse he would have been at the mercy of his pursuers.

Satisfied that one dead man would deter the other seven, he turned his horse and headed back to town on the run. He had to get there before loss of blood made him fall out of his saddle.

"JESUS!" Jim Priest shouted when he saw Len Unger.

Priest was the first to reach Unger. He dismounted and checked his fallen comrade.

The others caught up and looked down at Priest.

"One shot, through the chest," Priest said, looking up at them. "Clean."

They all looked up at the rapidly dwindling figure of Sam McCall.

"Ah," Hitchcock said, "let him go."

"Yeah," Priest said, standing up, "maybe he let us go, huh?"

Sam stopped only long enough to press his bandanna to the wound and tie it there with his belt. Either it was getting dark, or he was in danger of passing out. If he passed out he only hoped that the horse would find its way back to town.

"It's getting dark," Serena said, looking out the front window.

"She's worried about Sam," Jubal said to Dude Miller.

"You're not!" Miller asked.

"Sam can take care of himself," Evan said.

"Sure," Serena said, folding her arms beneath her breasts, "we saw that earlier in the week, didn't we?"

"Serena," Miller said, "take it easy."

"I'll take it easy when he gets back," she said, turning back to the window.

"Maybe she's right," Evan said to Jubal. "Maybe we should go and look for him."

"Sam's all right, Evan," Jubal said. "He don't need us to look after him. I still think he woulda handled all seven of those—"

"Someone's coming," Serena said, suddenly. "On a horse."

Evan looked at Jubal and said, "Why wouldn't he take his horse to the livery?"

Rising, Jubal said, "Why don't we go ask him?"

The four of them went out the front door to meet whoever was approaching. Serena was the first out the door, and as the horse was reined in she ran up to it.

"Sam," she said, putting her hand on his thigh, "we were so worried."

She felt something wet and sticky on her hand but before she could say anything Sam suddenly started to fall toward her.

"Sam!"

"Watch out!" Evan said.

He moved Serena out of the way in time to catch Sam before he hit the ground. Jubal rushed forward and took some of his older brother's weight.

"What's wrong with him?" Serena asked.

"He's been shot," Evan said. "Jube, get the doctor."

"Dude, help Evan," Jubal said.

"I'll get the doctor," Serena said.

"No, Serena," Evan said. "Stay here."

Dude Miller came forward and took Sam's legs from Jubal, who left to get help.

"Let's get him inside and see how bad he's hurt," Evan said.

Serena went ahead and opened the door, and Miller and Evan carried Sam in.

"Is he all right?" she asked anxiously.

"He's unconscious," Evan said.

"Should we take him upstairs?" Miller asked.

"No, no, put him on the sofa," Evan said, "on the sofa. Serena, get some water and some clean cloths."

Serena ran into the kitchen while Evan located the wound. When he found it he removed Sam's belt and bandanna and tore Sam's pants so he could look at it.

When Serena came back she said, "Shouldn't we wait for Doc Leader?"

"At Doc's age it could take him some time to get here," Evan said. "I just want to see what we've got."

He grabbed a cloth, wet it, and washed the area around the wound.

"How bad?" Serena asked.

"Could be worse," Evan said. "It could have hit his horse."

"What's that supposed to mean?" Serena demanded.

Evan looked at her and said, "It means if the bullet had killed his horse he wouldn't have been able to get away."

Serena looked contrite and said, "I'm sorry."

"Don't be," Evan said.

He took another cloth, folded it, and pressed it to the wound.

"Serena, hold this here," he said, "we've got to slow the bleeding until Doc arrives."

Serena got down on her knees next to the sofa and pressed

her hand to the wound. The torn pants legs was soaked in blood, and Evan tore it the rest of the way down and folded it away from Sam's leg so he could check for breaks.

"His leg isn't broken," Evan said.

"Glad to hear it," Doc Leader said, entering the room. "Now everyone out except Serena."

"Doc—" Serena said.

"And if you're gonna stay, you're gonna have to keep quiet."

Doc hunkered down next to Serena, then looked up at the other men.

"You heard me... out!"

Evan looked at Miller and Jubal and said, "Let's make some coffee."

Evan, Jubal and Miller were sitting at the kitchen table when Doc Leader came in.

"He's fine," Doc said. He put a basin down on the table. It contained bloody water and a spent bullet. He wiped his hands on a white cloth. "The wound is clean, I got the bullet, and there's no infection. He'll be fine. Who's payin' my bill?"

"I am," Evan said..

"I should—" Miller said, but Evan cut him off.

"He's my brother."

"We'll pay the bill," Jubal said, standing up.

Doc Leader nodded and said, "Put him upstairs in a bed and leave Serena with him. She'll be a better nurse than any of you."

"All right, Doc," Evan said, "thanks."

"Don't thank me until I tell you how much I'm charging.

"Doc," Evan said, "I don't care how much you charge."

Doc Leader grinned and it wasn't a pretty sight.

"You're gonna be sorry you said that."

CHAPTER FIFTEEN

When Sam woke up the first thing he saw was Serena's face.

"Thank God," he said.

"What?" she asked.

"I thought when I opened my eyes I'd see one of my brothers," he said. He closed his eyes for a moment, then opened them. "I much prefer this."

"Sam," she said, "I think that's the sweetest thing you've ever said to me."

"I must be delirious," he said, and passed out again.

————

THE NEXT TIME he woke up he saw Evan.

"I knew it was too good to be true."

"Serena sat up all night with you," Evan said. "But now she needs some sleep."

"Yeah, okay."

"You want to tell me what happened?"

"Yeah," Sam said, "they improved by one."

"What?"

"Eight of 'em this time."

"Eight?"

"Yeah. They were running me down, feeling brave. I killed one of them..." He trailed off, his mouth going dry.

"Put the fear of God into the others, huh?"

"Yeah, fella I killed got off a shot, though. I must be gettin' old."

"That's more than a lot of people can say," Evan said. "You want some water?"

"Yeah, thanks."

Evan lifted his brother's head and held the water glass to his lips.

"Thanks."

"Get some more rest, Sam," Evan said. "You lost a lot of blood."

"Gotta get up..."

"Yeah, sure," Evan said, "later."

"Later..." Sam said.

When Serena walked into the room Sam was sitting up, reaching for his pants. It was a clean pair that had come from the Miller store.

"What do you think you're doing?"

"I think I'm tryin' to reach my pants," Sam said. "When I reach them I'm gonna try to put them on. Do you wanna watch?"

She folded her arms and said, "What happened to that sweet man who was here last night?"

He looked up at her and let his arm drop because he couldn't hold it out any longer.

"He's here someplace," Sam said. "Will you help me get my pants?"

"I would help him," she said, "but I don't know about you."

"Please..."

She dropped her arms and approached the bed.

"Sam, you shouldn't be getting up."

"If you don't help me, I might fall once or twice, but eventually I'll make it."

"You'd do that, wouldn't you?"

"Serena," Sam said, "it's just a leg wound. I've been shot before."

She stared at him and then said, "I don't know why that hadn't occurred to me before. How many times have you been shot?"

"Serena—"

"How many?"

"Four, maybe five."

She stared at him in disbelief.

"You don't even remember?"

"Okay," he said, "it was five. *Now* will you help me get dressed?"

"I'll get you your clothes," she said, picking up his pants and flinging them at his face, "but you can dress yourself."

As she stalked from the room he pulled his pants from his face and said, "That'll do."

Serena had already alerted Evan and Jubal that Sam was dressing. Dude Miller had gone back to work full time and was at his store.

"Maybe one of you should go up and help him," she said, "so that he doesn't fall down too many times."

"He'll be fine," Evan said.

She stamped her foot, surprising them, and said, "That's what you said last night, and was he all right?"

"I only meant—"

"I know what you meant," she said. "I'll be in the kitchen making coffee."

"What is she so mad about?" Jubal asked.

"She's a woman."

"What does that mean?"

"Jube," Evan said, "you've made it to twenty-four and you don't know what that means?"

Jubal was about to answer when they saw Sam coming down the steps. He looked steady enough and they both remained seated rather than offer him a hand.

"You're looking fit," Evan said.

Sam reached the floor and limped to a chair.

"I feel like hell."

"You should have stayed in bed."

Sam settled himself in the chair and said, "I'd feel worse up there."

"I've told Jubal what happened," Evan said. "Is there anything you'd like to add?"

"Yes," Sam said. "I don't believe there's any gold on Pa's old land."

"No gold?" Jubal asked.

"Then what do they need a geologist for?" Evan asked.

Sam told them about the mud he'd found at the stream and the water hole.

"There was black mud on your pants and your boots."

"Yes."

"What does it mean?" Jubal asked.

"Oil," Evan said.

"Oil?" Jubal asked.

Evan looked at Sam.

"Am I right? Is that what you're thinking?"

"Yes," Sam said. "I saw the geologist run some tests, and then he took some of the mud back to the ranch with him.

"*Oil*" Evan said. "No wonder Burkett wanted that land so badly."

"But...how did he know there was oil?"

"Probably the same way we found out," Sam said. "He probably did a lot of looking around before deciding what land he wanted."

"Did Pa know, I wonder?" Evan said.

"I was wondering about that myself," Sam said. "I have a theory."

"What theory?"

"We all knew Pa," Sam said. "We all agree he wouldn't kill Ma and then kill himself."

"That's right," Evan said, and Jubal nodded.

"But if he thought his life was in danger, what would he do?"

After a moment Evan said, "I think he'd try to leave us a message."

"A message?" Jubal asked. "How?"

"Yes," Sam said, looking at his brothers, "how? That's for us to figure out."

At that moment Serena entered, carrying a tray with three steaming cups of coffee on it.

She offered the tray first to Evan, then to Jubal, and finally walked over to where Sam was seated. For a moment he thought she was going to dump it in his lap, but in the end she held the tray out to him until he took the cup from it.

"Thank you."

"Hmph," she said, and went back to the kitchen.

"What's she so mad about?" he asked.

"She's a woman," Jubal said.

"Ah," Sam said, "our little brother is becoming worldly, isn't he?"

Jubal smiled, and Evan frowned at him.

"Sam, where should we look for this message?"

"As I said, that's something we'll have to figure out together."

"What about the house?"

"What house?" Sam asked Jubal. "The big one?"

"No, I mean the house they were living in when they were... killed."

"That's certainly a possibility," Sam said. "We should check the house."

"And where else?" Evan asked.

They all thought about that for a while and then Sam said, "There might be a couple of places."

Sam and Evan exchanged a rather meaningful glance that Jubal caught.

"What?"

"Well," Evan said, "there was a certain area where Pa used to take us hunting when we were younger—uh, Sam and me."

"Could be he'd leave a message there someplace, figurin' we'd find it."

"Out in the open?" Jubal asked. "Rain might ruin it, or an animal."

"Under a rock, maybe," Evan said.

"Or in a hollowed-out log," Sam said. "I suggest we check the house first."

"And I suggest we do it together, Sam," Evan said. "I don't know if Burkett's men were acting on their own this time, but there certainly seems to be a lot of people who want you dead."

"I agree, Sam," Jubal said, grinning. "It looks like you need more guarding than Serena."

"Serena can take care of herself," she said, entering the room with a cup of coffee of her own. "I have a gun in my room."

"What kind?"

"A two-shot derringer."

"That's not going to stop anyone with any real resolve," Evan said. "You'd have to place both shots just right."

"Evan, why don't you take Serena to the gunsmith's shop today and get her a real gun—something she can handle, but something with stopping power."

"You're the gun expert," Evan said. "Why don't you take her?"

They all seemed to ignore the fact that only the night before he'd been shot in the thigh.

"All right, I will," Sam said. "My leg could use the exercise."

"Your leg," Serena said, "could use some rest. Evan will take me."

Sam looked at Evan, who simply shrugged.

"We might as well go now," Serena said, "before he closes."

"What time is it?" Sam asked.

"It's almost five," Serena said. "I'll fix dinner when I get back."

"Almost five?" Sam asked, dismayed. "The whole damned day is gone. Why didn't you get me up sooner?"

"You needed the rest!" Serena said as a parting shot. She and Evan went out the front door.

When they were gone Sam rubbed his aching leg and glared at Jubal.

"Don't look at me. She wouldn't let us wake you up."

"Big, strong men," Sam said, still rubbing his thigh. "Who patched me up?"

"Doc Leader. I had to drag him over here to do it, and he charged—well, a lot."

"Who paid?"

"Me and Evan."

"I owe you.

"Yes, you do."

Sam finished his coffee, set the empty cup aside, and stood up.

"What are you going to do?"

"Go upstairs," Sam said. "When Evan gets back we can ride out to the house."

"You going to sleep?"

"No," Sam said, "I'm gonna clean my guns."

As Sam negotiated the steps slowly Jubal thought that sounded like a damned good idea.

———

EVAN AND SERENA argued and finally settled on a .34-caliber Colt Paterson. It had stopping power but was light enough for Serena to control. They bought her a holster for it.

"I feel silly," she said, trying it on.

"Better to be silly than dead," Evan said.

"I'm not a fast gun."

"A holster is just something to carry a gun in," Evan said. "You're not required to get it out quickly, just efficiently."

"Did Sam tell you that?"

"Actually, no," Evan said. "It might surprise you to know that I've had a few gun battles of my own and survived. I was always able to make my first shot count by not rushing it."

"You've killed people?"

"You forget what happened earlier this week."

"That was different."

"It was? How?"

"It was self-defense."

"I've only ever killed in self-defense, Serena."

"I don't know if I could—"

"Serena," Evan said, "what do you suppose would have happened if you'd been wearing that gun the night those three men dragged your father from the house?"

Without hesitation she said, "I would have killed them!"

She looked shocked at her own words and he grinned.

"See?"

"Shut up."

Sam had his guns laid out on the bed and was cleaning the rifle when Evan entered the room. The rifle was his own Winchester, and not one from the gunsmith shop.

"Did you get her fixed up?"

Evan sat on the bed and watched his brother work on the rifle.

"Yes. We got her a Colt Paterson, .35 caliber."

"Good choice."

"She wanted something bigger, and I wanted her to have something smaller. We compromised."

"Compromising with a woman is a real bad habit to get into."

"Don't worry," Evan said. "I don't intend to make a habit of it."

He took out a deck of cards and began to deal a game of solitaire on the bed while Sam picked up his pistol and began to clean it.

"You know," Sam said, "I always envied your ability with a deck of cards."

"What?" Evan asked, surprised.

"I like to play poker," Sam said, "but I'm no damned good at it. I haven't got the patience to sit out a hand and wait for the next one."

"You can work on that."

Sam shook his head and said, "I'm too old a dog for that."

There was a few moments of silence and then Evan said, "That's funny."

'What is?"

"That you should envy me."

"Why?"

"Well, more than once since we arrived I've felt sort of... resentful of you."

Sam looked up from what he was doing, then put the gun down and sat across from his brother.

"Resentful? Why?"

Evan told Sam what had taken place in the saloon at the poker game, with the loser backing down because Evan was "Sam McCall's brother." Then he told him that the same thing had happened when he ran into John Burkett, Chuck Conners, and the geologist.

Sam stared at his brother and then said, "I guess there ain't much I can do about that, Evan."

"I know," Evan said. "It's just that it hasn't happened very often. Now, I sort of wonder why."

"I suspect you've always been able to take care of yourself," Sam said. "In the circle you travel in, you must have a rep of your own."

"I guess I do," Evan said. "I can't imagine what it's like to carry the rep you do."

"It keeps people at a distance," Sam said. "I can count my friends on the fingers of one hand."

"Well, so can I, and I don't have a rep to blame it on."

"Maybe it just runs in the family. Pa never had that many real friends that I can remember."

"No, and I don't guess that Jube does, either," Evan said. "I suppose we're lucky to have one another."

Sam laughed and said, "Maybe we just like each other because we never see each other."

"That could be."

Sam stood up, picked up his gun, and slid it into the oiled leather holster. He strapped the gun on and then picked up the rifle. Sensing what was coming, Evan collected his cards and put them away.

"Let's take that ride out to the house," Sam said.

"Can you ride?"

"Don't worry," Sam said. "I'll manage to stay mounted."

In the end, gun or no gun, they decided that Serena would go with them. When they reached the house and dismounted they all heard Sam groan as he put his weight on his right leg. He'd managed not to moan aloud when he mounted, but this time the sound escaped from him before he could stop it.

Evan and Jubal ignored the sound. Serena opened her mouth to say something, then thought better of it.

They entered the house and took the place in at a glance.

"There aren't many places something could be hidden," Jubal said.

"There are no floorboards," Evan said. "Let's try the drawers, and under the tables. Check and see if there are any loose stones on the fireplace."

"I'll check outside," Jubal said.

Serena walked around, looking in things like sugar bowls and teapots.

Sam and Evan started at the same point and worked their way around in opposite directions. When they came face to face they both had the same thing to report.

"Nothin'," Sam said.

They looked over at Serena, who shrugged and shook her head.

"I'll check outside with Jubal," Evan said.

When they were alone Serena said, "Maybe we're looking in the wrong places."

"We're lookin' anywhere a piece of paper could be hidden," Sam said, "and that's anywhere."

Sam walked about studying the hard-packed dirt floor, checking to see if there was anyplace where something might have been buried. He was finished when Evan and Jubal came back in.

"Nothing outside."

Sam looked up at the ceiling and said, "Just for the sake of being thorough we'd better check the roof."

"Who's going to go up on the roof?" Evan asked.

"Well, I can't," Sam said. "I've been shot in the leg, remember?"

Evan looked at Jubal.

"Why me?"

"Because you're the youngest."

"What does that mean?"

"Your balance is better," Evan said. "You're the least likely to fall off."

"Oh, never mind all this," Serena said. "I'll go up on the roof. Jubal, help me up."

The roof was low, and it took only a boost from Jubal to get Serena up.

"Check the chimney," Sam said. "There might be a loose stone."

They waited while Serena checked the roof, and then when she was ready to come down both Evan and Jubal reached up for her and helped her.

"Nothing?" Evan asked.

"Nothing."

"We'll have to check that area you said Pa liked to hunt," Jubal said.

"Yes, but we'll have to do it tomorrow," Evan said. "It'll be dark soon."

"If you men want to eat," Serena said, "we'll have to get back so I can cook."

"Why don't we go somewhere and eat?" Evan suggested.

"You have something against my cooking?" Serena asked.

"Of course not," Evan said. "I just thought you could use a break."

"Well," Serena said, "it doesn't sound like a completely bad idea. Where shall we go?"

"Is there anyplace decent to eat?" Evan asked.

"Well," she said, thoughtfully, "there is one place."

"The hotel?" Jubal asked.

"Oh, no," Serena said, making a face, "certainly not. There's a small cafe run by a friend of mine."

"Well, then," Sam said, "let's get back to town."

He didn't want to let on how weak he felt, or how much his thigh was aching. When they got back to town he'd beg off from dinner. He had no appetite.

No appetite for anything but revenge. His wound, and the sickly feeling that accompanied it, could not extinguish that.

CHAPTER SIXTEEN

Normally a patient man, Coffin was becoming impatient. A man could have just so much food, drink, gambling and women—even when they were all free.

Lincoln Burkett had given Coffin an unlimited line of credit wherever he went in town. Coffin, to the surprise of the merchants involved, did not abuse the privilege. It was plain to see what kind of man Coffin was, and the townspeople moved out of his way when he walked down the street, much the way they moved for Sam McCall. McCall, however, had come from Vengeance Creek, and they had known his parents. Coffin was a stranger, and no one knew what to expect from him.

They certainly didn't expect what they got.

When he ate in the hotel dining room or a restaurant, he was courteous and quiet. When he drank in the saloon he did so alone, and when he played cards he did so quietly and efficiently.

When he went to the whorehouse he treated the girls well, and though he did not have to pay he always gave them something.

In the span of a few days Coffin actually had some of the people of Vengeance Creek liking him.

Now he was growing impatient. He never liked staying in one place too long.

———

COFFIN WAS HAVING dinner in the cafe when Evan, Jubal, and Serena entered. Dude Miller had opted to stay home, and as he had planned, Sam had begged off and gone to his hotel room. Miller had offered him a room at the house, but Sam had refused. If some of Burkett's men came for him again—which seemed more likely every minute—he didn't want Dude Miller or Serena caught in the crossfire.

In the morning, if he felt strong enough, Sam planned on riding out to see Lincoln Burkett. If the man really wanted him dead, he'd give him the chance to do it himself.

As they entered the cafe Jubal saw Coffin, who nodded to him.

After they were seated Serena asked, "Who is that?"

"That's Coffin."

"Lincoln Burkett's hired gun?" she asked. "Eating here?"

"Where would you have him eat?" Evan asked.

"I don't know..." Serena said. "With his reputation you'd think he wouldn't want to eat with...with..."

"Decent people?" Evan asked.

"I was going to say that," she admitted.

"What about Sam?" Evan asked. "Should he be allowed to eat here?"

"That's different."

"Why? He has a reputation."

"But I know Sam," Serena said. "I know he's not like that."

"Maybe if you knew Coffin you'd decide that he wasn't like his reputation, either."

"I don't understand you," Serena said. "Isn't he here to kill Sam?"

"We don't know why he's here," Evan said. "We do know one thing: when Sam was pinned down in that telegraph office, Coffin helped us."

Serena looked surprised.

"Why would he do that?"

"Maybe he was just saving Sam for himself," Evan said. "Maybe he couldn't see a man dying that way, at the hands of seven men, all of whom were too cowardly to face him alone."

Serena compressed her lips and then said, "I don't think I'll ever understand men."

"I reckon that makes us even, Serena," Jubal said.

"Why don't we eat?" Evan suggested. "I'm starved."

Coffin recognized Jubal as Sam McCall's brother, and the other man was Evan McCall. He hadn't gotten a good look at either of them on the street that day, but he had seen Jubal in the saloon with Sam McCall the day they had talked, and he'd seen Evan out at Burkett's place.

Coffin wondered idly if Sam's ability with a gun was a family trait.

————

AFTER HE FINISHED his dinner Coffin walked over to the table where Evan, Jubal, and Serena were still eating. He was holding his hat in his hand.

"Hello, boy," he said to Jubal.

"The name's Jubal."

"Sure, Jubal," Coffin said. "I didn't mean any offense."

"None taken, Coffin," Evan said. "Is there some reason why you came over here?"

"As a matter of fact, there is," Coffin said, switching his gaze to Serena. "I came to pay my respects to the lady. Ma'am, I do believe you're the prettiest woman I've seen in a long time. I just wanted to tell you that."

Serena stared at Coffin for a few moments and then said, "Thank you."

"Are you Sam's woman?" Coffin asked.

"Why do you want to know that?" Evan asked.

Coffin smiled, and Serena noticed that the smile touched his lips, but not his eyes. His cold gray eyes made her shiver inside.

"Just curious, that's all."

"Well," Evan said, "if you have to know, she's Jubal's girl."

"Jubal, eh?"

Both Jubal and Serena gave Evan quick looks and then tried to mask them.

"Lucky lad," Coffin said, then added, "Oops, sorry. That's just like calling you 'kid,' isn't it?"

Jubal didn't answer.

"Well," Coffin said, "I'll be on my way and allow you to finish your meal. Ma'am?"

He put on his hat and walked out. Serena couldn't keep herself from staring at his gun as he went out.

"Is he very good with his gun?" she asked.

"That's what they say," Evan said.

"Better than Sam?"

"There's only one way we'll ever find that out" Jubal said, and Evan gave him a warning look.

"Is that going to happen?" Serena asked.

Neither Evan nor Jubal answered her this time.

"Of course," she said, answering her own question, "of course it will. If you keep pursuing Lincoln Burkett, it will happen. And why shouldn't it?"

"Serena—" Evan said, but she wasn't listening.

"The whole town knows they're both here, and they want to see it. If it happens, it will put this town on the map, won't it?"

"Serena—" Jubal said, but he didn't have any luck either.

"I'll bet you two are curious about it, too. I'll bet they're curious about it themselves. I'm probably the only one who doesn't want to see it happen."

"Serena!" This time they tried it together and managed to get her attention.

"What?"

"Eat your dinner," Evan said, "and stop worrying about things you have no control over."

She looked down at her plate and pushed it away.

"I've lost my appetite."

"Well, I haven't," Evan said. "It may not be as good as your cooking, but it'll do."

Evan started to eat, frowning at Jubal until he started as well.

As Coffin was approaching the hotel he stopped to light a cigarette. He knew that all of the McCall brothers had rooms in the hotel, and since the hotel only had two floors there was a fifty-fifty chance that Sam McCall's room was on the same floor as his.

In the past Coffin had drawn his gun only for money. Now, however, he was starting to wonder if he could avoid doing it just out of curiosity. He was itching to try McCall.

He dropped the cigarette to the ground and stubbed it out deliberately. He'd give Burkett a little more time to do what he had to do, and then Coffin was just going to have to do what *he* had to do.

Sam McCall was looking out the window. He saw Coffin pause for a cigarette, staring at the hotel. The man was probably thinking the same thing. They couldn't be more than some feet apart when they were both in their rooms. Sooner or later they'd have to close the distance between them, whether it was because Coffin was working for Burkett, or simply because it was inevitable.

Sam had to admit to a lingering curiosity about Coffin.

He had to admit to it, but he didn't have to give in to it. He turned and limped back to bed.

Evan walked Serena home while Jubal went to the saloon, where Evan would meet him later.

They walked at a leisurely pace, in silence for most of the way. As they approached the house Serena stopped.

"What is it?" Evan asked.

"Evan, why don't you and your brothers just leave town? Forget all about this place."

"We will," Evan said.

"After you find out who killed your parents."

"That's right."

"Couldn't the official verdict be right?"

"You don't believe that any more than we do, Serena. What's your point?"

She hesitated a moment and then blurted out, "I don't know that finding out who killed them is worth being killed yourselves."

"Take a moment to think about that, Serena," Evan said. "What if it was your father?"

"I see your point."

"We appreciate your concern, we really do... and your help. If you'd rather just back away from this whole thing we'd understand. In fact, we'd like for you to do just that—"

"No," she said, shaking her head, "I'm here to help you, when you need me—and my father feels the same way. All right?"

"Yes," Evan said, "all right. Let's get you home, now, shall we?"

They walked to the door, where she inserted her key and opened it.

"See you tomorrow," she said, turning to him.

On impulse Evan bent and kissed her on the mouth. She didn't seem surprised, but she didn't particularly participate, either.

Evan straightened and looked at her. He was about to apologize for taking the liberty when she stretched and kissed him quickly on the mouth.

"Good night," she said, and slipped inside.

Jubal was standing at the bar holding a beer when he saw John Burkett enter with three men. The tallest of the three was Chuck Conners, Burkett's foreman.

Jubal turned his back to the room. He was certain that Conners would know who he was. As it turned out, he hadn't turned his back soon enough, and John Burkett had seen him.

"My friend," Burkett called. Jubal tried to ignore him but in the mirror he could see Burkett crossing the room toward him. Conners and the other two men followed.

"Chuck, I want you to meet the hombre who helped me out at Louise's. Hey," John Burkett said, touching Jubal's shoulder, "I didn't even get your name."

As Jubal turned Chuck Conners said, "I can tell you what his name is."

"How would you—"

"His name is McCall," Conners said. "Jubal McCall."

"McCall?" John said, staring at Jubal.

"Sam McCall's brother."

John looked at Conners, then turned to Jubal and said, "Why, you—what were you trying to do? Get into my confidence?"

Jubal smiled and said, "No harm done, friend. I did keep you from getting your head knocked off."

"Now let's see if you can do the same for yourself," John Burkett said. "Grab him!"

Jubal threw his beer into the face of one man and pushed another away. Conners, however, was bigger and stronger. He got behind Jubal and pinned his arms back.

"Hold him, Chuck," Burkett said. He threw a punch that landed solidly in Jubal's belly. He followed that one up with a blow to the face, bringing blood from Jubal's lip.

"Can we get in on the fun?" one of the other men asked. His face was dripping with beer.

"Be my guest," Burkett said.

The other two men positioned themselves in front of Jubal. Apparently they were going to work on him at the same time.

"Hey—" the bartender said.

"You stay out of it!" Burkett barked at the man, who subsided. As far as he was concerned, he had done all he could.

"You're gonna feel this all the way down to your toes, boy," the man with beer on his face said.

Both men drew back their fists, and at that moment the man who was slumped in Conner's hands came to life. He backed up, pinning Conners to the bar, then lifted both feet and kicked out at the two men. He caught both of them in the chest, driving them backward.

"You son-of-a-bitch!" cried John Burkett. He went to draw his gun, but the move was arrested by a loud voice.

"I wouldn't do that, Burkett!" It was Evan McCall.

Burkett looked over and saw Evan standing just inside the batwing doors, gun in hand. Men who were sitting in the line of fire scrambled for safety.

"Tell your friend to let my brother go."

"There are four of us, McCall, and only two of you," John Burkett said.

"That may be, Johnny boy, but I'll make sure I kill you first." Evan paused a moment to let that sink in and then said, "The next move is up to you."

Conners was still holding on to Jubal. The other two men had regained their balance and were watching John Burkett, waiting for him to move.

"John!" Conners said.

"What?"

"This isn't the time or the place," the foreman said. He released Jubal's shoulders. "Let's go."

"Want a drink."

"We'll get one someplace else."

John Burkett was still staring across the room at Evan, his shoulders high with tension.

"John!" Conners said, "Let's go." He started for the door, then turned and looked at the other two men. "Let's go, boys!"

The two men looked at Burkett one more time, then shrugged and followed Conners.

"A wise move, Conners," Evan said.

"Your time will come, McCall," Conners said to Evan. "You and your brothers."

"Better get junior out of here before he does something rash."

"If he was going to do it, he would have done it by now," Conners said. "Just between you and me, I don't think he's got the *cojones* for it." He walked out, followed closely by the other two men.

That left John Burkett in the room alone to face Evan and Jubal, and he was starting to realize that. His eyes suddenly acquired a hunted look.

"Come on, John," Jubal said, "Forget it. I'll buy you a drink."

Burkett looked at Jubal and said, "Keep your damned drink. The next time you get in my way, nobody'll stop me. I'll kill you."

Jubal picked up his beer from the bar and raised the glass to Burkett, who stormed across the room past Evan, and then out.

Evan holstered his gun and joined his brother at the bar.

"Can't leave you alone for a minute, can I?" he said, leaning his elbows against the bar so he could continue to watch the room. Now that it was clear there would be no shooting, men were reclaiming their seats and going back to what they were doing. Evan, though, cautiously continued to survey the room.

Jubal wiped the blood from his lip with the back of his hand and said to the bartender, "Two more beers." He looked at his brother and said, "You got here just in time."

Evan smiled and said, "It's the old McCall timing. We all have it"

CHAPTER SEVENTEEN

In the morning Evan and Jubal told Sam about the incident as they walked to the Miller house for breakfast.

"Well, it sounds like we won't be gettin' any information from Johnny Burkett in the future," Sam observed.

"I guess not," Jubal said.

"Evan," Sam said, "you get the feelin' that we might all be targets now, instead of just me?"

"From what Jubal told me, John Burkett was just upset that he'd been fooled. I don't think he and the other men came to town looking for one of us."

Sam nodded. He felt the same way, but wanted to see how Evan felt.

"Jube?" He spoke to Jubal as an afterthought, not wanting to offend him by not asking his opinion. He had long since stopped thinking of his younger brother as just a boy.

"I agree, Sam."

"Then we're all agreed."

When Serena admitted them to the house she frowned at Jubal and said, "What happened to your lip?"

The three brothers exchanged glances and then decided to tell her about the incident.

"Where's your father?" Sam asked.

"In the kitchen."

"Let's go in there."

348 • ROBERT J. RANDISI

Sam didn't want to have to explain it to her and then repeat it to Dude Miller.

They had been able to smell breakfast cooking as soon as they entered. In the kitchen the smell of frying food was stronger still, and they all experienced hunger pangs of one degree or another.

"You could have been seriously hurt," she said to Jubal afterward.

"Evan got there in plenty of time."

Evan could tell from the look on her face what she was thinking. If not for two kisses, he might have been there before Jubal could be hurt, at all.

"Everything turned out all right," Sam said. "Let's talk about something else."

"You have something in mind?" Evan asked as they seated themselves at the table.

"Yeah," Sam said. "I'm goin' out to see Lincoln Burkett today."

"What?" Jubal said.

"That's madness!" Serena said.

"Do you think that's wise?" Dude Miller asked.

Evan looked at his older brother and said, "Do you want me to go with you?"

"No," Sam said, "I'll go alone."

"Why go at all?" Serena asked.

To the room at large Sam said, "I'm tired of being shot at and chased. If Burkett wants me dead I figure to give him a chance to do it himself."

"And if he tries?" Serena asked.

Nobody answered and Jubal finally said, "Sam will defend himself."

"And if he doesn't try?"

This time Sam answered.

"Maybe it'll force his hand."

"Meaning what?" she asked. "That he'll finally send Coffin after you?"

"Maybe."

"That's what you want, isn't it?" she said to Sam, angrily.

"You want to stand out there in the street with Coffin and see who's best!"

"I want to get this over with," Sam said. "I want to find out once and for all if Burkett killed our folks for what was on their land."

"What's on their land?" Dude Miller asked.

The McCalls had not yet confided to the Millers what they had discovered.

"We think there's oil on the land, Dude," Evan said.

"Oil?"

Sam told Miller about what he found, and about the geologist.

"Lord almighty," Miller said, "no wonder Burkett wanted that land—but your father couldn't have known, else why would he have given it up?"

"That's something we still have to find out," Sam said.

"And what happens if you find out that Burkett didn't kill your parents?" Serena asked.

"That would mean someone else did," Sam said.

"And we'd have to find whoever did," Evan added.

"And what about Burkett?" Serena asked. "Does that mean you'd forget about him? I mean, if it turns out he didn't kill them, and he didn't force the land from them, would that be the end of things with him?"

The brother exchanged glances and then Evan said, "We don't know, Serena."

"Serena," Dude Miller said, "if Burkett didn't kill their folks, then they don't have any business with him."

"The town—"

"We'd be back where we started, honey," Miller said. "Us against Burkett."

"And we'll lose," Serena said, twisting a dish towel in her hands. "I'd rather just pick up and leave than go on fighting, Papa."

"Why don't we wait and see what happens before you decide to leave *I*" Evan said.

"Sure," Serena said, throwing her towel down to the floor, "wait until one, or two, or all of you are dead. That's when it will be over."

She stalked out of the room then, leaving the four men speechless.

"I'll get that food off the stove before it burns," Dude Miller said.

Jubal walked Sam to the livery, while Evan stayed at the

house with Serena. Dude Miller walked with them as far as his store.

"Don't be too hard on Serena, Sam," he said before they parted company. "She's grown very fond of the three of you, and she doesn't want to see anything happen to you."

"I don't hold that against her, Dude," Sam said. "I just hope she understands what we have to do, and why we can't walk away from it."

"I guess we'll just have to wait and see about that," Miller said, and entered his store.

Sam and Jubal proceeded to the livery, where Swede brought out Sam's coyote dun.

"I wish you'd let me ride with you," Jubal said as Sam mounted up, "at least part of the way."

"I'll do this alone, Jubal," Sam said.

"Why do you have to do it alone?"

"Because this is what I do, Jube," Sam said. "This is what I do."

Coffin was looking out his window when Sam rode by, heading out of town. He had a feeling he knew where Sam McCall was going. Hell, if he was in McCall's shoes he might not have waited this long to confront Lincoln Burkett. Evan McCall's visit to Burkett hadn't accomplished anything. Maybe Sam McCall's visit would stir things up some.

Coffin decided maybe he'd take himself a little ride as well.

As Sam rode up to Burkett's house he attracted the attention of the men at the corral, the men in front of the barn, and a couple of men who were on the porch.

One of the men on the porch was Chuck Conners. When he spotted Sam McCall riding up he turned away from the man he was talking to and descended the steps to wait for him.

"Don't bother dismounting, McCall," Conners said. "You ain't wanted here."

"I want to talk to Burkett."

"He don't want to talk to you."

"Why don't you let him make up his own mind about that?"

"I'm the foreman around here," Conners said. "I make most of the decisions around here."

"Not this one."

"Now look—"

"Are you prepared to keep me from seein' your boss, Conners?"

"I am."

"Well then, get to it."

"What?"

"I said get to it," Sam said. "Go for your gun."

There were eight or ten men watching the proceedings now, and Conners' eyes flicked right and left, taking in that fact.

"Now wait—" he said.

"You think you can stop me?" Sam asked. "But, you see, I intend to see your boss, and—"

"I—I got enough men here to stop you."

Sam took a moment to look around. Most of the men who were watching were wearing sidearms.

"You sure do have enough—this time."

"What do you mean?"

"I mean you've tried sendin' seven men after me, and then eight. Now you've got about eleven, countin' yourself. Maybe you'll do it this time, but there's one thing you should know."

"What's that?"

"If I only get off one shot, it'll go right into your brain. Ninety-nine times out of a hundred that's a fatal shot. How do you feel about those odds, Conners?"

Chuck Conners stared at Sam McCall, then looked around at his men, who were waiting for him to call the play.

"Come on, Conners," Sam said. "Make a play or tell your boss I'm here."

There was a tense moment while Conners weighed his options, but he was saved from having to make the final decision.

"He doesn't have to tell me you're here, McCall," Lincoln Burkett said. He was standing in the open front doorway. "I can see that for myself."

"You willin' to talk to me, Burkett, or are you gonna call the play here?"

"Oh, I'll call the play, all right, McCall," Burkett said, "when the time comes. I think you've killed quite enough of my men. Chuck, let him by."

"But boss—"

"Let him come in. I want to talk to him."

Sam dismounted and handed his reins to a startled man

standing nearby. He brushed past Conners and climbed the steps. He heard Conners beginning to climb the steps behind him.

"Not you, Chuck," Burkett said. "I'll see Mr. McCall alone."

"Boss, I don't think—"

"Don't worry," Burkett said as Sam McCall reached him, "I'll be safe enough, won't I, McCall?"

"That depends on you, Burkett," Sam said, and slipped past him into the house.

Sam knew the way to Burkett's office. Evan had told him which room it was. He was waiting there for Burkett, already sitting in front of the man's desk.

"I see you've made yourself at home," Burkett said, moving around to the other side of his desk. "Can I offer you a drink?"

"No."

"Let's get to it, then," Burkett said. "Why are you here?"

"Like you say," Sam said, "I've killed enough of your men. I think it's time for you to try and kill me yourself."

Burkett laughed.

"Why would I want to do that?"

"Either you kill me," Sam said, "or tell me what happened to my parents."

"I intend to do neither," Burkett said. "Actually, I won't do the first, and I can't do the second because I know nothing about it."

"That's bull."

"That might be what you think," Burkett said. "I'll tell you the truth, the sheriff questioned me after your parents were found."

"Why would he do that?"

"Well, we had only made the deal for his ranch a month before. I guess the sheriff felt that was sufficient—"

"That's more bull," Sam said, interrupting him. "You own the sheriff, just as sure as you own the whorehouse and whatever other businesses you own."

"Who told you I own the whorehouse?"

Sam smiled.

"It's a badly kept secret, Burkett," Sam said, "but never mind. I think you should know I've sent for a federal marshal."

"You... have?" Burkett's face betrayed him for just an

instant. He didn't like the idea of a federal marshal poking his nose in his business. "When will he be arriving?"

"Soon," Sam said, "very soon."

"And what do you expect him to accomplish?"

"Once he looks at the evidence I've put together, I expect him to arrest the killers of my parents."

"Evidence?"

Sam stood up.

"I haven't been here all this time without accomplishing something, Burkett."

"And your brothers?"

"They don't know what I have," Sam said. "I'm tryin' to protect them."

"That's admirable," Burkett said. "A man should take care of his family."

"I'm glad you feel that way, Burkett," Sam said, moving toward the door, "because that's exactly what I've been trying to do all along—and what I'll continue to do. Uh, before I go, are you sure you wouldn't like to try for that gun in your desk?"

Burkett's eyes momentarily flitted to the desk drawer where he kept his gun.

"Uh, no, I don't think so."

"That's a pity," Sam said, and left.

Outside he found that the men who had gathered to watch him and Conners face off had not yet dispersed.

Even Conners was still there. The man he'd given his horse to was still holding the reins, and he took them back.

"Thank you."

"Did you accomplish anything?" Conners asked.

From astride his horse Sam looked down at the man and said, "I got done what I came to get done. Ask your boss about it. He'll tell you. In fact, I think he wants to see you."

Sam wheeled his horse around and rode away from the house, leaving behind a bunch of puzzled men and one very confused foreman.

———

"I WAS GOING to send for you," Burkett said when Conners entered.

"McCall said you wanted to see me."

"He did, eh?"

"Uh, do you want to—"

"Yes, yes, of course I do," Burkett said. "Close the damned door."

Conners did so and moved closer to the desk-

"What did he say?"

"He said he had evidence."

"He can't."

"I know," Burkett said, "but he also said he's sent for a federal marshal."

"That must be what he was doing in the telegraph office that day."

"If I ever find out who was behind that..." Burkett trailed off. "The man has killed eight of my men, Chuck...eight! And now he's got federal law coming in."

"What do you want done?"

Burkett took a long moment to light a cigar to his satisfaction. He was regarding the glowing tip when he finally said, "Get Coffin."

CHAPTER EIGHTEEN

Sam rode back to town and left his horse with the Swede at the livery.

During the ride back he was very alert. There was no telling what Burkett would do. Sam hoped to push the man into taking some kind of obvious action, but he didn't really expect it to be *immediate* action. Nevertheless he remained alert for another possible ambush.

As he approached the town he found himself wishing he could just by pass it and keep on going. He had never liked Vengeance Creek. It had always represented a prison for him, a place he thought he would never escape from if he didn't leave early. That was why he'd left in the first place. He had always regarded Vengeance Creek as a small town that would never grow up, and while he was here he had seen nothing to change his mind. Maybe a lot of people felt that way. Maybe that was why most of them accepted Lincoln Burkett as a savior, and not a conqueror.

Now he was back here and once again he felt imprisoned. There was no way he and his brothers could leave until they found out the truth, but who knew when that would happen—or if? What if they never found out the truth? Would he never be able to leave?

As he rode down the main street to the livery he felt as if the sides of the street were closing in on him, as if everyone on the street was watching—and most of them were. He and Coffin in the same place would have raised the tension of any town, and Vengeance Creek was no different. They were waiting for what they felt was an inevitable explosion.

After leaving the horse at the livery he started back to the Miller house, but then he made a detour to the saloon. Over a beer he thought about Coffin and about the townspeople of Vengeance Creek. If the town was his prison, then the town's people were his jailers. As curious as he himself was about Coffin and himself, he would have liked to leave the people hanging, deprive them of their entertainment. He wondered if he and Coffin could avoid a showdown.

He thought about Serena, but quickly dispelled her from his thoughts. Long ago he had resigned himself to the fact that there was no woman in his future. A woman would want him to settle down and, convinced as he was that he would someday die a violent death, it would not be fair to a woman to ask her to marry him, anyway. Serena and Evan made a nice couple, but he didn't think his brother would stay in Vengeance Creek any more than he would when this was all over.

Maybe Jubal...

Jubal still had time to make a life for himself. He was still young enough to change the direction his life was taking. Serena was only four years older than he, so maybe he could make his future here.

In Vengeance Creek?

Sam shook his head, finished his beer, and left the saloon.

Coffin hadn't tailed Sam McCall to the Burkett house. He had known he was going there, so he stayed far enough behind so that McCall wouldn't sense him there. He was watching from a distance when McCall faced off against Conners and made him back down in front of all his men. He was still there when McCall came back out after talking with Burkett. Coffin watched as Sam rode away, back to town, and then he approached the ranch.

He was riding up to the house when Chuck Conners came out of the house. Conners saw him and stopped short.

"Looking for me?" Coffin asked.

"How did you know?" Conners said. "I was just about to send someone to town to get you."

"Well, I'm already here," Coffin said, dismounting. "I had a feeling Burkett would be wanting me."

"Come on inside," Conners said.

The foreman called a man over to take Coffin's horse and then lead the gunmen into the house to Lincoln Burkett's office.

"Are you back already?" Burkett asked as Conners entered. A split second later he saw Coffin enter behind the foreman and frowned.

"What—"

"He came riding up to the house," Conners said. "He said he thought you'd be looking for him."

"That's all Conners," Burkett said, and Conners left.

Coffin sat in a chair and kept his eyes on Burkett.

"How did you know?"

"It was McCall come riding out here? I figured he was going to push the play a little."

"Well, he did."

"How?"

"He says he's got some evidence."

"Where would he get evidence?"

"I don't know."

"Then he probably doesn't have any."

Burkett rubbed his jaw and said, "I can't take that chance. I've got too much at stake here."

Coffin didn't know what Burkett had at stake, and he didn't care. In fact, he didn't even know what kind of "evidence" they were talking about. None of that had anything to do with him.

"You want me to take care of McCall?"

"Can you?" Burkett asked. "I mean, can you take him?"

"I don't know."

"What do you mean, you don't know?" Burkett said. "I thought you were the best."

"Maybe I am," Coffin said, "and maybe he is. That's what we're gonna find out."

"And what happens if he kills you?" Burkett asked. "What do I do after that?"

"There are other men with other guns, Burkett," Coffin said. "Somewhere there's a man who can take McCall if I don't. You'll just have to keep looking."

Coffin started for the door.

"When will you do it?"

"When the opportunity presents itself," Coffin said. He

turned at the door and looked at his employer. "When the time is right."

"And when will that be?"

"You'll know about it when it happens."

"But I want to watch!" Burkett shouted as Coffin started down the hall.

"I don't need an audience!" Coffin called back, and kept walking.

Burkett sat back in his chair and fretted. He had sent for Coffin with the understanding that he was the best man for this job. If McCall killed him, who else could do it?

He heard someone else in the outside hall and left the office to see who it was. He was just in time to see his son heading for the front door.

"John!"

John Burkett stopped, his shoulders slumped.

"Where are you going?"

"To town," John replied without turning.

"I don't think that's wise."

"Why not?"

"It might not be safe."

"I'll be fine."

"Take someone with you, then."

John opened the door and said, "I'll be fine, Pa."

John Burkett's ego was still stinging from the last time he had taken someone to town with him. They had seen him humiliated.

"John, you're not intending to go after McCall, are you?"

John Burkett turned and looked at his father.

"Not Sam McCall, if that's what you're worried about," he said, "but I want the other one, the one they call Jubal."

"Well, don't do anything rash," Lincoln Burkett said. "Wait until after..."

"After what?"

Burkett didn't answer.

John Burkett took his hand off the doorknob. He left the door open but stepped back into the entry hall.

"Have you done it?" he asked. "Have you sent Coffin after Sam McCall?"

Lincoln Burkett hesitated a moment, then said, "Yes."

"Well, it's about time," John Burkett said. "When's he going to do it?"

"Soon."

"Today?"

"He didn't say."

"Well, hell, I wanna be there when he does it," the younger Burkett said. "That might be the perfect time for me to take out the other one, Jubal."

"And what about the middle one?" the father asked. "Evan?"

"He's a gambler, not a gunman," the son said. "I'm not worried about him."

"He stopped you once."

"He had the drop on me, Pa," John Burkett said. "That won't happen again."

"John—" Burkett said, but this time his son walked out and closed the door behind him.

Burkett decided to give his son a head start and then have Conners send some men after him. None of this would be worth the effort if John got killed. He was trying to build a future here for his only son. If the boy would only realize that...

When Sam reached the Miller house no one answered the door. He found each of his brothers in their hotel rooms, which was just as well. He didn't want Serena to hear about his conversation with Burkett.

He found Evan first, and then they went to Jubal's room. They stayed there while he told his story.

"I don't know that I like this, Sam," Evan said. "It's not as if you weren't a big enough target already, but you just about painted a bull's-eye on your back this time."

"Well," he said, "with the two of you to watch my back, I haven't got much to worry about, have I?"

"That's for sure," Jubal said enthusiastically. "You can count on us to watch your back, Sam."

"Thanks, Jube." Sam frowned then. "Aren't one of you supposed to be with Serena?"

"She's at her father's store, helping out," Evan said. "I'm supposed to meet her there soon."

"Oh."

"Sam," Evan said, "you know that the biggest threat to you isn't going to come from behind you."

"I know that."

"You mean Coffin?" Jubal asked.

"That's right," Evan said.

"We all could take care of Coffin," Jubal said to Evan. "We all could bushwack him the way Burkett's men tried to bushwack Sam."

"I don't like bushwackers," Sam said, "I don't care who they're bushwacking."

"I don't mean kill him," Jubal said. "We can just cut him out of action for a while."

"Jube may have a point here, Sam," Evan said.

"No," Sam said, "I'll take care of Coffin."

"Or he'll take care of you," Evan said.

Sam looked at his brothers and said, "It's gonna happen sometime."

"Are you resigned to that?" Evan asked. 1 am.

Evan stared at Sam for a few moments and then said, "Maybe I don't understand you any more than Serena does."

"Maybe not," Sam said, "but if you had a big poker game you wouldn't let me play in your place, would you?"

"That's not the same," Evan said. "I wouldn't be playing for my life."

Sam shrugged and said, "That's the nature of the way we both ended up living our lives. The stakes in my life are slightly higher than in yours."

It was agreed that Evan would go and meet Serena as planned while Sam and Jubal rode out to the section of the ranch where their father had liked to hunt.

As they rode out there Jubal said, "Pa never took me hunting."

"We took you with us sometimes," Sam said, "but you were too small to remember."

"Really? What did you hunt?"

"Jackrabbit, mostly," Sam said. "Once in a while we'd get us a buck. Once we all came across cougar sign and tracked the animal to its lair."

"Who got it?"

"Pa did, on the dead run. He was the best shot I ever saw with a rifle."

"Still?"

"Hell, yes, still."

"Better than you?"

"He was always a better rifle shot than me."

"Better than some of your friends?"

"Friends?"

"Hickok, Ben Thompson, Bat Masterson."

"What makes you think those fellas were friends of mine?"

"I read... guess I shouldn't believe everything I read, huh?"

"I know those fellas, for sure," Sam said. "Knew Hickok real well, although we never did like each other all that much. Man shouldn't die the way he did, though, at the hands of a back-shootin' coward."

"Is that how you expect to die, Sam?"

Sam looked over at his little brother.

"I expect to die from a bullet, Jube. I prefer that it not come from behind, though. I pray it doesn't."

"What's it like?" Jubal asked.

"What?"

"Not being afraid to die," Jubal said. "When I was up on that scaffold I was so scared I coulda shit, except they woulda liked that."

"What makes you think I ain't afraid to die?"

"The way you talk about it."

"I expect it, Jube," Sam said. "I expect there ain't a whole lot I can do about it. That don't mean I ain't afraid of it."

"I thought you wasn't afraid of nothing" Jubal said.

Sam laughed.

"It's no shame bein' afraid, Jubal," Sam said. "A man who says he's never been afraid is either a fool or a liar. If you were afraid up on that scaffold, that's only natural. Hell, when I saw you up there with that rope around your neck I was plenty afraid."

"Why's that?" Jubal asked.

"You're my brother."

"Yeah, but we don't really know each other, Sam," Jubal said. "In fact, we're almost strangers—or we were before this started."

"That don't make no never mind, Jube," Sam said. "You're still my brother. Fact that we ain't seen each other in years don't change that."

"Guess I ain't never had the chance to tell you I was proud to be your brother," Jubal said. "Anytime I ever heard anyone talking about you I always wanted to tell them you was my brother."

"You didn't?"

"Naw. For one thing I didn't figure they'd believe me. Later, I started to figure that maybe I was proud of you for the wrong reasons. Still, from what I seen of you since you and Evan got me off that scaffold, I'm right proud to call both of you my brothers."

"Well, we feel the same, Jube," Sam said, slapping his brother on the back.

"Maybe we should stay in closer touch after this is over," Jubal said.

"Maybe we should" Sam agreed.

But they both knew that wouldn't likely happen. When this was over the three of them would go their own ways—at least Sam and Evan would. Sam was over forty, Evan closing in on it, they were set in their ways. Jubal might very well leave Vengeance Creek with one of them, but Sam would make damned sure it wasn't him. He didn't need Jubal around when the lead started flying his way. He didn't want his brother around when that last piece of lead found its way to his heart. He'd be much better off with Evan, maybe even learning to play cards.

There was more money in gambling than there was in gunplay, that was for damned sure.

When they finally reached the part of the ranch Sam wanted he reined in.

"We used to hunt this section here, for a few miles around."

Jubal looked around. It was mostly flat land, rocks, and clay, some Joshua trees, and black chaparral.

"If he wanted to leave us a note, where would he leave it?" he asked. "We can't be turning over every rock and looking under every bush."

"It would be someplace where the sun and the rain couldn't get at it," Sam said.

"Also somewhere an animal wouldn't get at it."

"A hole, maybe," Sam said.

"A chuck hole? Nah..." Jubal said.

"Let's ride," Sam said. "Maybe somethin'll come to us."

So they rode.

―――

AFTER A COUPLE of hours they reined in and dismounted near a water hole. While the horses drank their fill they each took a drink and topped off their canteens, doused their heads, and wet their bandanas, tying them around their necks.

"We likely to run into anybody around here?" Jubal asked.

"No," Sam said. "Most of this clay is buckshot land, not good for much of anything. Might not even be that many jackrabbits around here any more."

"What about cougars?"

"Maybe," Sam said. "The big cats know how to survive. There's water, and there's rattlers, and an occasional rabbit, I guess..."

Sam's voice trailed off suddenly, and Jubal noticed a funny look in his eyes.

"What is it?" Jubal asked. "You just thought of something, didn't you?"

"Cougars," Sam said.

"What about them?"

"A cougar's lair is usually a sort of cave, the inside of a rock formation."

"Ain't no mountains around here, Sam."

"No, but there's that lair Pa and I tracked that cat to," Sam said. "Pa would know that I'd remember that."

"You think that's where he left us a message? In a cougar's lair?"

"It's as good an idea as any," Sam said.

"Do you remember where it was?"

"Gimme a minute," Sam said, looking around. He wasn't really looking around, though, as much as he was looking inside himself.

"I think I've got an idea," Sam said. "Let's mount up and try it."

"I'm game," Jubal said, "but what do we do if that cat is there when we get there?"

Sam grinned and mounted up.

"We'll do just what Pa did," Sam said. "I just hope I'm almost as good a shot as he was."

CHAPTER NINETEEN

John Burkett found Coffin drinking a beer, sitting alone at a table in the saloon.

Actually, Burkett wasn't looking for Coffin, but he recognized him as soon as he entered the saloon. He bought himself a beer and carried it over to Coffin's table.

"Mind if I sit?"

Coffin looked up.

"Burkett, right?"

"That's right."

Coffin didn't say anything after that, which John Burkett took as no objection to him sitting.

"I understand my old man gave you the go-ahead."

"What go-ahead is that?"

"To kill Sam McCall."

Coffin smiled a humorless smile.

"Just like that, huh?" he asked. "Kill Sam McCall."

"Well, you can, can't you?"

"Sure I can," Coffins said, "and he can kill me just as easily."

"You saying you can't take McCall?"

"I'll tell you what I told your father, boy," Coffin said, "that's what we're going to find out."

"What about his brothers?"

"Secondary concern."

"Huh?"

"They are only a concern of mine if I kill McCall. If he kills me..." Coffin's voice trailed off and he shrugged.

"What happens if Sam McCall won't fight you?"

"He will."

"But what if you won't? Will you shoot him in cold blood?"

"I have never shot a man in cold blood in my life, kid."

"I didn't say you did," Burkett said, "but if McCall won't draw, that's what it will be. If that happens you'll go to jail."

"I thought your old man owned the law in this town," Coffin said.

"Hah!" Burkett said. "My old man will be the one to insist that the sheriff arrest you. He won't be able to let you go free after you've shot Sam McCall down like a dog."

Coffin frowned at John Burkett. He knew the kid was playing a game, but he couldn't figure out what it was.

"What's your angle, kid?"

"I know how to make sure Sam McCall fights you."

"How?"

"Kill one of his brothers," John Burkett said, "preferably the gambler, Evan."

"Why him?"

"Because I want the other one."

"Why?"

"That's between him and me," Jubal said. "Meanwhile, if you kill the other one Sam McCall will come after you. Then when you kill him you can claim self-defense, for sure."

Coffin stared at his beer. He knew McCall would fight him if he called him out, but there was a chance that he wouldn't, especially since McCall knew he was working for Burkett. Refusing to fight him would be a way for the man to give Lincoln Burkett another headache.

"I'll tell you what," John Burkett said. "I'll make it easy for you. You kill for money, right?"

"Sometimes."

"I have some money," Burkett said. "I'll pay you to kill Evan McCall."

"What?"

"How much do you want?" Burkett asked. "A hundred? Two hundred? No, a man like you would charge more than that, wouldn't he? What's my father paying you for Sam McCall?"

"That's between him and me."

"All right," John Burkett said, "A thousand. I'll pay you a thousand dollars to kill Evan McCall."

Coffin studied the young man for a few moments and then said, "Pay me up front and you have a deal."

Burkett smiled and stood up.

"I'll go to the bank right now."

"I'll be waiting right here."

John Burkett left the saloon, happy as a kid on Christmas morning.

———

SAM REINED IN HIS HORSE, and Jubal looked at him eagerly.

"Is it near here?"

"I think so," Sam said. "Come on, it can't be much farther."

Jubal hoped not. Sweat was running down his back, and his shirt was sticking to him.

"I hope there's water near this cat's lair," he said, half to himself.

When John Burkett returned to the saloon he was happy to find Coffin still sitting there. It looked like he was even working on the same beer.

Burkett approached the table and dropped a white envelope down on it. Some of the other men in the place looked over curiously, but when they saw that whatever was taking place was happening at Coffin's table they quickly averted their eyes.

"There's your money," Burkett said. "Do it...now."

"Sam McCall's out of town."

"Evan McCall is over at Dude Miller's store, mooning over Miller's daughter."

"She's pretty enough to moon over," Coffin said. "Tell me, what will you do if Evan McCall kills me?"

"That can't happen," John Burkett said, and then stared at Coffin and asked, "Can it?"

Coffin laughed softly and said, "Not hardly."

"When Sam McCall comes back to town and hears that you killed his brother, he'll come looking for you for sure."

Coffin picked up the money, stood up and stuffed the envelope into his shirt.

"I won't be hard to find."

———

"JUST A FEW MINUTES MORE, EVAN," Serena said, apologetically. "I'm just helping Pa with his inventory."

"Take your time, Serena," Evan said. "I'm not in a hurry."

Evan was looking over some of the items on Dude Miller's shelves when Coffin entered.

"There you are," Coffin said.

"You looking for me?"

"I'm looking for a McCall," Coffin said, "and I guess you're it"

"I'm... what?"

"I've decided to kill a McCall today," Coffin said, just as Serena came through the storeroom door.

"Are you crazy?" Serena asked him.

Coffin turned to her and touched his hat.

"No, ma'am," Coffin said, "I'm just doing what has to be done." Coffin looked at Evan and said, "I'll be waiting for you outside, McCall."

"And if I don't come out?"

"If you don't come out," Coffin said, "I'll come in here and get you. If I do that, the place might get damaged. Heck, the little lady might even get hurt."

With that Coffin turned and walked outside. Evan took out his gun, checked the loads, and slid it back into the holster. He eased it in and out a few times, just to be sure it wouldn't stick.

"My God," Serena said, "you're not going to do it, are you?"

"Do what?" Dude Miller asked, entering the room. "What's going on?"

"Coffin has called Evan out," Serena said. She looked at Evan and said, "Isn't that what they say, he 'called you out'?"

"I suppose so."

"And he's going," Serena said to her father.

"Dude," Evan said, "keep her inside."

"Evan—"

"Just keep her inside. All right?"

Dude Miller nodded and said, "All right."

Evan eased his gun in and out of his holster one more time and then walked to the door. His heart was beating so hard it sounded like thunder in his ears.

———

"THERE IT IS!" Sam said. "That's the cat's lair."

"Are you sure that's it?" Jubal asked.

"Yep," Sam said, "I recognize the rock formation."

They both stared at the formation of rocks that amounted to a small hill. Halfway up there was a wide crack between two rocks.

"That's where it was," Sam said, pointing. "Halfway up. See it?"

"I see it."

Sam dismounted and started walking toward it.

"Sam!" Jubal called.

"What?"

"What if there's a cat in there?"

Sam stopped short and turned to face his brother.

"You're gettin' smart in your old age, little brother."

———

THE TOWNSPEOPLE already knew that something was happening. Coffin was standing in the street, waiting, and that was a sure tip-off. They didn't know who he was waiting for, but they were lining up to watch.

Evan McCall stepped out of the store onto the boardwalk and looked at Coffin. The way the town was built, neither man would have the sun directly in his eyes when they were facing each other.

Small *consolation*, Evan thought. This *is crazy*. I *can't out-draw him*. He was convinced his only chance was to draw sure and easy and make his first shot count. He knew that Coffin would get off the first shot, he just had to hope that it wouldn't be a fatal one. He needed time to get off one shot.

It was his only chance.

Sam and Jubal gathered up as much brush as they could find, and then they climbed the rocks together. Jubal held the brush while Sam lit it, and when it was flaring well he tossed it into the lair, and they scrambled back down to the ground.

Sam grabbed his rifle from his saddle and they settled down to watch. If there was a big cat in there the smoke would drive him out eventually.

"This is the way Pa did it," Sam said, holding the rifle in both hands. When the cat came out he'd come out fast, and Sam was going to have to be just a fraction of a second faster.

Evan walked out into the street and faced Coffin. Dude and Serena Miller moved to the window to look out.

"I thought he was gonna kill *Sam* McCall," somebody said.

"When McCall finds out about this," someone else said, "he's gonna have to."

Evan had never been in quite this situation before. He knew Sam had, many times, but most of the gunplay Evan had been involved with had either been in saloons and gambling houses, or long distance, like the telegraph office incident. He'd never faced a man this way before.

Hell of a time to try.

"Be ready," Jube said.

"Shhh."

"Just be ready—"

"I'm ready," Sam said, "no, be quiet—there!"

They saw a streak of brown as a big cougar came shooting out of the cave. He leaped into the air in panic, trying to get down to the ground as quickly as possible.

Sam fired, and the bullet struck the cat while it was in the air, jerked it as if it were a puppet on a string, and dropped it to the ground, dead.

"You got it!" Jubal said, excitedly. "Just like Pa, huh?"

"Yeah," Sam said, feeling oddly proud of himself, "just like Pa."

Evan heard the shot and knew that he had no chance. He had just touched his gun when he felt the bullet punch him in the chest. His entire body went numb and he stood for a moment transfixed, wondering if Coffin would fire again.

He didn't have to.

"Evan!" Serena screamed. She avoided her father's grasp and ran out into the street, falling to her knees by Evan McCall.

"Evan," she said, lifting his head into her lap, but it was too late for any last words.

Evan McCall was dead.

She felt hands on her shoulder; her father was lifting her to her feet.

"Come on, Serena," Miller said, "come inside."

"All right," the sheriff called, "some of you men lift the body and carry it to the undertaker's."

Miller had gotten Serena up onto the boardwalk when she suddenly whirled around. She didn't have to look for Coffin, he was still standing in the same spot.

"You're a dead man, Coffin!" she shouted. "When Sam McCall comes back you're a dead man, I promise you that."

Coffin looked at Serena and although he spoke in a low voice, everyone heard what he said.

"One of us is, I promise you that, ma'am."

Sam and Jubal waited for the brush to burn out and for the smoke to clear. It took nearly forty minutes for that, because there wasn't much of a breeze to help it along.

"All right," Sam said, "let's go in."

"I hope there's not another cat in there," Jubal said as they climbed up to the lair.

"If there is," Sam said, "the smoke killed it for sure."

As it turned out there were three more cats inside, all cubs. Apparently, they had been too young to escape and the smoke had killed them.

"Damn," Sam said when he saw them.

"Couldn't be helped, Sam," Jubal said. "We didn't know they was there."

"Yeah," Sam said, "yeah."

Jubal was carrying a makeshift torch they had fashioned from a branch they'd found nearby and now Sam lit it with a lucifer stick match, striking the match on his thumbnail.

"Let's look around," he said.

They each took one side of the lair, which was so low that they had to crouch down and, eventually, get down to their knees.

"I don't see anything..." Jubal complained.

"Look for cracks in the wall," Sam said, running one of his hands over the wall while he held the torch in the other.

"Wait a minute," Jubal said, "wait—bring that torch closer."

Sam turned and joined his brother, holding the torch as high as the ceiling would allow. The ceiling was so low they could feel the heat of the flames.

Sam watched as Jubal tried to work his hand into a good sized crack.

"There's something here," he said, "but I can't seem to—

wait, wait, I've got it—" He pulled something from the crack and said, "I've got it!"

"Let's look at it outside," Sam said, and started backing out.

When they got outside Sam dropped the torch and reached for the item in Jubal's hand. It was some sort of a leather case, the kind his father used to keep letters in.

"Open it," Jubal said.

Sam opened it. There were no letters inside, but there was one piece of paper which had begun to yellow around the edges. He took it out and saw the handwriting on it.

"It's Pa's writing," he said.

"Are you sure?"

Sam held the letter so Jubal could look at it and they both saw the word "Pa" signed at the bottom.

"We've got it," Jubal said, "but what's it say?"

"I'll read it out loud," Sam said, and proceeded to do so.

After Sam read the letter they mounted up and headed back to town hell bent for leather. They wanted Evan to hear what was in this letter, and then they would all decide exactly what they were going to do about it.

Part Four

SIEGE

CHAPTER TWENTY

W hen Sam and Jubal returned to Vengeance Creek they could feel that something had happened while they were gone. There were still people standing in groups along the street. When Sam and Jubal passed, people suspended their conversations to stare at them.

"What the hell happened here while we were gone?" Jubal asked.

"I don't know," Sam said, looking back at some of the people, "but I aim to find out. Come on. We'll leave the horses in front of Dude's store and find Evan."

They rode over to Dude Miller's general store and tied their horses to a post. As they approached the store Sam suddenly stopped short.

"That's funny," he said. "He closed early." It was only three P.M., and Miller usually kept his store open at least another three hours.

"You don't suppose he got beat up again, do you?" Jubal asked.

"We'd better check the house."

They remounted and rode to the house. When they dismounted they didn't bother tying off their horses. They mounted the porch and Sam found that the door was unlocked. They exchanged glances and then hurried inside.

They heard Serena crying as soon as they entered, and then saw her and Dude sitting on the sofa. Dude had his arm around

Serena. Sam couldn't see her face. If any of Burkett's men had hurt her...

"What's going on?" Jubal asked. "What's happening?"

Both Miller and Serena turned to face them, and Sam was taken aback by the look of pure horror on Serena's face.

"Serena?" he said.

All she could do was cover her open mouth with both hands and stare at him.

Sam looked around and said, "Where's Evan?"

"Sam—" Dude Miller said, but he stopped short.

"Dude, Serena?" Sam said. "Where is Evan?"

Finally, Serena lowered her hands from her mouth and stood up.

"Oh, Sam..." she said.

"Serena?"

"Sam, oh Sam," she said, moving toward him slowly, "he's dead."

"What?" Sam wasn't sure he'd heard right—he *hoped* he had not heard her right. "What did you say?"

"H-he's dead," Serena said again, "I still can't believe it h-happened, but h-he's dead, Evan's dead..."

"What happened, Serena?" Jubal demanded.

"Tell us what happened," Sam said, his face a mask of stone.

Dude Miller rose and stood behind his daughter, his hands on her shoulders.

"It was Coffin, Sam," Miller said. "Coffin called him out into the street."

"And Evan went?" Sam said, in disbelief.

"He's dead?" Jubal asked.

"He's dead, boys," Dude Miller said. "Coffin cut him down before Evan could even touch his gun."

"Evan was no gunman," Sam said coldly, "he had no business facing Coffin."

"Sam..." Serena said.

Jubal turned to bolt from the room and Sam grabbed him.

"Where are you going?"

"I'm going after Coffin!"

"No you're not."

"Then we're going after him—"

"You're stayin' right here, Jube," Sam said.

"Sam, he killed Evan!"

"I know," Sam said. "I know he did, and he's gonna pay, but you're stayin' here."

"Like hell I am—" Jubal said, pulling free of Sam's grasp. He touched his gun and said, "I'm gonna kill the son-of-a-bitch."

He started past Sam and Sam grabbed his arm, spun him around, and hit him. Serena gasped. As Jubal started to fall Sam caught him, lifted him up and laid him on the sofa. Then he took Jubal's gun from his holster and gave it to Dude Miller.

"Don't give it to him when he wakes up."

"Where are you going?" Miller asked.

"I'm gonna give Coffin and Burkett what they want," Sam said.

"You're going to let them kill you, too?"

"I'm not Evan, Serena," Sam said. "He didn't belong out there. I do."

"Sam—" she said, reaching for his arm, but he was already on his way to the door.

"Papa—" Her eyes and her voice beseeched her father to do something.

"Honey," he said, shaking his head, "it's got to be this way."

She stared at him for a moment, then looked down at the unconscious Jubal. Lying there quietly like that, he looked like a little boy. She leaned over and touched his cheek tenderly.

"And what if Coffin kills Sam?" she asked. "Does Jubal go after him next?"

"I don't know, honey," Miller said, "I just don't know."

True to his word, Coffin was not hard for Sam McCall to find. He was sitting in a wooden chair in front of the saloon. Standing alongside him was John Burkett and two or three Burkett men.

Sam walked briskly toward the saloon, and Burkett and his men straightened up. Coffin continued to lounge in his chair, sitting with it tilted back against the wall.

"Sam—" he said as Sam mounted the boardwalk, but he got no further. Sam hooked the front of the chair with his foot and pulled. Coffin went down on his back, the chair splintering beneath him. Sam quickly bent and removed Coffin's gun from his holster, tucking it into his own belt.

When he straightened Sam looked at John Burkett and his men and said, "Stand still and don't interfere!"

"You took his gun," John Burkett said. "You can't kill him in cold blood."

"I'll kill the first man who touches a gun," Sam said to them, and they all leaned away from him, holding their hands as far from their guns as possible.

Coffin had struck his head when he'd fallen and had not yet fully regained his senses. Sam leaned over, grabbed him by the shirt front and hauled him to his feet. Holding him with one hand he began to strike him with the other, vicious forehand and backhand blows that jerked the man's head right and left. Blood began to trickle from smashed lips, and then it flowed down over the man's chin. Still Sam McCall held him by the shirt and struck him, back and forth, until finally he was too tired to continue. He turned Coffin around and shoved him out into the street, where he fell onto his back. He was conscious, but his eyes were glazed and the lower portion of his face was a mask of crimson.

Sam went into the street after Coffin and hauled him to his feet again. Instinctively, Coffin covered up, fearful of more blows, but Sam was finished with him—for now.

"Walk!" he said, pushing the man.

"Where are you taking him?" John Burkett demanded.

"To jail."

"For what?"

"For killin' my brother."

"It was a fair fight!" John Burkett called after them.

"That the way you saw it, Coffin?" Sam asked as he continued to push the man toward the jail. People who were watching sidestepped to get out of their way.

Coffin wiped his mouth on his sleeve and frowned down at the blood. He was only now beginning to understand what had happened.

"Was it a fair fight, Coffin?" Sam demanded again.

"He had a gun."

"Sure he had a gun, but he was no gunman and you knew it. Why'd you do it, Coffin?" He slammed his palm viciously into the man's back, staggering him. "Why'd you do it? Did you get tired of waitin' on me? Or did Burkett tell you to do it?"

"The kid—" Coffin said through mashed lips.

"What?"

Coffin tried to speak more clearly, but his tongue had been cut against his teeth and was swelling up some.

"The kid, he paid me."

"The kid? John Burkett?"

"That's right—"

Sam turned quickly, just in time to see John Burkett aiming his gun at his back. He drew and fired, in fear for his life. In fear of dying the way Hickok had died. He fired by pure instinct, and the bullet sped straight and true across the street, striking John Burkett in the heart.

Sam turned back to Coffin then, who was watching him. The man was grinning, and Sam could see the film of blood on the man's teeth.

"Oh, the old man's not going to like that, Sam." Coffin said. "You better give me my gun and let me kill you right now."

"Keep walkin'," Sam said. "You're gonna hang for killin' my brother."

"Ha!" Coffin said. "Not in this town. Burkett owns the sheriff."

"There's a federal marshal due here any day," Sam said. "You're gonna wait in a cell until he gets here, and then I'm gonna turn you over to him."

"The sheriff will never go along with it."

"If he doesn't, I'll kill him."

Coffin fell silent for a moment and then said over his shoulder, "You would, wouldn't you? And what about Burkett? He won't let me stay in jail."

"If he tries to get you out, I'll kill him, too."

"All this killing," Coffin said, "when the one you really want is me. Come on, Sam, give me my gun and let's get it done."

Sam holstered his gun, spun Coffin around, and grabbed him by the shirt with both hands. He pulled Coffin real close to him so that he wouldn't miss a word.

"No gunplay for you, my friend," he said evenly, coldly. "You're not gonna get off that easy. I'm gonna watch you dance at the end of a rope, Coffin, kicking and screaming until you die. I'm gonna make sure your neck doesn't break. I'm gonna watch you strangle at the end of that rope. Whataya think of that, Mr. Gunman?"

Coffin stared into Sam McCall's eyes and felt fear for the first time in years.

"That's no way for a man to die, Sam," he said, softly.

"You're not a man," Sam said, releasing Coffin's shirt.

"You're slime, Coffin, and slime dies at the end of a rope. Now... walk!"

Sheriff Kelly jumped to his feet when the door to his office slammed open. Coffin staggered through the door and Sam entered after him.

"What's going on here?" Kelly demanded. He noticed that Sam McCall had his gun out, and this did not please him. He started to sweat profusely.

"I want this man in a cell, Sheriff!" Sam said.

"You can't just—"

"This man killed my brother," Sam said, cutting him off. "You know that. In fact, you might even have watched him do it."

"I didn't—"

"I have a federal marshal coming to town," Sam said, although he still didn't know if the man would ever really get there. "You're to hold this man in a cell until he arrives."

"Look—"

"You are not to let him out for any reason."

"Mr. Burkett won't—"

"If you let him out," Sam continued, "I'll kill you."

Kelly's mouth snapped shut.

"Is that clear enough for you?"

Kelly tried one last bluster.

"You c-can't threaten an officer of the law l-like that."

"I'm not threatenin' you, Kelly," Sam said. "I'm makin' you a solemn promise. If you let him out before I tell you to, I will kill you. Do you understand?"

Kelly nodded jerkily, his voice failing him.

"Now, toss me the keys to the cells."

Kelly opened the top drawer of his desk and groped for the keys. Finally, he yanked his eyes away from Sam's gun long enough to find them and he tossed them over.

"Let's go, Coffin."

Coffin, resigned to the fact that he would be spending a short time in jail, obeyed. He knew Burkett would have him out in no time. After all, Coffin was the only man who could stand up to Sam McCall and get Burkett's revenge.

As they reached the doorway to the cells Coffin stopped

short and said, "You'd better go and tell Lincoln Burkett that his son is dead, Sheriff."

"What?" Kelly said. "J-John's dead?"

"He tried to backshoot me while I was takin' Coffin, Sheriff. There were witnesses."

Actually, Sam had his doubts about witnesses coming forward to back him up. They would, after all, be going against Burkett if they did that. Sam had decided, though, from the moment he learned that Evan was dead, that he would be taking matters entirely into his own hands. If he had to answer to the law later, so be it.

He put Coffin in a cell, locked the door and came back out to the sheriff's office. He holstered his gun and undid the gunbelt for a moment. Kelly watched as Sam looped the key ring through the gunbelt and then buckled it again.

"Wha—"

"I'll hold onto the keys, Sheriff," Sam said, "this way you won't be tempted."

"Look, McCall," Kelly said, "if you killed Burkett's son—"

"Oh, I killed him, all right. He's still lyin' out there in the street."

"Oh, Jesus—" Kelly said, rushing to the window. "I'll have to have him taken to the undertaker's—"

"No," Sam said, "you'll stay right here with the prisoner."

"But the body—"

"I don't want John Burkett's body at the undertaker's while my brother's body is there, Sheriff. Is that understood?"

"But Mr. Burkett—"

"I don't care about Mr. Burkett."

"H-he'll kill me!"

"He'll kill you later," Sam said. "If you don't do as I say I'll kill you right now. You have a choice."

Kelly swallowed and said, "With a choice like that, I'll take later—but who'll tell Mr. Burkett?"

"There were some men with John Burkett," Sam said. "Lincoln Burkett will know about it soon enough."

"He'll come after you."

Sam grinned coldly and said, "I'm countin' on that, Sheriff."

As Sam started to leave Kelly said, "Wait—what am I supposed to do?"

"Get your deputies to help you with Coffin. You're gonna have to keep Burkett's men out of here."

"W-What?"

"They'll want to try and break him out. It's your duty to stop them."

"Oh, Jesus—" Kelly said, but Sam McCall was already out the door. Sheriff Kelly fell into the chair and put his elbows on the desk and his head in his hands.

———

SAM WENT BACK to the Miller house and told Jubal, Dude, and Serena what he had done.

"You didn't kill Coffin?" Jubal demanded, outraged. There was a bruise on the right side of his jaw.

"No."

"Why not?"

"There was no need."

"He killed Evan."

"I know that, Jube."

"But you killed John Burkett."

"He tried to backshoot me," Sam said. "That was self-defense."

"I don't understand you," Jubal said. "You had a chance to kill Coffin...unless you were afraid to face him."

"Jubal!" Serena said.

"No, no "Jubal said, waving her protestations away, "that's it, isn't it? Big Sam McCall is afraid that he can't take Coffin."

"Open your eyes, son," Dude Miller said. "He did take him."

"But he didn't kill him!"

"When the federal marshal gets here," Sam said, "he'll place Coffin under arrest. Coffin will give the marshal Lincoln Burkett."

"But John Burkett paid Coffin to kill Evan," Dude Miller said. "You said so yourself."

"And Lincoln Burkett paid Coffin to kill me, only he didn't get the job done." Sam looked at Jubal and said, "Believe me, Jube, this is the way to do it. This way we'll take them down together."

"If you had killed Coffin we could have gone out to Burkett's ranch and killed him, and *then* they'd be taken care of."

"That ain't the way Evan would have done it," Sam said, "and it wouldn't have been Pa's way. You read Pa's letter."

"What letter?" Miller asked.

"We found a letter from Pa," Sam said, "but we can talk about that later. Jube—"

Sam reached for Jubal, but the younger man pulled away and started to walk out.

"Jubal!" Sam snapped. "I need you."

"You don't need me," Jubal said. "You got it all figured out by yourself."

"Where are you goin?"

"Out."

"Jube." Sam crossed the room and grabbed his brother's arm. Jubal tried to pull away but Sam held him tightly.

"Burkett's gonna come for me, Jube, and he's gonna try to get Coffin out of jail. The sheriff isn't gonna hold up under this. You and I are gonna have to stand against Burkett and his men until the marshal gets here."

"Which is when?" Jubal asked.

"I don't know."

"This is madness," Serena said. "The two of you can't hold off Burkett and all of his men."

"There are three of us," Dude Miller said.

"Pa!"

"Dude," Sam said, "I'm gonna hold you to that."

Dude Miller nodded.

"What are we gonna do?" Jubal asked.

"We're gonna occupy the jail" Sam said, "and we ain't comin' out until the marshal gets here. Serena?"

"Yes."

"I'll need you to send another telegram. We're gonna have to make damned sure that marshal is on his way."

Serena took a deep breath and said, "I'll help any way I can, Sam."

Sam thanked her and looked at Jubal.

"Jube?"

Jubal thought it over a moment, and finally said, "I'm with you."

Sam smiled and said, "I knew you would be."

"But if things go wrong," Jubal said, "the first thing I'm gonna do is put a bullet in Coffin's head. Agreed?"

"Agreed," Sam said. "I'll even help you."

———

THE THREE MEN who had been standing with John Burkett had a decision to make. They could ride back to the ranch and tell Lincoln Burkett that they had let his son be killed, or they could mount up and just keep riding.

In the end they decided that their jobs were too good to just walk away from. If Burkett fired them, that would be another thing, but they couldn't just walk away from these jobs. Besides, Burkett wouldn't kill them. He was going to need all the men he could put his hands on to get his revenge on Sam McCall.

They knew they were going to have to work fast.

They were going to have to fortify the jail, stock it with food and water, and get it ready to withstand any and all attempts to enter it before Lincoln Burkett arrived with his men.

Luckily, Dude Miller gave them free access to his store, which had most of what they needed: canned food, blankets, sheets, coffee, and whatever else. He even had wooden shutters, which they nailed up over the windows, leaving only space enough to shoot through.

Ed Collins at the gunsmith shop also pitched in, giving them all the ammunition they'd need for their guns and offered to stay inside with them.

"No, Mr. Collins," Sam had told him, "I think we'll need someone on the outside who's on our side."

Collins argued, but in the end he saw the wisdom of that.

They also went over to Doc Leader's to get what they would need to tend to bullet wounds. Doc thought they were crazy, and he bitched and moaned, but he gave them what they needed.

"Don't be expectin' me to come over there and tend to you, though," he told them. "I may be an old man, but I ain't in any hurry to die."

"Don't you worry, Doc," Sam said, "we'll tend ourselves."

They lugged all the equipment over to the sheriff's office under the watchful eye of the whole town. The sheriff didn't help, preferring to stay behind his desk and fret about his safety.

They were all in the office when the door opened and a well-fed, jowly, officious-looking man in his fifties stepped in.

"Mr. Mayor," Kelly said.

Sam turned and looked at the mayor of Vengeance Creek, whom he had not yet met.

"Which of you is Sam McCall?" the mayor asked.

"I am."

The two men locked eyes, and to Sam's satisfaction it was the mayor who looked away first. Obviously the man was not looking forward to the conversation that was coming. He had probably been elected by the town council as spokesman.

"Mr. McCall, I am Mayor Eustace Tenderberry. Uh, we on the town council cannot...condone what you are about to do."

"Oh? And what is it I'm about to do?"

"Well, sir, uh, you are about to turn this town into a battle-field. What's worse, your opponent is the town's most prominent citizen."

"Mr. Mayor," Sam said, "what is about to go on between Burkett and me is our business. I'm sure even he would not want you interfering in it."

"Nevertheless," Tenderberry said, "for the safety of our town, and of Mr. Burk—uh, I mean of all our citizens, I'm afraid we must ask you to leave. Sheriff?" the mayor said, looking at his lawman. "You will escort Mr. McCall and his brother to the town limits."

"Mayor," Kelly said, gaping at the man, "are you crazy?"

"Sheriff!" Mayor Tenderberry said. "Either you do your duty or I must ask you to hand over your badge."

"Well, shit," Kelly said, "that's the best offer I had all day." Hurriedly he unpinned the badge from his shirt and dropped it on the desk. On his way out he said to the Mayor, "Now *you* escort him to the town limits."

The mayor watched the sheriff leave and then turned to face Sam McCall.

I'll, uh, ask you again—" The man stopped when Sam took a few steps toward him and flinched, as if he thought Sam was going to strike him. Dude Miller and Jubal watched with interest.

"Mr. Mayor, I suggest you go to your town council and tell them you tried your best to get my brother and me to leave, but it didn't work."

"B-but—" the mayor stuttered, "but—we don't have a sheriff now!"

Sam smiled humorlessly, walked to the desk, and picked up the badge.

"Now you do."

"What—"

"Unless you want the job?" Sam held out the badge to the man.

"No, no, no—" the man said, his face flushing.

Sam pinned the badge on.

"Jube, you're a duly sworn deputy. So are you, Dude."

Both men nodded.

Sam turned to the mayor and said, "Mr. Mayor, my men and I will do out best to protect the town and our prisoner until the federal marshal arrives."

"And when will that be?" the Mayor asked.

Sam turned to Serena, who had sent a telegram to Austin, Texas, where the man was supposed to be coming from.

"The reply said that the marshal had to go to Fort Worth first on an emergency. He should be here in three days."

"There you have it," Sam said. "In three days' time this will all be over."

"Three days," the mayor said, looking dubious and shaking his head. "Three days," he repeated, and left in a daze.

Sam looked at Serena, Dude and Jubal, and Jubal said, "Or less."

Sam knew what he meant.

When Lincoln Burkett heard the news of his son's death he sat very still. The three men standing in front of him, and his foreman, all stood still and stayed very quiet. This was not the reaction they had anticipated.

"And Coffin?" Burkett asked then.

"Sam McCall took him to jail," one of the men said.

"No gunplay?"

"McCall didn't give Coffin no chance," the man said, explaining how McCall had jumped Coffin without giving him a chance to go for his gun.

"All right," Burkett said, "all right. Conners, get the men together."

"All of them, sir?"

"All of them who are willing to fight," Burkett said.

"And those who aren't?" Conners asked. After all, most of the men had signed on as ranch hands.

"Fire them."

"Yes, sir." Conners turned to the other men and said, "Get out. Pass the word."

"Sure, boss."

After the men left Chuck Conners looked at Burkett and asked, "Are you all right, sir?"

"I'm fine, Conners." Burkett looked up at his foreman. "Are you worried that you see no grief? Well, I'll save you the worry. This is not the time to grieve, this is the time for revenge. Grief will come later. Understand?"

"Yes, sir."

"Conners, pick one man and have him ride into town and look things over."

"Yes, sir."

"We won't move until he comes back."

"Right."

"Get out, now," Burkett said. "I have to think."

Conners nodded and left.

Burkett sat behind his desk, wondering why he felt so controlled. There was no rage, or grief, there was no feeling at all. There was just the realization that there was something that had to be done.

Later he'd worry about emotions.

Right now his concern was revenge.

Once the jail was set up for their three-day—at *least* three-day—siege Sam turned to Dude Miller.

"All right, Dude," he said, "Out."

"Hey, wait."

"Your help is appreciated up to now, Dude," Sam said, "but from here on in it's up to me and Jubal"

"I want to help."

"You have, but I don't want you to risk your life," Sam said. He looked at Serena, and then back at her father. "That's something that Jubal and I have to do, Dude, not you, and not Serena."

"Sam—"

"Pa," Serena said. "He's right."

"Dude," he said, "go home with Serena—and for God's sake keep her away from here."

"He doesn't have to keep me away," Serena said. "I'm not a child."

"No, you're not," Sam said. "Dude?"

"All right, I will."

"And keep an eye out for that marshal."

Dude nodded.

"All right, out with both of you. From this point on, nobody in and nobody out."

Serena walked over to Jubal and kissed him on the cheek. His face flushed. She turned and looked at Sam.

"Take care of him, all right? And of yourself."

"We'll take care of each other," Sam said. "We're the only family we have now."

"No," she said, "that's not true."

She turned and went out the door. Miller started to follow her out. He stopped before leaving, turned, and said, "Good luck."

"Thanks"

Dude Miller walked out, and Jubal closed the door behind him. He turned to Sam and said, "We're gonna need it."

CHAPTER TWENTY-ONE

S am made a pot of coffee and sat behind the sheriff's desk with a cup. Jubal sat across from him. Sam began opening drawers and looking inside.

"What are you looking for?" Jubal asked.

"Ah, found 'em."

Sam took his hand out of a drawer and tossed something at Jubal, who caught it with one hand. When he looked at it he saw that it was a deputy's badge.

"Put it on," Sam said.

"You know," Jubal said, pinning it to his chest, "I can't believe the way this has turned out. We're the law in Vengeance Creek."

"It is an 'odd' twist, isn't it?"

"I don't think odd covers it."

They ruminated over their coffee for a few moments and then Jubal said, "When Burkett comes after us, he'll be breaking the law."

"That's right."

"And then we'll have him."

"Right again, but not for murder—and we'll only have him if we survive."

"Hey!" Coffin called from his cell.

Jubal cocked his head at Sam, but Sam said nothing.

"How about some of that coffee?"

"Bring him a cup," Sam said.

"All right."

"Make him stand against the wall while you put it on the floor in front of the cell."

Jubal looked at Sam and then nodded. He hadn't thought of that. He took the coffee into the back.

"Smells good," Coffin said.

"Stand against the back wall."

"You think I'd waste good coffee—"

"Look, Coffin, I'd just as soon kill you as look at you. Now stand against the back wall!"

Coffin obeyed, and Jubal set the coffee cup down in front of the cell. When he stood up he stared at Coffin, the man who had killed his brother. Earlier, when they had first heard about Evan's death, he had been ready to kill this man. He couldn't understand how Sam could not have killed him.

It would be easy to do now. Just take out his gun and fire. So easy...

"Are you going to wait until it gets cold?" Coffin asked.

Jubal looked down at the coffee and had the urge to spit into it. Instead he turned and walked stiffly back into the office.

"You've been a sheriff before, haven't you?"

"Once or twice."

"I've never worn a badge," Jubal said. "It feels sort of funny."

"The badge gets heavier and heavier the longer you wear it. Luckily we won't be wearing them very long."

"I don't get it," Jubal said suddenly, and Sam knew he was changing the subject.

"What?"

"How could you not have killed him?"

"I don't know," Sam said, shaking his head. He put his coffee cup down and rubbed his hand over his face. "I intended to kill him. I went there to kill him. When I saw him I just kept walking toward him, and I was thinking, 'This is what Burkett wants.' I guess I didn't want to give it to him... you know?"

Jubal studied his brother for a few moments, then said, "Yeah, maybe I do."

"You want some dinner?" Sam asked.

"I am hungry. What's on the menu?"

"Beans."

"Sounds great."

"Yeah," Sam said, "don't it."

As Sam opened a can and set in on the potbellied stove Jubal asked, "What's Burkett likely to do?"

"If I was him," Sam said, "I'd send a man into town to look us over first, see how things were laid out."

"What's to see?" Jubal said, "We're in here and he's out there."

"Well, when he knows it's that simple he'll come for us...unless..."

"Unless what?"

Sam turned to face his brother and said, "Unless he wants to make us sweat."

"You think he will?"

Sam shrugged.

"If he does that it'll work in our favor."

"How?"

"If he waits long enough the marshal will get here," Sam said. "It's not likely, though."

"He knows about the marshal?"

"Yep," Sam said, "smart me told him."

"It must have seemed like a good idea at the time."

"Thanks," Sam said. "Hey, you want these real hot?"

"It don't matter. Warm'll do."

Sam used the coffee cups to hold the beans and handed Jubal a cup and a fork.

"What about him?" Jubal asked.

Sam sat behind the desk and said, "If there's any left..."

―――――

LATER THEY SET up the sleeping arrangements, four hours on and four off. They decided to play some checkers before one of them went to sleep. The board was a contribution of Dude Miller's.

Over the board Jubal said, "I just thought of something."

"Tell me."

"The marshall's going to be coming alone, right?"

"Probably."

"What's to stop Burkett from waiting for him and ambushing him?"

Sam looked at Jubal. It was a sharp observation, and he gave it some thought.

"It's a good point," he said, finally, "but I don't think he will."

"Why not?"

"Well, there are several directions the marshal could come from. Burkett would have to use too many men to cover them, and he's gonna want to use those men on us. No, I think he's gonna try and take us before the marshal gets here."

"Tonight?"

"Not tonight," Sam said. "He's got to get his information first. Sometime tomorrow, he and his men will come."

"And we be ready?"

"As ready as we can be."

The man Chuck Conners sent into town for Burkett was Jackie Doaks. Doaks rode in and headed straight for the saloon. It was there that he heard the story about Sam McCall, Coffin, and John Burkett.

He circulated around town and gradually put together the setup. It was almost eleven P.M. when he mounted his horse and rode back to the ranch. He had watched the

McCall brothers carry supplies into the jail, and it was clear that they intended to spend some time in there.

Maybe a long time.

When Doaks gave Conners the story, Conners took it in to Burkett.

"They're not stupid," Burkett said. "They know we'll be coming for them, and they've decided to barricade themselves in the jail."

"How do we get them out?'

"Oh, there are any number of ways," Burkett said. "I'd like to try and get them out alive first. I want to put my hands on Sam McCall."

"And if that doesn't work?"

"Then they'll die in there."

"What about Coffin?"

"Coffin didn't do the job," Burkett said. "As far as I'm concerned, he's dead already."

Conners stood still and quiet and waited for his instructions.

"All right," Burkett said. "I want all the men to have a good breakfast in the morning before we go to town. Tell Cook to make it a big spread."

"Yessir."

"Some of them won't be coming back."

Jubal took the first watch. He started out by playing solitaire, then walking to the window and looking out every so often. Once or twice he went in the back and looked at Coffin while he slept. He was tempted to put a bullet in the man, but he knew that he and Sam had to stay together on this.

He went back into the office and sat behind the desk. He started thinking about Evan, about how little they knew each other. How could three brothers grow so far apart, he wondered? How could they let that happen— and worse, leave their parents behind to die?

When this was over he was going to have to see what Sam wanted to do. If he wanted to split up—well, he'd abide by his wishes but maybe, just maybe, he'd want to stay together. Maybe they'd stay, or they could leave and ride together.

And what about Serena? There were times when Jubal thought she was in love with Evan and times when he thought she loved Sam. What was going to happen there? How did Sam feel about her?

These were all questions that could be answered only after this was all over—if they were all around to ask and answer them.

―――

SAM TOOK over at 4 A.M. He went through many of the same motions Jubal had before him. Coffee, solitaire, the window; he even spent a few minutes looking at Coffin, thinking the same thoughts.

Finally he settled behind the desk, his feet propped up.

His gun was holstered and his rifle across his lap.

He thought about Evan, as Jubal had. He wondered if he and Jubal were thinking the same things. They probably were. After all, they were brothers, weren't they? Sure, they and Evan, three brothers who hadn't seen each other—

Sam stopped and dropped his feet to the floor. He was sure that Jubal had already gone through this. There was no point in his mulling it over again.

He walked around the room a few times, then set up the checkerboard and started playing a game against himself. When he got tired of that he finally got around to thinking about Serena.

She was a fine girl who would make some man a fine wife. Maybe she would have made Evan a fine wife. As far as Sam went, there wasn't room in his life for a wife, fine or otherwise... but if there were...

He watched the boarded-up windows, waiting for the first hint of daylight. Burkett and his men might come with the light, or they might wait until later.

Sam wondered how long they'd be able to hold out against Burkett's superior numbers. With all the supplies they had inside, Burkett could still outwait them. He wouldn't have the time to do that, though, so he'd have to find a way to force them out.

Fire came to Sam's mind first, and then explosives.

He wondered how long it would take Burkett to think of one or both of them.

"What's for breakfast? Jubal asked, sitting up and rubbing his hands over his face.

"What else?" Sam asked. He was standing at the potbellied stove. He turned and grinned at his brother. "Beans. Want 'em hot?"

"Ah, warm's okay."

While Sam dished out the beans Jubal poured water into a bowl and washed his face. When he was done he accepted the cup of beans from Sam.

"Coffin still asleep?"

"I guess," Sam said. "I'll give him some beans if there's any left."

Sam walked over to where Jubal was sitting on his cot and handed him a cup of coffee.

"I found extra cups last night."

"Good, we can eat and drink at the same time. We're living in style."

"Yeah," Sam said, settling himself behind the desk.

"Tell me, Sam," Jubal said, "what were you thinkin' about last night, while I was asleep?"

"Oh, probably the same things you were thinkin' about. Mostly about Evan."

"Yeah, Evan," Jubal said, shaking his head. "I was thinkin' about you, too... I mean, about us."

"Yeah?"

"Where you gonna go after this, Sam?"

"I don't know," Sam said. "I don't usually know where I'm headin' next."

"What about your future? Don't you have any goals?"

"Goals," Sam repeated. "Now there's a word I haven't thought about in a long time. No, Jube, I'm afraid I'm plumb outta goals at my age. I guess it'd be nice if I was just left alone for the next twenty years, if I didn't have anybody tryin' to kill me, or if I didn't have to kill anyone else. I guess those're my goals."

"They're not bad goals."

"What about you? What're your goals?"

"I don't rightly know."

"You're only twenty-four, Jube," Sam said. "You've gotta have goals."

"What was your goal when you were twenty-four?"

"I don't know...probably something stupid like wanting to be the fastest gun in the West."

"You accomplished that."

"Maybe I did," Sam said, "but when I got there it didn't mean anythin' to me any more. I hope you're smarter at twenty-four than I was."

"Well, I think I'm smarter than I was before I went up on that hangman's scaffold."

"I hope so."

"Did you think about Serena last night?"

Sam shifted uncomfortably in his seat and said, "Some."

"She's a nice woman, huh?"

"Real nice."

"Make a fine wife, huh?"

"You gonna ask her?"

"Hey, no, not me! I thought maybe you."

"Not me, Jube," Sam said. "There's no room in my life for a woman. You're young, though. Why wouldn't you ask her?"

"She's older than me."

"So?"

"How'd we get on this subject?"

Sam smiled at his brother's discomfort and said, "You brought it up."

Jubal put his spoon in his cup and laid it on the floor with a clatter.

"She wouldn't have me."

"Why not?"

"Ah, she'd probably be comparing me to you and Evan all the time."

"I don't think so," Sam said. "Maybe when this is all over you should stay around a while, let her get to know you better."

"Stay here?" Jubal asked. "In Vengeance Creek?"

"Why not?"

"Sam, I left here."

"Well, do yourself a favor," Sam said. "Look at your reason for leaving, and see if you still want to go."

"Hey!" Coffin shouted from his cell. "Do I get some breakfast?"

Sam got up, walked over to the can of beans on the stove, and looked inside.

"Yeah," he said, "he gets breakfast."

———

"WHAT'S THAT?" Jubal said sometime later.

"Sounds like horses," Sam said, "a lot of them." They each went to a window and looked out the gun-port in the shutters. Lincoln Burkett was riding down

Main Street with about thirty men or more. They were riding at a leisurely pace, seemingly without a care in the world. The tip-off was when they rode past the jail each man turned his head and looked at it.

Sam found it interesting that Lincoln Burkett was the only man who didn't look. He already knew they were there.

"It's gonna start," Sam said. "Any minute now."

CHAPTER TWENTY-TWO

B urkett sent some of his men to look the town over. One of the men, Bud Poke, came back and said he had found Tom Kelly.

"Show me," Burkett said.

"He ain't wearin' a badge, boss."

Burkett looked at Conners and said, "Go and see the mayor."

"Right."

Burkett and Poke walked over to the cafe where Kelly was having breakfast.

"Looks like you lost your badge, Tom," Burkett said.

Kelly looked up from his meal at the two men.

"Mr. Burkett—" Kelly said, starting to get up.

Burkett put his hand on Kelly's shoulder and pushed him back down, then sat across from him.

"Tell me what happened..."

———

CONNERS MET Burkett coming out of the cafe.

"Kelly's not sheriff any more," Burkett said. "He gave up his badge rather than face McCall. Damn it!"

"You ain't gonna like this, boss," Conners said. "Sam McCall's the new sheriff."

"What?"

"The mayor says he picked up the badge when Kelly put it down. There was nothing he could do about it."

"That incompetent—well, if McCall thinks this is going to change anything, he's wrong."

"But...he's the law now."

"He wasn't elected," Burkett said, "and the mayor will swear afterward that he didn't appoint him. Badge or no badge, Sam McCall is a dead man."

"What do you see?" Sam asked.

He was seated behind the desk while Jubal was positioned at a window.

"Nothing," Jubal said. "The town looks quiet. I guess Burkett and his men must have put their horses in the livery."

"The Swede wouldn't be able to accommodate that many horses," Sam said. "They're probably in a corral behind the livery."

"Same thing."

"He hasn't even got a man watching the jail?"

"Not that I can see through this hole," Jubal said. "If I open the shutter—"

"Forget that," Sam said. "He's probably got a man up on a rooftop. If you open that shutter you'll be dead."

Jubal turned and looked at Sam.

"You don't think the fact that you're now the sheriff will keep him from—"

"I wasn't elected, Jube," Sam said, "and I wasn't even appointed. I don't know that I'd stand up in court as sheriff of Vengeance Creek."

"Why did you take the badge, then?"

Sam shrugged. "It shut the mayor up, didn't it?"

"Yeah," Jubal said, "I guess it did."

"You want some coffee?"

"I'm up to here with coffee. I could use a beer, though."

"Sorry, no beer."

"I could go down to the saloon and get two—"

"If you walk out that door," Sam said, "you're a dead man."

"I guess I could do without a beer."

"How about lunch?"

Jubal made a face and said, "Beans?"

Sam nodded.

"I'll skip it."

"I could open a can of fruit."

"Wait a minute—"

"You want the beans?"

"No," Jubal said, "something's happening."

"What?"

"Come and see for yourself."

"All right," Burkett said to Conners, "set the men up the way we discussed."

"Right, boss."

"I'll be at the saloon. Let me know when they're all in place."

"Yessir."

Conners turned to the men, who were all gathered by the corral behind the livery, and said, "All right, boys. Take up your positions. There's to be no shooting until you hear it from me or Mr. Burkett. Understood?"

They all nodded.

"Then get moving."

Sam took up position at the other window, and he and Jubal watched while Burkett's men moved into what was obviously prearranged positions across from the jail.

"Counting?" Sam asked.

"Twenty? Maybe more?"

"The rest must be on the rooftops."

"Did you see Burkett?'

"No, not yet," Sam said. "He'll come along later, to give us a chance to come out quietly."

Jubal looked at Sam and said, "Have you been through this before?"

"Once or twice," Sam said, "in different surroundings, but the basic situation was the same."

"What did you do those times?"

"Hold fast and wait for help to arrive."

Jubal frowned.

"Isn't that what they did at the Alamo?"

"Let's hope that's the only resemblance to this situation."

When Chuck Conners entered the saloon Lincoln Burkett was seated at a back table with a bottle of whiskey. It was early enough that he was the only customer in the place. Burkett had not yet gone to the undertaker's to see his son's body. He wouldn't do that until he could tell his dead son that he had killed Sam McCall.

Conners approached the table and waited to be noticed. Burkett poured himself another drink and downed it before doing so.

"Well?"

"All the men are in position, sir."

"All right," Burkett said, picking up his hat and standing up. "Let's get this done."

Sam and Jubal were at their positions at the windows, holding their rifles, when Lincoln Burkett strode into view across the street, Chuck Conners at his elbow. Conners, like all of the other men, was holding a rifle. Burkett had no rifle, and his handgun was in his holster.

"Hello in the jail! McCall!" Burkett called out.

"I hear you, Burkett," Sam replied.

"Come on out, McCall," Burkett said. "Let's finish this like men."

"Sure," Sam called out, "me against thirty of your men."

"Just you and me McCall," Burkett said.

"He's lying," Jubal said.

"Of course he is."

"McCall!" Burkett shouted. "I'll let your brother come out. I have no quarrel with him."

Jubal looked at Sam, who seemed to be considering the offer.

"This is Jubal McCall, Burkett!" Jubal shouted. "I'm staying right here."

"You're a foolish young man."

"No," Jubal said, "your son was a foolish young man. He tried to backshoot my brother, and he paid for it."

"Then you'll both die!" Burkett yelled. Burkett turned to his men and said, "Fire!"

"Down!" Sam said.

Sam and Jubal hit the floor as lead began to rain down on the jail. From inside it almost sounded like rain. Chunks of lead chewed up the wooden shutters, but they stayed in place, relatively intact, except that a lot more light was shining through them when the shooting stopped.

"Is it over?" Jubal asked. He lifted his head and wood splinters fell off it to the floor.

"For the moment," Sam said, brushing himself off.

"How are we ever to get off a shot?"

"Quiet, Jube," Sam said. "Let's here what he has to say."

"McCall!"

"We're still here."

"Send out Coffin."

"Why?" Sam called. "So you can have another gun? No, thanks. I'm holding Coffin until the federal marshal arrives, and then I'm turning him over for the murder of my brother."

"Your brother, my son," Burkett said. "They're both dead. How many more have to die?"

"That's up to you, Burkett."

Sam and Jubal heard Burkett shout, "Fire!" and they ducked down again.

When the second volley of shots sounded Serena bolted for the door of the store. Her father, moving more swiftly than even he thought he could move, grabbed her by the arms, stopping her.

"Let me go!"

"We'll have to stay here, Serena," Miller said. "We can't give Sam anything else to think about, and if you're on the street, that's what you're going to do."

"Someone has to help them."

"And you're that someone?" Miller asked. "Are you going to take a rifle and go out there and help them? You'll do more harm than good out there, Serena, believe me."

As most of the townspeople had done, Dude Miller had closed his store, locked it, and remained inside. There was no one on the street except Lincoln Burkett and his men.

As they stood there, eyes locked, the second volley of shots ceased and it became quiet again.

"I want to hear what they're saying, Papa."

Dude Miller frowned, but he said, "All right. Let's open the door a crack."

They did so, and found that they could hear both Lincoln Burkett and Sam McCall.

"You can't hold out, McCall. We'll chew that building to pieces."

"Go ahead and chew, then," Sam called back. "We ain't comin' out."

"You know," Jubal said. "It'd be a lot simpler if you had killed Coffin and we had John Burkett in here."

Sam looked at Jubal and said, "Sorry I didn't think about that yesterday."

"I was just saying," Jubal said, "not criticizing."

"I understand, and I agree."

Sam sneaked a look out the window. The bottom half of his wooden shutter had been blown away. He only had time for a short look because as soon as they saw his head a couple of men started firing. He ducked back down.

"Burkett's got his men well schooled," Sam said. "I don't even have time to get a shot off at him. He's probably got two men on each window with orders to shoot as soon as they see someone."

"So then we can't fire back."

"Not with any effectiveness."

As he said that the third volley of shots commenced. With parts of the shutters gone the lead was able to enter the office. The coffeepot leaped off the stove, lead imbedded itself in the walls, and one or two slugs managed to hit something and ricochet off.

"That's great," Jubal said. "Now we have to worry about being hit by a ricochet."

Sam didn't reply.

"McCall," Burkett called, "I'm giving you some time to think over your position—but don't take too long!"

All of a sudden holing up in there didn't seem like a very good move. What they should have done was leave town with Coffin and meet up with the marshal somewhere along the way. Still, if they had done that they could have been ridden down by Burkett and his men. At least here they had cover—for as long as the building was standing.

"What do we do if they rush us?" Jubal asked.

"That's a strong door, it should hold for a while," Sam said. "First man through the door knows he'll be dead. Burkett's gonna have to find someone who wants to come through first. That'll take some time."

"Sam," Jubal said, sitting with his back to the wall, "I don't see how we can hold out for two more days."

"Well" Sam said, scratching his head, "maybe he'll get here early."

"And maybe Christmas will be early, too."

One of the things they had established early on was the lack of a back door. It seemed then that this would work in their favor. Now Sam was thinking of another way out of the jail.

"What are you thinking?" Jubal asked.

"I'm tryin' to think of another way out of here."

"What good would that do?"

"Well, if we could slip out it might take Burkett a while to decide that we were gone. By the time he decided to storm the jail we'd be long gone."

"To where?"

"On the trail," Sam said. "Maybe we could meet up with the marshal."

"If this marshal is riding alone, he ain't going to do us much good."

"I don't think Burkett would kill a duly appointed officer of the law. That would undo everything he's accomplished here so far."

"Well, the only other way out is through those barred windows in the cells," Jubal said. "We just have to find a way to get those bars off."

"Well, then," Sam said, "let's look around the office and see what we can find to do that with."

"Why are you giving them time?" Chuck Conners asked Burkett.

Lincoln Burkett stroked his jaw and said, "I just thought of an easy way to get them out of there."

"We can set the jail on fire."

"No," Burkett said, "that would endanger the buildings around it."

"What about dynamite?"

"Same thing." Burkett looked at Conners and said, "I'm supposed to be a good citizen of this town. How would it look if I burned it down?"

"What are we gonna do, then?"

"There's one person in this town they might come out for."

"Who?"

"Grab two men and follow me."

"The shooting has stopped," Serena said.

"For now."

"What do you think—" Serena started to ask, but she stopped short when four men appeared at the door.

"Wha—" she said, but the man in front pushed the door open and she staggered back.

"What's going on here?" Dude Miller demanded.

The fourth man to enter was Lincoln Burkett.

"What do you want, Burkett?"

"I need your daughter's help, Miller."

"My daughter?"

"Yes" Burkett said, "I think the McCall boys would come out if she asked them."

"I won't ask them."

Burkett frowned at her.

"I was hoping you'd cooperate, but that doesn't matter. You're coming along anyway."

Burkett waved his arm, and the two men with him and Conners grabbed her arms. .

"Hey!" she said.

"Let her go—" Miller started, but Chuck Conners stepped in front of him and hit him once on the jaw. Miller slumped to the floor, unconscious.

"Papa!" Serena cried. She looked at Burkett and asked, "Why are you doing this?"

"As I said," Burkett replied, "I need your help with the McCalls."

"To kill them?"

"That's up to them. Take her outside," Burkett said to the men holding her. "Let's see how Sam McCall reacts to this."

CHAPTER TWENTY-THREE

There were no tools in the office. No hammers, no crowbars, nothing.

"How's anyone supposed to escape?" Jubal demanded, annoyed.

"I think that was the idea, Jube," Sam said. "At least, the original idea."

"So what do we do now?"

"I have a suggestion," Coffin called from the back.

"Watch the window," Sam said to Jubal, and then went in the back to talk to Coffin.

"What do you have in mind?"

"Simple enough," Coffin said. "Give me a gun and let me help."

"That's simple enough," Sam said. "I give you a gun so you can kill me."

"Now, Sam," Coffin said, "we both know that Burkett's not happy with me. After all, I didn't do the job. If he kills you, he'll kill me, too. If you give me a gun you and I are worth any ten of his men."

"Which leaves twenty for Jubal to handle," Sam said. "Somehow that doesn't seem to even the odds up much, does it? Sorry, Coffin. You're just gonna have.to stay an observer."

"If I'm going to die," Coffin called out as Sam went back into the office, "I'd rather it be with a gun in my hand."

"Anything happening?" Sam asked Jubal.

"They're doing the same thing we're doing... waiting for Burkett. Wait, there he is."

Sam hurried to his window.

Burkett was standing across the street, partially obscured from view by a buckboard. Still, Sam probably could have gotten off one shot. He touched the gun in his holster.

"McCall!" Burkett called. "I've got someone out here you might be interested in."

"What the hell is he talking about now?" Jubal asked.

Burkett waved his arm and suddenly Serena Miller was pushed out from behind the buckboard. She stood in the open, and Burkett stepped out next to her. Behind her and to her right was Chuck Conners.

"Serena," Jubal said.

"What do you want, Burkett?"

"I see you're interested in talking now," Burkett said.

"Just get to it, Burkett."

"You come out and I'll let the girl go."

"And if we don't come out?"

"I'll turn her over to my men."

The threat was either one of violation, death... or both.

"I wonder..." Sam said, looking around at all of Burkett's men.

"What?" Jubal asked. "What?"

"Well, most of Burkett's men probably hired on as hands, and not as hired guns."

"What's your point?"

"I think if I'm standing out there all by myself, he's gonna have to kill me himself. I don't think his men will do it for him."

"What about his threat to Serena?"

"Well, there might be a few of his men who wouldn't mind taking her into an alley, but I don't know how many men he's got who would be willing to kill her."

"So what you're saying is that you're going to go out there alone."

"Right."

"To get killed."

"Wrong."

"Then what?"

"Hopefully," Sam said, "I'll be able to reduce this whole

thing to Burkett and me." He took out his gun and checked the cylinder, to make sure it was fully loaded.

"And if not?"

"Just stay in here and watch, Jube," Sam said. "With any luck you'll still be able to deliver Coffin to the marshal for killing Evan."

"And with no luck?"

"We'll all be dead within the next fifteen minutes."

Sam stood up, taking most of his weight on his uninjured leg. The other was far from completely healed, but he wasn't about to let it stop him from doing what he had to do.

"I'm comin out, Burkett!"

"No, Sam," Serena called, "don't come out. He'll kill you."

"I'll cover you from the window," Jubal said. "If you go down, I'm going to kill Burkett."

"Sounds fair to me."

Sam walked to the door, opened it, and stepped out.

Once outside Sam felt very vulnerable. There were at least thirty guns pointed at him. He was putting a lot of faith in Burkett's men being ranch hands and not killers. Of course, there were those men who had chased him that day, but maybe they'd be less willing to fire at such a stationary target.

"All right, Burkett," Sam said, "I'm here."

"Where's your brother?"

"Like you said before," Sam said, "you have no quarrel with him."

Burkett thought it over and decided not to argue the point. Sam McCall was out in the open. He could deal with the other one later.

"Let her go."

"Not yet, McCall."

"Then what now?" Sam asked.

"Now you drop your gun."

"I don't think so, Burkett," Sam said. "If your men are gonna kill me I want a chance to take some of them with me—or are you gonna do it yourself? Yeah, there's an idea."

"Shut up, McCall."

Sam raised his voice.

"With most of the town watching they can all testify that thirty men gunned me down. That's murder."

"Remember," Burkett said, "you have your gun."

"One against thirty?" McCall said. "Even though it's my gun, it's still murder. Are you all gonna go to jail—or are you gonna let your boss do his own killing?"

Sam looked around and saw Burkett's men exchanging glances.

"Come on, Burkett," Sam said, "if you do it yourself at least you can claim self-defense."

"Good try, McCall," Burkett said, "but if you gun me you're as guilty of murder as you say Coffin is for killing your brother."

Sam frowned. Damn the man, but he was right.

"Well, go ahead then, Burkett," Sam said. "Give your men the order to murder me."

Burkett looked around at his own men and saw the dubious look on some of their faces.

"Go ahead, Mr. Burkett," Chuck Conners said, "some of us will back you."

"Of course," Sam said, "my First bullet will go right through your heart, Burkett"

Burkett suddenly froze, as if he realized that Sam McCall could draw and fire and kill him before he could even move. What good was having Sam McCall dead if he couldn't see it?

"Call it, Burkett."

Sam saw the look of fear on Serena's face. When the lead started flying he hoped she was smart enough to duck beneath the buckboard.

"Wait," Burkett said. "I have a better idea."

"I'm listening."

"One of my men against you."

"What stakes?"

"Everything," Burkett said. "I'll withdraw my men from town."

"And Coffin?"

"He'll be yours."

"And the killing of your son?"

Burkett made a face and said, "You lost a brother, I lost a son. Maybe well can stop it there."

Sam didn't believe him, but for the moment it was the best offer he had.

"All right," Sam said. "Pick your man."

Burkett spoke without hesitation.

"I pick Coffin."

Sam was about to refuse, saying that Coffin was a prisoner.

"I'll agree, on one condition," Sam said.

"What?"

"Let her go now"

Burkett looked at Serena for a moment, and then he spoke to Chuck Conners.

"Let her go."

"Make him bring Coffin out first, boss."

"No need for that, Conners," Burkett said. "Mr. McCall is a man of his word—aren't you, Sam?

"Jubal?" Sam called.

"Yes, Sam?"

"When Serena is safely away, bring Coffin out."

There was a moment's hesitation. Sam knew Jubal would have liked to argue the point, but there wasn't time.

"All right, Sam."

"Don't give him his gun yet."

"Right."

Sam looked at Burkett expectantly.

"Go ahead, little lady," Burkett said, "go back to your father."

Serena threw one last glance at Sam, and then ran from the street. She didn't go far, though. Her father had recovered and had come down the street to see what was happening. She ran into his arms, and they both stood there to watch. Dude Miller had one hand around her shoulder. In his other hand, down by his leg, he held a rifle.

The door to the jail opened and Coffin stepped out, followed by Jubal, who had his gun in his hand and Coffin's gunbelt over his shoulder.

"Stop," Jubal said, and Coffin stopped.

Sam turned so he was half facing Burkett and Coffin. Some of the townspeople had gotten brave and had come out onto the boardwalks to see what they had been waiting all week to see. Burkett's men, seeing all the witnesses, began lowering their rifles.

"Give him his gun," Sam told Jubal.

"But Sam—"

"Do it, Jube."

Jubal, shaking his head, took Coffin's gunbelt from his

shoulder and handed it to the man. Coffin grabbed it and buckled it on, then faced Sam.

"This is a big mistake on your part, McCall."

"This is what you've wanted all along, Coffin, so let's just do it."

Coffin stepped down into the street and said, "You can't fool me, Sam. You've been wanting this, too. You want to see which of us is better just as much as I do."

Sam didn't answer. He watched Coffin carefully as he walked out into the middle of the street.

Jubal, relieved of the responsibility of watching Coffin, chose now to watch Lincoln Burkett and his foreman closely. If and when Sam killed Coffin, Jubal didn't think Burkett was going to accept it.

Burkett, watching as the two men squared off, said to Conners in a low voice, "If McCall kills him, I want him dead."

"Right, boss."

Conners turned and indicated to his men that they were to watch him. He had kept the men he could be sure of—Priest, Granger, and some of the others who had chased McCall that day—on the ground with him.

Except for Jubal, who was watching Burkett and Conners, all eyes were on the two men in the street.

"Who calls the play?" Coffin asked.

"Never mind that," Sam said. "You just move when you're ready."

They were close enough that Sam could watch Coffin's eyes. If they'd been further apart he would have kept his eyes on his right shoulder, waiting for it to dip. The eyes, though, would narrow even before the shoulder clipped.

Even though Coffin's eyes did narrow before he moved, Sam was surprised at how fast he was. Coffin had possibly the fastest move he'd ever seen, and even as he drew and fired his own gun he couldn't help but admire it.

Sam's bullet struck Coffin high in the chest. Coffin's finger spasmed, jerking the trigger of his own gun, firing a round into the ground by his foot. For a moment time stopped for Coffin and he stared at Sam, admitting to himself the fact that the man had not only outdrawn him, but had done it by a wide margin. Even though he had seen Sam McCall's move twice before, he was shocked.

"Shit," he said, and died before he hit the ground.

Jubal raise his rifle and shot Chuck Conners as he was drawing his gun.

"Fire!" Lincoln Burkett shouted...

———

IT's easy to get thirty men to agree to fight rather than lose their jobs. It's easy to get them to fire their rifles at a building, at a jail with two men inside it. It's harder, however, to get thirty men to fire their guns at another man. Killing a man isn't an easy thing to do, and men who make their living punching cattle or breaking broncs can't moved so easily into killing.

When Burkett shouted "Fire!" thirty men heard him, but only about eight actually drew and began to fire. The others lowered their rifles and watched....

The minute Burkett shouted, Dude Miller pushed Serena into a doorway and raised his rifle. He fired at the nearest man with a gun in his hand.

Ed Collins came out of his gunsmith shop with a rifle in his hands and ran toward the action. If there was ever a time for this town to get out from under Lincoln Burkett's thumb, this was it.

Swede Hanson had known since the day the McCalls arrived that it would come to this, lead flying in the streets. He had cleaned his old Navy Colt every day since then, and now he had a chance to use it. He'd been standing in a doorway, watching the action, and now he stepped out and raised his gun...

Sam would have preferred to turn as soon as he fired, but he had to make sure that Coffin would go down. As the man started to fall he turned, saw Chuck Conners fall, and leaped for cover just as Lincoln Burkett shouted his command to his men.

Sam noticed right away that not all of Burkett's men had obeyed his command. He also noticed that there was some covering fire coming from different directions. With a glance he identified Dude Miller and Ed Collins. He didn't find out until later that Swede Hanson had also been firing.

Lincoln Burkett also noticed these things. He especially noticed that less than half of his men had obeyed his command.

He didn't like the odds.

He ran up onto the boardwalk, behind his men, and started running down the street.

"Sam!" Jubal shouted. He had taken cover behind a horse trough and was now pointing at the retreating figure of Lincoln Burkett.

"I'll get him!"

Sam got to his feet and fired as he ran. He stayed on his side of the street, passing Jubal, until he was clear of the jail and Burkett's men, and then he crossed the street and took up the chase.

He reloaded as he ran, keeping Burkett in sight ahead of him. Burkett, at his age, would normally not have been able to stay ahead of Sam, but Sam's leg wound kept him from running at full speed.

The thing that worked in Sam's favor was that Burkett had chosen a direction that was away from everything. He was running away from the livery, and the saloon, he was even running away from his ranch, which was south of town rather than north. This indicated that the man wasn't running toward anything, he was simply trying to get "away."

That wouldn't happen, Sam swore to himself. Not by a long chalk.

He ignored the burning pain in his thigh and increased his speed. He was closing the gap between himself and Burkett. Burkett saw this as he looked over his shoulder, and he panicked. Gun in hand he turned and fired at Sam, but his shot was so hurried that he missed by a wide margin.

Sam saw the man riding down Main Street just as Burkett fired at him, and he saw the badge on the man's chest. The appearance of the man slowed his reaction, and Burkett fired again. This time the bullet fell short, kicking up dirt in front of Sam's feet. This reclaimed Sam's attention and he fired once, accurately. The bullet hit Lincoln Burkett high on the right shoulder. It was an unhurried shot, because it was obvious that Burkett was inept with a gun, therefore it was a well-placed shot. Burkett's hand opened and the gun fell to the ground. He went to one knee, clutching at his shoulder.

Sam reached him just as the man on horseback did.

"Marshal Carson?" Sam said, looking up at the lawman.

"That's right," Carson said. He was a burly man in his thirties, with a heavy mustache and steely eyes. "Are you Sam McCall?"

"That's right."

"And this man?"

"This man is the reason I sent for you, Marshal."

The sound of firing was still clear from down the street but had fallen off some.

"Seems I arrived a little late," the marshal said.

"No, marshal," Sam said, looking down at Lincoln Burkett, "you arrived just in time"

EPILOGUE

With the arrival of the federal lawman, activity died down. The men who had lowered their rifles to watch now scrambled for their horses, not wanting to be involved any further if it meant jail.

Jubal, with the help of Dude Miller, Ed Collins, and Swede Hanson, had done a pretty fair job on those of Burkett's men who had agreed to fight for their boss—that is, until they saw him hightailing it out of there. A few of them lay dead or wounded on the street, and the others had thrown down their guns. They weren't fighting any more for a man who had lit out.

Burkett and his men were taken to the jail, where they were stuffed into cells. Doc Leader was sent for to see to the wounded ones.

The marshall's horse was taken to the livery stable for him as he entered the sheriff's office. With him there were Sam, Jubal, Dude Miller, Serena, and Ed Collins.

Marshal Frank Carson seated himself behind the sheriff's desk and pinned his eyes on Sam.

"Are you the sheriff here?"

"Not elected, or appointed—"

"Then I'd appreciate it if you would take off that badge." Carson looked at Jubal and said, "That goes for you, too."

"Yes, sir."

They both removed the badges and set them down on the desk.

"Who are you people?" Carson asked, looking at the others.

Dude Miller made the introductions.

"Where's the sheriff?"

"We don't have one at the moment," Miller said.

"The mayor, then?"

"I suspect he's hiding underneath his desk," Ed Collins said.

"Do any of you people sit on the Town Council?"

"No," Miller said, "they wouldn't have Ed and me."

"Why not?"

"We wouldn't kowtow to Lincoln Burkett."

"Burkett..." Carson looked at Sam. "That's the man you shot as I was ridin' in, right?"

"Right."

"What's his position in the town?"

They all started talking at once, and Carson waved his hand for them to quiet down.

"Ma'am, for no other reason than that you're the prettiest one here, why don't you try tellin' me what this is all about?"

"From the beginning?"

Carson frowned and asked, "How far back are we goin'?"

"Pretty far back," Serena said.

Carson sighed and signaled for her to begin. He didn't have anything else to do at the moment.

———

WHILE SERENA EXPLAINED to the marshal everything that Lincoln Burkett had done since he'd arrived, Jubal made coffee and set a cup at the marshal's elbow. The man acknowledged him with a nod of thanks.

From there Serena went on to explain what had happened to Joshua and Miriam McCall, and then everything since the arrival of Sam, Evan, and Jubal.

"Where is Evan McCall?" Carson asked.

"He's dead," Sam said. "Burkett had him killed by a man named Coffin." He didn't bother telling the lawman that John Burkett had had Evan killed. To Sam it was all the same.

At Coffin's name the marshal perked up.

"I know that name. Where is Coffin?"

"Sam killed him," Dude Miller said.

"Outdrew him clean," Jubal said.

Carson looked at McCall and said, "Well, I guess you're everything your friend Murdock said you were."

"I hope not" Sam mumbled, and drank some coffee.

Serena continued her story, filling the marshal in on all the facts and most of the supposition that had gone on during the week.

When she was done Carson asked for another cup of coffee and waited until he got it to speak again.

"As I understand it, then," he said, looking at Sam and Jubal, "your parents were killed, and you didn't believe the official verdict. Rather, you believe they were murdered."

"That's right."

Doc Leader entered the room at that point and Carson looked at him.

"Well, Doctor?"

"Nobody back there's gonna die in the next twenty four hours. They can stay there, if that's where you want them."

"That's what we're discussing nqw," Carson said.

Someone was shouting from the back, and Carson asked the doctor who it was.

"Who is that?" Carson asked.

"That's Lincoln Burkett," Doc Leader said. "He's lookin' for someone to scare, I reckon."

"Tell me, Doctor," Carson said, "you examined the bodies of Joshua and Miriam Burkett, didn't you?"

"I did."

"What was your verdict?"

"I didn't give the verdict."

"Who did?"

"The sheriff, Tom Kelly—but I suspect he was told by Lincoln Burkett."

"Burkett gave the verdict?"

"If you ask me," Leader said, "yeah."

"Well, what did you think? Did Joshua McCall kill himself?"

"You're askin' me?"

"That's right. Does that surprise you?"

"It sure does," Doc Leader said. "Nobody asked me before."

"Well, you're bein' asked now," Carson said.

"No, he didn't kill himself, and I doubt that he killed his wife."

"On what do you base your findings?"

"There were no powder burns around his head wound," Leader said. "If he had shot himself at point-blank range, the hair around the wound would have been singed. It was not."

"So then he was killed by someone else?"

"Yes."

"Would you put that in writing for me, sir?"

"I'll be happy to."

"Thanks, Doc," Sam said.

Doc Leader scowled and said, "I suppose I owe it to you. I was as cowed by Burkett as anybody in this town. Does me good to see him in jail."

"It's where he belongs," Jubal said.

"Well, we haven't established that, yet," Marshal Carson said.

"What?"

"We've established that someone killed your parents," Carson said, "but not who."

"It had to be Burkett," Serena said. "Remember, he ended up with the McCall ranch."

"I know, and I know you told me there's oil on the land, but there's still no proof that Joshua McCall didn't make a legal agreement with Burkett to sell the land, and the house—"

"I have proof," Sam said.

Carson looked at him.

"What proof?"

"A letter," Sam said, "written by my father before he died."

"Where is the letter?"

"Right here."

Sam took it out of his shirt and handed it to the lawman.

"Where did that come from?" Serena asked.

"We found it yesterday," Sam said, "but in all the excitement we didn't have a chance to tell anyone."

They all stood silently as Carson read the letter. He looked up at them when he was done. Dude and Serena Miller and Ed Collins had expectant looks on their faces.

"According to this," Carson said, "Joshua McCall was coerced into trading his land for a worthless shack because of a threat to his wife."

"I knew it!" Jubal said.

Sam looked at Serena and said, "Burkett told Pa he'd have

Ma raped and killed if he didn't agree. Pa wanted to stand up to him, but Burkett had too many men."

"Your father's men," Serena said, "the ones who wouldn't work for Burkett, were run off, so he was alone."

"That's right."

"It also says here," Carson said, "that in the event of his death we—you," he amended, looking at Sam and Jubal—"and your brother should consider that he had decided to call Burkett's bluff and go to the law."

"Pa probably decided to go to the law outside of Vengeance Creek, and Burkett found out about it and had him and ma killed."

"And they tried to make it look like Pa did it himself," Jubal said.

"Does it say there whether or not your Pa knew about the oil?" Dude Miller asked.

"No," Sam said. "My guess is Pa didn't know anything about it."

"He never knew what a rich man he was," Miller said.

"Well," Carson said, folding the letter, "if this handwriting can be identified—"

"It can," Miller said. "I've got samples of Joshua's hand-writing in my store." He looked at Sam and said, "i.o.u.'s after they moved into that shack. Your Pa wouldn't take charity, he insisted in giving me an i.o.u. for everything."

"That's just like Pa."

"Well then, with what happened here today," Carson said, "I think I've got enough to hold Lincoln Burkett over for trial. I'll send for a circuit judge and we'll hold the trial right here."

"Good," Serena said. "I want to see him go on trial."

"You people had better get out of here and let me get started with my job," Carsori said. "It looks like I might be here a while."

Dude Miller, Serena, and Ed Collins all made for the door.

"Uh, McCall—" Carson said.

Both Sam and Jubal turned.

"Both of you, stay a minute."

They waited until the others had left.

"I'll need deputies while I'm here," Carson said. "I've got a full house back there. You interested?"

Sam and Jubal exchanged glances, and when Jubal nodded, Sam said, "Sure, Marshal, count on us."

"Pickup your badges, then. Sam, I'm namin' you interim sheriff of Vengeance Creek."

Sam hesitated, then picked up the badge.

"One more thing."

"What's that?" Sam asked.

"I want you to understand that I don't know if we have enough to convict Burkett for having your parents killed—not without a witness. We all can get him for trying to kill you, and for stealing your father's ranch, but murder? Don't count on it."

"That's all right, Marshal," Sam said. "If he gets convicted on the other charges he'll go to jail—and we'll be around when he gets out."

"And if he doesn't go to jail," Jubal said, "we'll still be around."

"If anythin' happens to him, I'll have to come after you two," Carson said, pointing his index finger at them.

"That's something we understand too, Marshal."

"All right, then," Carson said, "suppose you two fellas get out on the street and try and put this town back in order."

"Yes, sir."

They headed for the door. Jubal opened it but Sam turned to face the marshal again.

"Marshal?"

"Yeah?"

"What about the ranch? Who does it belong to?"

"Nobody, right now," Carson said. "I impounded it, but if everythin' can be proven—and with the help of this letter and Burkett's actions, I think it can—the judge should probably be returnin' the ranch to you fellas. You better decide what you want to do with it."

"Burkett's got a lot of money..." Sam said.

"I hope you're not implying that either I or the judge can be bought."

"I'm not implying anything, Marshal," Sam said. "I'm just sayin'..."

Carson eyed Sam critically and said, "All right, Mc-Call, I understand what you're sayin'."

Sam nodded and followed Jubal outside.

"What are we going to do now?" Jubal asked.

Sam looked up and down the streets of Vengeance Creek.

"Well, we're stuck here until the judge comes to town. Who knows when that will be?"

"And then after that, if we get the ranch, we're going to have to stay around and figure out what to do with it."

"Well, you could live on it," Sam said.

"We could live on it," Jubal said. "Maybe even you and Serena—"

"Whoa, boy, don't be jumpin' to no conclusions."

"Don't call me boy!" Jubal said. "I see the way you look at her—"

"Whatayou know about lookin' at a woman, you young PUP?"

"I know enough..."

They started down the street, Sam walking with a slight limp, still arguing about who might many Serena and who might live on the ranch, and who knew what about women, two brothers who were closer now than they had ever been in their lives—and as close as they might ever be.

A LOOK AT: DOUBLE THE BOUNTY

Decker Bounty Hunter Book One

A MAN SEEKING JUSTICE...

He almost paid the ultimate price for a crime he didn't commit. Now Decker will make sure the innocent have nothing to fear... but the guilty won't stand a chance against the Bounty Hunter...

According to numerous eyewitnesses, Brian Foxx held up a bank in Wyoming and one in Arizona -- on the exact same day at the exact same time. Decker has no idea how Foxx pulled it off, but he's got a legend of his own to maintain: he always gets his man.

Robert J. Randisi delivers an action-packed depiction of the dangerous life of a bounty hunter in Double The Bounty.

AVAILABLE NOW

ABOUT THE AUTHOR

Randisi was born and raised in Brooklyn, N.Y., and from 1973 through 1981 he was a civilian employee of the New York City Police Department, working out of the 67th Precinct in Brooklyn. After 41 years in N.Y, he now resides in Laughlin, NV, 90 miles South of Las Vegas, on the Colorado River, with his 25-year partner-in-life-and-crime, Marthayn Pelegrimas.

He is the author of the "Miles Jacoby," "Nick Delvecchio," "Joe Keough," and "Dennis McQueen," mystery series, and the co-author of the "Gil & Claire Hunt" series. He has been nominated four times for the Shamus Award from the Private Eye Writers of America, in the Novel and Short Story categories.